INTERNATIONAL FTA

INTERNATIONAL FTA

Mike Manley

authorHOUSE®

AuthorHouse™
1663 Liberty Drive
Bloomington, IN 47403
www.authorhouse.com
Phone: 1 (800) 839-8640

Published by AuthorHouse   06/04/2015

ISBN: 978-1-4969-5633-0 (sc)
ISBN: 978-1-4969-5634-7 (e)

Library of Congress Control Number: 2014921305

Print information available on the last page.

This book is dedicated to my parents the reverend doctor Joshua Iroegbu Nwangaga and the late Mrs. Dorothy Nqangaga, George Pleasant Jones, Joe Dublin, Regina Paige, Christine Morrill, Divine Jones (Rochester) and finally the Almighty God who made it possible.

CHAPTER ONE

1985

R ev. Joshua Nwanta and his wife, Dorothy sat in the living room of their family home located in the compound of the church in Towson, MD. The previous weeks had been very stressful due to numerous problems their children were having in school. The six children were all born in Towson at the same hospital.

Just days before, the eldest son, Theo came back from school smelling like marijuana. When asked, he tried to deny it by saying he was around some kids who were smoking it. On the other hand, the eldest of the three girls, Ada, came home late one night, smelling like male cologne and when asked, she claimed it must have been in the seat she was sitting in.

All this unchristian-like behavior from the children of an African minister, not only violated the Ten Commandments but also the Nigerian Ibo culture.

"Do you think we ought to take these kids home, honey?" Mrs. Dorothy Nwanta asked her husband as they watched the daily religious program on television.

"I don't know. It's kind of tough raising kids in a country they have never been to. But with the way things have been going lately, we could consider it." Rev. Nwanta responded.

Suddenly, there was an interruption in the regular television program. The news that followed was more than shocking.

"A deadly shooting today at Towson High School in Baltimore County has left four teenage students dead and twenty injured. The shooters were also students in the school and are believed to be members of a secret cult who idolized Charles Manson and Jeffrey Domer. According to eye witnesses, the three white male students' dressed in all black outfits, walked into their classroom late, armed with what looked like AK47 assault rifles and opened fire. Some students were able to escape uninjured while others weren't so fortunate." The female news reporter paused for a moment and continued. "These kids were from rich families and no one seems to understand why they chose to take the wrong path. The only information we have now is that they believed the only way to become famous in America is through violence and they have done just that. The question is: Has violence taken over other justified and credible means to fame in the American Society? Stay tuned to this station as more information unfolds in this tragic story." The reporter concluded and turned the broadcast over to the anchor.

The sudden news had left the couple in a state of shock as no words were exchanged between them for a few minutes.

Mrs. Nwanta was the first to speak in a tone that showed deep concern and paranoia since her three eldest children were enrolled in the school where the shooting had occurred. "Well don't just sit there; we got to get down there. Let's go!" She said and rushed to the bedroom to get ready, followed by her husband.

Fifteen minutes later, the couple was on the premises of Towson Town High School. The thickness of the crowd that had now formed told them they were behind schedule. The crowd was made up of concerned parents, news crew, fire fighters, police officers and paramedics. They had no choice but to wait like the rest of the concerned parents. The county police had placed a yellow tape separating the crowd from the main building of the school.

The news crew continued to scramble for information from parents who weren't in the least interested as their mind were preoccupied by the event of the day.

After thirty minutes of anticipation and waiting, an announcement by the school principal was made over the intercom, instructing parents on how to check with school authorities about their children. After that, he told them that the school was closed until further notice.

It took another thirty minutes for the Nwanta's to find their children and take them home.

Later in the evening after dinner and special prayers by Rev. Nwanta, Mrs. Nwanta didn't waste time in voicing her opinion and feelings. She stood up from the dinner table and walked over to her husband who didn't eat due to fasting which he had started for the victims of the shooting. "I think we should go back home with the kids. This country is becoming too violent and the kids are going off course. We can't control their behavior once they leave out that door. Home is better." She looked over at the children who were still sitting. "Honey, they are too precious to me. If you don't want to go, we'll go without you." She finished and turned and rejoined the children.

They began to sing hymnal songs reflecting the victims of the shooting, followed by more prayers.

Rev. Nwanta didn't take long to make up his mind since his family came first after God. But the plan he had in mind would take at least twelve months and the kids would have to be transferred to a nearby Catholic High School in the meantime. He got up and joined the rest of the family in singing and praying.

After fifteen minutes of praying and singing to the almighty God with his family, Rev. Nwanta laid out his plan to return home, stressing to the family that it was not easy to just pack up and go back to a country you haven't been to in twenty years. "I will talk to the Bishop about replacing the outgoing Bishop of Aba Diocese and that means we would reside inside the church compound of Saint Thomas Cathedral. Meanwhile, I have to finish the family home in the village so that we can all be comfortable when we get there, okay." The holy man concluded and the kids were excited but Mrs. Nwanta wasn't happy about waiting for twelve months.

"I guess I have no choice," Mrs. Nwanta said in agreement.

CHAPTER TWO

The Journey

Rev. Nwanta accomplished his goal and the entire family was now on their way home.

The departure section of Dulles International Airport in Northern Virginia was quite busy due to heavy summer vacation travelers. The children Theo, Ada, Olu, Chinne, Nwoke and John were seated in a bench by the boarding gate waiting for the British Airways flight to London with a final destination of Nigeria.

Theo was the tallest and oldest at eighteen. He stood 6ft. and muscular, brown skin and most girls considered him cute.

Ada was fifteen and quite pretty with her dark complexion. She always wore her hair in a corn-roll and related to her African culture well, at least better than her highly westernized siblings. Olu was very westernized and religious. Her light brown skin and plum figure made her the heaviest of the family. Chinne was tall for her age and very active in all school sports activities. Nwoke and John were the youngest and most rebellious. However, they were growing and the more they learned about the motherland, the less they wanted to go.

"I'm sure going to miss all my friends" Nwoke mumbled under his breath as he sat next to his little brother, John. He then looked at the four year old. "Do you really want to move to Nigeria?"

"Not anymore. Daddy said it's real hot and I don't know anybody there." John responded with a tone of disappointment in his voice."

"Well, I'm sure you're going to make some new friends when you get there."

Their conversation was interrupted by their mother after the announcement for boarding was made over the intercom. "Okay kids, everybody get up. Didn't you hear that?" She grabbed her carryon, followed by her husband and the rest of the family.

They boarded the flight to London Heathrow International Airport. After a five-hour layover in London, the flight took off to Murtala Muhammed International Airport in Lagos, Nigeria. The entire trip lasted eighteen hours. They had no problems clearing through the Nigerian customs authority after retrieving their luggage from baggage claim.

"Well, we're here kids, you all ready?" Rev. Nwanta asked as they stood in the arrival section waiting to exit the airport in a taxi. He didn't see any happy faces except that of his wife.

Despite the disappointing response, he proceeded to inquire about ground transportation to the local airport. As he walked around by himself, he could see some developments to the airport and he still remembered certain things even though some things such as restrooms, bars and mini-restaurants had changed for the better.

The economy had obviously improved from what it was twenty years before when he was just twenty-four years of age. After studying the busy surrounding briefly and realizing the city was dangerous and it was common to be picked up by armed robbers in a fake taxi, he decided to take precaution. He quickly went back to check on his family and after seeing his wife and the children safely conversing amongst each other he approached a security checkpoint a few feet away from where the family was.

The uniformed guard noticed the Reverend wearing a white clerical collar and wondered if there was a problem. "How can I help you, Reverend?" asked the tall hefty security officer as he studied the shorter man of God.

At five feet nine inches, men over six feet didn't intimidate the man of God. "Yes, you may." He responded, adding a Godly kindness to his voice. "Can you please advise me on how I can get a safe transportation for my family to the local airport?"

The security officer smiled and felt his weapon by his waist. "No problem. I can tell you've been away for a long time, Reverend."

"Yes, I have." Rev. Nwanta replied with a smile." I am also happy that English is the main language here, unlike other countries."

"Just go outside and ask any parked black and white taxi but do not get the ones circling the loop without any visible taxi number written on the side." The security officer instructed, pointing at a fleet of parked taxis on the curbside of the ground transportation loop.

"Thank you very much my dear and God bless you." Nwanta walked away, feeling safe and welcome.

The country was made up of three dominant tribes; Ibo, Yoruba and Hausa. There are at least one hundred ethnic groups speaking indigenous dialects but English remained the major language. It was colonized by the British and granted independence in 1960. This explains why Christianity and English language became dominant over the traditional religion. But Islam is still dominant in the Northern states among the Hausas. The British education system was also adopted.

Rev. Nwanta quickly returned to where the family was. "Come on kids, we got to go." He said and motioned to one of the airport attendants to bring them a wagon to haul their luggage outside to the cab.

They were driven to the local airport where they boarded local flight to Port Harcourt Airport in the Eastern part of the country. The flight lasted forty five minutes.

The village of Ubakala in Umuahia was about two hours from the airport so; they took a taxi van and headed home. Halfway to the village, they ran into a tropical thunderstorm which usually threatened all moving vehicles on the road. It wasn't unusual to have thunderstorms every other day during the summer months. The taxi driver pulled over to the side of the road to wait for the rain to subside.

Only the Reverend and his wife had seen such powerful thunderstorm and lightening with heavy torrential down-pour. All they could hear was the sound of heavy rain and thunder.

Nwoke was startled by one particular thunder. "Hey ma, is that hail?" he asked.

"No, it's rain. A different kind of rain," his mother responded from the back seat.

Rev. Nwanta, who was sitting on the passenger side of the first seat with the driver wondered if the rain and delay was actually a blessing in disguise. It was going on three o'clock in the afternoon and anything could've been waiting on the way home. He prayed by himself briefly. "You know, I forgot this was rainy season. You see, I've been away for twenty years." He informed the skinny dark skinned driver.

The driver was shocked and wanted to know if the man ran away because of the civil war. "Are you serious, sir?" Twenty-one years in another man's country without visiting home? Were you afraid of the war?" he asked, studying the Reverend and then checking the rest of the family through the rear-view mirror?

"Because I received a full scholarship for my bachelors and masters degree in Theology."

"Where?"

"In the United States. After that, I worked as a minister following my ordination and later on, my wife joined me."

"So the children are all U.S. Citizens?"

"Yes. They have never been to this country."

The driver turned his head and studied the kids and their mother. He knew he had to increase the fee since his passenger had dollars. "Sir, I have to charge extra due to the time I have wasted. Time is money in Nigeria."

"Well, I am not worried about the money. Just get us home safely and God will bless you immensely." Rev. Nwanta responded, wondering what religion the man belonged to.

The storm lasted about thirty minutes and the driver pulled off immediately accelerating to 120 kilometers per hour. Since there were no posted speed limits in the country, he was able to cut the trip by twenty minutes after wasting thirty minutes. Mathematically, he only lost ten minutes and the Rev. was aware of this but didn't want to argue.

A right turn off the Aba-Umuahia expressway took them to the village of Ubakala, where Rev. and Mrs. Nwanta were born and raised.

The small dirt road captured the attention of the kids.

Nwoke was the first to ask questions. "Hey dad, why are those people walking with flip-flops on and carrying that thing on their heads?" He asked as the van passed two women who appeared to be coming from the farm.

"Because that's their way of life. It's not cold, so they don't need shoes only when they are leaving the village but right now they are working at the farm." Rev. Nwanta answered.

Chinne also made an obvious observation. "Why are the roads so small and dusty?" she asked.

Mrs. Nwanta decided to answer, "These are pathways for villagers to walk and ride their bicycles to market and farm. They are not roads. The main roads are in the townships, Okay?"

Rev. Nwanta intervened by instructing the driver to turn left into a long driveway that led to their newly constructed home.

The villagers who got the news of the Nwanta's arrival from America were already waiting inside the huge compound. They obviously organized a welcome home party for the highly respected family.

Rev. Nwanta was surprised as he saw what his relatives had planned. He quickly paid the driver double the fare and thanked him.

The driver was astonished and helped the relatives and caretakers of the family remove the luggage from the taxi-van. "Thank you, so much sir. You have just given me a vacation for the next three weeks.I have never been paid this kind of money before. Thank the Lord for American dollars." He bowed down on his knees to the minister of God and then happily got back in his taxi and drove off.

Amidst drum beats, singing and dancing by the villagers, Rev. Nwanta led his family into their new home.

They were surprised at the luxury they saw. The house was a split-level brick home, sitting on one and half acre of land surrounded by trees and carefully planted flowers.

In the living room while observing the inner backyard, Nwoke quickly ran to his father. "Hey Dad! This is nice, but can you tell those people outside to stay there?" he cried, not feeling comfortable around the strangers who looked and dressed differently from what he was used to.

"No, I cannot. They are part of your family and you must learn to be friends with them. Why can't you be like your brothers and sisters? Now let me show you all to your rooms."

He then began showing the entire family one by one to their rooms. The house was made up of a large kitchen with an island and eat-in nook. It had a three-car garage in the 7000 square ft. building, a family library full of traditional religious books, seven bedrooms, including a first and second floor master suites, ceramic floors and the latest modern appliances with central air conditioning system.

The cheap labor makes it possible for the minister to afford such an expensive home. Well, one could not forget the power of American dollars when changed to the local currency; the Naira.

After everybody was settled in their rooms, Rev and Mrs. Nwanta came outside to the main compound and addressed the crowd of about one hundred people. Everyone referred to each other as brothers and sisters. The Rev. Then prayed for everyone and dedicated the home to his late parents. He briefed them on what he went through to get where he was and also that none of it would have been possible without God. The man of God stressed how important it was to get your education by building a solid foundation in elementary school.

After the ten-minute speech from the highly respected man of God, the celebration continued. The kids had never seen anything like it; different drum beats and the way the villagers dressed, complemented by the singing and dancing in the traditional Ibo language now it excited them and they wanted to be a part of it.

They joined them for about forty minutes and retired to their rooms, but the celebration continued through the night.

Visitors continued to come to the Nwanta's residence over the next few days as the family had now become outstanding members of the village. They were treated differently due to their western lifestyle which the kids where now working on changing to suit their heritage.

CHAPTER THREE

After one month in the village, the Nwanta's moved to Saint Thomas Cathedral Church in Aba. Aba is a town forty five minutes from the village of Ubakala and known for its commercial status. The kids continued to adjust to the new culture by mixing with fellow Ibo born children.

As the new Bishop of Saint Thomas Cathedral, there were many activities Rev. Nwanta was directing and this opened the way for the children to further learn the language and adapt faster to the environment.

The children were enrolled in the summer program of St. Thomas Ascension Seminary which taught children from first grade to twelfth grade. A private tutor helped them learn Ibo as fast as they could but it wasn't possible to master the tribal language in a matter of months. It would take close to a year for the American kids.

The school year began in September and all the kids had no problems blending in with other kids their ages. Theo and Ada were the closest to the twelfth grade and they had a hard time adjusting to the new English system of education which required a lot of essay writing as opposed to multiple choice. As a result, a private tutor was employed by the Church to teach them English writing and math skills which were a little different from the American system.

They all lived in the dormitory except Nwoke and John. Boarding school was a requirement to help instill strict discipline in students.

Aba was a commercial city and extremely busy. The traffic would be less troubling if the roads were bigger. This also made it very dangerous as armed robbers and con-men were common but for some reason, religious organization such as churches and Christian schools were never a target for law breakers.

One day while watching the news, a story about an armed robbery that took place at a bank not far from the church compound frightened Mrs. Nwanta so much that she began to wonder if things were even safer in the motherland. At least the U.S. had very strict laws to punish violent criminals unlike Nigeria where criminals could buy the law through bribery.

For the first time since their return, flashbacks and memories of that dreadful day in Towson led her to question her decision to return home.

One day, Nwoke had just been driven home by the family driver and he had a reputation for yelling his dad's name unlike John who was still in kindergarten.

"I'm home, dad!"

Mrs. Nwanta was the only one who heard him this time from the top of the stairs but she wasn't strong enough to pick up the twelve year old like her husband. "Okay, Nwoke. You got your homework?" she asked and gave him a hug then looked the young boy deep in the eyes for any signs of trouble since he was the only one known to get in trouble at school.

"In my book bag," Nwoke responded, innocently. "Now where's daddy?"

"He's in a meeting, now, go change your clothes and go to the study for your homework, okay."

Nwoke did as he was told. He wasn't too happy about being set back one grade due to the kids inability to speak ibo language fluently. Now instead of graduating high school at eighteen, they would all be nineteen the year they finish high school.

One week later, school recessed for Christmas. The driver picked up the kids from the dormitory and brought them home.

Theo was the first one to get out the Peugeot 505 Station wagon. "I'm so glad we are home for three weeks," he said out loud.

Nwoke who was standing on the balcony heard him and quickly responded. "I'm not. I wish it would last forever," Nwoke responded, rebelliously and disappeared to his room.

All the kids got out of the vehicle and took their luggage to their rooms.

Ten minutes later they all gathered in the family room, including Nwoke.

"Mom, can you tell me why there's no snow in this country? I think I prefer a white Christmas than hot Christmas," Nwoke said to his mother who seemed happy to have the kid's home for Christmas.

Mrs. Nwanta faced her twelve year old boy. "Now young man, can you tell me the meaning of "Why" in Ibo language?" She asked politely with a smile so as not to further upset him.

Nwoke looked around the big room at his brothers and sisters as all eyes focused on him, then back at his mother. He let out a little smile and this was Mrs. Nwanta's intention when she asked the question. As a former school teacher, she was well versed in children behavior and how to correct it. "I know you got to be kidding, Mom. That's one of the first words I learned when we first got to the village."

"So what does it mean?" She repeated, feeling the reverse psychology technique working as the defiant son was now smiling and friendlier than when he first walked into the living room. "Gini," he finally answered, looking at his mother in the eyes and then studying his brothers and sisters who were very attentive to the session.

"Good. Now, you kids enjoy yourselves and find something productive to do." Mrs. Nwanta left the room.

Theo was busy thinking about Joy, the girl he met in the village when they first arrived in the country. He had already changed into his American attire and hoped she would come over like she did whenever school recessed. She had an aunt in the town, but if she didn't, he would just have to see her in the village when they went home for Christmas.

They all sat in the living room, watching traditional African movies depicting the lifestyle and also produced in Nigeria until the cook and the maid announced dinner. Nwoke was the last one to get up and go to the dining room as he wondered how he could get back to Baltimore or Towson. At twelve years of age, he knew he probably would have to wait till he graduated high school before he could return to the U.S. He planned to use college as an excuse and that meant getting good grades to impress Mom and Dad. His thought process was broken when the maid walked into the room and asked him if he was going to eat. He caught himself immediately, got up and joined the family for dinner.

A week later, as the family was packing up to travel to the village for the Christmas celebration the report cards arrived by mail. All the kids passed their subjects with flying colors and this was a major improvement from the previous semester. This impressed Rev. and Mrs. Nwanta as it showed the kids had now adjusted quite well to the education system.

Rev. Nwanta spoke up before they all got in the vehicles. "All of you will get your Christmas wishes and it must be reasonable," he emphasized the word "reasonable". "Now, let's go." He ordered the two drivers to get in the cars and make the trip a pleasant one.

The family left the church compound and headed for the village for the Christmas celebration.

CHAPTER FOUR

– 1989

Four years had now gone by without any negative incident from any angle for the Nwanta's and Mrs. Nwanta now believed she did make the right decision.

Summer vacation had just started, but it was called the long vacation in Nigeria and it wasn't unusual for students to travel to other countries if they could afford to but, Rev and Mrs. Nwanta weren't going to risk sending any of the kids to the States. The chances were they may not return.

Nwoke had just turned sixteen and girls were becoming interesting to look at. He had also met a male friend who may be considered his best friend and they both shared the same interest. The only difference was that his friend. Uzo Otu was born and partly raised in London, England. The two boys had become so close that fellow students thought they were brothers.

Nwoke made it a habit to go to Uzo's house daily and Uzo also returned the favor. Today he was at Uzo's earlier than usual.

Uzo's fathers' house was a villa with a six-car garage in the back of the main building. It had a waterfall, swimming pool, and a second pool in the basement. The kitchen had granite countertops, subzero stainless steel appliances and large breakfast room, Italian marble floors throughout the entire house. A pool house that included all fitness equipment, first and second floor master suites, both with luxury baths and huge walk-in closets. Tray ceilings and stamped concrete side-walk and patio and a mahogany double-door front entrance. The 10,000 square ft. villa sat on three acres of land in the government reserved area (GRA) of Aba. This was the most expensive area of the state, exclusively for the wealthy. Nwoke still had no idea what Uzo's father did for a living but he travelled to London quite often.

"Uzo, I'm going to build a house just like this when I grow up," Nwoke said as they passed through the parlor on their way to the East balcony that overlooked the main building.

A look inside the kitchen revealed granite countertops, subzero stainless steel appliance. A large breakfast room, Italian marble floors throughout the entire house. A gym that included all fitness equipment. First and second floor master suites and a third one in the basement with luxury baths, tray ceilings and stamped concrete sidewalks and patio. Fifteen bedrooms that included six guest houses. The mahogany double front doors set a standard in the neighborhood.

Uzo was very tall at 6'4" for his age and Nwoke 5'7" figure made him look like a midget. Uzo was light brown skin and slim like an NBA player as opposed to Nwoke's stocky figure.

They sat down next to each other in the balcony and observed the main street which wasn't busy at all in the upscale neighborhood.

"Man, where are your sister and her buddies?" Nwoke asked. He had taken a liking to Uzo's sister, Ije but didn't let Uzo know.

"I don't know. She does have some pretty good looking friends from what I've seen. I saw one stop by earlier in a little Toyota. She's driving at sixteen.

"Say what?" Nwoke turned his head, surprised that a sixteen year old Nigerian girl was driving.

"Yea, you heard right. She might have been mixed with something," Uzo said with a British accent and intonation.

"Stop! You think she might be in the same school with us?"

"I'd never seen her, but I'm going to find out soon, chap."

"Yeah, right," Nwoke responded doubtfully with a grin.

"I tell you what, I'm glad I only have one sister and one brother. I wouldn't want any boys to lust after my sister."

"Me too, I got three of them. Let's go to my house. Saint Thomas road is a lot busier than this dead part of town. Plus they got choir rehearsal tonight and that's about ninety percent females," Nwoke suggested, fed up with looking at trees and occasional vehicles.

"Oh, Okay. Let me tell my mom, because I think you're right for once and I'd have to agree that your place does have much more action than this." Uzo got up and left to tell his mom.

He returned ten minutes later in a different outfit. "You ready, yo?" He liked to tease Nwoke with American slang every so often.

"Stop the fake American, yo."

The two boys descended the stairs and walked across the backyard to the 'boy's quarters of the villa to get an available driver to transport them.

"Dike! Dike!" Uzo yelled to the driver that was in his room with the door open.

Dike was his favorite of all five drivers. "Okay, give me a minute!" He disappeared back into his room. Five minutes later he was dressed and ready.

Uzo and Nwoke proceeded to the main gate to wait for the driver. Six minutes later, a white Mercedes 420S, pulled up in front of the iron gates and they got in. The driver drove them to the Bishop's mansion at Saint Thomas Cathedral in the town. The two young adults got out and headed straight for the balcony.

The view from the balcony to the main road named after the church was a very busy road for pedestrians and taxi drivers. It could be compared to a street in the busy part of Manhattan in New York City.

4:30PM in Aba meant rush hour and a lot of pedestrian traffic since the city didn't have a door to door taxi service like the U.S. If one wanted door to door, they would have to pay a rate that's very abnormal.

"This is the perfect time to sight-see, man. We should have been here from the get-go." Uzo commented as he sat down and stretched his legs to get comfortable.

Nwoke followed suit. "Hey, check her out." He said, pointing at a pretty honey complexioned young girl who looked to be about fifteen years old.

The girl had swaggering strides to supplement her looks.

"You want to go try your luck?" Uzo asked.

"Nah, I like them a little taller than that." Suddenly giggling sounds and chuckles made the two boys turn around to face Ada, Chinne and Olu who stood behind the front window of the living room watching and listening to the two female hunters.

Nwoke was upset. "Don't you all have something better to do with your time?" Nwoke asked in a loud voice, standing up and upset at the invasion of his privacy by his bored sisters. "If you guys don't leave us alone, I'm going to have to tell mom."

The girls quickly disappeared since their mother had told all family members not to bother Nwoke unless he initiated it. This was all in an attempt to make Nwoke stop thinking about going back to the U.S. But lusting after girls from a holy compound, was not Godly and Nwoke knew this.

But Chinne could not resist the temptation of letting her little brother know how she felt about the ungodly act. "Shut up, boy!" She yelled from across the living room. "You all ain't got no business looking at girls from a church compound. Don't you know it's a sin?"

Nwoke quickly turned around, surprised that big mouth Chinne had to add her two cents to it after the other two sisters had left. He wasn't very happy. "Oh, give me a break! I know your boyfriend, okay and I also know what you've been doing with him when you go over there to see his sister."

Chinne was now furious since she didn't know how the defiant little brother got his information. "I'm gonna smack you," she moved toward her irritating brother.

Ada come from nowhere and intervened. "Stop it you two," she said as she stepped between the two younger siblings.

Uzo just watched, enjoying the little drama.

"C'mon Chinne. Remember what ma told us," Ada dragged her little sister out of sight.

+ Just as soon as they resumed their sight-seeing adventure, a female voice interrupted them from the living room once again.

"Hello, you guys," said the feminine voice.

They both turned their heads to see Joy, Theo's girlfriend coming through the living room. She looked exquisite.

"Hello, Joy. What brings you to town?"

"Hello, Miss," Uzo said with a smile, admiring the pretty woman.

"Hi and you must be Uzo."

"Yes and you must be Joy."

"Well, of course," she gave him a smile and turned her attention back to Nwoke. "Your brother, to answer your question."

Theo entered the balcony and grabbed her right hand. "Let's go," he said and led her through the balcony to the front stairs leading down to the parking lot. The two lovers walked hand in hand like they were still on campus. They were now third year students at the University of Nsuka where he had officially engaged her for marriage just before the summer vacation.

The two boys, tried once again to get back to their leisure duty. But the sound of two females entering the living room with the doors wide open caught their attention.

"Don't step so hard on the floor with those heels' Nwoke said without turning to see who it was.

Uzo turned and what he saw was better than any they've seen across the street all day. "Yo, look."

Nwoke turned and was also interested in the girl who accompanied Chinne into the house.

"I should introduce myself," Uzo thought out loud.

"Go ahead," Nwoke encouraged.

Uzo thought about it, but when he remembered what had just transpired between Chinne and Nwoke, he decided against it. He would wait for a better day without Chinne and hopefully, that wasn't going to be too long. "Yo, watch when I start driving. It's going to be pure hell out there. I promise you. The entire town will feel my presence," the British-born young boy concluded as they refocused on the female traffic on Saint Thomas road.

Nwoke didn't say a word since he knew his day of driving will also come.

Ten minutes later, the girls left for choir rehearsal in the church.

"Hey, who was that beautiful girl I just saw and I know you saw her too," Uzo asked.

"Oh, I don't even know. She just goes to choir rehearsal with Chinne. I think she might be from London or at least born there. I heard her accent once. Forget her; I think she's a church girl."

"Why you think that?"

"Look at that," Nwoke pointed at two pretty teenage girls walking past and holding hands.

"C'mon man. Let's go for a walk ourselves instead of sitting here," Uzo suggested.

"Good idea. Just up the street and back."

They got up and headed for the stairs when sudden thunder and lightning proceeded torrential downpour of a tropical storm. This was typical of the summer months and the boys quickly retrieved to their previous position to continue where they left off. But now, there weren't much pedestrian traffic as most of them hopped into taxis while others took cover under commercial buildings.

Report cards for the last semester came by mail the following day and, to everyone's surprise, Nwoke was the only one to get all A's and this impressed Rev. and Mrs. Nwanta. Nwoke now knew he was on the right track to returning to where he was born.

But, the journey was going to take a lot more than he thought.

CHAPTER FIVE

1992

At the age of eighteen, Nwoke had been driving for a little over two years and he enjoyed every bit of it. His father had bought him a 1991 Volkswagen Golf to help make him as comfortable as possible. He and Uzo were always gone from school to different all-girls' secondary schools on parties and inter-house sports competition. This wasn't common in the country, but as the children of the upper-class in an upper-class school, they could afford to do it and it brought them a lot of attention since there were only ten other students who had vehicles in the entire school.

Uzo's Mercedes 190E placed him in a class by himself and he and Nwoke had twin sisters for girlfriends. The girls were the school principal's daughters. Their names were Helen and Deborah.

Helen and Deborah were average height for eighteen-year olds, honey coded complexion and kept a modest look of naturally braided corn-rolls. Their figures weren't voluptuous but slender and attractive.

Today was a sunny day in May and Nwoke and Helen were in the library studying for the General Certificate of Education finals (GCE).

"Hey Helen, what's up with you and that math book?" Nwoke asked, sitting opposite his girlfriend, Helen.

"I don't know. You tell me, Einstein." Helen answered, not raising her head from the text book.

Coincidentally, Helen's parents were from the same village as Nwoke's. Nwoke met her for the first time at the monthly village meeting which was hosted by the Nwanta's a year before. But he had no idea she and her sister were students at the same school until he spotted her again two weeks later on his way to his geography class.

"What do you think is up, American boy?" Helen asked after getting no response from her previous answer. She was trying to solve the geometric problem on her own, without Nwoke's assistance. "Why don't you just focus on your geography and let me do this." This time she lifted her head and looked at him.

"Okay, if you say so, my dear."

"Can you save the jokes for later, please. I'm really trying to concentrate here."

Uzo and Deborah walked in, holding hands and headed for the table Nwoke and Helen were seated at.

"Yo, Yo, Yo, Wazzup?" Uzo announced as he took the empty seat next to his buddy while Deborah sat next to her sister.

"What's up?" Nwoke asked.

"Trying to get an A in this geography," Uzo answered, opening his big geography text book.

"Shit, that's easy, yo."

"Maybe to you. I have a hard time remembering time zones and ethnic groups around the world. But the land formation is easy and so are plantations."

Deborah wasn't in a study mood. She had enjoyed her moments with Uzo and it filled her with cheers and smiles. "Hi Nwoke and what's going on sis?" she intervened.

"Nothing sis," Helen replied, studying her sister closely. "Where are you two coming from?" her mind went straight to sex in the back seat of Uzo's Mercedes.

"The usual, ha ha ha," Deborah answered with a smile.

"Okay, enough talking, you guys. It's study time. I think this is a library, if I remember correctly," Nwoke intervened as they all got the message. He bent his head and began to study.

Others followed suit.

School let out for the vacation in early June and students vacated the premises of St. Thomas Ascension Seminary for their various homes across the country. Some even traveled abroad.

Nwoke, Uzo, Helen and Deborah were now awaiting the results of their GCE, If they all passed with C's and or better, they would become eligible for the University entrance exam also known as Joint Admissions and Matriculation Board Examination(JAMB). But attending university in the country was the last thing on Nwoke's mind. He wanted to follow his father's footsteps and attend Towson State University. He was ready to approach his father for that purpose.

Upon arrival in his Volkswagen at the church compound, Nwoke parked his car, removed his school luggage and made himself comfortable in his room once again. Afterwards, he found his father in his study.

"Hey son, how was school this term?" his father asked, standing up to face the smartest child in the family. He noticed Nwoke had grown slightly taller than himself. "It's been a while since I saw you. You're taller than me, just like Theo."

Nwoke's mind was already set on what he came to his father's study for. "Well, dad you've been so busy since we came back from Towson."

"But I still saw you all at dinner during vacations. Well, I guess that's not enough, cause little John's also grown before my eyes. What's on your mind?"

"I wanna go to college in U.S. Well, your former school, Towson State."

The Bishop of Aba diocese studied his young son very closely and wondered what it was that made him want to return to the U.S. so badly. He had tried his best to make the family as comfortable as possible and even more comfortable than they were in Towson with the assistance of maids and drivers. He was twenty-four in 1964 when he travelled to the U.S. on a church scholarship to attend college and become a minister of God. But that was a different generation than the generation of today, especially in America. It was the violent life style of young Americans that led them to return home and it wouldn't make sense for him to go against the wishes of his wife and the purpose of the trip back home seven years ago. Moreover, a young adult without guidance of parents will be as lost as the one who never had any parents at all. This eighteen year old standing before him now seemed too wild and too young to be in a U.S. college without a guardian. All kinds of thoughts went through his mind. He even thought about informing the minister that succeeded him and also his nephew, Alo who also lived in Towson after graduation from Morgan to guide him if he were to change his mind and keep the boy focused on attending college. His worst fear was not to make any decision that could make the intelligent kid lose focus.

After about five minutes of silence, Rev. Nwanta came to the conclusion that he needed more time and his wife would have to get involved in reaching a decision. "Okay son, I don't wanna keep you waiting since you just got home, but let me talk to your mother first. But remember, we do have some of the best universities in the world right here in Nigeria and I want you to think about it." The Reverend concluded.

"When are you gonna let me know something?"

"Soon. Just go ahead and enjoy your vacation for now," he replied and Nwoke left the room.

Minutes later Mrs. Nwanta entered the study and closed the door behind her. She noticed her husband was buried in deep thought. "What's the problem, honey?" she asked, removing her glasses and putting her right hand on her husband's back, rubbing it gently.

"Nwoke says he wants to go back to the U.S. and attend college. That's not even feasible."

She stopped massaging his back and walked over to the window. "Oh, I see," she responded thoughtfully." I thought he was happy here with his friend, Uzo and that made him forget about the U.S. This isn't good. He's the smartest one in the family and we must keep an eye on him."

"Maybe, we should think about it and make some calls. After all, he'll be in a respectable college and not high school. Plus he wants to be a business major," Rev.

Nwanta responded and got up off the chair and joined his wife in looking out the window. "Honey, Towson does have a good Business school, but he'd have to live on campus and spend weekends at the minister's house on the church compound and travel home for the summer vacation, he concluded, waiting for his wife's response.

"Maybe, he should live on the church compound and come home during breaks. That's if we let him go but honey, I brought all of them back for a reason and I don't wanna contradict that. Let's think more about this."

Uzo turned his Mercedes 190E into the iron gates of the Cathedral Church compound and parked. The car was his eighteenth birthday gift, brand new from Leventis Mercedes of Aba. It was black with all leather interior, fully loaded and sitting on twenty-two inch wheels. He stepped out of the car, checked himself on the side-view window and proceeded upstairs into the mansion. "Hello, girls. What's happening with you all righteous beauties?" Uzo greeted as he walked into the family room where Chinne, Ada and Olu were sitting, watching 'Coming to America. He could have passed for an American NBA player at 6 foot 7 inches.

"Damn Uzo!" exclaimed Ada. "Do you grow everyday?"

"I believe so my dearest beautiful one," answered Uzo, jokingly.

Ada liked Uzo, but she didn't think it was morally appropriate to date your younger brother's best friend. "So, where are you two headed today?" She looked him over from head to toe and then gave him a sexy smile while Chinne and Olu watched.

"You know Nwoke just got in and I think he's in his room, unless you wanna watch 'Coming to America' with us," Olu added.

"No, I think I'll pass. I've seen it too many times. We are on a mission to celebrate the beginning of long vacation," Uzo answered dismissively with a grin and headed for Nwoke's room.

"I'll bet you are," Ada said as they watched the tall clean figure disappear through the door he came in.

They refocused on the movie and chuckled at a scene in which Mr. MacDowell sent the little dog after Darryl.

In Nwoke's room, Uzo talked about doing it with Deborah and how much different it was when compared to the more voluptuous new girl he'd just met named Regina. He had only known her for two weeks. Nwoke didn't pay too much attention as he was preoccupied with what his father had said and what the man's final decision might be.

By watching a lot of American movies, Uzo had now began to immitate the lifestyle of most of the characters. "Yo, you heard what I just said?" Uzo asked, touching his friend on the shoulder.

"Some of it," Nwoke finally responded, still propped up on the bed.

Uzo noticed Nwoke wasn't himself so he asked, "you okay?"

"I guess. My pop is now having second thoughts about sending me back to the U.S. He doesn't seem to trust an independent young adult in the U.S." He sat up and noticed how fresh Uzo looked.

"No big deal. You wanna come to London with me, then? I know I'm going and ain't no ifs or buts about it. My father has a nice house there."

"That would be a last resort, but first, let me see what he says." Nwoke got up, feeling a little better about his second choice if his father said no. He went to his closet to pick out something fresh to match Uzo's outfit. As he reached inside the closet, he turned his head to get a second look at what Uzo was wearing. "Damn, yo! You look like you play for the Chicago bulls," he pointed out as he surveyed the six-seven Uzo and his fresh outfit that looked like something out of a brand name sports store in a Baltimore city black neighborhood.

Uzo had on a black T-shirt by Nautica, fat gold chain, blue denim shorts and fresh pair of Air Jordan's to cover his size fifteen feet.

"Did your dad shop for you in the U.S. or what?" Nwoke asked, not sure how he could match what he saw.

"Always, You know he goes to New York a lot from London."

Nwoke found something close but not as fresh. He had bought the outfit in Aba.

"That looks good," Uzo said as he saw what Nwoke had in his hands. "Plus one of dad's business partners who lives in New York plans to open up an American sports-clothing store here in Aba, selling this kind of shit, You know what I mean?"

Nwoke still wasn't sure what Uzo's father did for a living to be so rich. "Okay, American boy. I'm sure chicks haven't seen those yet." Nwoke got dressed.

"Well, just call me Michael Jordan for today. See my gold pen to write down numbers, addresses, names and maybe sign a few autographs with?" Uzo took out a gold pen out of his right hip pocket and showed Nwoke.

Nwoke smiled and led the way downstairs to the car. He felt content in his Ralph Lauren shirt and prewashed

Polo jeans shorts with a pair of Air Nikes he'd only wore once.

The two spoiled rich eighteen year olds stepped into the shiny baby Benz and took off into the busy town to celebrate the temporary freedom from school.

Nwoke checked the digital clock on the stereo of the car. "It's only three P.M., man. What's the business in this new machine of yours?" he asked as he flipped through the CD and cassette case to pick out a good one. He stumbled on the new DasFX and inserted it into the player and turned up the volume to the max as Uzo turned up the air conditioner to let all four windows down to attract girls.

"I never thought I would ever get used to this hot weather. Let me slow down to ten miles per hour so we can get a better view if it doesn't start raining" Uzo yelled over the loud rap tune: 'Microphone checka' which now filled the air.

"I say we go get the twins," Nwoke said and turned the volume down. With his right hand on the volume, he checked the right side of the street for any pretty pair of school girls looking for some fun, when he saw none, he turned the volume back up to the max.

The subwoofer on the stereo vibrated the ground.

This time, Uzo turned the volume down to a tolerable level so they could decide on what the agenda was for the day. "Yo, I say we can always see the twins. Here's the plan; I'll pretend to be an NBA player and you're my agent, straight from New York or Chicago."

"Great idea. What do you know about NBA?"

"C'mon we might play rugby in London but we watch the NBA playoffs and finals."

"Okay, we have to do it out of town so that we don't bump into somebody we know."

"Which town did you have in mind?"

"The closest,"

"I saaay Owerri....plus they got some pretty fly bitches."

"Okay then. Owerri it is," Uzo replied and pulled into a gas station on Ehi road. "Let me fill up the tank and we'll be on our way." He pulled by a pump in the empty gas station and turned off the engine.

The attendant filled up the tank and walked over to the driver side door for payment. Uzo paid him, but the teenage attendant, who couldn't have been no more than fourteen, didn't leave. He continued to stare at Uzo after seeing the stack of one hundred naira notes.

Uzo realized the boy wanted a tip. "Okay little boy. Here chap," he said as he handed the boy a one hundred naira note.

"Thank you, sir," the boy said and immediately went to the car behind Uzo's.

The Mercedes pulled out of the gas station and turned right on Ehi road which joined Aba-Owerri rd.

Step on the accelerator, man." Nwoke said and changed the CD to EPMD's 'Crossover'.

The Mercedes sped past a few females strolling along the busy road. Some looked like they needed a ride while others looked like they were looking for a good time. The transportation system in the country consisted of taxis, buses and vans. The newer model of 505 Peugeots and luxury buses which made long distance trips. Uzo continued to feed the cylinders with patrol as the speedometer button touched 160 kilometers per hour on the expressway leading to Owerri.

They arrived Owerri at about 4:15PM and pulled straight into the taxi-park, otherwise known as a taxi-stand in the U.S. This was where all the taxis and commercial vans loaded their passengers. The drivers took turns loading passengers.

They got out and Nwoke immediately approached a short, stocky dark skinned taxi driver whose turn to load hadn't reached.

"Oga, wetin de happen?" Nwoke asked in broken English which was another means of communication in the country, spoken and understood by all citizens. This meant 'what's happening.'

"Nothing, my brother," responded the driver.

Nwoke and Uzo moved closer to the man and he looked up at Uzo and shook his head. Uzo asked, "Oga, I beg, where are the good-looking girls in Owerri? We are from Aba and we're just visiting for today."

"Right here, my friends. Are you from America?" the taxi driver asked and took a bite off his meat pie.

"No, but we were born abroad, You mean here in the park?"

"Yes, they usually come here to board taxis all the time when they're leaving town," the man responded in proper English as he tried to impress the two rich-looking kids. This surprised Nwoke and Uzo since most of the taxi drivers were not educated.

"Well, we're from out of town and we wanna meet girls staying here, not leaving," Nwoke replied.

The taxi driver studied the young adults and wondered why such good-looking rich kids would travel out of town just to meet girls. He knew they could have all the girls they wanted. If anything, Aba probably had more girls than Owerri, since it was the commercial capital of the state. His thoughts were broken by two pretty teenage girls who looked to be about eighteen years of age, strolling by and heading for the six-passenger van that was loading for Aba.

The girls caught the attention of Uzo and Nwoke and Nwoke immediately rushed to stop them from getting into the van as he tapped one of them on the shoulder.

The girl turned immediately. "Why are you touching me?" she asked as she faced Nwoke, startled.

Then Uzo walked up to where they were and both girls studied the six-foot-seven Uzo from head to toe.

"Well, me and my friend here wanted to talk to you and your buddy," Nwoke turned on his best American accent as he pointed at Uzo.

"Well, hello to you," responded the second girl with a tone of admiration of Uzo and Nwoke who seemed somewhat different from what they were used to.

"Hi, pretty," Uzo greeted with a smile.

The two girls now stood side by side as they studied Uzo and Nwoke. They were about five-foot four inches, both of them slender with very attractive figures that wasn't too curvy. One was lighter complexioned than the other.

Uzo decided to take control of the conversation. My name is Uzo and this is my friend, Nwoke." He looked to his right side at Nwoke who was staring at the darker girl whom he had tapped on the shoulder.

The two girls appeared to be impressed by the English accent and American accent and intonation coming from the two boys.

"We are pleased to meet you and glad we ran into that taxi driver over there," Nwoke said and pointed at the taxi driver whom they were talking to. He also admired the long natural permed hair they wore.

The two girls each had a carry-on which meant they weren't going to stay very long wherever they were headed.

"My name is Blessing and this is my friend, Chichi," the light-skinned girl introduced as other passengers began walking around the four young adults into the loading van.

"Why don't we all get out of the way. I think the driver might be getting a little irritated," Nwoke suggested, moving a few steps away from the van as the other three followed.

"So, where are you two going?" Uzo asked.

"Aba, to visit my uncle for a couple of days," Chichi said, looking at Nwoke and observing his outfit.

Most of the males in the country wore slacks and button-up long sleeve shirts and dress shoes or sandals. Uzo and Nwoke reminded the girls of something out of an American rap music video.

"Let me make a suggestion," Uzo said, standing above everyone but paying close attention to Blessing and turning on his best American accent with a British flava. "We live in Aba and we would be glad to give you two a ride if you're willing to show us around Owerri for a couple of hours. Actually, we just came to sigh-see."

The two girls looked at each other and immediately thought these two kids must be rich and foreign with an Ibo name. They had been friends for so long that they could read each other's mind. They were interested but they had a habit of playing hard to get. But deep inside, Chichi wanted to forego their usual routine of playing hard to get since Uzo and Nwoke were different from the boys they were used to, who deserved hard time.

"But my uncle is expecting us and our parents know what time we are supposed to be there," Chichi said and looked at her partner for any sign that may point to the contrary but saw none, so she continued, "I don't think that's a good idea," she lied, knowing the contrary was true. She waited for a response from either Uzo or Nwoke.

"And what time are you supposed to be there?" Nwoke asked, believing that's why Chichi didn't think it was a good idea.

"9pm," Blessing intervened, ready to put an end to the dialogue that could make them miss out on some good guys they could learn from.

"I'm sure that's not a problem. It's only 4:30pm and if we leave Owerri by seven, I don't see why we shouldn't be in Aba before eight. Where in Aba does he live?" Nwoke asked.

"Azikiwe road," Blessing answered, cutting her eyes at her friend, indicating she was ready to go with them.

"Oh, I think that's one of the roads behind the church, if I'm not mistaking," Nwoke said, looking at Blessing for an answer.

"You sure? Uzo asked.

"Positive, yo."

"Okay then. I guess we can take a chance with you strangers, what do you think, Chichi?" Blessing said as she looked over at Chichi, smiling to confirm their willingness to go with the boys.

With her own pleasant smile, Chichi said "fine with me." She shrugged, studying Nwoke from head to toe. "Mmmm, so where are you guys from?"

The four young adults began walking toward Uzo's car.

"Well, I was born in Towson Maryland which is in the United States but my friend here was born in London England and plays professional basketball for the New York Knicks and I am his agent," Nwoke lied, avoiding eye contact with the girls who only watched soccer and had only seen an NBA game on commercials or when they can get to a home with satellite television.

"Oh, really? For how long?" You two look rather too young for all that."

Uzo looked at the two girls who now seemed smarter than they gave them credit for. "I'm twenty one and Nwoke is twenty." He continued to justify the lie.

The two girls exchanged looks in doubt of what Nwoke had just said but didn't seem to care. There was no mention of age since they were all legal at eighteen..

They got to where Uzo's Mercedes was parked. Uzo pressed the keyless entry button and the car made a bleep-bleep sound and they all got in. Blessing and Chichi sat in the back while Uzo and Nwoke sat in the front.

The girls were obviously impressed by the cleanliness and comfort of the Benz.

What kind of music do you all listen to?" Uzo asked and started the engine.

Nwoke grabbed the CD case.

"Hip hop, soul and soft rock or country," answered Chichi as she sneaked up her hand and tapped Blessing on the shoulder, indicating high impression of the Americans.

Nwoke continued to flip through the CD's and cassettes. "You ever heard of Mary J. Blige or Janet Jackson? Those are the only soul and R and B we have," he said.

The car approached the gates and they all waved to the taxi driver that spoke to them when they first got there.

"You know that man?" Chichi asked.

"We met him here just before you guys got here.

The stocky taxi driver watched the car pull out and waved back, shaking his head and smiling at how easy today's teenage girls were.

"We know Janet Jackson and her family very well, but is Mary J. Blige the new girl that sang "Real love?" Chichi asked.

"Yeah, she's new. I think this is her first album." Nwoke found the CD and inserted it.

"Can you put it on "Real love?" Blessing begged Uzo, pointing her finger at the dashboard.

Nwoke pressed the button and skipped to 'real love'.

Uzo wasn't sure which way to turn. "Now, which way, girls?" he asked.

Blessing had forgotten they were supposed to be showing the strangers around town. But she immediately gathered her thoughts. "Where do you think we should go, Chichi?"

"Let's just go to our school and just ride around, even though it's empty but at least they'll know where to come get us when school starts back.

Nwoke wondered what made the two girls think they would be in the country till September. "What's the name of your school?"

"Government Girls Secondary school, Owerri," Chichi responded.

Uzo turned his head and looked at them briefly.

"Good idea. Just turn left coming up and go straight, it'll be on the right side," Blessing said afterward, Uzo tuned the volume on the stereo back up.

The girls had seen the video of the song on VCR at a friend's house and they loved Mary J. The pop culture in Nigeria was highly influenced by American pop and hip-hop culture.

They rode through the empty boarding school and the girls showed them a few more places of attraction, including Alvan Ikoku college of Education which was a very popular teachers' college and since about seventy percent of teachers in the country were females, Nwoke and Uzo wished they had just gone to the school for older women instead. There were summer school students still on campus and many were attractive.

There weren't too many teenage attractions in the town since it was the administrative capital of the state, unlike Aba which was the commercial capital where all the fun was. They left the town at exactly 5:30PM and headed for Aba.

The ride lasted about forty minutes as Uzo made his way through the heavy traffic after exiting Aba-Owerri road. The time now was 7:10PM

"You guys must try to visit us on October 1st, Independence day and I promise you won't go back to Aba," Chichi informed their out of town partners.

"Oh, yeah? We'll be sure to keep in touch after tonight, okay?" Uzo lied, knowing this was going to be a one-time deal.

"You all wanna get something to eat?" Blessing asked, turning her head to look at Uzo.

"What do you have a taste for?" Nwoke asked, surprised at the American slang Blessing just used.

"Pepper-soup and French fries. If we can find ice cream, fine but if not, then ice-cold soda will do just fine," Chichi intervened.

Uzo nodded and turned the volume of the CD player back up, bopping his head to the beat of Pete Rock and

CL Smooth's 'Reminiscence' which Nwoke had just changed to.

They stopped at the next fast-food joint called 'Finger licking'. Everybody ordered what they had a taste for and they spent about thirty minutes eating and then got back in the car.

Nwoke's parent's had travelled to the village for the weekend which was normal once a month. All kinds of thoughts went through his mind as they sat down in the car, but when he remembered his nosy sister and their lectures on God, all thoughts of taking the girls to his house vanished immediately. He then remembered Uzo saying something about his parents traveling to Lagos for a week to a family member's wedding.

"And where's your place, if I may ask?" asked Chichi.

"In the GRA and Uzo and I have a summer home there but we got a couple of relatives and caretakers who stay there all year long," Nwoke lied with a straight face.

The sound of GRA immediately got the attention of the girls and they became convinced that these were young millionaires they had just ran into. They weren't going to let the opportunity go by just like that. They exchanged looks and signals in approval of Nwoke's suggestion but didn't want them to know how excited they were about it.

"Okay, we'll go with you guys as long as you promise to get us to my uncle's house by 9PM," Blessing said and relaxed in the comfortable leather seat. She looked at Uzo and then studied his long, muscular legs.

Uzo took notice immediately. "Great, I promise to have you at your uncle's by, at least, 9PM, so don't worry about it," he said and started the engine and turned the air-conditioner on full blast to counter the one hundred degree temperature outside while Blessing was now in complete control of the CD case.

Twelve minutes later, they were pulling up at the big, fancy gates of Mr. Otu's mansion and Uzo beeped the horn so that one of the caretakers could come and let them in. The girls were overwhelmed by the million-dollar mansion and even more so when the little caretaker ran out of the boy's quarters to open the gates, Uzo pulled the baby Benz beside his father's big 420s Mercedes which was alongside six other luxury automobiles. The entire environment in which the girls found themselves in, smelled of luxury and wealth. The more they noticed, the more they believed Uzo and Nwoke were actually who they claimed to be. They wondered how much an NBA player in the U.S. made. They were dumbfounded and neither one uttered a word as they got out of the car and followed Uzo and Nwoke to the rear entrance stairwell, located outside the building.

"Hey, Uzo, can I talk to you for a second?" he asked, opening the car door and stepping back outside for privacy.

They went outside and walked behind the car.

"What's up with your place? You know how my family acts about this kind of stuff, especially my sisters."

"That's alright. My parents should be in Lagos till next week and I can handle my little brother and sister."

They both looked at the two girls through the rear window of the Benz and caught them looking back at them.

The girls smiled so intimately and the two female hunters knew they were going to get lucky.

"Remember, we are only in the country for a month since the NBA season just ended," Uzo reminded Nwoke before they went back to the car.

They joined the girls in the car and Nwoke spoke up. "Hey, pretty mamas, since you still got a little more time to kill," he said and glanced at his watch. The time was 7:50PM. "I thought maybe we could perhaps stop by my place for a minute. "He and Uzo kept their eyes on the girls to see what their reaction would be.

Uzo's younger brother and sister were sitting in the family room with the stereo on full blast, playing 'hip-hop-hooray' by Naughty by nature.

Uzo led them into the family room. "Sit down or dance, you all!" he yelled through the very loud sound as they entered the party-like atmosphere.

Neither girl started dancing, instead they both sat down. Nwoke sat next to Chichi while Blessing sat by herself. Uzo walked over to one of the end tables where the remote control unit was and grabbed it. He turned down the volume with the hope it would make his curious brother and sister leave the room. But it didn't as the two watchful eyes appeared to wonder what their older brother was doing with the strange girls in their parents' home. This was a first time for Uzo to behave in such fashion.

Uzo noticed this and didn't want the little brats to blow his cover, so he decided to be kind. He called them outside to the balcony and told them he needed some privacy and they agreed, but still suspicious. But, they gave him his wish by hanging around on the balcony. Uzo returned to the room, relieved that he didn't have to introduce his siblings. "You guys want something to drink?" he asked, noticing the look on the girls' faces immediately he entered the room. He wondered if they already knew that those were his siblings since they were so young. He then walked over to the small bar and got some sodas and a couple of beers. There was no law regulating alcoholic beverages in the country.

The two girls looked across the big room at each other, sending their familiar signals indicating that they now got the message. These were just some spoiled rich kids who were born overseas. But they weren't gonna let that spoil their day. So, they decided to go along with the flow.

The couples danced to the beat of 'Dr Ore's G-thing and then switched over to Whitney Houston's Body guard soundtrack—'I'll always love you'.

Nwoke danced across the big room, looking for something to drink while Blessing and Uzo were in the corner dancing in each other's arms. He reached for a bottle of Heineken that Uzo had placed on the table from his father's bar, got a can opener, popped it and took several gulps, frowning his face in disgust. "Yo, what do people see in these drinks? It is so bitter!" This was Nwoke's first time tasting beer and the look on his face made everybody break out in a laughter. He put the bottle down and grabbed a bottle of coca cola to wash off the bad taste in his mouth.

Whitney Houston's 'I'll always love you' went off and Nwoke took charge this time as he replaced the song with Michael Jackson's 'Liberian girl'. He then slowly walked over to Chichi and grabbed her, squeezing her body tight against his. She didn't hesitate to return the favor by putting her arms around him without applying any pressure in return. Their chests pressed against each other as he rocked her back and forth slowly, with their feet sealed to the floor. The hormones in the two young adults began to pump blood to their vital organs which involuntarily caused their lips to meet. They kissed passionately to the surprise of their partners who could no longer continue to watch. Uzo and Blessing began to imitate them.

Nwoke wasted no time when Liberian girl stopped playing. He quickly grabbed the remote and skipped to 'I just can't stop loving you'. He then returned to where he left off by engaging her in a tongue-kiss. Uzo did the same.

"Are you shy?" Uzo asked Blessing after the long kiss.

"Yes. This is my second time with a boy," she lied to impress the rich kid.

This made Uzo even more interested and he immediately thought about replacing Deborah. "Oh, really?" He stopped dancing and stared at her, then realized from the look in her eyes that she might be lying but he could care less. After all, he just wanted some and he wanted it right then and there.

The sudden sound of love tunes by their older brother which had never happened before, made Uzo's younger siblings curious. They were still on the balcony and they became nosy and wanted to find out what was going on behind the drawn curtains of their family room.

"Hey, let's go take a peek," Nwogu suggested with a grin on his face.

"Why?" Ije asked, staring at the drawn curtains.

"Cause I just think it's strange they're listening to dad's CD and a love song for that matter."

"Oh, okay. I guess you're right," the pretty brown skin fifteen year old Ije said.

The two curious studs turned and took slow, cautious strides toward the window.

Mike Manley

"Hey, over there in the corner," thirteen-year old Nwogu said as he peeped through the crack between two curtains.

Ije followed her younger brother's gaze. "Oh! My gosh!" she exclaimed as she saw her brother Uzo locked in a tongue-kiss with his hands on Blessing's breast while hers were wrapped around his neck.

Then the two virgins scanned the room and found Nwoke in the far end opposite corner, walking through the door that led into the guest room and closing it behind him as Chichi led the way. They exchanged looks and returned their focus on their older brother and his partner.

Uzo and Blessing walked through the doors leading out of the family room to his own room.

"Where do you think they're going?" Nwogu asked, looking at his older sister for answers he already knew.

"I guess to his room to finish what they started."

"I wanna see."

"I wonder how you're gonna do that. His window faces the water tank," Ije informed the curious thirteen-year old.

Nwogu was disappointed but determined to find out what his brother was up to with the strange girl. "I wonder if he broke up with Deborah?"

"I don't think so. They were just together the other day."

"I got an idea." The little boy turned and made his way through the family room to the rear balcony and, studying the big water tank which stored water from rainfall during the long rainy season, the five foot-five inch tall Nwogu reached for the big iron pipe that held the aluminum tank in place and pulled his one hundred and thirty five pound figure to the iron rod that held the four pipes together. He peeped around the big square tank with his hands around it through the open blinds of Uzo's room window. His mouth opened wide in shock at what he saw, but nothing came out.

"What's wrong?" Ije asked in a whispering tone in order not to alert the love-making couple inside the room.

Nwogu almost fell backwards when he heard his sister's voice in such a low tone as he had no idea she was standing in the rear balcony, watching him. The shocks from both his sister's voice and what he had just witnessed in his older brother's room, made his mouth shut and dry. Instinctively, he couldn't answer her question but kept his curious eyes at the window.

Inside the guest room, Nwoke and Chichi were already on their second round of heated sexual intercourse as Chichi continued to want more. She moaned and groaned in ecstasy as Nwoke pounded her in a doggy-style position on the Berber carpeted floor.

In Uzo's room, the two young adults were engaged in a sit-down position as their arms were locked around each other in unlimited climax that gripped the two young adults. Slick Rick's "A teenage love' was playing on Uzo's portable CD player and the volume was loud enough to absorb the sound made by Ije and Nwogu's footsteps around the water tank. The two young adults were sweating profusely, despite the central air conditioning in the mansion and in the heat of the moment. Blessing mumbled the words, 'I love you' as the two lovers screamed, reaching climax.

The two wanna-be basketball player and agent had the time of their young lives. Time was now running against them as they struggled to get the girls to their destination. But to Uzo's surprise, Blessing didn't appear to be worried since she knew exactly what to tell her uncle, after all they were supposed to be traveling by public transportation which wasn't all that reliable.

After a twenty-minute ride to Azikiwe road to drop the girls off, Nwoke and Uzo decided to wait and see what the reaction of Blessing's uncle would be. They exchanged addresses and phone numbers, knowing that this was going to be the last time they saw the girls. The two females got out of the car, feeling very happy and content with themselves. After ten minutes of waiting without the girls coming back, Uzo started the car and began to back out of the parking space, but a sudden knock on the window stopped him.

"Hey you two! Thanks a million. Well, see you all later." Blessing screamed through the window with Chichi standing beside her, smiling.

Azikiwe road was right next to the church and Uzo dropped Nwoke off at the compound as the two boys rejoiced their encounter with Blessing and Chichi.

Three weeks passed and Nwoke still hadn't heard from his father about attending college abroad. He continued to wait for their answer, anxiously.

"Honey, I think he should go to school here, like his siblings," suggested Mrs. Nwanta as she sat on the foot of the bed in the large bedroom, waiting for her husband to join her.

Reverend Nwanta finished putting on his pajamas and walked over to the bed. "I'm leaning toward that, dear," agreed the Reverend as he sat down next to his wife. "The university of Nsuka is better than any school in Maryland and we can keep an eye on him."

"Good. That's why I love you so much, my dear. I really didn't want that boy in the 'States all alone, running wild and free.

The righteous couple concluded that their smartest son, Nwoke, would not be returning to the U.S. for college or anything else. The couple prayed and went to sleep.

It was a hot, rainy Saturday morning when they woke up. A knock on the door startled the couple and they wondered who could be at their door at 7:00AM in the morning.

"Yes, come in," Mrs. Nwanta said.

Nwoke opened the door and let himself into his parent's bedroom.

"Hi, Nwoke. You're up early and I think I know why you're here."

Nwoke stood not far from the door after shutting it behind. "Dad told you?" he asked his mother, disregarding his father's presence.

"Yes and we'll be out in a few minutes. See you in the dining room," a sleepy Mrs. Nwanta said and laid her head back down.

"See you, son," Rev. Nwanta said and began looking at the ceiling, hoping that the decision would not lead his son to do wrong.

"Okay, then. I'll be waiting." Nwoke turned and walked away.

Breakfast was served around 9:35AM and the family, excluding Theo who was now working in Benin, ate and went about their separate ways.

Reverend and Mrs. Nwanta remained in the dining room with Nwoke.

Rev, Nwanta decided to take control of the situation, "Okay son. I'm sorry I didn't get back to you sooner but, it's been a rough three weeks, I must admit," The Rev. continued to study his son's facial expression and then, glancing over at his wife who was seated to his right, paying close attention. "You know it's always like this whenever schools let out for long vacation because of the extra-curricular activities to keep students out of trouble." He took a sip of tea and continued," why don't you join the teenage bible study group?" You can bring all your friends."

"Nah, we're too busy for that. Plus we have the membership at Aba country club," Nwoke replied, sarcastically, wondering why his father was beating around the bush instead of going straight to the point.

"C'mon son. You're never too young or too busy for God."

"Yeah, I know. I'll make time one of these days and come with Uzo," Nwoke lied, hoping the positive answer will influence the minister to make a favorable decision. "So, what school am I going to in Baltimore so that I can write my letter of admission in time?"

Rev. Nwanta didn't want to just come out and blatantly refuse, so he decided to use a different approach. "Not sure yet but, I'm inclined to agree with Towson State since they have a good Business school."

Mrs. Nwanta just listened and kept looking at Nwoke to see if his expression would change since young adults tended to have mood swings, especially if they don't get their way. She studied Psychology and perfectly understood young adults as a former school teacher. She also knew they could be violent, that's why she didn't want to intervene as she liked the route her husband was taking.

"When are you gonna be sure, dad?" Nwoke looked at both parents with piercing eyes.

This sent a cold chill through Rev. and Mrs. Nwanta.

"Why do you want to go back to the U.S. so badly, son?"

"I asked a question first."

"Okay, it was going to be soon, maybe today." The Rev. didn't want to further upset the young adult.

Mrs. Nwanta decided it was time for her to intervene. "Right, son. There's no hurry. You still haven't received your GCE result yet," she added, focusing on Nwoke's reaction.

Getting nowhere in the dialogue, Nwoke stormed out of the dining room, fed up with his parents delay tactics which they've always used, even when doing his Christmas shopping as a little child. Money wasn't a problem since the Diocese of Aba paid for all minister's children's education, no matter what level or what country. He stepped into the shower, washed himself quickly, got dressed and went downstairs to his car.

"Hey, Nwoke. Where are you going?" asked little Johnny, who was outside, playing with other kids.

Nwoke got in his car, completely ignoring his little brother. He started the car and selected the CD '187 on an undercover cop' by Dr. Dre and Snoop dog and inserted it into the player, raising the volume to the max as Johnny's friends and John himself heard the music and abandoned what they were doing. They watched Nwoke pull out of the compound onto the main road, disappearing into the traffic that was already beginning to build up.

Fifteen minutes later, Nwoke beeped his horn three times at Uzo's gate.

Uzo so happened to be leaving out and heard the familiar horn and turned around as he was about to open the door to his Benz. "Hey chap, what's up?"

"Nothing, man. I think I wanna go see the twin. What do you think?"

"I don't care. You know mom still ain't here, so I'm pretty much in control of where and what I do and we better make the best of it since it ain't gonna last forever."

"I guess I'll leave my car here, then."

"Good idea, but pull inside the gate."

Nwoke drove the Volkswagen through the already opened gates and parked it. They got inside and before Uzo could turn the CD player on, Nwoke interrupted him.

"Hold on a second, yo. My dad might be getting cold feet about sending me back to the 'States."

"Why?" Uzo turned his head and studied his best friend.

"Cause it doesn't take three weeks or one month to decide if your son should go away to college or not, does it?" Their eyes met.

Uzo started the Benz and steered it through the gates and out of the compound. "Yeah, but you're talking out of the country yo. That ain't easy for parents to do."

"Look who's talking! Didn't your parents say you could go back to London at will, but you chose to stay here for college?"

"Yes. I kind of like it here. I got respect I can't get in the U.K., so what's so good about the white man's country?"

"Yeah, you're right about that part but I like a variety of girls, man, plus this all-year heat and no snow is not normal."

Uzo proceeded up the road, heading for Helen's house. "Oh, I see. Well, I don't like snow all that much and the cold weather is not really for black people, you know. Plus, I got an aunt and two cousins living in the same area where my father's house is and they keep an eye on my Pop's house." Uzo slowed down as they got closer to Helen's house. "You think they're home?"

"Who? The twins?" Nwoke responded, still buried in his thoughts.

"Of course I'm talking about them. Wake up, man." Uzo smiled. "I really did like Chichi though but, I can't deal with two girls on a serious tip like that but I plan to hook up with her again, one day."

"Maybe we should've called first."

"Well, too late now. Let's just go for the ride anyway. Who knows, we just might meet another two pretty ones.... hah," Uzo joked, checking his face in the rearview mirror.

Nwoke's mind wasn't in a joking mood but preoccupied by what his parents told him. "I wanna get back to where I was born and, maybe marry Helen one day."

"Marry? Get real, yo."

"Yeah. That's right.I think I love the girl."

"The other day, you were in love with Chichi and now you love Helen. Do you know what love is?"

Nwoke was surprised at Uzo's tone of voice and the direction he was going. "Look at you, sounding like my father. Do you know what love is, nigger?"

Uzo wondered if his friend was really getting angry. "I didn't say I did. Just my observation," he responded and turned the CD player back on and inserted LL Cool J's 'Mama said knock you out'.

They arrived at Helen's house ten minutes later. Not quite sure what they were going to do after the brief disagreement so, they decided to just sit in the car with the music turned down low about half a block from the small bungalow.

"I agree," Uzo replied.

Helen's father was the principal of the private school which was owned and operated by Saint Thomas Cathedral. The principal and staff of most secondary schools in the country were required to reside on school premises.

Helen came strolling out of the back-yard ten minutes later with a trash bag and set it on the side of the house for the trash-man. She was only wearing a wrapper and a blouse with some slippers. One could tell she hadn't been out of the house yet. She looked up the street and appeared to recognize the black Benz parked on the side of the deserted road with what looked like two boys inside and walked toward it. "Now, I know you wouldn't have been sitting there for too long and, Nwoke, where have you been?" She said as she stood outside the passenger side door, looking at Nwoke's negligence of her since school let out.

Nwoke avoided eye contact with the pretty face, knowing he had done the pretty decent girl wrong by cheating on her. But then, who's to say she hadn't done the same? The guilt vanished suddenly when Nwoke looked at Uzo and saw his reaction to Helen's remark which was the same as his. His older brother, Theo had told him that girls were really worse and slicker than boys.

Nwoke turned his head and looked her straight in the eyes. "You could've came over or called yourself."

"Oh, I'm sorry for being so rude, Uzo, what is up? Your friend has been treating me so bad since school closed. Have you talked to Deborah?"

Uzo wasn't sure what to say since he's done exactly the same thing as his friend.

"No, I haven't and I'm sorry we've just been busy trying to get Nwoke's papers ready for college in the U.S. Where's she?" He looked straight through the windshield to see if Deborah was anywhere in sight, but no sign of her.

"I think she's still in the bathroom."

"So what are you girls up to?" Uzo asked.

"Nothing, just going over to some girlfriend's house, that's all." She smiled like there might be some hidden agenda behind her claim.

Nwoke and Uzo exchanged looks, wondering if the twins had been doing exactly the same thing they'd been doing. They didn't believe her for a second and now they were determined to ruin whatever their plans were for Saturday night.

"Well, I'm not gonna keep you guys waiting. I gotta get in the shower and Deborah is probably done already."

"Oh, I'm sorry. I hope we didn't interrupt anything," Nwoke waited for a response.

Helen decided to ask a rhetorical question to counter whatever the boys were trying to do, "You all want to go with us?"

"Where? Your girlfriend's?" Nwoke asked, studying her expression, knowing that she couldn't be possibly serious."

"Yes and what's wrong with you two hanging out with a few girls? Anyway, let me go get into the shower." She turned and walked back to the house without waiting for a response.

"Okay, we'll wait right here!" Uzo yelled as she continued to walk away.

Twenty five minutes later, the twins came out of their house, looking exquisite and their mother, who had been watching the interaction between Helen and Nwoke through the window, continued to watch her pretty daughters leave with the two rich kids from abroad. She was actually glad that her daughters were involved with the boys since she knew their parents well and Nwoke's father was from the same village as they were.

"You two look beautiful today," Uzo complemented, turning his head to look at the two girls as he reversed the vehicle.

"Thank you so much, Uzo," the twins responded in unison. They looked at Nwoke who had no comment.

"We're just gonna go to the country club and maybe, the movies later. Is that cool with you two?" Uzo suggested and looked at Nwoke for approval.

"So, we're not going to my girlfriend's?" Helen asked, disregarding the suggestion by Uzo.

Nwoke intervened. "No. I don't wanna be around a bunch of girls at their house."

"That's right," Uzo supported and shifted the gear to Drive.

"Wow Nwoke, you seem kind of irritable today," Deborah said.

"He's mad about something and won't share it with me," Helen said.

Nwoke ignored the comments and found the CD case for some music to ease his mind. He decided on Eric B and Rhakeem's 'Don't sweat the technique'

"Aba country club will be fine, "Helen spoke up over the loud sound.

Uzo smiled and steered the vehicle in the direction of the Aba country club.

CHAPTER SIX

The results for the GCE exit exam came out in July and Nwoke scored all A's in both the GCE and Saint Thomas High School certificate. The fall semester was about to begin in one month and Nwoke had high hopes that the excellent grades will help his parents make up their minds immediately. But, it didn't. Instead it made them want their smartest son to attend medical school in the country. They told him to take the JAMB and select the University of Nsuka as his first choice. This meant no U.S. college for Nwoke. He agreed, but he also had his own plans.

After the brief meeting as Nwoke was leaving the family room, his mother had one last thing to add.

"Nwoke, it's not that we don't love you. We just don't want to lose you to the violence of the youth in America. Now since you've been back, have you heard a gun-shot or anyone getting shot?" Mrs. Nwanta asked.

Nwoke didn't respond to the question. "Very well then. I'll see you all later. I'm gonna go over to Uzo's and hang out for a few hours." He left the family room.

It took him fifteen minutes to get to Uzo's house but, the Benz 190 wasn't anywhere in sight and he wondered where Uzo could have gone without him. They were so used to each other being home whenever either one popped up that they never bothered to call each other before going. He beeped the horn to see if anybody would come out other than the caretakers.

Three minutes later, Ije came down from the rear stairwell. "Yes Nwoke." She walked up to the gate and studied Nwoke, wondering what he and her brother were up to today. She remembered what she had seen last time when her parents were away. The thought kind of turned her on.

"Hey pretty thing, where's your brother?" Uzo asked, noticing for the first time since he'd been coming to the house, how sexy Uzo's sister was. Today she had no bra as her nipples were hard and showing under the tight t-shirt she had on. Nwoke was now tempted.

"He said to tell you to meet him at the country club if you happen to show up." Ije noticed how Nwoke was staring at her breasts and wondered if the horny boy even heard what she'd just said. Nevertheless, she gave him an encouraging sign with her eyes.

"Oh, I see. So what's up with you for today? You are looking quite beautiful."

She moved closer to the iron fence and her hard nipples were now pointing through the iron bars. "Nothing, why? What's up with you?" The bold fifteen-year-old Ije asked, looking the family friend in the eyes in a leading gesture which he just couldn't resist.

Nwoke didn't want to betray his best friend and had to make a decision right then and there. He scanned the building to see if her parents or nosy little brother was home but he saw no sign of life in the main building. "You wanna go for a ride around the GRA? That's if you're not busy." Nwoke knew it would have been degrading if the little girl turned him down so he held his breath in anticipation of some heated sex with his best friend's sister.

"Sure. Why not? I'm bored anyway," Ije said and opened the side door by the gate just enough to squeeze her slender figure through the small opening. She willingly accompanied Nwoke into the small Volkswagen Golf.

Nwoke's heart was racing as he had so much that was going through his mind. He hoped Uzo didn't happen to be coming around the corner. "So, where's your boyfriend? I know you got one," Nwoke asked as he put the car in motion. He studied the moisturized legs of the fifteen-year old and his penis immediately became erect and he wondered if she was still a virgin.

Ije kept her eyes on the pathway that led to the main street but used her peripheral vision to monitor Uzo's eyes.

"Ain't got one. Too much trouble and they might just be trying to get to my parents' money, I don't know. My mom told me not to trust these Nigerian boys cause they can be very deceitful."

Nwoke figured he might be the only one right for the girl and wondered why he wasn't going out with her. She had been there in his face all along and he couldn't even see it. He was sure Uzo wouldn't mind if it was official and if he told him he liked his sister. He wouldn't mind if Uzo went out with one of his sisters as long as he knew about it. He turned left and headed for the empty school compound, avoiding the twin's house.

"You haven't told me where we're going?" Ije said, studying Nwoke and looking down between his jeans and, after noticing the lump between his legs, she quickly looked away. She pretended she didn't know what Nwoke wanted even though she led him on.

"We gonna go take a look around the school compound, park somewhere, listen to some music if you don't mind," Nwoke said as he drove past the school library and headed toward the dorms which was located down a hill about a half a block from the classrooms. The campus of Saint Thomas Ascension Seminary was sitting on a twenty-acre piece of land and the buildings were spread out all over, including a soccer field that was one hundred yards long and fifty yards wide.

Nwoke parked the Volkswagen behind the dorms which faced the woods and picked out 'The Chronic CD by Dr. Dre and inserted it into the player and turned the volume down so they could talk at the same time. He then turned and looked at her and realized how pretty she really was. Ije was light brown skin, she wore her hair in a long natural pony tail with perm. Her eyes were sleepy and she stood about 5'6". Her long legs were now stretched out in the front seat, uncovered by the tight jean shorts she wore. The silky smoothness of her legs gave Nwoke an instant erection. Her cup-size breasts and flat stomach gave her an athletic look that Nwoke wasn't aware of."I think we have so much in common and I'm definitely not going to scam your parents for some money. My family has enough," he said.

Ije turned her head and looked at him, "You're just realizing that?" she said and rolled her eyes slowly away, She then opened the passenger side door, got out and stood up and stretched with a yawn, showing her behind to Nwoke who was still sitting in the small car as she did so.

Nwoke couldn't take anymore, so he adjusted the volume of the music and stepped out of the driver side of the car, rapping to the lyrics of 'Bitches ain't nothing but ho's and traits' as he walked around to the passenger side where Ije was still standing, facing the woods and rocking her hips to the beat of the song. He came behind her and wrapped his arms around her chest from the back.

"You know that song is disrespectful to women around the world," she commented as she stood still without even turning her head.

Nwoke changed his mind suddenly and told the fifteen year old to put her clothes back on as he did the same. He started the car and left the area as his conscience kept telling him it was wrong.

He arrived at the country club ten minutes later with the music of Dr. Dre still blasting out of the small Volkswagen, feeling like a new man. For some reason the secrecy of the sexual encounter seemed to make a big difference than sex with Helen or Chichi. He couldn't let Uzo know about this. Nwoke made up his mind to keep it a secret for now and never to bring Helen around Uzo's house where Ije might see her and start trouble. At six feet, he didn't want to risk fighting a physical encounter with the six-eight Uzo since his chances would be extremely slim.

He stepped out of the car and met Uzo. They worked out every other day but today wasn't one of those days. It was their day of pleasure and relaxation and they were gonna do it with the twins.

Not knowing exactly what the first words out of his mouth was going to be, he quickly gathered his thoughts and uttered the first words so as not to look guilty of any wrong doing. "Yo, how could you leave without me? I went to your house and Ije told me where you were," he said as they walked back into the club toward the swimming pool.

"C'mon yo. I thought you already know that Fridays were our fun day and to meet here or I meet you," Uzo replied, sounding tipsy. He had begun to take a liking to the way alcohol made him feel, even though he still didn't like the taste.

Nwoke was shocked when they got to the pool.

"Hi, Nwoke, where's your swimming trunk?" Helen asked as she swam her way to the corner of the pool where Nwoke and Uzo were standing.

Nwoke's heart dropped since he had no idea that Uzo had picked up the twin on his way to the recreation center. He composed himself and answered with a guilty conscience. "Oh, hi Helen. It's in my locker." He immediately turned and headed in the direction of the male dressing room, avoiding prolonged eye contact with his girlfriend.

In the dressing room, the thought of what he had done consumed him and he wasn't sure if he wanted to stay in the company of Helen and Uzo. The full guilt of the spontaneous encounter with his best friend's little sister hit him and he almost broke down as he realized he really loved Helen. The brief scene with Ije was more of a lust in the heat of the moment than anything else. He was now confused. Confronted with two problems, eighteen year old Nwoke, had betrayed his girlfriend just around the corner from her house.

He finished dressing for the pool by putting his swimming trunks and no tank-top to show off his muscular frame, just like Uzo out by the pool. He figured this was a good time to start drinking since he'd tried it before and didn't like it, but now he had the urge to force it on himself. He gathered himself and walked out of the male dressing room to join the crew. "Let me have a Heineken, please," he told the waiter of the pool area, his eyes hidden behind some sun-shades.

"You okay, yo? You took forever changing into the swim trunks," Uzo asked, taking a sip of his Guiness and studying his friend who now looked more like an undercover agent.

Nwoke took a seat next to Uzo and shortly after, the waiter brought the bottle of Heineken and he paid him. He took a big gulp and wished he could feel it instantly. "Yeah yo, my parents think I should stay here and go to medical school."

"Well, like I told you before, you can come with me to London. Money ain't a problem," Uzo replied.

Nwoke picked up his Heineken again and this time, drank the entire content of alcohol for the first time in his life. "I'll think about it, buddy," he replied as the alcohol was now beginning to take effect.

Helen and Deborah made their way back to where Nwoke and Uzo were sitting.

"Are you guys coming in the pool or what?" asked Deborah as she and her sister took their seats next to the two spoiled rich kids.

"What's up with the sun shades, Nwoke?" Helen asked as she wasn't used to seeing him in sunshades.

"Nothing. I'm just sick of the sun so I decided to shade it, you know what I mean, baby?" Nwoke replied as he observed the pretty twins looking quite seductive in their bikinis. The alcohol seemed to make the paranoia disappear momentarily. He was beginning to feel like superman, ready for whatever. "Watch this," he said and stood up, walked to the pool and jumped in.

Uzo was surprised and immediately joined his buddy.

"See that? All of a sudden they decide to swim after leaving us to swim by ourselves," Deborah commented to her sister.

"I tell you what, we're gonna let them swim by themselves. Let's get something to eat," Helen said and got up, followed by her sister.

Forty minutes later, they were on their way to Imo Hotels for more pleasure as alcohol had taken control of the teenage boys. Helen and her sister didn't drink, so they remained sober.

Nwoke no longer had any second thought about what he did with Ije as he took Helen into the hotel room and carried her to the Queen-sized bed. With the help of alcohol, he pounded her with a passion and desire she had never experienced before.

"Nwoke, what's gotten into you?" Helen managed to ask under heavy breathing.

"You, baby. You, Helen," he replied as he dominated the helpless girl and re-established the love they almost lost.

The next day at the bishop's mansion inside the compound of Saint Thomas Cathedral, the Reverend Joshua Nwanta sat in his study, taking a few minutes to consider the idea of Nwoke studying at the same college he attended. He remembered how he was a twenty-four year old on a church scholarship, studying Philosophy and Theology in the U.S. The problems he faced without his parents there to help or guide him morally in a foreign country was hard to overcome. But he fought through temptation that could have led him to the wrong path with the help of the almighty God. His teenage son could never handle the pressure like he did. Moreover, he was more disciplined as a married young man which the eighteen-year old Nwoke wasn't. The church only paid his tuition and fees, but he had to work on the church premises to pay for boarding and send some money home for his wife and parents. When his wife finally joined him and started having children, he had to work two jobs while studying full time in order to maintain his scholarship. He then had to move out of the church rooming house into a two bedroom apartment in order to accommodate the growing family and as more children were born, he moved to a four-bedroom town house while studying for his PH.D in Theology. After graduating and getting ordained as a minister, the Holy Trinity church in Towson offered him a Deaconry position with housing benefit and he accepted and moved back to the church compound.

If he was to allow his eighteen-year old son to return to the U.S., there was the likelihood of the young adult being lost in the fast college life of the American society and he may take the wrong path in life. The Reverend was still meditating when the door opened and Mrs. Nwanta walked in and broke his meditation.

"Hey, honey," she said and walked behind his chair and began giving him a shoulder-massage as he acknowledged her presence.

"Hello, my dear. Nwoke must attend university here in Nigeria," he said firmly without turning his head as he was enjoying the little massage therapy.

"Of course honey. I agree one hundred percent. I thought we told him that."

"Yeah, but I just thought about the entire situation and felt maybe we were wrong but we're right in our decision. I believe it is best for the family and himself," he reiterated.

Two weeks passed and Nwoke became more obsessed with attending college in the U.S. for a better life. He had a dream about attending an all-white college in Maryland and sleeping with white girls and Asian females in the same school. When he woke up, he decided to try again and see if his parents had a change of heart and if they didn't, he would take Uzo up on the offer to go to London first and then make his way to the 'States.

At the dining table during family breakfast, Nwoke asked his father in the presence of his siblings to see if he could get some support. "Hey dad, you know any white colleges in the state of Maryland?"

The girls and little John all looked at him and wondered what was behind the question but none of them said a word. They just listened carefully.

"Yes, of course, son. There are quite a few. You got Towson, Villa Julie and Goucher in Baltimore county, and then University of Baltimore county but the greater percentage of the students are white. You really don't have an all-white college per say, but you could find an all-black.

Everyone at the dining table, including Mrs. Nwanta continued to pay close attention.

"Well, I had a good dream about one of them and it was a small one so you think it might've been Towson?"

Reverend Nwanta studied his son closely, trying to make sense of the conversation. "Well, Towson isn't all that small, but it could've been Baltimore or Goucher which are much smaller than Towson.

"I was a student, a freshman with an undeclared major."

"Oh yeah?"

"Yes, but I'm still gonna be a businessman, no matter what major."

"Son, you already know you're gonna have to study whatever major you choose right here in Nigeria like your older siblings," Rev. Nwanta concluded and looked around the room to see the reaction of his children to what he said, but the kids were trying to hide their amusement as they could no longer eat their food.

Nwoke got up and left, feeling dejected, rejected and defeated.

After Nwoke left the dining room, everyone started giggling and laughing but Rev. and Mrs. Nwanta had to put a stop to it.

"It's not funny, kids. Your brother is caught up on this America-thing and it could lead him to do something much more serious and bad." She expressed seriousness and continued. "So, stop it and if you notice any suspicious behavior on his part, let me or your father know, you hear me?"

The children agreed in unison.

The Reverend now intervened." I was just making sure I haven't lost my sense of fatherhood. Your brother went to college here and now has a good job and Ada is about to graduate, so I really don't see why the stubborn child doesn't want to adjust to his motherland." He sipped on his cup of tea and looked at his wife who gave him the look he needed to move on.

"Hey, dad, it wouldn't be a bad idea if Nwoke went back to the 'States so I can go there for summer," little Johnny said.

"Finish your food, son," the minister replied and got up and left the dining room.

Nwoke deliberated in his room for about an hour and dosed off. When he woke up, it was almost 2PM. He quickly got himself together and went downstairs to his car. As he opened the door to his Volkswagen, he remembered Ije and something inside his inner senses told him to run away with her to London but, the thought quickly died as he remembered why he was going to their house. Since the heated encounter with the fifteen-year old, Nwoke hasn't stopped thinking about her. He started the car and pulled out of the compound of the church. Halfway to Uzo's house, it dawned on him that he might have more feelings for Ije than he did for Helen. This scared him quite a bit.

It took him a little more than thirty minutes to arrive at Uzo's as he drove extremely slow, thinking about everything humanly possible to lift the burden of his return to U.S. from his best friend. He really wanted to do it himself but nothing materialized. Just before he got out of the car, a thought came to his mind; doesn't Ije have access to the same money as Uzo? But the thought quickly vanished when he remembered her age. Uzo was the first son, also known as 'Opara' in Ibo language and they got priorities on anything over the rest of the family. He beeped the horn twice to let Uzo know he was there but, deep inside, he wished Ije would come out and open the gate so he could see her.

Minutes later, his wish came through as the fifteen-year old descended the front stairwell slowly, knowing that Nwoke would be looking at her long legs and probably missed her like she missed him. "Hello dear, are you looking for my brother or....?" She asked in a sexy voice with a warm smile, hoping that Nwoke would say no that he was actually looking for her and that he missed her so much.

Nwoke was in fact, hoping that nobody else was home so that he could, perhaps get a quickie. "I did miss you and I wish the situation was different," he said in a low voice. "Where's Uzo??" His eyes shifted to the main building as he wondered if she was gonna open the gate or just talk through the iron bars. She opened the gate and let Nwoke in. "He's upstairs somewhere."

Nwoke parked and walked beside her as they talked." He could smell the freshness of the girl as she got closer. He figured she must have just got out of the shower.

"I missed you too," she said and cut him a look. "On second thought, I think he might be working out in the family gym. Go ahead and I'll see you later."

Nwoke went to the gym while Ije proceeded back inside the mansion. The gym was quite big and full of all kinds of foreign exercise equipment imported from either the U.S. or Japan. Solo flex, free iron weights, treadmill and Stairmaster were neatly arranged a few feet away from the pull up bar. Uzo saw Nwoke enter as he struggled with two hundred and twenty-five pounds of free weight on the flat-bench. "Can you please give me a spot, it's my tenth rep," Uzo begged.

Nwoke quickly moved to render his assistance. "Okay, man, puuuush push," he encouraged as he grabbed the bar with both hands and helped his friend place the weight in position. "You shouldn't do that without somebody around, yo. You know better than that," he cautioned.

"I heard your horn, that's why I increased the weight. So what's up with you?"

"Nothing, I just wondered."

"You wanna get in on a set?"

"Nah, I'm okay, besides, I prefer the country club where there are girls and women to impress," Nwoke said in a depressing tone.

Uzo stood up from the bench and grabbed the towel and started wiping himself. "Okay man, what's wrong? I've never seen you refuse to work out and you've worked out here with me so that's not the reason."

The two boys had always worked out together, four or three days a week whether in school or out of school. Today was not one of those days. To Nwoke, this was a day of future planning and decision making.

"I need to talk to you about what you suggested earlier," Nwoke said.

Uzo immediately understood why the depressive state of his best friend. "Oh I see, so what's the problem because that's not a real problem. I told you that." He said, callously.

"But where's the money? This isn't gonna be a nickel and dime trip, you know." Nwoke knew Uzo's father had plenty of money but so did his own father. Your parents' money isn't yours and if you wanted to make it yours, you would have to steal it and that wasn't the way Nwoke was raised. No situation was desperate enough to make him steal anything from anyone, ever!"

"My dad doesn't have the problem that your dad has about where his first son goes to college. He'll let me have whatever amount I consider appropriate, besides he has an account in London that any of us can access at any time the bank is open," Uzo said and started arranging all the free weights.

Nwoke helped him put everything where they belonged. They both stood there and thought about how they were going to pull this off without the permission of Nwoke's parents.

"You still got your U.S. passport, right?" Uzo asked.

"Yeah, but not with me. My parents got it."

"You can get it, right? Cause from what I gather, you may have to run away."

"You don't think I know that? Of course I'm gonna have to run away and then when I'm gone, they just might send me some money. What do you think?"

"I agree. Good thinking but now you gotta go get it and I don't think that's going to be easy."

Uzo's last comment sent Nwoke into a deep thought and he was still lost in trying to find a means to get a hold of his blue passport when Ije broke it up.

"Hey, you guys still working out?" Ije asked as she entered the gym.

"No," Uzo replied and left.

"See you later," Nwoke said and followed Uzo.

Ije assumed the Stairmaster as she thought about Nwoke. She had nothing under her sweat pants.

Since money wasn't a problem or even an issue of concern in the Otu's residence, all Uzo had to do was ask and his parents would do whatever that was within reason to see he got what he wanted as the 'Opara' of the family, which meant first son.

Nwoke continued to wonder what Mr. Otu did for a living. Uzo's father was the owner of the company but there was nothing visible or tangible to support the claim.

"Well, this wasn't the time to care about how Mr. Otu made his money as long as it was going to help him get out of Nigeria and return to the country of his birth.

Nwoke drove back home with the thought of how he was going to find his passport. But Ije's image was still in his mind and he didn't want his best friend's sister to distract him from executing his plan. He managed to refocus on finding his U.S. passport which he had no idea where it was. He parked the Volkswagen in its usual spot and slowly ascended the steps to the second floor with the hope of solving the one problem that had been disturbing him since he refused to live in the hot country without twenty four hour television station or cable. A country where telephone was a privilege.

He went to his room and thought about where his parents would keep the family passports. Then his thought wandered back eight years when they arrived at Murtala Muhammad International Airport, then it suddenly hit him; even though he was only 12 years old at the time, he could still remember his mother putting all their passports in her pocketbook after the customs cleared them. Nwoke stood up and quickly walked out of the room to the long rear balcony that connected his parent's bedroom. He stopped at the door and listened to see if anyone was inside the bedroom and when he heard nothing, he tapped lightly on the wooden door just to make sure. After a few seconds, he turned the door knob and entered the room, slowly and cautiously. Carefully, he searched for his mother's pocketbook but it was gone and the one he saw was different. He then looked inside the closet and saw two big leather suitcases and his mother's carryon with the British Airways tag still intact. He grabbed the carryon and walked back to the bed and placed it on it.

He attempted to open it but it was locked so he stood up straight and scanned the large room, praying that no one would come in. He saw a picture of a white Jesus Christ on the wall and paused for a minute, but when he remembered that Jesus Christ could not possibly be a white man, he proceeded. There was a set of keys on the table and he took it and tried three keys on the carryon but it wouldn't open. The fifth key which was also the smallest, opened the carryon and to his delight, the passports were laying on top of a bible inside the small carryon. Nwoke found his passport among eight U.S. passports belonging to all the family members. When he opened the first page, he noticed the expiration date was still valid. It would expire in two more years. He put it in his pocket, closed it and returned it where he got it. He then put the keys back where he got them and left the room, closing the door quietly behind him. Nwoke walked to the living-room to see if there was anyone there but it was empty as the maid had just finished cleaning up. He then went to the phone and called Uzo first to see what he wanted him to do next.

Uzo answered after three rings. He told Nwoke to come back to his house so that they can talk about how to proceed.

Nwoke thought about hiding the passport in his room, but decided against it for some reason. He took it with him to Uzo's house.

As he parked his car outside in front of the mansion and got out, he saw Uzo's mother coming down the front stairwell and he hesitated, not sure what he was going to do under such duress. There was too much guilt weighing on his conscience at the moment and he had to find a way to maintain control of himself. He thought about all the bad things he had done and planning to run away with her which could implicate Uzo. Now, he wasn't sure if he could face Mrs. Otu right then and there, but it was too late to do anything else as Mrs. Otu had already seen him.

"Hello Nwoke, how are you? I haven't seen you in ages," Mrs. Otu said, waiting for Nwoke to walk into the compound.

Nwoke heard her but pretended to be locking his car doors, avoiding eye contact with the woman. "Oh, I've been busy studying, Mrs. Otu," he replied with a quick smile and then turned and quickly walked into the compound past her."

Mrs. Otu called the driver and walked over to the Range rover, dressed in expensive lace wrapper and blouse to match with the head-tie. The jewelry she had on must have cost at least fifty thousand British pounds or more which was equivalent to one hundred thousand U.S. dollars. "Nwoke, come here, you haven't greeted me," she yelled after she noticed Nwoke was almost inside the house.

Nwoke stopped and turned around. "Oh, I forgot. Good afternoon, ma'am."

"Good afternoon, my dear," she replied and carefully studied the distant eighteen-year old. "Why are you standing so far away?"

Nwoke moved closer, now feeling more nervous than ever as the nosy woman's eyes checked for signs of misbehavior. "Is Uzo home?" he managed to ask

"Yes he is," she said as the driver started the Range rover. Nut she completely ignore the running vehicle as she wondered what the young adults were up to. "So what have you been studying and doing with your holidays?"

Nwoke wondered why she wouldn't just get in the vehicle and go where she was going. He immediately wished he had left the passport at his house. "Chemistry and swimming at the country club keeps us busy enough, ma'am."

The driver came out of the driver side door and walked around the rear passenger door and opened it for her.

She saw the open door and ended her cross-examination of the young adult. "I'll talk to you another day, Nwoke and greet your parents for me." She entered the SUV and the driver closed the door.

Uzo waved and let out a sigh of relief. He walked into Uzo's room to find Uzo watching music videos via satellite. The Redman and EPMD video on 'yo MTV Raps' made Uzo lose temporary focus on why he was even there, coupled with the interrogation by Mrs. Otu.

Uzo noticed his presence but kept his eyes on the video. "Time for some action."

"Yo, that's how we're gonna be, soon. All those video bitches around us, looking so good and delicious," Nwoke said and took a seat.

The video ended and commercial followed.

"So, what's up?"

"I got it right here in my pocket and I want you to keep it safe for me in case my parents start looking and asking questions. Can I trust you?"

"Of course. Where is it?"

Nwoke gave him the passport and Uzo put it away in his closet.

"Okay now, I just gotta let my old man to know that I plan to return to London in a few weeks, but meanwhile, we're just gonna live life to the fullest with Nigerian girls and take a lot of pictures and videos."

"For what?" Nwoke asked.

"So that we can show our friends in the U.S. and London that some of our girls look better than the ones on those videos.

"You're right, we need to change the perception they have of Africa. You know they still think it's a jungle and we run around like Tarzan," Nwoke said.

CHAPTER SEVEN

On the morning of September 7,1992, the individual results of the University entrance exam, which was also known as The Joint Admissions and Matriculation Board exam for all West African students[JAMB] was released to all secondary schools in the country. Nwoke woke up, stretched out with a morning yawn and walked over to his portable CD player on the table, got the CD case beside it and flipped through them and found 'Death Certificate' by Ice Cube. He inserted it and skipped to the popular track 'It was a good day'. He turned up the volume enough to keep the sound in his room. He then walked into his bathroom, rapping to the lyrics.

Twenty minutes later, he was ready for the day as he looked forward to returning to Towson. He could remember the mall not far from the church compound where they lived. He then went to the dining room, ate breakfast and called Uzo. "You up?"

"Not really, but I am now. Why what's up?" Uzo answered on the other end of the line and in a sleepy voice. "What time is it?"

"Eight in the morning and today is the day, son."

"What day and what are you talking about?"

"Our JAMB grades will be posted at the school today. It's September 7th and the new school year starts in a couple of weeks."

"Oh, that's right! Let me get ready, but you can start coming over. I should be ready by the time you get here."

"Okay, I'll see you in a little bit." Nwoke hung up and went downstairs to his car and drove to Uzo's house.

When he got there twenty minutes later, Uzo was already waiting outside. He stopped in front of the house and Uzo jumped in.

"Let's go get the twins," Uzo said.

They went to the twins' house, picked them up and drove to the school to check their result and university postings.

This was a big day in the lives of all the students that graduated from secondary schools in the country aspiring to further their education to the college level. The crowd consisted of all one hundred and fifty students and their relatives and friends who accompanied them either by giving them a ride or wishing them good luck. Some arrived by taxi and this contributed to the congestion of the school compound.

They took turns checking the bulletin board and for their names and grades. Fortunately, all four love birds passed.

After congratulating each other, they went back to the twins' house and waited for them to inform their mother since their father was at his office monitoring the anxious students.

"Hi, Mrs. Oha," Nwoke greeted as he saw Helen's mother and noticed how close the resemblance between mother and daughter was.

"Oh, hello boys and I'm sure you all did well on the JAMB, judging from the excited looks on your faces," Helen's mother said, cheerfully as she walked up to Nwoke and Uzo while her daughters had gone to the back room. "So, Nwoke, you're going to be a doctor, hah?" She was even happier now that her daughter just might be married to a doctor, possibly an American trained doctor. She lit up a smile.

"Yes, ma'am," Nwoke lied, knowing that going to medical school in Nigeria was the last thing on his mind.

"Great." She then turned to face Uzo?"

"I'm just gonna be a business man after I major in Business Administration.

"Good."

Helen and Deborah came back out to the living room.

Mrs. Oha studied the four young adults and she could remember her days as a young girl and how she had given her then boyfriend who is now her husband, such a hard time before giving him some. She hoped her daughters would do the same but she also knew things had evolved to a different life style with the new generation and she just had to endure it and not ask any embarrassing questions. "So you guys going out to celebrate?"

They all looked at her, knowing that wasn't really what she meant to ask. They looked at each other and decided to play along with the older and more experienced woman.

"Yes ma. We'll probably just go to Nwoke's church and study the bible. Today is bible study day, remember?" Deborah answered and sat up.

Mrs. Oha knew the kids were lying but didn't want to spoil the festivity mood the young couples appeared to be in and let'm go about their business.""Okay, see you kids later, then.

The four lovers got in the car and went to Uzo's house. Uzo informed his parents and picked up his car. Deborah got out of the Volkswagen and joined her boyfriend in the Mercedes while Helen remained inthe Volkswagen with Nwoke as they drove the two vehicles to the church compound so that Nwoke could drop off his car and also let his parents know about his admission into the medical school.

Nwoke knew the news of his admission to Medical school would hurt his parents more, knowing he would probably go to a pre-med school and then Medical school if they had sent him to the U.S. where his heart was and always will be.

They arrived at the church compound and Nwoke quickly parked and ran upstairs, leaving his friends downstairs. "Hey, dad! Hey mom." He yelled from the top of the stairs. He couldn't wait to see their expression when he told them he's been admitted to the best School of Medicine in the country.

"Yes Nwoke, what is it and why weren't you at breakfast this morning?" asked Nwoke's mother, still in her night gown and looking rather concerned.

"I got a distinction on the JAMB and I was also admitted to school of Medicine Nsuka," Nwoke said and gave his mother a hug.

His mother embraced him as other members of the family emerged from all over to find out what the noise was all about. They congratulated the smartest member of the family.

"That's wonderful, my son. We're all so proud of you and that's why we want you to become a medical doctor before our eyes," Mrs. Nwanta said as she let go of her son and studied him with her right hand on his shoulder.

The Reverend came out of his study and joined in the celebration. He studied all his children carefully and briefly, realizing what a great gift God had given him and his wife, more especially, the smartest student in the school of Saint Thomas, Nwoke Nwanta. "Son, I am very proud of you and I want you to know this is why we want you here in the country with us so that you can remain focused and not get distracted by materialistic tendencies which were very prevalent in the U.S.." He moved closer to Nwoke and placed his right hand on his fore-head. "Especially, college campuses can be very sinful and easily destructive. Do you understand?" the blessed man lectured as all family members listened.

Nwoke looked his father in the eyes. "There are distractions here and everywhere else too, dad," he argued and turned to look at his siblings who were very quiet and attentive. "But that's just fine." His father let go off his shoulder and he turned and went back downstairs to rejoin his friends in Uzo's car. When he got in the Benz, he noticed three impatient-looking faces and realized how long he had taken to return. "Let's go," he said as he sat in the back seat with Helen.

Uzo pulled out of the church compound and turned up the volume on the stereo as the Reggae sound of Shaba Rank's 'Mr. Lover man' filled the small Benz.

"Nwoke, are you okay?" Helen asked with her mouth in Nwoke's ears due to the loud music. "You don't look too happy."

"I'll be alright," he answered, avoiding her eyes and not letting her know what the problem really was.

"Ar you sure?" Helen was now becoming more concerned about her boyfriend's demeanor as he went from being cheerful to depression.

Nwoke thought for a few minutes and concluded it wouldn't be fair to hide the truth from the girl he loved. "Well, they won't let me go back to the 'States."

"Go back to the 'States?"

"Go back to the 'States? Is that how you feel about me?" Helen now sat up in the back seat, staring at Uzo for answers but got silence instead.

Uzo studied the couple through the rearview mirror and adjusted the volume of the stereo accordingly as he noticed that things were getting heated in the back seat. "What's up, you two?" he asked.

Deborah turned her head to look at her sister who was looking out of the window.

"I think she's mad because I wanted to go back to U.S. and I haven't told her." Nwoke responded.

"Calm down, Helen. We were planning on taking you two with us as a surprise gift. That's why he's mad?" Uzo intervened as he made a left turn to join Umungasi road.

Deborah cut in. "Oh really? Why haven't you told me, sugar?"

"It was going to be a surprise," Uzo lied and leaned over and kissed his girl her, knowing deep inside that very soon, she won't know where to find him. But he planned to keep in touch after settling down in London.

Helen believed Uzo and immediately expressed her apology but Nwoke remained quiet to make her feel guilty. Not getting any response, she leaned her head on his shoulder to see if that would work as Uzo weaved the Benz through heavy traffic.

"I think we should go to the club tonight. What do you think?" Uzo asked, checking everybody's expression.

"That sounds perfect. Let's go to the one next to Aba country club; 'Club 4AM...yeah, that's it; Club 4AM," Nwoke suggested and added, "any objection?"

All you could hear now was the angry sound of Shaba Ranks as nobody objected to Nwoke's suggestion which meant that was the final decision for the celebration of their entrance into the universities.

"C'mon, you all. Let's go shopping for the special occasion tonight. We gotta stand out, you know what I mean?" Uzo suggested, smiling. "My treat." The richest one of them all concluded.

Helen and Deborah looked at each other as if they weren't sure what they had just heard.

"Can you turn that down a little, Uzo?" Helen spoke up from the back seat, raising her voice. "Now, Uzo, what did you just say?"

"I said I'm treating everyone to shopping for the club tonight so we can all stand out in the crowd. That's what I said," Uzo reiterated, firmly, making sure everyone understood what he meant.

"Are you serious?" Deborah asked, studying her boyfriend who was already heading in the direction of expensive clothing store chains. She knew Uzo's parents were rich but not Uzo himself.

"What do you mean am I serious? Money is nothing to me and my allowance is whatever I want it to be."

"Which store?" asked Helen with excitement in her voice and eyes. No one had ever taken her and her sister shopping to a store of their choice and told them to pick out whatever they wanted; they'd always had a limit on what they could buy as far as clothes and shoes were concerned.

Uzo slowed down as they were now passing through a major road full of upscale clothing and shoe stores, mainly Boutiques. "You two pick the store. Any of them will be just fine."

Helen looked at Nwoke for approval and got it.

"Don't you all worry about me. I'm good. I got plenty of clothes," Nwoke said, so as not to lose his self-respect and pride in front of his girlfriend. "I'll pay for whatever you get, Helen."

Uzo looked at his best friend through the rearview mirror and wondered why he made the comment. But then he understood and didn't want to cause any further problems. After all Nwoke's father was rich too. He just didn't have access to his father's money like Uzo did. Plus Nwoke was from a holy environment, much different from his.

"Then take us to the 'Paris Boutique'," Helen suggested and pointed a few yards ahead.

"Oh yeah. Good choice, sister," Deborah supported.

Uzo pulled up and parked by the side of the road right across from the 'Paris Boutique'.

Nwoke didn't plan this, so he didn't bring enough money with him. He really wanted Uzo to take him back to his house so he could get some more money. "Uzo, can we go back to my house real quick?"

"What for?"

"I forgot something."

Uzo got the message. "Not right now, maybe after shopping. Hey, don't worry about nothing."

Nwoke asked him to walk with him while the girls did their shopping. He then told Uzo he would pay him the money once they got to his house but he needed to hold some for now to make it look like he paid for Helen's clothes.

The twins shopped for one hour. They came to the door of the store and waved at Uzo and Nwoke who were outside waiting. Uzo paid Deborah's bill while Nwoke paid for Helen's. The total bill was eighteen thousand naira which was the equivalence of nine hundred dollars at the exchange rate of twenty naira to one dollar.

They got back in the car and Uzo pulled off.

"What time is it, yo?" Nwoke asked Uzo as he now sat in the front with Uzo to allow the happy girls to chit-chat with each other.

"Right in front of you, yo." Uzo pointed at the digital clock on the dash. "What's wrong with you?"

"Nothing," Nwoke replied, a little nervous about the money and their plans.

"I hope you ain't worried about that. That's what friends are for."

"Okay. Let's just go." He now felt better since he couldn't think of what to tell his parents to get that kind of money out of them.

Helen decided to intervene. "We don't know how to thank you guys," she said, looking at Uzo and Nwoke. "I love you and I don't ever want us to part."

This touched Nwoke and for once, he began to reconsider going away to another country for college. But he kept quiet. "I love you too," he said and turned to face the road.

Uzo dropped off the twins so that they could get ready. Then he drove Nwoke to the church compound. But before Nwoke got out of the car, he came up with an idea.

"Yo, I think we should go ahead and attend the first year and leave just in time for summer '93. Plus I can get some money for school 'cause I just don't feel comfortable putting everything on you."

Uzo agreed to the new idea since he wasn't the one pressed to go overseas. Plus they could get a taste of college life in Nigeria before leaving.

The four love birds went to the club and had a time of their young lives.

CHAPTER EIGHT

1993

After one year of college in the country, Nwoke and Uzo confirmed within themselves that Nigeria was not the place for them. Nwoke was able to save up enough money to, at least, sponsor himself even though Uzo insisted on fulfilling his promise of bearing the entire expense for the overseas venture.

One week after school recessed for the summer, Uzo and Nwoke made their final arrangements to leave the country for London. Uzo did not have to lie to his parents but Nwoke, on the other hand, had to tell his family he was traveling to Lagos with Uzo for a month on vacation. Uzo's family driver drove the two boys to Portharcourt International Airport where they took a local flight to Lagos local airport.

"I'm sure goingto miss Helen," Nwoke told Uzo in the back of the taxi to the Marriot International Hotel in Ikeja that Uzo's father had recommended for his son to stay since there was a British Airways ticketing and reservation office located inside the lobby.

"Same here. After that night at the Imo hotels, I really think I fell in love with her," Uzo confessed as he looked out the window and noticed how crowded the city was. He concluded within himself that he couldn't live in Lagos permanently."I just might fly her to London to live with me.

Nwoke thought about Ije for a minute, not picking up the last words that Uzo said and then, his thoughts wandered over to Helen and he made up his mind that he would keep in touch if future situation permits him to.

The scenery of the city was like that of downtown Manhattan, except for the many high-rise buildings in Manhattan. There were international tourists and business men of all races going about their businesses and the city appeared to be over crowded. All classes of indigenous people from hustlers to civil servants, made the pedestrian traffic heavier than it should be. There were pan-handlers and hawkers in some parts of the town since they were not allowed into the upper scale areas of the city. The hawkers threatened to take over the shopping system as they ran to each car that was stuck or moving slowly in heavy traffic. Sometimes petty thieves would blend in and snatch gold chains off your neck.

The taxi pulled up in front of the five-star Marriot hotel and Nwoke handed the driver a five hundred naira note and he and Uzo got out. The bellboy grabbed their luggage and brought it to the reception area and set it down. Nwoke tipped him and he went back to his post.

The pretty white female receptionist studied the two young adults and seemed to wonder if they were by themselves or if their parents were outside. "Are you ready, sir?" she asked, looking at the front door. Obviously, she wasn't used to seeing young adults by themselves, especially black ones.

Uzo looked down on her as he mounted above the reception desk. "Yes we're ready, ma'am," he said in a British accent to match hers.

"How many rooms, sir?" For a second, Uzo thought he was back in London as the white female brought back memories with the Oxford accent.

"Can we get one suite with two bedrooms?" Uzo asked as Nwoke watched,

Nwoke was busy studying the young woman who looked to be about twenty five. Her blonde hair and petite figure made her seductive as she stood behind the counter. She was about Nwoke's height.

She noticed Nwoke but focused her attention on the tall Uzo. "And how will you be paying?" she tapped several keys on the computer keypad.

"Cash," Uzo answered and looked at Nwoke. He then reached in his front pocket and pulled out a stack of cash.

When Nwoke saw how thick Uzo's stack was, he was glad he didn't have to pull out the expense money his father had given him since it was much smaller in size than what he had just seen. Again, he wondered how Uzo's father got so rich.

"Okay, cash is fine and do you have your passports? That's the only form of identification we accept."

The two boys went into their carryons and brought out their foreign passports and handed them to the lady. She inspected them and gave them back. "That'll be six hundred dollars, three hundred pounds or twelve thousand naira." The receptionist distinguished the various international funds they accepted and their equivalence.

Uzo actually had some pounds on him as well but chose to pay in the local currency and save the pounds for London till he can get to the bank of England. He counted twelve thousand naira in one hundred naira denominations and handed it to the pretty woman with a smile.

She returned the smile, wondering if Uzo was a basketball player in the U.S. "You must be in the NBA of the U.S.," she said.

"You're right and I'm his agent," Nwoke intervened.

"I see," she replied and looked at Nwoke, then she counted the money and put it in the drawer.

"You do have room service, don't you?" Nwoke asked, looking at the woman to establish his presence.

"Well, of course my dear," she responded and looked up at Uzo. "Can you just sign here and here. The latter is for me as an autograph. What team do you play for?"

Uzo was more than pleased to answer. "New York Knicks."

"You have a few months to rest up, correct?"

"Yes. We didn't get where we wanted in the playoffs." Uzo signed in both spots and the second ona card for the pretty receptionist.

"And that'll be room 456 which is one of our executive suites with two master bedrooms for your comfort. Enjoy your stay and my name is Madelyn and if you need assistance with anything, just dial zero to reach me." She gave Uzo the keys, completely ignoring Nwoke and called the bellboy to escort them to their suite.

"Thank you very much and may I ask where you're from?" Nwoke said.

"Oh, I'm from Wales," she answered with a grin on her face and then she gave Uzo a sweet smile.

Uzo smiled back as the bellboy came and helped with the luggage to the elevator.

"You know what, yo?" Nwoke said.

"What," Uzo replied as they waited for the elevator with the short skinny bellboy beside them.

"Lagos is okay and I think you can hit the white girl."

"I think so too. I'm gonna see about that later. We still gotta find out what else is out there, if you know what I mean."

"Tonight, then."

"Yes," Uzo responded and smiled.

The elevator doors opened and they got in. Minutes later the doors opened on the fourth floor and they got out. The bellboy carried the two big suitcases on a cart while Uzo and Nwoke held on to their carryons. The bellboy led the way to the suite down the hall.

Uzo stepped in front of the bellboy after he stopped and opened the door with the keys he was given.

Nwoke walked through the small living-room into another room with a private bath. "Hey, I think I'll take this room 'cause I like the view." Then he went to the other room that Uzo was already in and noticed the two rooms were similar with satellite television reception and VCR.

"Lagos seems to be the only city with cable and satellite for international reception," Uzo said to Nwoke as he entered the room

"Maybe so, but we haven't been to all the major cities in the country," Nwoke answered and immediately walked to the phone and called Helen.

Helen answered after three rings. "Hello."

"Hello, my love and how are you today?" he asked.

"Oh my God! Mom it's Nwoke calling from Lagos," she exclaimed on the other end of the line.

Nwoke figured she must have called his house and was told he was in Lagos.

"I'm so sorry that I didn't let you know, baby. But I was in a hurry and Uzo was, too. So, tell your sister Uzo wanna speak to her after you finish,"Nwoke said.

"I wanted to see you 'cause I missed you so much and I can't believe you traveled all the way to Lagos without letting me know first hand. That was mean and there's no excuse for it. I even thought, maybe that's why Uzo made the comment at the club, when he said this may be the last time we go out together, remember?" Helen recanted.

Nwoke knew that the explanation could go on forever, so he decided to cut it short. "Okay, Helen. Uzo wants to speak to Deborah." He handed Uzo the phone without saying another word to Helen.

Uzo apologized to Deborah but she wanted to join him in the big city, even though her parents wouldn't allow such. Uzo used that as an excuse to get off the phone. "Okay, I'll call back to see if they let you come to Lagos, okay?." He hung up the phone, thinking about the receptionist and what their plans were for the night. "You ready to go back downstairs and book that flight?" he asked Nwoke after putting the phone down.

"Sure," Nwoke replied, feeling guilty of not paying for anything. He wanted to find a way to reward his best friend for all he had done for him so far. But he knew this was not the time to be thinking about fifty thousand naira to his name that his father had given him and that was chicken change compared to what Uzo had and what they were facing ahead.

The two best friends went back to the ground level floor to the British Airways branch office for reservation and ticketing. There was nobody waiting in line at the counter.

"Yes, may I help you?" asked the clerk who was a middle-aged black lady seated behind the desk with a computer in front of her. She studied the two teenage boys standing before her. She gave them the look that told Uzo and Nwoke that they were either too young or didn't belong where they were.

"Yes, ma'am," Uzo answered and took two steps forward toward the woman, followed by Nwoke. "We wanna make reservation to London on the next available fight, please," Uzo said.

The woman heard the British accent and knew her instincts were right. "Very well then. Sit down my dear." She motioned the two boys to the two chairs in front of her. Her opinion of them was now different as she appeared to express respect for the spoiled rich kids traveling without their parents.

Uzo and Nwoke turned their heads simultaneously when they heard an American couple arguing about the NBA finals as they walked pass the counter.

"Now, young men. When would you like to travel?" the clerk asked, catching their attention which seemed temporarily lost.

"Oh, I'm sorry ma'am. When is the next available flight?" Uzo asked as he and Nwoke turned their heads to face the woman once again.

She studied them again, wondering if in fact the young boys were drug dealers running from their boss. Then she faced the monitor and started punching some keys. "May I ask why you two are in a hurry to leave the country?"

Nwoke wondered why the woman was being so nosy. Then he remembered his mother telling him about tribal differences and that the Yoruba tribe did not like the Ibo tribe because of the civil war and the Ibos' intelligence. "Oh we're not in a hurry, ma'am. We're just going on vacation for the summer and we wanted to get all the time we deserve before school starts," he replied while Uzo listened. He tried to control his temper as he wondered why the woman was asking questions unrelated to her specific duties.

"Okay, let me see your passports."

They reached in their pockets and handed her the passports. A U.S. citizen didn't need a visa to enter the United Kingdom. She studied the two passports and, satisfied with the authenticity, she proceeded. "Okay, let me see what I have available. This is economy-class ticket, I presume?"

The two boys nodded.

She typed a few more keys, waited a minute and punched some more letters, there was printing sound and she handed them back their passports and walked over to the printer to retrieve the receipt.

Nwoke and Uzo noticed the woman was very curvy and sexy.

The clerk then sat back down, retrieved two tickets from the drawer and took two labels from the printed receipt and pasted them on the tickets. "Okay boys. That'll be forty thousand naira or one thousand pounds for the two of you."

Uzo decided to pay in British pounds this time. He reached inside his shorts' front pockets and brought out his wallet, counted one thousand pounds and placed it on the desk.

The clerk, wearing an expensive wedding band on her left hand, accepted the cash. She counted it and took the rubber stamp on her desk and stamped the two economy class tickets for the young adults and handed them their tickets.

"Thank you ma'am," Nwoke said, happy to be on his way out of the country as he stood up.

"Thanks a lot, ma'am" Uzo followed and he and Nwoke turned to leave.

While waiting for the elevator, Nwoke glanced at the ticket. "Well, today is Thursday and I think that's enough time, don't you?"

"Sure, it is."

"C'mon, let's check the directory over there." Uzo pointed to the lit directory board next to the elevator and moved toward it as Nwoke followed.

"Hey, see that?" Uzo pointed at the directory that was lit up with little diagrams and listings of the big hotel. "They even got a bar and lounge in the basement. We should go there tonight.

Nwoke glanced at his watch and it said 6:10PM. Yeah, but it's still early so why don't we just step into town and get good view of the city and then go to the bar when we get back."

"Sounds good to me."

Instead of going to the elevator, the two best friends walked toward the exit sign, checking their pockets to make sure they had the keys to their suite and they did.

"I think the safest way is to jump in one of the hotel private taxis and just let the driver drive us around for a flat fee since we just wanna sight-see," Nwoke suggested and checked his back pockets to make sure he had enough cash in case he needed to pay the fare, knowing full well Uzo wouldn't let him spend his pocket change, anyway.

"That's why I like you so much, buddy. You always come up with great ideas!" Uzo said.

They walked through the front revolving doors and one of the bellboys noticed the young adults and quickly attended to the visitors who appeared in need of assistance. "Hello my friends. How can I be of assistance again?"

Uzo and Nwoke remembered the skinny bellboy from the last time he helped with their luggage to the room. They told him to get an air-conditioned taxi to show them around town.

The bellboy took his whistle that was hanging around his neck and blew it for the first taxi in line to come around.

A clean white Mercedes 280 with windows wound up swung around the corner from the hotel taxi stand like someone was chasing it. The driver pulled up in front of the hotel entrance and got out. "Hello, my very good friends," the chubby but very clean dressed driver greeted, knowing that this was going to be a good fare. There were no bad fares that came out of the five-star international hotel chain. He immediately walked around to the passenger side and opened the rear door for his customers, taking notice of Uzo's height.

Nwoke tipped the bell-boy and they both thanked him and got in the cab. The driver shut the door, walked around to the passenger side and got in.

"How are you boys today and where would you like to go?" the cab driver asked as he sat down and turned his head to face his young passengers.

Uzo and Nwoke exchanged looks and Nwoke replied to the driver's question. "How much time do you have and what time do you get off work?"

The driver looked elated, knowing that these where probably young rich kids who knew nothing about taxi driving. He figured he may have just hit the jackpot. "I have as much time as you need," he said.

"Good, we just want to see the city for a couple of hours. Can you handle that?" Nwoke asked.

"Of course I can. That is why I am here; to serve you."

"How much is that going to cost us? We would like a flat rate before you pull off." Nwoke had heard of taxi drivers ripping people off by driving around unnecessarily to prolong the ride and he didn't want to be a victim.

"You are my brothers and I will help you see the best of Ikeja and maybe part of Victoria Island." He now turned his head forward, avoiding the question as the airconditioner pumped out cold air in the one hundred degree temperature. He shifted the gear selector into the first and began to release the clutch while depressing the accelerator.

Uzo stopped him. "Now, hold on a second here. You haven't told us how much this ride is gonna be and you are already pulling off.

The Mercedes jerked Nwoke and Uzo as the driver stepped on the brakes suddenly. "Just give me one thousand naira and that should take care of everything and if you want to tip me, fine, but if not, it is also fine."

Uzo looked at Nwoke and nodded. "Okay, that's fine but make sure we see the best," Uzo replied, knowing they could have negotiated for less.

Nwoke also approved with a nod of his own to the driver.

The chubby cabbie matched on the accelerator while simultaneously releasing the clutch as the older Benz rolled off into motion. One could tell the driver kept up the maintenance by the way the engine sounded.

Ikeja was a middle-class town in Lagos where the busiest airport in the country and the entire west Africa was located. The driver drove slowly through the heavy traffic which was a part of everyday life in the crowded city. This gave Nwoke and Uzo the opportunity to get a good view.

On the main street, the hawkers besieged the taxi with all kinds of goods but Nwoke and Uzo weren't interested in buying anything. The driver also informed them that it was not safe to pull out cash in the car while the hawkers walked alongside the vehicle. The young hawkers were known to snatch whatever they could get their hands on, including necklaces and cash. Unfortunately, the only way to pay was to wind the windows down in the stop-and-go traffic.

"So, where are you guys from?" the taxi driver asked.

"We are from the eastern part of the country," Nwoke answered.

"But you two don't sound or even look like you live in this country."

"Oh, that's because we were born and partly raised abroad, but we've been living in Nigeria for the past eight years and now we're on our way back to where we were born." Nwoke didn't want to go into too much detail. He immediately turned the question around. "And what about you?"

"Well, I'm from Lagos state, born and raised," the driver replied as the taxi came to a complete stop in the heavy traffic.

"So, do you like it here and how long have you been driving a taxi.? Uzo intervened.

"I've been driving taxi in Lagos for about fifteen years now and I just got this position with the hotel five years ago. I wouldn't mind driving taxi in New York or London. Is that where you two are from?"

Uzo and Nwoke were surprised the taxi driver guessed the city where they were born since they only told him the countries.

"Why?" Nwoke asked.

A teenage hawker suddenly flashed what looked like a gold-plated watch through the rear passenger window, but when he saw Nwoke and Uzo, didn't pay any attention, he kept moving to the car behind them. Then came an ice-cream hawker, followed by a fruit hawker, each passing left and right as the taxi moved about five feet and stopped again.

"Because the exchange rate is quite impressive," the driver replied.

It took about thirty minutes before the traffic started moving up to a tolerable speed and Nwoke and Uzo noticed that the city was more developed than either Aba or Owerri. They passed by several high-rise buildings and a few foreign company logos and car dealerships of different makes and models. The city was live with people who dressed and looked like people in the U.S. and Western Europe. Where is the pride of Africa and its heritage, Nwoke thought to himself. The age of majority influenced the changing culture of the country. There were a lot of pedestrians who appeared to be moving faster than automobiles due to the time-consuming heavy traffic. Jeans and tennis shoes seemed to be the dominant wear for young males between the ages of thirteen and thirty.

The taxi had now entered into the upscale suburb of Victoria Island and the scenery changed drastically.

"Look, yo." Uzo pointed at a stretch limo with dark tinted windows that went by in the opposite direction, followed by a Rolls-Royce.

"I see, maybe I wouldn't have been so desperate to return to the U.S. if my dad had moved to this place. Hey, driver, where are we?"

"Oh, I'm sorry but this is Victoria Island or Ikoyi. The rich live here," the driver replied.

Uzo was impressed. "Is it part of Lagos State?" he asked.

"Yes. A lot of oil refinery employees live here that's why you see the mixed race of people."

The area was cleaner and less crowded than Ikeja and there wasn't a whole lot of pedestrian traffic and no hawkers at all.

The number of expensive cars that filled the roadway led Uzo to ask the driver another question. "So all these people are working class citizens?"

The driver made a right turn and headed toward the coast of the Atlantic ocean. "Not really. I would say about sixty percent are employed in very high-paying positions by either government, foreign banks or oil companies and the other forty percent are young drug pushers.

"Drug pushers?" Nwoke intervened, getting curious.

"That's correct. The people that take drugs to America or London and sell it for big money." The cab turned onto a residential neighborhood with nothing but a couple of mansions. "Have you heard of Gabriel Ogar? That's his house over there." The cab driver pointed at a lavish villa beside the Atlantic ocean coast on several acres of land.

"No, we haven't. Who the hell is he?" Nwoke asked.

"Well, he is one of the richest drug dealers in the country and the most wicked. He has people all over the world working for him."

But Nwoke and Uzo had never heard of the man. They knew about marijuana and that was it and to them, it was cheap and anybody could afford it.

"You mean you can make that kind of money selling drugs like marijuana cause that's all we have in Nigeria?" Nwoke asked, applying his intelligence a little bit while Uzo paid attention.

The driver accelerated a little after passing the villa. He checked the two innocent boys through the rearview mirror. "No, I mean heroin. You've never heard of heroin?"

"No, have you, Uzo?" Nwoke turned his head to look at Uzo.

"I saw a movie in the U.S. about how it can actually kill people who use it," Uzo responded.

"Well, these people are not the users,"the cabbie continued. "They are sellers and they sell very large quantities in exchange for powerful currencies such as Euro, dollars or pounds."

"Where do they get it?" Uzo asked.

"Thailand or Afghanistan."

Nwoke again asked an implicit question. "You seem to be very knowledgeable in the business. Have you ever tried to sell some?"

Again, the thirty-something year old taxi driver studied Nwoke in the rearview mirror, feeling like he was under cross-examination as the taxi turned back onto a main road. "I have many friends and relatives who did and some made it big while others got caught and are in prison, getting old." The driver shook his head, regretfully as he continued to lecture the young adults on the advantages and disadvantages of dealing illicit drugs. "The consequences outweigh the benefits, my brothers, especially in the United States.

The last statement by the taxi driver lingered through Uzo's mind and he wondered if that was what his father did, but then dismissed the thought when he remembered the quality of the electronics equipments his father imported.

Nwoke, on the other hand, sat there and thought about what it would be like to come back richer than his father and his uncle in Towson and maybe Uzo's father all put together by moving heroin. But the thought of getting caught and going to prison for a long time without being with any girls quickly made him dismiss the idea.

"Hey, what are you dreaming about?" Uzo asked as he tapped his best friend on the shoulder.

"Nothing, I think we better head on back to the hotel," Nwoke suggested, consulting his wrist watch.

"Okay, driver, let's call it a night. It's almost 9PM and we wanna check out that lower-level bar and lounge at the hotel. How much do you think one of those gated homes we saw in Victoria Island costs?" Nwoke asked, thinking if he ever made it big in life, he would return to Nigeria to live in the upscale neighborhood.

"About three hundred thousand American dollars will get you one and if and whenever you decide to get one, let me know. My brother is in estate management here in Lagos." The taxi driver reached inside his glove compartment and took out business cards and handed them to Nwoke while controlling the old Benz with his left hand as they headed for the hotel.

Twenty minutes later, the taxi pulled up in front of the Marriot International hotel. The driver got out of the car without even waiting for his money from his passengers, walked around to the rear right passenger side door and opened it to let Nwoke and Uzo out.

"Wow, I've seen it all today. I'm so glad we came up with that idea. I'd never thought my country was so pretty in some parts," Nwoke said after stepping out of the car. "Thanks a lot for the joy-ride that could possibly change my life in the future."

Uzo got out after Nwoke. "Thanks a lot too, sir and you never told us your name," Uzo said and reached in his back jean pocket to pay the man when Nwoke intercepted his right hand and paid the driver himself with his left hand, handing him one thousand naira.

The driver had never seen anything like it before where two people fought to pay the fare. He was used to seeing the opposite.

The same bellboy who had helped them earlier, stood at the doorway and watched in amusement as the driver gladly accepted the flat-rate fare with the two hundred naira tip."

"Thank you and my name is Fola

"Okay, Mr. Fola I'm Nwoke and that's Uzo. Thanks a lot for the tour of Lagos. We'll be in touch."

"I will see you guys again, my brothers..." Fola got back in the taxi and was gone forthe rest of the night as he had made more than he usually made in one day.

"Sorry buddy, I just couldn't keep letting you pay for everything. It makes me feel worthless."

"I understand, but I want you to understand it's no problem on my part, okay," Uzo replied as they both entered the hotel and headed for their suite to change their clothes.

It took them thirty minutes to shower and dress. Uzo had on a black Armani slacks to go with white Ralph Lauren long sleeve shirt while Nwoke wore blue Geofrey Beene long sleeve shirt with some prewashed jeans over some Hush-puppies. He didn't want to wear Gatas like Uzo.

The two young boys now looked like young men on a business trip. They were smelling fresh from the Geofrey Beene Grey flannel cologne as they stepped out of the suite into the elevator.

Stepping out of the elevator which opened into the bar on the lower-level, their eyes met two beautiful girls who were just a few feet ahead of them into the bar. The women must have just got off the elevator minutes before them. Neither said a word to catch their attention, even though the urge was there.

The bar and lounge were big and the dance floor was the size of a night club. The place was elegant and classy, perhaps too mature an environment for the teenage boys. But, with the way they were dressed, they could pass for twenty one or older, at least so they thought. The number of guests told them they might have got there a bit earlier. The time was now 10:00PM. The few guests already seated were older couples in their forties and older and would probably leave early. They were probably on vacation or business of some kind and didn't show signs of noticing anything different in the age of Nwoke and Uzo. Since there was no curfew law in the country, most people didn't really care and this gave the young adults more confidence to mingle.

"Nwoke made an observation and let his partner know. "Hey, over there, he pointed to where the two pretty black girls had just taken their seats.

"Yeah, I see. How old you think they are?" Uzo asked, acknowledging his best friend.

"Oh, I don't know, maybe twenty."

"Well, I can handle that. They can't be that much older than we are."

"Besides, age ain't nothing but a number," Nwoke quoted from the popular American saying. He remembered Ije who was two years younger than he was and wondered if Uzo had done one of his sisters without him knowing about it.

"Let's go sit by the bar, yo," Uzo suggested and began walking towards the bar area.

They took their seats in the middle of the bar where the cash register was. The music was low and they weren't used to this kind of mature environment. They wondered if they could ask the DJ or whoever to turn it up.

Nwoke asked the bartender but the young man said he had no control over the volume.

"There are only four couples dancing on the floor, look," Uzo told Nwoke who was busy studying the female bartender.

Nwoke looked without interest. "Okay, they're dancing out of tune to that Whitney Houston song. She's pretty."

"Who?"

"The bartender."

Uzo checked her out and their eyes met as she headed toward them from the end of the table.

"May I help you?" the white girl asked with a smile. She looked to be in her mid twenties.

Uzo noticed her accent could've been from any of the English-speaking European countries.

"Yes, give me a Heineken," Uzo said, feeling like the mature environment required mature drink. He looked at Nwoke to see if he'd follow suit and he did.

"And I'll take a Guiness stout," Nwoke followed, studying the white chick who looked very attractive and seductive. "Thanks." He smiled.

There were two bartenders and the second one was a black male in his early thirties who could have been Nigerian. He was counting money with his back turned to the customers.

She served the drinks. "You chaps need any cups?" she asked with an English accent.

"Nah," answered Nwoke as Uzo shook his head, eyes fixed on her breasts, which were quite enticing.

She quickly noticed but said nothing as she turned and walked away to attend to other customers.

Nwoke watched her with interest and wondered what it would be like to do it to a white girl. The more he thought about it, the more he wanted to find out.

Uzo's interest was at the two young black girls that had come in at the same time they got off the elevator. "Yo, why don't we just send a bottle or two of Champaign to those women over there, near the dance floor," he suggested, turning his head to look at the women.

Nwoke quickly shook his head in disagreement. "No, I like the bartender more."

"Now, you like older women. She's at least seven years older than you and you are not gonna be able to do anything with her tonight."

"Never say never. Like I said, age ain't nothing but a number," Nwoke said and took the bottle of Guiness and drank a big gulp, eyes fixed on the bartender's behind as she served other customers. He frowned his face. "This stuff is as bitter as hell."

"But it's supposed to be good for you, especially if we can score tonight, then you'll really see the benefit. I just can't tolerate that bitter taste, that's why I'm drinking Heineken." He took a sip from the bottle and waved at the female bartender for more service.

"Hey, what are you doing?" Nwoke asked.

"Don't worry, I'm sending a bottle of Champaign to those two over there. I think they notice me."

"Now, what movie did you get that idea from?"

"One of those American movies and it worked."

"Good for you but leave me out of it. I got my eyes on the bartender and I'm staying on top of my game. I never had a white bitch before and this could be my last chance in Nigeria."

"Neither have I and I'm not crazy about them either. They're all over London."

The bartender came over. "Yes, what can I do for you?"

"What brand of Champaign do you have?" Uzo asked, studying the girl that's got his partner's attention. He concluded she was indeed quite attractive.

"All kinds. What brand do you want?" Her pure British accent convinced Uzo she must be from England and this made him feel at home.

Nwoke paid close attention.

Uzo was lost in memories of London for a minute. "Can you send a bottle of Moet to those two black girls over there?" He pointed at the women.

"Okay, and who may I say sent it?"

"Uzo."

"Anything else?"

"No. That's it for now." Uzo finished his drink and asked for a second bottle.

The bartender studied Uzo and noticed how long his legs were, but didn't pay much attention to Nwoke. She turned and left to fill the order.

Nwoke sat quietly and observed, applying his intelligence to the situation as he watched the Caucasian beauty pick up the bottle of Moet and walk briskly over to the table where the two women were sitting. She placed the bottle of Moet on the table with a note and looked in the direction of the bar where Uzo was seated with Nwoke and said something. The women followed her gaze and waved at Uzo, smiling. The bartender then walked back to the bar, giving Uzo and Nwoke a second look. She then wrote something on a small notepad which was the tab on the young adult's bill. She turned her head and gave Nwoke and Uzo a second look to see if they were looking at her behind and they were.

"I think I got'm yo," Uzo said as he waved back at the two girls and smiled back.

The girls waved him over to their table in a gesture of invitation to join them. He stood up and walked slowly over to the table where the women were.

The pretty girls noticed how tall Uzo was and studied him closely.

"Hello beautiful ladies. I'm Uzo." He sat down opposite them, smiling.

"Hello, I'm Cynthia and this is my friend, Mary," the honey-coded complexioned one said.

"Hi," Mary said and smiled. "Thanks for the Moet." She was a little darker than Cynthia and both of them looked like they had minor extensions to their hair in the form of expensive weave. Her skin was glowing and one could see that she took good care of herself and probably rich to be staying at the five-star hotel.

Cynthia looked well maintained too as if she was an international business woman. "Do you play basketball?" she asked, showing some interest in the tall young adult. She couldn't quite make out Uzo's age.

From past experience, Uzo wasn't going to lie about who he was so he said, "I wish I was in the American NBA but I'm just tall for nothing."

"Don't say that. You are tall for something and you can still be an NBA player if you are determined. After all, how old was Hakeem Olajuwon when he started playing basketball for the first time?" How old are you right now?"

Uzo had hoped she wouldn't ask that question. He hesitated and made up his mind to lie about it, at least for the time being to score the anticipated one-night stand. "I'm almost twenty, what about you?"

"I'm twenty-two and Mary is twenty-three." She looked over at Nwoke sitting at the bar and then at her friend, sitting beside her.

Uzo finished what was left of the Heineken, hoping it would help calm down his teenage nerves which was now sending sweat across his forehead.

"Are you afraid of talking to an older woman? And is that why your friend is scared to come join us?" Mary intervened, staring at the young Uzo to see if she can shake him up a little but at the same time admiring his courage to step up the plate without his friend.

"Of course not. Actually, we're both a little mature for our age even though age ain't nothing but a number. So what are you up to?" Uzo was now feeling the effect of the two bottles of Heineken and this gave him a sense of security and confidence.

"Nothing. Just trying to pass a little time before the next flight. We are flight attendants. Can you open the bottle for us, please?" Cynthia asked as she finished the drink in her cup, testing the young adult's manhood.

Uzo had never opened a Champaign bottle before but, he had seen it done by his father. He grabbed the bottle opener, inserted it into the top of the Moet bottle and twisted and pulled to a loud pop.

"Thank you. That's very good for a twenty year old. I would have probably spilled it all over my clothes." She smiled and rolled her eyes at him as she held her cup for a refill while Mary kept looking over at the bar.

Uzo understood he had to pour the drink for the two ladies as a mature gentleman. He did so, gently, unconcerned about what his partner was up to. "So, what Airline you guys work for?"

"British Airways. We've just got here this afternoon and we're going back to London Saturday night," Cynthia replied and took a sip from her cup.

Uzo almost let out a scream like an excited young boy but he maintained his composure, not wanting to expose his real age. He glanced at the bar to see what Nwoke was doing and it looked like his partner was having fun as he kept his eyes on the pretty bartender. "That's the flight we're on."

"You and who, your girlfriend?" Cynthia asked.

"No. My buddy over there." He pointed at Nwoke who was now talking to the white woman.

"What a coincidence," Mary cut in after seeing Nwoke engaged in a conversation with the white bartender whom they were familiar with from being there several times in the past. She also finished whatever drink that was in her cup and held it up for Uzo to refill with the Moet which he happily did. "So, where are you girls from?"

"I was born in London and my friend was born in the 'States."

"Well, we're from Liberia but employed by the British Airways," Cynthia replied, exposing her perfect dentition.

"And why is your friend still over there?" Mary cut in again, looking over at the bar which was now getting crowded.

"He'll join us shortly," Uzo said and stood up, "and if you'll excuse me, I'm gonna get me another bottle of Heineken and I'll be right back." He left for the bar.

The two girls watched the tall figure walk away and then started talking to each other.

Uzo came back five minutes later with another bottle of Heineken and immediately sat down and began drinking without hesitation. He was now feeling pretty sure of himself and felt like he was superman from the effect of the alcohol. He was also happy he didn't have to drive, all he had to do was catch the elevator to the fourth floor and find room 456.

Cynthia and Mary finished the Moet one hour later and also began to feel the effect of the alcohol. Now they were used to it and were also the legal age required in other countries with laws limiting alcohol sales and consumption to the age of twenty one and above.

The dance floor was now almost full as more and more guests continued to arrive. Young and old, white and black, middle-Easterners and Hispanics, were all mixed up in the partying crowd. The music was now louder and the environment was beginning to look like and international festival and this put Uzo in a dancing mood.

Even though the DJ wasn't playing his kind of music, the effect of the alcohol made the music sound good to Uzo.

"Hey, you all want to dance?" Uzo stood up as he put the empty bottle down and stared at the two tipsy females before him.

Cynthia and Mary, feeling tipsy but not intoxicated, immediately stood up and followed Uzo to the dance floor.

"Oh, goodness! You make us look like midgets!" Cynthia commented. "How tall are you?" She was looking up at the 6'8" Uzo, shaking her hips with Mary following behind them.

"I'm six-eight," Uzo said out loud over the loud dance tune.

"So, you play basketball for your school?" Cynthia asked on top of her voice, looking Uzo up and then down to his waist, concentrating her focus between his thighs and then back up.

Uzo didn't want to tell her he just got out of High school so he said, yes and began moving his hips rhythmically to the dance tune and scooping low enough to the 5'5" height of the two dance partners. The DJ must have noticed the tallest person on the floor was a young adult and decided to change the music to 'Keep ya head up' by Tupak Shakur, which immediately changed the mood of all dancers and some spectators as more younger guests joined the crew on the floor.

"That's what I'm talking about," Uzo yelled through the loud sound of Tupac as the girls began shaking their hips excessively, attracting a little attention from some dancers. The silk-dress Cynthia was wearing was now revealing her voluptuous figure as she kept shaking her behind and her breasts.

Mary wore a pair of tight-fitted jeans that revealed a more slender and moderate figure.

At the bar, Nwoke sipped his third bottle of Guinness and the fourth one was unopened. His attention was still on the bartender who appeared too busy to hold a conversation. He glanced over at the table where Uzo and the two women were sitting and his heart skipped a beat when they weren't there. He began scanning the dance floor, knowing he couldn't miss Uzo's tall figure. He spotted his best friend in the middle of the dance floor, dancing intensively with the women he sent the Moet to. He now felt leftout and decided to finish the third bottle of Guiness and drink the fourth later. Just as he did so, the bartender walked toward him and stopped. "What's up, sweetie?"

"What's up with you and where is your tall friend?" she responded, looking a little tipsy herself.

"On the dance floor," Nwoke replied as he studied the pretty white woman. "What's our bill 'cause I don't think we're gonna drink any more tonight. My tall friend and crew seem a little over the edge. Look." Nwoke pointed at Uzo on the dance floor as Uzo continued to shake his shoulders and body for the two women who appeared to be enjoying the entertainment.

"Oh, wow!" she exclaimed, eyes fixed on Uzo and crew.

"Yeah, see what I mean?"

"Okay, give me a second," she turned and walked to the register, rang up the tab and walked back to where Nwoke was seated. "Fourteen hundred naira. We also take American Express card, dollars and British pounds in cash."

Nwoke wanted to impress her, so he didn't bother to cross-check the bill as he was overwhelmed by the beauty of the white woman. He reached in his front pocket as he stood up and brought out a stack of cash, counted two thousand naira in one hundred naira notes and gave it to her. "Is there anyway I can get in touch with you?"

"Sure." She took a pen that was on the table and scribbled a phone number on the back of the receipt. "That's my number and the number here at the bar. I noticed you've been watching me. "She smiled seductively.

"Nwoke returned the smile and accepted the receipt and looked at the paper, wondering if she gave him the right number. "So, what are you doing after work tonight?"

She looked at him and Nwoke could tell she was wondering how old he was."

"How old are you?"

"Eighteen and how old are you?"

"Twenty four and too old for you." She smiled and started walking away but Nwoke stopped her with his famous line.

"Age ain't nothing but a number, you know."

The familiar line caught her attention and she turned to face the young adult once again. "Nothing," she answered, staring him deep in the eyes to see if he would buck.

"What time do you close? I'm leaving for London Saturday night and when I call you, it's gonna be from there or the U.S.

"The bar is open twenty four hours and the shift change is at 2:00AM or you can call me on the number to my room."

The employees of the international hotel chain who were nationals of other countries lived in the hotel but Nigerians could live outside the facility.

"Can you just come up to room 456 before you retire to your room tonight?"

She heard the bell for service on the other end of the bar and turned her head to the left, then to the right and saw a couple waving at her for refill since her co-worker was busy. "We are forbidden from visiting guests but I'll try, bye." She turned and walked away to attend to a customer who desperately needed her attention.

Nwoke couldn't believe his ears. She was going to break the rules for him? He wondered why. Was she just a freak or up to something? Maybe she was a gold-digger. How many times had she done this with other guests before him? All kinds of thoughts raced through his mind but since he was only gonna be in the hotel for a few more hours, he didn't care. He sat up off the high stool and went to join his friend on the dance floor to the music of Janet Jackson's 'Love will never do without you' which was now playing on the crowded dance floor.

Uzo was happy to see his friend a little more sober than he was. The mixture of Moet and Heineken might have been too much for the young adult. Nevertheless, they all danced together as couples and Nwoke could tell from the way Mary was shaking her behind that she had enough alcohol in her. Nwoke was now happy to have an option if the bartender didn't show up. Then, it hit him; he didn't even know her name. He quickly retrieved the piece of paper she wrote her number on and saw 'Joyce' and put it back as he continued to dance. Yo, you ready to go upstairs?" he asked the very tipsy Uzo, raising his voice over the loud music.

"We can, but where is the white girl?" Uzo yelled back, laughing but only Cynthia and Mary heard him as the music absorbed the voice.

Nwoke didn't think it was funny, so he looked at the girls to see what their reaction to the joke was, but they were busy dancing and probably didn't hear everything. He tapped Mary on the shoulder to see if she would follow him toward the elevator and she did.

Minutes later, Uzo and Cynthia joined them at the entrance of the elevator where the unfamiliar couple were having an introductory conversation. Seconds later, the elevator door opened and the four drunks got in. Minutes later, they got out on the fourth floor. Cynthia staggered a bit as she took the first few steps out of the elevator. They stopped at room 456 and Nwoke opened the door and let everybody in. Mary and Cynthia giggled their way into the suite but there was nothing funny.

Nwoke knew from the condition of the women, they weren't quite themselves as alcohol had taken control of their minds. He figured he could control the entire situation. He checked the clock in the sitting room and it said 1:34AM and he knew the bartender would be arriving in about twenty five minutes if she was for real.

"This isn't our room. Our room is not this big and nice," Mary said in a dragging voice as she sat down next to her friend

"I know," Nwoke agreed and sat down next to her.

Cynthia walked over to the love-seat, kicked off her shoes and sat down, staring at Uzo.

Mary was already seated but when she saw Cynthia kick off her shoes, she did the same. "Wow! This is a whole apartment," she exclaimed as she studied the spacious suite with intoxicated judgment. She placed her right leg over the armrest and looked at Nwoke who was busy wondering if Joyce was going to show up or not.

"Can we get some music?" Cynthia asked, stretching across the love-seat and looking at Uzo.

Uzo started to join her in the love-seat but instead, picked up the remote to the stereo to fulfill Cynthia's request. He began by turning on the television to MTV via satellite but they were showing a music game show so, he found a slow-jam station on the radio and left it there.

Nwoke continued to watch the big screen T.V. with Mary sitting beside him, not sure what to do with her as she kept seizing him up, wondering what was between his legs.

Across the room, Uzo and Cynthia wasted no time getting closer as he grabbed her and started tongue-kissing her on the sofa. She responded with the passion of an intoxicated horny woman molesting a teenage boy. Uzo had never experienced such intense kissing in his young life and that was when he realized that the myth about older women was true. With the alcohol working his erect penis, he picked up the pretty honey-coded complexioned woman and carried her into his bedroom.

"Come here, boy. Let me undress you and teach you some things, okay," Cynthia said in a rather alcohol-influenced voice. They began to have sex.

The steamy sexual intercourse was interrupted by a knock on the door.

Nwoke immediately got up off the bed and put his jeans on without his boxers and ran to the door to see who was knocking at 2:20AM. Mary lay there, shocked at the speed her young lover ran out of the door with, wondering if he was in some kind of trouble.

Nwoke opened the door to face the pretty bartender. "Oh, hi Joyce," he said, smiling.

Joyce smiled and studied Nwoke's muscular build and then the lump in his jeans between his legs. "Hi, remember me?" she asked, now looking him in the eyes.

Nwoke wasn't sure what to do, whether to let her in or ask her to leave. "How could I forget, come in, Joyce." He opened the door to let her in.

"So, tell me, what's your name again or did you already tell me?" she said as she stepped inside the apartment.

"Nwoke; pronounced: wokey."

"I'm just going to call you Wo for now. I like your physique and I really think you're sexy." She began to pace the floor with a switch to her steps, showing the tight jeans that revealed an athletic buttocks. She studied the suite like she knew there was another woman inside. "I was surprised when you invited me to your room 'cause black guys don't usually ask me out. I guess they feel they don't have a chance with a white girl and a foreigner at that.

"I didn't think I had a chance but I thought it was worth trying and now here you are, so what's up?" Nwoke wondered what she had in mind and if she was for real or not. It couldn't be that easy, he thought.

"Nothing, I just came to see what was up with you. I knew you liked me when you didn't go with your friend in pursuit of the other women. You just sat at the bar, watching me instead of watching them. "She turned to look at his facial expression and reaction to what she said.

Nwoke was surprised she knew all along. "Well, you're different and very pretty."

Their conversation was interrupted by Mary's voice from the bedroom.

"Hey, Nwoke baby. Are you coming back to bed or are you going to leave me all by myself?"

Joyce knew from the sound of the voice, whoever that was in the bedroom, was drunk.

Suddenly, Uzo and Cynthia started to moan and groan again and this attracted Joyce immediately.

"Wow, what are you two doing here? You guys stay pretty busy, I see," Joyce said with a smile and moved closer to Nwoke, looking him deep in the eyes.

Mary wandered out of the room, naked, disregarding the white female who looked shocked. "Are you coming back into the room or not, Nwoke?" she asked with a seriousness to her tone.

"I'm sorry. I didn't know you had company," Joyce said, looking at Mary and then at Nwoke, not minding the situation since Nwoke wasn't her boyfriend.

Nwoke, now caught between a rock and a hard place, had no choice but to introduce the two women to each other. "Okay, Mary I'm sure you've seen Joyce before and Joyce, this is Mary.

Mary studied the white woman from head to toe. Due to the alcohol, she couldn't really make out if she was the receptionist in the lobby or the bartender since they both had blonde hair and about the same age. But then she recognized her from her voice after Joyce said hi. "Yes, I remember her. She was the one that brought us the Moet."

Joyce response was the opposite since all black people looked alike to the Caucasian race. "No, I don't remember her. I get a lot of customers that come through daily and I don't pay much attention." She studied Mary briefly and turned her focus back to Nwoke.

Nwoke remembered his father telling him that all blacks look alike to white people, but he could care less at the moment. His penis rose once again after seeing

Mary naked with hard nipples. They engaged in a heated threesome.

The three-way sexual intercourse lasted for another two hours with the horny freaks trying all kinds of experiments to achieve multiple orgasms.

Nwoke and Uzo woke up to find the three girls gone. The time was now 9:00AM

"Yo, it was a dream last night; I had my first three-some," Nwoke informed Uzo who had no idea that the bartender had come over after all.

"You're joking, right?"

"Come in here for a second." Nwoke led Uzo to his room and showed him two separate female underwear with mucus on them.

Uzo studied the underwear in total disbelief, "you sneaky thing. You could have come to my room and got me and Cynthia to join." He held on to the underwear.

Nwoke smiled at him and looked at the underwear in Uzo's right hand. "Sorry, but you can'st have that," he reached out for Uzo to hand him the underwear and he did. "My friend, I was too busy enjoying myself to think about somebody else, besides, you guys were making all kinds of noise, disturbing the peace. "He broke out in a loud laughter.

"Okay, since that's how you feel, I think I got a hangover and I'm gonna go lay back down, "Uzo said and started walking to his room. A piece of paper on top of the entertainment center to his left caught his eye. He picked it up and it read: 'Hey baby, I'll see you on the plane Sat night, Cynthia.' A smile lit up his face as he went back to his room and laid back down since the flight wasn't until the next day.

On the other hand, Nwoke, who didn't have too much to drink, didn't have any headache or hangover and decided to watch television which had reception of all major channel around the globe, including CNN International, MTV and BBC. He now felt complete since his dream of being with a white girl had now been fulfilled. But he still wanted more as he thought about the encounter; it was almost an appetizer. He'd seen it on x-rated movies but this time, he'd actually lived it and, wow, he thought to himself; white and black girls are all the same but it seemed like the white girls cried more and wanted more. He sat back and smiled, feeling on top of the world and looking forward to the journey ahead.

The two boys spent the entire day indoors, watching different movies and music videos. They tried all kinds of international foods with room service. Uzo tried to contact a couple of his child-hood friends in London but the numbers had changed or disconnected. Nwoke did the same and also got the same result so they decided to talk to Cynthia and Mary but unfortunately, the women couldn't come over again. They spent the second night alone.

Saturday came and Nwoke was the first to wake up. He ordered breakfast and looked forward to the day. His demeanor was the same as a nine-year old on Christmas morning, waiting to open his presents under the Christmas tree.

Uzo got up later and also had breakfast. Since the flight wasn't till 8:00PM, the duo decided to go get some souvenirs from the hawkers in a taxi.

They went downstairs to the lobby and asked their favorite bellboy to get them Fola. Fola came within seconds from the stand and drove his favorite passengers to the same area where they had seen so many young hawkers and they bought several African artworks and some traditional clothings.

When they returned to the hotel, it was almost 4:00PM and they had to get ready for the 8:00PM flight.

"Okay yo, it's almost four O'clock," Nwoke said as they walked into the suite."

"I think I might be in love," Uzo said, setting his bag on the dining table.

"What?" With a one-night stand? That alcohol must still be working."

"So what? Don't you read love stories? People have gotten married the day after one-night stand, you know."

"Those are stories. Do you or someone you know, know anyone who actually got married after a one night stand?"

Uzo stopped in his tracks and thought for a few minutes. "It doesn't matter. I like older women and I dig Cynthia, plus she can come see me in London or wherever else I decide to go."

"Whatever. She ain't nothing like Joyce."

"Good for you. You had to work all night for that, anyway," Uzo said and went to his room.

"Okay, I'm gonna go take a shower and get ready and you go do the same, remember we have to be there at least by six."

By 5:00PM, the dynamic duo were ready as they gathered some miscellaneous items, closed their suitcases and called the receptionist to send the bellboy up. They were in the lobby by 5:15PM.

"Let me go say goodbye to Joyce," Nwoke said and left Uzo and the bellboy with the luggage. He went to the elevator and pressed the lower-level button. Seconds later, the elevator doors opened and he got in. Two minutes later the doors opened into the bar and lounge and Nwoke stepped out. He saw Joyce sitting in the bar with only three customers and he figured it probably didn't start getting busy till much later, so he gladly walked up to greet her. "Hello, my dear," he greeted with a smile, leaning over the bar.

"Oh hi, Nwoke. Are you just about ready to leave me, dear?" Joyce asked, jokingly, looking at her young one-night stand.

"Yes, but I'll be back and I'm gonna keep in touch. I got your number and maybe one day you can come visit."

"I'd love that," she said as she walked around through the small opening and hugged him. Then she kissed him on the lips.

Nwoke grabbed her and began tongue-kissing her, ignoring the three customers who couldn't help noticing the love birds.

"Bye," she said after he let go.

"Bye, bye." He stepped back, still looking her in the eyes, lustfully. "Well, I'd better hurry.

The two parted and Nwoke got back in the elevator and went back upstairs where Uzo and the bellboy were waiting.

"Get us a taxi to the airport, please," Nwoke instructed, leading the way out the revolving doors, followed by Uzo and the bellboy.

"Okay, sir," the same bellboy said as he rolled the luggage on the curbside and blew his whistle for the next taxi in line to pull up to the front of the lobby.

"Did you check us out and turn the key in?" Nwoke asked.

"Of course, I did that while you were downstairs kissing your one-night stand.

One minute later, a Peugeot station wagon pulled up and the bellboy helped the driver load the two suitcases in the trunk. Uzo tipped the bellboy and the two travelers got in the taxi.

In the heavy traffic, it took the driver thirty minutes to get to the airport which was only a few miles from the hotel. The time was now 6:15PM when they finally got out of the taxi on the curbside of Murtala Muhammed International Airport which they both remembered coming through as children years before. Uzo paid the fare and they got out.

Nwoke looked around for a cart that would fit the two leather suitcases as they held on to their carryons and, soon enough, a young teenage boy pushed one to them.

"Thank you, little one," Uzo said to the little boy who couldn't have been no more than fourteen years old.

The boy lifted the two heavy luggage and placed them on the cart and asked, "which Airline, sir?"

"British Airways, son," answered Nwoke as the boy who seemed very strong for his age, pushed the cart toward the terminal of British Airways. Nwoke and Uzo followed closely behind.

The little help pushed the cart into the terminal and placed it in line for a position and then turned and looked at Nwoke and Uzo.

Nwoke looked at Uzo and said, "Let me handle this." He reached inside his pocket and gave the little boy a one hundred naira note, admiring him with an encouraging smile, sending the boy a message that he should continue to do positive things like that.

"Thank you so much, Oga," the little boy rejoiced as he left the terminal area.

The airport was busy as usual with people from all ethnic backgrounds, including Arabs, Indians and indigenes, just to name a few. One could tell the travelers were mainly businessmen who probably had some kind of interest in the oil-rich African nation.

Their turn came shortly and they were confronted by an overweight female customs inspector. "Open your luggage, sir" she said, looking up at Uzo who was mounting over her.

Uzo, who had never been through this without his parents, obeyed the woman's orders and opened the luggage and the small carryon for the customs officer inspection.

She inspected the content of the big box, lifting through Uzo's clothes and all his personal possessions thoroughly. "Okay, now place it on the scale, sir and please hand me your passport."

Uzo did as told.

She finished inspecting the passport and then tagged the two-piece luggage and said, "now, let me have your ticket,"

Uzo didn't know the ticket was inspected too and it was in the carryon and he quickly took the carryon and opened it, then retrieved the B.A. ticket and handed it to her.

She accepted it, inspected it for authenticity and handed it to the British Airways check-in clerk at the counter. The clerk stamped it and gave him a boarding pass.

"You have a safe journey, young boys," the mean customs inspector said but this time, with a smile.

Nwoke, who was behind Uzo witnessed all that went on and quickly retrieved his ticket and made sure his passport was in his hand as his turn came. He went through the same process and joined Uzo at the boarding gate as they waited for departure.

CHAPTER NINE

London

The Boeing 747 British Airways Jet was full as usual and Nwoke and Uzo quietly sat next to each other, waiting to catch a glimpse of Mary and Cynthia whom they hadn't seen yet as they were greeted and shown to their seats by a couple of white employees.

The announcement to fasten seatbelts came over the intercom minutes later and then the plane moved to the runway for take-off. Five minutes later, it was airborne and the unfasten seatbelt sign came on. The passengers got lose and started moving around to the restrooms and repositioning their carryons on the overhead carryon compartments.

"Soda or alcohol refreshments," Mary announced repeatedly on the left side of the aisle as she walked down from the top, pushing a small beverage cart.

Cynthia came down the right side, making the same announcement.

"Yo, look: it's Cynthia and Mary," Nwoke said and pointed at Mary as she came down the aisle.

Uzo was busy trying to adjust his headphones so that he could watch the movie or listen to some music. "Oh yeah?" He looked up the left aisle from the end seat he was seated and saw Mary, but couldn't see Cynthia on the right side only heard her voice. He smiled to himself contently.

Fifteen minutes later, the two familiar flight attendants were at Uzo and Nwoke's row but Mary served them, while Cynthia served the row straight across.

"Peanuts, soda or beer?" Mary asked, smiling as her eyes met both Uzo and Nwoke but kept to her duties.

"Both," Uzo said out of turn and blew a kiss at her.

"Soda and peanuts for me," Nwoke said and also blew her a kiss.

Mary smiled and looked at Nwoke, not understanding why Uzo would even blow her a kiss. She served both of them and proceeded to the passengers behind them.

Across the aisle on the right side, Uzo and Nwoke could now see Cynthia who looked quite cute in her navy-blue and white uniform just like Mary as she blew both of them a kiss and smiled. She was very serious in the discharge of her duties. She was gone to the next passenger in two minutes since the passengers she was attending to didn't want anything.

The sight of the two beautiful flight attendants quickly brought unforgettable memories to the minds of the two young adults.

Nwoke particularly thought about the three-some with Joyce and wondered if Mary was concerned about it or felt somewhat demeaned.

They both wondered how often the two female strangers had such encounter. The thought of them performing the same sexual acts with other men, hurt them to their hearts as they had caught feelings for the experienced women.

"You think maybe that was the first time they did that or do you think they do it in different countries?" Uzo asked the intelligent Nwoke who seemed to have answers to everything.

"No, I just can't see them sleeping around like that. But they can't keep steady boyfriends, traveling around the world like that. I'm sure of that."

Uzo thought for a second and nodded his head in agreement. "That makes a lot of sense, buddy. You see why it's so good to have Einstein as a travel companion?" Uzo complemented and grinned at his intelligent friend.

Nwoke thought about the possibilities of Uzo's question and then thought of different excuses for the one-night stand, doing what they did to men around the world. He came to the conclusion that the best way to find out was to ask them at a more convenient time should the relationship go any further.

It was against the Airline's policy for an employee to engage in a personal conversation with passengers aboard the flight at any given time during a scheduled flight while on duty.

Nwoke and Uzo were determined to see both women in London, possibly at Uzo's father's house.

"Let's drop them a note the next time they pass by for anything," Nwoke suggested.

"There you go again with another great idea."

"Can you remember your father's address?"

"Not right off but, I got it written down in my address book which is in my carryon. Let me find it. "Uzo got up and reached for the overhead carryon compartment and retrieved his carryon. He opened it and got his address book and a notepad with a pen. He then replaced the carryon in the overhead compartment.

Nwoke took the notepad from him and wrote a brief message with Uzo's address after Uzo read it out to him. He folded the piece of paper and held on to it.

The two travelers plugged their headphones in and focused on the movie screen in front of them. In the economy class, there weren't much options on the six-hour flight so they had to make due with whatever convenience that was available.

It wasn't until thirty minutes later that Cynthia and Mary made their rounds to pick up empty bottles and trash and Nwoke gave the note to Mary. She quickly put it in her pocket without reading it as she continued to do her job.

An old white woman who was sitting directly across the row to the left of Nwoke, saw him hand Mary the note and smiled at him, then turned her head to face the movie screen.

"That lady remind me of aunt B on the Andy Griffith show. You all watch that in London?" Nwoke said as he looked at Uzo.

The flight brought back childhood memories as the two boys sat in their seats and reminisced about their pre-teen days in the western world. They wondered what their childhood friends were doing as adult teens.

They still had quite a few hours to go on the flight and the more preoccupied their young minds were, the less they would feel the length of time.

At the Saint Thomas Church compound in Aba, the Rev. Nwanta and his wife sat in the dining room after dinner, wondering if Nwoke made it to Lagos alright since he hadn't called and it's been two days.

"I wonder why Nwoke hasn't called since he got to Lagos to let us know he made it okay," Mrs. Nwanta said to her husband who was sitting next to her.

"You know how kids are. He probably called his girlfriend and will call us later, besides, he's only been gone a couple of days.

Little Johnny ran into the room, looking like he'd just ran ten miles after playing outside. "Hey mom, when is Nwoke coming back?" the twelve year old asked, showing signs of missing his older brother. He and Nwoke were very close.

"Don't know, son, but soon I hope."

"I wanna play Dominoes and he's the only one that can play."

"Go play with Chinne."

"That's alright. They ain't no good at Dominoes, they just wanna play checkers.

Rev. Nwanta didn't know what to tell the twelve year-old since he had never played the game himself. "Teach one of your friends, you never know, they just might learn to beat you or go get a novel or scripture and read. Bye." He got up and left before Johny could respond.

Mrs. Nwanta looked at her youngest child and repeated what her husband had just said.

The flight to London Heathrow airport lasted exactly six hours and five minutes. Uzo and Nwoke had no unusual encounters with the British Customs as they checked out.

They went to ground transportation for a taxi to Uzo's father's house.

The United Kingdom is a union of four countries; England, Scotland and Wales, make up Great Britain, capital London. Mild climate, influenced by the warm Gulf Stream which flows across the Atlantic from the Gulf of Mexico, then past the British Isles. Most winds from the southwest bring rain, but the rainfall decreases from west to east. Winds from the east and north bring cold weather in Winter. Population is about 59,778,000, area-94,202 square miles. Religion is mainly Anglican and Roman Catholic make up about thirteen percent. The Government is constitutional monarchy.

"Yo, I've never been to London but I see the steering wheels on these cabs are on the right side, just like in the movies. How in the world can they do that?" Nwoke commented as he stood outside with Uzo, waiting for the next taxi to pull up.

"That's how it's always been, chap." Uzo was too excited to be answering some silly question. He felt at home. "We think Americans drive on the wrong side of the street. If you know your history, you would know that Nigeria used to drive on the right side of the street too," Uzo lectured.

A taxi pulled up in front of them and the driver got out.

"Hello," Uzo said to the overweight taxi driver as he stepped out to help with the luggage.

"Hello, young chaps." The cab driver put out his cigarette and opened the trunk to allow Uzo and Nwoke to put their suitcases inside the spacious trunk. "So, where are you young boys going this early in the morning?"

The time was 3:00AM and most passengers waited until day-light before leaving the airport. The inexperienced travelers didn't know.

"Number 14 W. Manchester street," Uzo replied and got in the back seat, ignoring the out-of-shape white cabbie.

Nwoke followed suit after placing his suitcase in the trunk.

The driver closed the trunk and walked around to the driverside and got in. "Very well, then," he said and started the vehicle.

"Please take the shortest route," Uzo said as the taxi pulled off.

"I will, I assure you. I don't cheat my passengers.

"Nwoke, who was listening, felt like he was watching an old English movie due to the accent that now changed the entire atmosphere of the ancient city.

The driver turned on the radio to block off whatever the black young adults had to say.

Except for the left-handed driving, London looked like an ancient city from back in the eighteenth century, but one could tell that the infrastructure had been updated, even though the buildings were of ancient architecture. The people looked just like people in New York or Chicago, made up of all races and culture. But, whites were the dominant race.

"What's up with the two-storey buses, yo?" Nwoke asked as a two-storey bus service passed by.

"Nothing, they just transport people around for a fee. It's a commercial bus service which I'm sure you have in the 'States," Uzo replied as he noticed a girl that looked like Deborah at the bus stop.

"I think I remember my father saying they got'm in New York for tourists.

Fifteen minutes later, through the nearly deserted roads, the taxi got off the main road and slowed down. Five minutes of neighborhood cruising and a left turn, brought them to Manchester street. The driver slowed down to a crawl as he checked the numbers on the isolated homes that looked expensive.

"I think this is my street. I remember my friend David lived right there." Uzo pointed at a house, excitedly.

Minutes later, the taxi stopped in front of a single brick two-storey house.

"Okay kids. That'll be fifteen pounds," the unfriendly cab driver said without turning his head to look at Uzo and Nwoke.

Uzo paid him and got out, followed by Nwoke.

When the unfriendly cabbie saw the twenty pound note, he hopped out of the cab with the hope of keeping the change."I'll get your luggage out, sir." He popped open the trunk and took the two suitcases out, placing them by the walk-way of the house.

"Okay, you can keep the change," Uzo said.

"Thank you chaps and enjoy the rest of the day." He got back in the cab and pulled off.

Uzo's father's house was modest. It looked like Mr. Otu lived low profile in London but extravagantly in Nigeria. It was a split-level brick building that sat by itself in a middle class neighborhood of west London. It was located in an area that would be considered suburb in the U.S.

Uzo turned and looked at Nwoke who wondered if Uzo lost the keys. "Oh, it's in my carryon." He opened his carryon and retrieved the bunch of keys that his father had given him which included the keys to the two vehicles; a Volvo 760 and BMW 525. He inserted one of the keys but the door didn't open, so he tried a second one and the door yielded. "We're in, partner." The 6'8" young adult picked up his suitcase with his carryon over his shoulder and entered the house he hadn't been in since the age of ten.

Nwoke followed. "This is nice, yo," he said, looking over the fine furniture displayed throughout the home.

"Thanks. C'mon, let me show you to your room," Uzo said as he led the way up the carpeted stairs to the guest-room.

This is just right," Nwoke said as they walked in the room. He set his luggage down. The guestroom was spacious and moderately furnished with a full bathroom and a 22 inch television set. He immediately grabbed the remote and flipped the t.v. on.

"And there are some new pajamas in the closet. I'm gonna go downstairs and order some food. What do you want?" Uzo said

"Pizza or Chinese is fine.

"Coming up and welcome to the lost life. It's just like the old days, isn't it, Americano?" Uzo left without waiting for a response. He went downstairs, opened the door and picked up a menu he had seen under the screen door. He studied it to see if it was a twenty-four hour service since it was so early in the morning and it was, so he ordered a large pizza and shrimp fried rice. He hadn't tasted neither in eight years. He then carried his luggage to his room which brought back many child-hood memories. The room now looked childish and he would need to update it as soon as possible.

They took showers and got comfortable in their pajamas and waited downstairs in the living room for the food to arrive.

"I'm gonna have to call home tomorrow to let them know where I am," Nwoke said as Uzo walked to the window to see if the delivery person was there.

Uzo then walked to the door and opened it, leaving the screen door so they could see the man or woman making the delivery. "Yes you should and I'm going to call my mom and dad too."

It was a nice breezy morning with temperature of about 75 degrees."

"You think it's a good idea to tell them you ran away with me?" Uzo asked.

"Well you didn't run away. Your parents were nice enough to let you go back to where you were born for college. You never know, that might make them feel better," Nwoke replied as he found the remote and flipped the television on.

"Yeah, I guess you're right. They might be upset at first, but when they learn you're with me, they might feel different."

"Let'm worry about it. I know I'm okay and I'll still get my college degree, no matter what and I will be something in life. Now, tell me this; you think Cynthia and Mary are coming?"

"I don't see why they wouldn't. In fact they should've been here by now," Uzo said and looked out the window again. "This is much better than the hotel room they get from B.A. Besides, that's their loss. You see," he walked away from the window to where Nwoke was seated. "Girls are no problem when you're rich with a car and a nice home like this."

"I don't know about that. Maybe most of the girls but not any of them, especially when they got that kind of job around the world, traveling for free," Nwoke replied.

"Well, that's along the same line of what I just said, isn't it?"

Nwoke thought for a few seconds and agreed.

Ten minutes after the conversation, a taxi pulled up and Uzo, who could see through the screen door, noticed the dome-light and jumped up, wondering if his father had followed them to London. "Yo, come look at this," he said to Nwoke as he walked up closer to the screen door and saw Cynthia get out of the taxi, followed by Mary.

"No, shit! This can't be happening so fast, man!" Nwoke exclaimed and pushed the door open to help Mary with her luggage while Uzo followed and picked up Cynthia's heavy suitcase.

Cynthia and Mary were lit up with a smile after seeing the two young adults rush to them like little boys excited to see their parents' home.

"You guys are quick, got your pajamas on already," Cynthia said, still in her uniform as she paid the cabbie and followed behind Uzo who picked up her suitcase out of the open trunk of the station wagon taxi.

Nwoke picked up Mary's suitcase and kissed her. She followed him behind Cynthia and Uzo.

"Look who's talking about being fast. Who would have thought that you two would have been here by now? Did you even make it to the hotel?" Uzo asked Cynthia.

"No, we don't have to, unless we want to. We don't really like staying in different hotels anyway," Cynthia replied as she entered the house.

Mary closed the door after Nwoke stepped inside with her suitcase.

"Oh, leave the door open. We're expecting the food delivery guy to pull up any minute now," Uzo informed Mary and Mary quickly pushed the door back open, leaving the screen shot.

"Did you order enough?" Mary asked after hearing the comment from Uzo.

"I think it'll be enough and if it's not, we'll just tell him to go back and get some more when he gets here," Uzo replied as he took Cynthia's luggage to his room. "C'mon Cynthia, come with me."

Cynthia followed Uzo to his room, changed her clothes and came back downstairs.

Mary did the same, behind Nwoke.

They all gathered downstairs in the living-room and past memories became apparent.

"Welcome, my dear and please forgive me for inviting the white girl to my room the other night," Nwoke apologized and hugged Mary, then engaged her mouth in tongue-kiss like a man who hadn't seen his first-time love in years and she surrendered with the same desire as the young adult.

"I missed you so much and I'm glad to be sober now. You are such a handsome young man. How old are you again?" Mary asked as she let go of Nwoke and looked him over, seeing how young he really looked since she didn't get a chance the other night.

Nwoke thought about it for a minute and she sensed he must be pretty young but it was too late to change anything about what had happened between them, so she started guessing his age to help him out.

"Seventeen....eighteen?"

"The latter...not the first one?" Nwoke said, deciding it was best to tell her the truth so she won't have to find out later on if the relationship should go further.

This turned Mary on some more. "You mean I did all that with an eighteen year-old?" she said, smiling and studying the young adult before her, undressing him with her eyes. "Well, when is your birthday?"

"December,"

"So, I'm almost six years older than you and I could go to jail in America for what we did. But that's okay, let's just forget it, I'm so hungry," She faced the television.

Nwoke looked at his older lover and wondered what her real motive was since she wasn't upset about him lying about his age like any other woman would be. He decided to be more thoughtful and more careful in his dealings with her to counter whatever her motive may be.

The doorbell had just rang as the food delivery man stood in the doorway. Uzo quickly ran to the door.

"How much?" Uzo asked, mounting over the little Asian-looking man.

"Six pounds and fifty shillings," the little delivery man said with a pleasant smile.

"Here's eight and you have a nice day," He paid the man and closed the door, this time he locked it with the chain. "Dinner is served, you all!" He set the large pizza and the large shrimp fried rice on the dining table in the dining room.

The four lovers devoured the slices of pizza and scalloped the shrimp fried rice.

Dinner lasted about thirty minutes and Uzo walked over to his father's bar next to the dining and brought out a six-pack Heineken and a bottle of Hennessey.

"Drink on, yawl!" Uzo announced as he set the drinks on the dining table. He then picked up the bottle of Hennessey and opened it, walked into the kitchen and brought four glasses and poured the Cognac halfway to the top of all four glasses and toasted. "To eternal love!" he said and took a sip, frowning to the taste. The Hennessey had a slight burning sensation unlike Guiness and Heineken. "How can they drink this stuff?"

"Don't worry, you'll get used to it, little boy," Cynthia teased as she took two quick sips and exhaled, smiling at Uzo and Nwoke. "I was the same way my first time but for now I think that's enough or you can mix it with coca-cola."

"That sounds good....I mean the soda idea," Nwoke cut in as Mary had already finished her cup.

"So what does your father do for a living?" Mary asked as the Hennessey began to creep in.

"Oh, he's an electronics dealer," Uzo replied and walked over to the kitchen to get a bottle of soda out of the refrigerator. A minute later, he returned with a bottle of coca-cola.

"Perfect for Henney, boy. You sure you haven't done this before?" Cynthia asked, giggling.

"I wish," Uzo said and mixed himself and Nwoke's cup under the direction of Mary.

"That must be pretty cool. He imports or exports electronics?" Mary asked as she grabbed a bottle of Heineken while Cynthia was still working on her cup of Hennessey.

"I believe both."

Nwoke drank the entire content of the cup of what tasted more like coca-cola than alcohol and didn't winch. "That tasted pretty good, Uzo. What are you waiting for?"

"Waiting for Cynthia to do something with hers," Uzo answered and emptied the entire content into his stomach, this time, without a frown.

They joked and drank for the next two hours and retired to their respective rooms.

In the guestroom, Nwoke kindly welcomed Mary inside, under the influence of alcohol. Mary gladly accepted but decided to take over.

"This is going to be different, young boy. Mama is gonna teach you some new tricks tonight. C'mon, let's take a shower," Mary said under the influence of Heineken and Hennessey, kicking off her shoes and immediately undressing. She went to her carryon and retrieved her bathing needs and took another look at Nwoke and switched her naked hips to the bathroom, knowing that the young adult would follow his penis instincts.

Uzo and Cynthia did almost the same thing except for Cynthia's special fantasy in the bath-tub as opposed to Mary's shower fantasies.

"First of all, Uzo baby, we have to make sure that the water is hot so we sweat while we're sitting inthe water and I mean.....sitting," Cynthia said, turning the bathwater on and adjusting it to the righttemperature for the situation at hand while the naked Uzo stood behind her naked behind and paid very close attention to the older woman.

The digital clock on the nightstand showed 11:35AM as Nwoke looked at it after turning over, away from Mary. He was still sleepy with a little hangover, "Oh shit! I gotta call dad and let'm know where I am," he said out loud to himself, subconsciously, waking up Mary.

"What?" Mary asked in a sleepy voice with her eyes closed and dosed back off like somebody talking in their sleep.

He stood up off the bed and walked over to the loud phone that was on the study table and dialed Nigeria. He waited a few seconds before he heard something on the other end. "Hello....hello....," he said repeatedly, trying to counter the static noise that was interfering with the international line. The line became clearer minutes later. "Is that you, dad?"

"Yes, it is and where are you, Nwoke, sounding so far away?" Rev. Nwanta asked on the other end of the international phone line.

"I'm in London with Uzo and I'm sorry I didn't tell the family."

"London? Are you kidding me? How—why? You were supposed to be attending Medical school here in Nigeria and now, you are where?"

"I'm going to Towson or Baltimore from here, or wherever my journey takes me, but I'm still gonna go to college when I get there."

The Reverend paused for a few minutes and sighed like somebody who'd just been defeated and had nowhere to turn. "Alright, just keep in touch, son and call me when you get to Towson but you should stay with your uncle, Alo and I think he still lives in Towson."

"Thanks, dad. Bye." Nwoke hung up the phone and then turned and looked at Mary who was now fully awake, staring at him. He walked back to the bed and joined her under the sheets.

In Uzo's bedroom, Uzo also woke up but a little later than Nwoke at exactly 11:50AM. He picked up the phone to let his father know he made it safely and that Nwoke was with him which he hadn't told him before leaving Aba. "Hell." He had a much more clearer reception than Nwoke had earlier. "Ije, is dad home? I'm in London. Let me speak to either him or mom."

"Okay, hold on," Ije said on the other end of the line.

Two minutes later, Uzo's father came on the line. "Hello, my son. How are you?"

"Fine. I just called to let you know that I made it here safely and I'm with Nwoke Nwanta."

Mr. Otu was quiet for a few seconds. "You didn't tell me you were taking Reverend Nwanta's son with you. Do his parents know?"

"Uzo now became scared. "No, I don't think so, I mean, he didn't tell them but, he's in transit to the U.S. for school, too."

"Oh, okay. So he's going back for school, just like you, hah?"

"Yes, so can you tell his father that he's okay?"

"Okay, I will or I might just wait for them to call me. How are the house and the vehicles?"

"The house is fine. The cleaning lady is doing a good job but I haven't been to the garage yet. You wanna hold on while I check real quick?"

"Yes, hurry up." Mr. Otu decided to hold on as the international phone bill accumulated.

Uzo quickly put his pajamas back on and ran downstairs and across the living room to the back and opened the door that led into the two-car garage. He saw the BMW 525 and the Volvo 760. Over to the left corner, he saw his bike from eight years before, still looking like

146

new and all his little brother's toys that he didn't want, in a big box that was open. Satisfied with what he saw, he ran back upstairs and picked the phone back up. "Yes dad, the cars are fine."

"Alright, son. Have you selected a school yet?" You know you must start school this Fall, that's what we agreed on, right?"

"Yes, I remember, but I still haven't made up my mind on which one to attend."

"How about Oxford? I can call a friend of mine and let him know that you will be coming to the admissions office very soon. His name is Frederick Mondale."

Uzo was silent for a few minutes since he really didn't want to go to school just yet. He just wanted to enjoy himself for at least a year without stress before studying full time, but he had no choice now. "Iguess it's okay but I don't wanna live on campus so can I just get an apartment close to the school?"

"I don't see why not as long as you promise to study. A college degree is very important in life, son, no matter what you decide to do."

"I Promise to study hard, dad," Uzo agreed, knowing that his father earned an Economics degree from Oxford.

"Very well son and tell Nwoke to get in touch with his father and I'll probably be there in a couple of weeks. Take good care of yourself." The international line died.

Uzo replaced the phone in its cradle and looked at Cynthia who was now staring at him with tired eyes.

"That was your father wanting you to attend college at Oxford? That's a good school."

"Yeah, I have to register by Fall. Well, I mean way before Fall. I just gotta take their special entrance exam which I know is very hard, "Uzo said and walked to the foot of the bed and sat down. He stared at the pretty woman who now looked more beautiful than before she went to bed.

Cynthia noticed how he was looking at her and responded accordingly. "Oh, poor baby, come to mama, "she said and flipped over the satin cover, revealing her naked, smooth body which the eighteen year old couldn't resist.

"You're gonna make me fall in love with you, Cynthia," Uzo uttered as he penetrated the twenty-two year old woman, forgetting the condom that was on the nightstand.

At exactly 12:40pm, Mary and Cynthia met downstairs in the kitchen to cook lunch. But Uzo came downstairs and changed their minds. "Hey pretty babies, what do you think you're doing? We're going out for lunch. It is almost one o'clock," Uzo said as he entered the Kitchen.

"Oh, okay baby, I'm gonna go get ready then," Cynthia said and disposed of what raw food they had on the kitchen countertop.

The two visitors, still in their nightgowns, started up the stairs after leaving the kitchen when Cynthia stopped all of a sudden, eyes fixed on Uzo's family picture which was on the wall at the beginning of the stairs. Mary's eyes followed suit.

"What is it?" Mary asked, following her friend's gaze.

They moved closer to the 12" by 12" picture.

"That, right there must be Uzo's father and he looks familiar but I just can't place him." Cynthia said.

"Oh, maybe he was just a passenger on the plane. We get'm all the time—you know the regular riders. His mother is pretty, so is his sister," Mary responded.

"The little brother isn't too bad looking either."

"Yeah, that's my family," Uzo's voice said from behind them. "Mary, where's Nwoke? I don't know what he's doing still up there. I'm about to go find out," Mary said and went up the stairs.

Nwoke had just finished talking to Ije and Helen when Mary entered. He was still fantasizing about Ije when Mary's voice broke the fantasy.

"Hey, Uzo said we're going out for lunch so let's get ready. Why are you up here by yourself anyway?" Mary said, studying the young adult for any suspicious activities.

Nwoke looked at her and said, "nothing, just thinking about what my father said. Let's get ready, then." He sat up on the bed and stood up and walked to the bathroom to take a shower.

Mary followed behind, dropping her night-gown as she walked, revealing a naked Mary.

The four lovers came down to the family room thirty minutes later and, as Mary walked past the living room again, she couldn't help noticing Uzo's family picture a second time. This time, it hit her and her heart skipped three beats as she realized that Uzo's father was the man they had served several weeks before, near the airport. "Oh my goodness!" She said to herself under her breath as shock waves went through her body. This was the opportunity she and Cynthia had been waiting for, she thought to herself. She wasn't going to let Uzo and Nwoke suspect anything just yet. The sound of footsteps coming toward her, broke her thought process.

"What are you doing? Aren't you coming to join us in the family room till the taxi gets here?" Cynthia asked as she came back to the living room, looking for her friend.

Mary turned quickly and looked at her and then, after making sure there was nobody else behind her, she got closer to her friend and business partner. "Hey, I think I recognize Uzo's father," she whispered. "Remember the man we served several weeks ago near the airport in a blue BMW and he wouldn't get out of the car?"

"Yeah, how could I forget? He's the only customer that never got out of his car for some reason. I knew there was something about the way his son spent money at the five-star hotel and he's only eighteen," Cynthia said and moved closer to the picture for better view.

Cynthia and Mary had been delivering heroin for Mr. Gabriel Ogar for almost two years now through their jobs as flight attendants for British Airways and never had the opportunity to make their own connection.

Uzo and Nwoke interrupted their secret conversation.

"Let's go, you girls. The taxi is outside," Uzo informed them, looking them over and wondering what they were standing in front of the family picture for.

"Yes, let's go," Nwoke seconded, leading the way out of the door like a hungry young adult who'd been playing outside all day.

While in the taxi, Cynthia couldn't bring herself to stop thinking about the new discovery they'd just made. Every so often, she would glance at Uzo and wonder what he knew about the game. Mary, who was sitting directly behind her boyfriend who was sitting up front with the Indian driver, kept studying the back of his neck, reading things into it, praying that he was a 'big boy' in the game too.

The ride to the Carnaby street shopping strip which is home to over thirty flagship fashionable boutiques by famous brands, lasted thirty five minutes. There were many bars, cafes and restaurants. Uzo paid the fare and they all exited the taxi. The restaurant was located on the first-level of the mall.

"So, when are you guys leaving London?" Uzo asked as they walked toward the entrance of a Gucci store.

Cynthia and Mary exchanged looks before Cynthia responded.

"Sooner than you think." She didn't want to be specific just yet, not until they found out what was really going on with the two strange young adults.

"What do you guys got a taste for today that they don't serve on the plane?" Nwoke asked, grabbing a hold of Mary's hands and squeezing it but not too hard.

"Seafood good, you guys?" Mary asked the two lovers in front of her.

Cynthia turned around and answered, "Perfect! I was just thinking about the same thing." She then turned and faced Uzo, still walking and holding hands. "That's fine, isn't it, honey?"

Uzo agreed and smiled at her as he almost bumped into a group of white teenagers who were headed in the opposite direction. "Oh, excuse me. I'm sorry," he apologized and then focused on the crowded surrounding.

They found the small seafood restaurant and ate lunch but when Uzo attempted to pay the bill, Cynthia stopped him and pulled out a stack of pounds and paid the fifty-pound bill which included a five-pound tip. She wanted to send a message and see if the young adults could put two and two together so that they can all get on the same page.

"Mmmm....impressive," Uzo said, wondering why Cynthia did that.

Nwoke, on the other hand, wondered how much flight attendants made for her to be walking around with what looked like at least five thousand pounds in large notes.

"Now, shall we go shopping, my dear? My treat," Mary said, holding Nwoke's hand once again.

"What?" Nwoke responded, shocked at the offer and wondered what was really going on with the two women. Could they be so in love already that they were willing to spend their hard-earned money on them? He thought to himself.

"Yes, you heard right. You can pick whatever you like and I'll pay for it, pretty boy." She smiled confidently and looked over at Cynthia, hoping that she would follow suit. She knew that if Cynthia did the same for Uzo, maybe the message would really get across and the boys would open up on what they were really doing in London.

"Same here, Uzo," Cynthia added, staring at Uzo, seriously.

"Why the sudden generosity?" Nwoke inserted with the tone of an investigator fishing for information.

"Nothing, we just don't want you to be doing everything for us, but maybe next time, okay?" Cynthia concluded and began marching through the crowded mall, looking for an upscale store to start with.

"You still haven't answered my question," Uzo reminded the two visitors.

"What question are you referring to?" Cynthia responded.

"How long are we going to enjoy your company this time?"

"Oh, I'm sorry. A couple of days more and then we're gone to the 'states."

"That's good. We're enjoying your company so far and I'm hoping this won't be the last time," Uzo said and spotted a Versace store to the right about fifty feet ahead. "Let's go there, you all." He pointed at the sign that read; 'Versace for men' in front of the store and they all entered.

"They shopped at the store for thirty minutes, then went to a Victoria Secret outlet and the women bought a few things. The shopping ended at the 'Athletic Footwear of London' and they took a taxi back to Uzo's house.

"You guys really get to see the world, don't you? Where else have you been?" Nwoke asked, sitting in the comfortable sofa in the family room, watching MTV London which showed music videos from the U.S. and London. They couldn't get BET since Uzo's father didn't install satellite since there was no one at the house to watch television. The cable network was enough for Mr. Otu when he was there.

Mary had just spent one thousand pounds on her teenage lover and felt good about it as she sat real close to him in front of the T.V. set. "I think we've been to all the major cities around the world in the past two years, we've been employed by the airline. There are also a lot of other fringe benefits that come with being a flight attendant, you know." Mary was now throwing hints at the unsuspecting young man who had no knowledge of the business she was into.

"Oh yeah? What kind of benefits are we talking about?" Nwoke became curious. "Well, I can't tell you just yet but I will." Mary looked over at Uzo and Cynthia who were deep into a conversation and weren't paying them any mind before she continued. "Does Uzo's father own a blue BMW?"

"Yes, I was just wondering if he was the man I saw at the B.A. Christmas party last year, that's all." But Nwoke was too smart to believe that was all that Mary had on her mind but he didn't want to press the issue at the moment. He felt it was better to keep having fun and with time, nature was going to take its course. But he sincerely hoped that the two women hadn't slept with Uzo's father at the Christmas party.

"Uzo stood up when Dr. Dre and Snoop Dog's G. thing video came on. "I gotta get my British License, but think that'll be after you guys are gone," he commented.

Nwoke began rapping to the lyrics."I got the CD but I'd never seen the video, girl!"

Uzo raised the volume with the remote and started dancing as he lip-sinked the popular American rap tune, joined by Nwoke as the two girls watched in excitement, realizing the boys were just like foreigners and not much African.

The partying went on for about two hours into the day but, no matter what they did or talked about, Mary and Cynthia still couldn't get their minds off what they'd just discovered about the very house they found themselves in. The longer they stayed at No. 14 West Manchester street, the more they knew that the young lovers they were now deeply involved with, had no knowledge of how the home was paid for. Cynthia and Mary were disappointed in the meantime and they figured this wasn't going to be their last trip. The two flight attendants-drug smugglers were determined to make good use of the innocent young adults as time progressed. It also made them uneasy knowing that, in the drug game, anything could happen at any time, including police raid of the house they were in at any given moment, but they were ready to take their chances. After all they had already made their drop before coming to Uzo's house from the airport. At the moment, they were as clear as the sky except for the large amount of cash they were carrying. Besides, they were only visitors waiting for their next assignment.

"Hey, Nwoke can I talk to you for a moment, please?" Mary said and grabbed Nwoke by the arms and took his unfinished bottle of Guiness and put it on the table. He followed her upstairs to the bedroom where she told him to sit down on the bed like a disobedient child who missed school. "So what are you gonna do for money when you get to the U.S.?"

"Well, I'm sure my dad will send me enough money to be comfortable on. I'm not from a poor family, you know."

"Oh yeah? What does he do for a living?" She hoped he was also a drug dealer but she was disappointed.

"He is a minister of the Anglican church in Aba, Nigeria which is a branch of the Episcopal Ministry of the United States."

"Oh, I see, but he is nothing like Uzo's father, though," Mary now sat down next to Nwoke, putting her arms around him as her soft breast pressed against his right

155

shoulder. "Nah, not even close from what I've seen. Not financially."

"Wouldn't you like to be independent of Mommy and Daddy now that you're by yourself?" Nwoke now wondered where this was leading to and decided to be a little more cautious in his answers since he already knew that the girls were up to something from the start. "Of course I'd love to be independent of them."

"I think I can help you become independent, Nwoke. I like you a lot and I'm sure we can do well together." She said and turned her head and kissed him on the lips.

Nwoke kissed her back, feeling a little rush of blood to his manhood but this was a serious matter and he didn't want to lose focus. He removed his lips from her and studied her facial expression for any sign of deceit but saw nothing but sincerity on the pretty face. "How?"

"Okay, let me show you something," She stood up and walked over to the closet where her luggage was and brought her carryon out and placed it on the bed and opened it. "look inside, "She said as she unzipped a small compartment inside the top cover of the coach carryon.

Nwoke's mouth went dry as he sat there, staring at the stacks of cash that were separated in pounds, dollars and Euros. "How did you get that?" Rob a bank?" he asked, scared as she began to look like a stranger who had just robbed a bank and escaped to Uzo's father's house for safety from the law.

"Stop joking, do I look like a bank robber to you? This is some of my money and also some of my partners who are in the U.S., London and Nigeria. You can become one of those partners if you want. It is a total of about five hundred thousand dollars if you break it down to that denomination."

"So, how much of it is yours?""Ninety thousand dollars is mine and you can get that too, when you get to the U.S. and even more after you meet some new customers and we start doing our own thing."

"What thing are you talking about?" Nwoke hadn't the slightest idea what his lover was talking about but he was very interested in earning that type of income without doubt.

"I am talking about moving heroin," she said and closed the carryon and put it back on top of the spacious walk-in closet. She then came back to the foot of the bed but this time she decided to stand over Nwoke and look him straight in the eyes." I mean to Maryland, particularly Baltimore which has one of the highest number of addicts in the United States and since you're not far from it in Towson, you can probably find a contact and just relax and collect your money; it's that easy."

"It sounds good and easy but I know nothing is that easy in the world and I'm gonna have to think about it. I've heard some terrible things about drug dealers, especially from taxi drivers at the Marriot in Lagos plus what I've seen in the movies like 'New Jack City' and 'Boys in the Hood', nothing is been good about the dealer. Look at 'Scarface', you've seen 'Scarface'? "I think so, but that's just made up stories. You wouldn't be in that type of danger."

"They've either gone to prison for a long time or died by gunshot." Mary looked at the young adult and almost gave up in trying to convince him but something inside her wanted her to persist. She studied him with surprise and respect and at the same time, wondered how a eighteen-year old could be so smart and mature. She continued her persuasive speech. "Listen, whatI'm about to tell you now stays in this room, you hear me?" She continued, now placing both of her hands on Nwoke's shoulders as she stood over him, looking him deep in the eyes. But, then she stopped short. "Nothing —just forget it." She didn't want to leak Uzo's father's secret since Uzo himself didn't even seem to know where his father's money came from. She didn't want to be the one to cause any kind of friction between the two best friends. If anybody was going to tell, it would have to be Uzo himself. "But I don't wanna forget it, I wanna take time and think about it, okay?"

"The door opened and Cynthia Walked in without knocking. "Hey, you guys, why did you two decide to leave us down there?""Don't you ever knock?" Mary asked, taking her hands off Nwoke's shoulders and confronting her friend who was obviously rude by not knocking on the door before entering.

"Oh I'm sorry. I just thought maybe you were doing the nasty so that me and Uzo can join you all." She laughed, leaving the door ajar. "So what is up?""Nothing, I was just talking to Nwoke about some business he might be interested in," Mary replied, looking at her friend and partner in crime who obviously understood what the discussion was about by the expression on her face.

"Well I came to tell you that Uzo said there is a nice African club here and that they probably won't ask for any Id's, so I'll join you all." He started laughing like it was a funny joke. "Well, I'm gonna leave you all to get ready while I do the same. See you in a bit," Cynthia said and left the room, closing the door behind her.

Everyone was dressed and ready by 9:00PM as they gathered in the family room, wearing all fresh outfits they had purchased earlier in the day. Uzo called a taxi and they waited for it to arrive and then took it to the club.

The four love birds had a time of their lives after bribing the bouncer at the door. The huge man told them that even though that was an African club, they still had to abide by the rules of the country it was located in.

They got back home about 4:00AM.

The sun's ray shone through the blinds of the guest room window of Mr. Otu's house on Sunday morning. Nwoke woke up but remained in bed, under the covers, thinking about what Mary had proposed to him the day before. After a night of partying in a different atmosphere than he was used to, Nwoke now felt even closer to the flight attendant. He had now fallen in love with the twenty-three year old beauty and really didn't want to let her go. He no longer remembered Helen in an intimate way and he realized that Mary was really his first love. He felt so different with her and didn't know if it was due to the age difference or what, but it felt good and he was determined to make an attachment with the business by any means necessary.

"Hey, wake up." Nwoke bumped her a few times to get the sleeping beauty's attention.

"Yes, dear," Mary said in a sleepy and tired voice. "I think I have a hangover again; I might have to stop drinking completely if I can help it." Mary said, studying the young adult for any suspicious activities.

Nwoke looked at her and said, "Nothing, just thinking about what my father said. Let's get ready, then."

Nwoke placed his hand on her forehead and felt a little warmth that was transmitted to his veins like electricity and he immediately knew it was true love between them.

"You want me to get you a cup of cold water with ice and see if that will help?"

Mary was now even more astonished at the young adult's maturity and felt maybe the relationship might go further than age would permit. "I guess you can, if you feel like going all the way downstairs."

Nwoke got up off the bed and ran downstairs and came back two minutes later with a cup of ice water. "Here, this should make you feel much better," he said and held the cup to her face.

She sat up and he put the cold cup to her mouth and she helped him pour it down her throat as she swallowed several times. "Thank you, dear," she felt emotional after thanking him and then realized this was a mature eighteen year old and she wasn't going to let anything get in the way of their road to progress.

"So, when are you guys leaving?" Nwoke asked.

"Sooner than you think." She didn't want to be specific just yet, not until they found out what was really going on with the two strange young adults.

"Can you not leave today?" Nwoke begged like a child whose mother was dropping him off at a new school.

"I wish I could make that decision, believe me I would stay with you forever but I must go today. We still got drops to make in Washington and Maryland, but I'll be back in two days." She got up and held the young adult, still naked.

Nwoke hugged her back, his nature rising to fullness as he gently laid her back on the king size bed and slowly slid the erect penis into her wet vagina. She let out a moan that made him pump her without mercy as a goodbye present.

Following the sexual encounter, Nwoke went to Uzo's room and knocked on the door.

"Come in," Uzo said.

Nwoke wasn't sure how to go about telling his best friend that he was about to change the plans they had together. He hesitated and then decided to change the subject. "Have you ever thought about making your own money and becoming independent of your father?" he asked, still standing in the middle of the floor.

"Why are you asking such a question?" Uzo studied him and wondered what he had been up to since he last saw him a few minutes ago.

"Nothing really, I just thought maybe it crossed your mind just like it just crossed mine."

Uzo could tell his partner wasn't being quite honest with him so, he decided to dig a little. "Where's Mary?"

"In the room."

"You know what, I'd been thinking about how they were spending money at the shopping center." He looked toward the bathroom door to see if Cynthia was still inside. "Did you find out where all that money might have been coming from? I know you and you are not the type to just let that go without getting some answers, so what's up?" He stood up from the bed and moved closer to him.

Nwoke started to tell him but something told him not to. "I don't know but I'm ready to get on my own, even if dad sends me money. I think I wanna count money like them and I will but, only after my bachelors degree."

"That's four years from today and I wouldn't start thinking about it. Anyhow, to answer your question, I like my life right now and I wouldn't wanna change it for nothing. I got money in my name to last me a lifetime so why would I wanna make more? That's being greedy."

"No, I don't think so. I think it's more like being independent. You might like depending on your father and asking for everything but in my situation right now, I'm just gonna try to do it myself and talk to them when I feel like it."

"So, what ideas do you have in mind? Mary's partner or Cynthia's?" Uzo grinned a little.

"Cynthia's? That's your girl."

"So Mary's or what?"

"Yeah. I'm gonna stick with her for the long term and I can't do it by staying here in London."

"What are you saying? Don't just get into anything. Remember what the taxi driver told us in Lagos? That kind of cash they got isn't natural for working people like them, so watch out. I know that I'm gonna stop Cynthia from whatever they're doing for money because I wanna spend the rest of my life with her. Don't let Mary know."

"Oh really? I'm beginning to feel the same way about Mary and I just might be going to the states with them to see about...............taking entrance exams for Universities and colleges.

"Hey, I think I'm in love, "Uzo confessed as Cynthia looked at him, still under the covers, and smiled.

"Me, too."

"Yeah? With Mary or Joyce?" Uzo laughed.

"I'm serious, but you're trying to be funny about it." Nwoke started pacing the floor, wanting Cynthia to hear him. "I don't know how it happened, but, I've never felt like this before, not even with Helen. I just don't wanna let her out of my sight." He turned and faced Mary, who had come into the room and just stood there, listening to the entire conversation.

Mary had tears running down her cheeks. They looked at each other and embraced for about one minute, then went back to the guest room and made love. After that, Nwoke asked her to make him a reservation on the same flight and she did so, using her employee status to put Nwoke in the first-class unit. By 6:00pm, all four love-birds went to the airport in a taxi for the 8:00pm flight. Uzo was only seeing them off since Cynthia promised to be back in a couple of days on the same flight.

"Make sure you come visit after you get yourself together, yo." Nwoke told Uzo as they sat in the check-in area of the airport, while Cynthia and Mary were already gone.

"You bet. We're definitely going to do that sooner than you think. She might have to quit that stupid job."

"Well, good-luck on the exams."

"Same to you. Don't you have to do the same thing there?"

"Yeah. Dad wants me to take the SAT and my uncle is gonna arrange for that."

"At least your plan worked and you don't have to hide anymore. You did it, buddy," Uzo said and stood up to check into the First-class unit of the British Airways flight destined for Dulles International Airport in the United States.

The flight left at exactly 8:00pm and Nwoke was in the seat all alone while Mary and Cynthia discharged their duties as flight attendants in the Economy-class unit. The seven-hour flight was packed as usual with mainly Caucasian passengers and Nwoke was the only black in the first-class section.

The flight arrived at Dulles at 8:00pm U.S Eastern Standard Time which was 1:00am London time. Nwoke checked out of U.S. Customs with his U.S. passport without a problem as a born United States citizen. He waited for Mary and Cynthia who came out one hour later since they had to finish their regular duties as employees of the airline.

Nwoke remembered very little about the airport but, certain things looked familiar as he stood in the Arrival area with his luggage. "I think I better call my uncle from here and let'm know that I'm here."

"Why don't you just come with me and spend the night. You can call him from the room," Mary suggested as they all stood there, trying to make up their minds.

Nwoke agreed and they caught the free shuttle for employees of the airport and flight attendants, to the Days Inn.

"What's your room number, Mary?" Cynthia asked as they stepped out of the shuttle bus, dragging their luggage into the lobby of the Inn.

"324." Mary responded.

"Oh, right next to mine. I'm in 323." Flight attendants always received free accommodation before the next scheduled flight to go back to where it originated. This was one of the best benefits that came with the job.

They showed the receptionist their vouchers and she gave them their keys. Cynthia went to her room and Nwoke and Mary went to Mary's room. After a few minutes, Nwoke called his uncle in Towson but, his uncle wasn't home as the answering machine came on. He decided to leave him a message. He then called Uzo and told him they got there safely. Ten minutes later, the phone in the room rang and Mary answered. Alo was on the other end of the line and Mary handed the phone to Nwoke.

"Hello, uncle. I wasn't expecting you to call back so fast." Nwoke could hear the sound of moving vehicles and automobiles in the background.

"Hey, little man. I know you've grown now. Which HolidayInn are you at?" Alo asked on the other end of the line.

"I'm at the one right here at the airport with my girlfriend."

"Your girlfriend already? Did you meet her here or did you fly her here, big boy?"

"Oh she's a flight attendant for the Airline I came on. I wanna spend the night with her so, can you just pick me up tomorrow?"

Alo agreed and Nwoke told him to come whenever he was ready before five O'clock. When Nwoke asked him where he was to have so much noise in the background, Alo told him he was in the car. In 1993, car phone wasn't common for the working-class citizens. It was a luxury to have one so he figured his uncle must be doing well as a social worker for the state of Maryland. The conversation ended.

"Excuse me, Nwoke. I got to go make a phone call," Mary said and left, leaving the eighteen-year old wondering why she couldn't use the phone in the room.

Ten minutes later, Mary came back. "I have to go somewhere real quick. Be back in about twenty minutes." She went to her main luggage, dug through several layers of clothes and other personal things. She then pulled a plastic compartment from the side of the luggage the same color as the luggage, retrieving several stacks of cash in dollars. Mary didn't bother to count it as if she already knew the amount.

Nwoke sat quietly and watched as if Mary was really trying to teach him something.

Then, reaching on top of the rack of clothes in the luggage, Mary got a black plastic bag and dumped the stacks of dollars inside and walked over to the small carryon and pulled out the handle. Inside the metal handle bars, were two rock-solid, beige-colored substance which she pulled out of each bar and placed them on the coffee table. She then went into the bathroom and got a roll of tissue paper, wrapped around each of the rock-solid substance that was already covered with see-through plastic wrap and put them inside the same plastic bag. The twenty-two year-old flight attendant then went to the phone and dialed extension 323 for her partner in crime. "You ready?"she looked over at the unsuspecting Nwoke. "Okay, I'm coming out, right now." She turned her swagger on and took the bag and headed for the door. But, before she closed it behind her, she turned to look at her eighteen-year old boyfriend. "I'll explain later." She closed the door behind her.

Nwoke, confused about what just transpired, tried to put two and two together, figuring that the beige substance had to be the drug, heroin, but what was the cash for? From his inexperienced analysis, Mary made drops in different countries on consignment from her boss and also collected money next time around. But, this time she had both in one bag. He planned to ask her when she got back.

Twenty minutes later, the door opened and Mary, still in her B.A. uniform, walked into the room, smiling. "Hi, baby boy." She sat next to Nwoke on the bed and kissed him on the left cheek.

Nwoke took his eyes off the TV he was watching. "Now, can you tell me what that was all about?"

"Now, my dearest boyfriend." Mary showed a happy mood and this brought an air of safety in the comfortable room. "The two beige-colored substance were raw heroin from Thailand and each stick was five hundred grams and the cash was for a friend of mine to deposit for me in my account. I have yours right here with me." She reached in her shirt-pocket and gave Nwoke a stack of ten thousand dollars.

"Wow! Mary, you didn't have to do this; first, you spend all that money at the mall and then you put me in a first-class flight and now, this? What's up?" He stared the older woman deep in the eyes for answers.

"I love you and I want you to be comfortable so that I can also be comfortable whenever I come to the 'States. Plus, I want you to be my partner."

"So, you want me to get an apartment?"

"Yes, please." She grabbed him and rolled the young lover on the mid-size bed, pulled down his jeans and put his hard penis in her mouth. Five minutes later, Nwoke reached orgasm and she swallowed. "Now, let's get ready for the night." Mary got up and started undressing.

Nwoke, who still hadn't given her a concrete answer, decided to follow suit.

In the shower, Nwoke asked Mary who packed the heroin in the handles of the carryon but Mary told him that she didn't know.

"All we do is take instructions. The organization is very big," Mary said inside the hot shower.

"This is dangerous, isn't it?"

"Sometimes but, if you're careful, you shouldn't have anything to worry about." Mary didn't want to scare the eighteen year old boy by telling him horror stories. They just needed to get rich together. She was getting very attached within such a short period and it wasn't her intention to get tied up with a boy.

They ordered room service of seafood, ate and had some drinks. This was now a different country where you had to be twenty one to drink alcohol but it was already too late as Nwoke was already drunk. The night began with Mary playing sexual games on the young Nwoke which he had never done before. This lead to a night of unforgettable sexual pleasure.

Morning came and they went down to the restaurant with Cynthia, who looked stressed due to the absence of Uzo. The trio had breakfast at the buffet and came back to Mary's room where they waited for uncle Alo to call. In the room, Cynthia and Mary decided to lecture Nwoke on the different aspects of the illegal business; its measurement, cost and means of smuggling. As an intelligent young adult, Nwoke quickly learned and figured out how much was worth having if one wanted to get rich.

Alo arrived in the Dulles area where the hotels were located at about 12:00pm and called the room. Mary answered and gave the phone to Nwoke. Nwoke told his uncle that they would be right down. Nwoke got his luggage and Cynthia and Mary accompanied him downstairs. They came out to see a silver colored BMW 750i. Since it was the only car parked in front of the Inn, Nwoke walked up to it and looked inside.

"Are you my uncle Alo?" Nwoke asked, studying the dark complexioned thirty something year old man with some Gucci shades on.

"Yes, Nwoke. I would never have recognized you. You were a baby when I saw you last. How are you?" Alo smiled and looked at the two women through his Gucci shades. "You must be his girlfriend."

"Yes, good afternoon, sir. I am Mary and this is my friend, Cynthia,"Mary introduced and shook his hands while Nwoke opened the back door and slid his carryon in the back seat.

Alo popped open the trunk as he studied the two women who were too iced-out to be flight attendants. He knew a hustler when he saw one."Nice meeting you two and I hope this will not be the last time. Thanks for taking care of my little nephew."

Nwoke closed the trunk after putting his luggage inside and walked over to the front passenger seat and sat down.

"You're not even going to kiss me goodbye?" Mary asked Nwoke who was already touching the stereo system and the different gadgets on the dashboard.

"I'm sorry, baby," Nwoke said and stepped out of the car and hugged and kissed Mary, intensely and got back in the car as Mary and Cynthia went back inside. He studied the car phone and the soft leather of the luxury automobile. "You still work for the state, uncle?"

"Off and on but, right now, I'm off." Alo smiled as he started the car and pulled off.

Nwoke then checked out his uncle's Rolex and necklace and figured his uncle was well-paid by the state. He admired the white long-sleeve Ralph Lauren shirt and prewashed jeans. Alo was dressed casual but looked expensive.

Five minutes later they hit the beltway, heading north.

"How many CD's can this Bose system hold?" Nwoke asked.

"Twelve. Why don't you go ahead and skip to what you like."

Nwoke skipped to 'Liberian girl' by Michael Jackson. Mary is from Liberia, unc and I love her."

"Now hold on, son. How old is she and what does she really do?"

"Age ain't nothing but a number. She's only twenty two. I thought she told you that she's a flight attendant?"

Alo didn't want to get in the way of the young adult's love-life so he left Mary's source of income alone. "I just think you're too young to be falling in love. Your dad wants you to get your degree first and you're supposed to be going to medical school after your pre-med, right?"

Nwoke nodded since he didn't want to talk over the romantic song as he thought about Mary.

Alo stepped on the gas pedal of the ultimate driving machine and the speedometer reached 90 miles per hour. Baltimore was one hour away from Dulles Airport.

"I just might change my Major, unc," Nwoke advised after the music went off and he reduced the volume of the crystal-clear sound.

"Why?"

"I don't think I wanna be in college for ten years of my life. I'm gonna get rich soon."

Alo looked at him and immediately understood where the conversation was headed and decided to change the topic. "Whatever you say. By the way, I broke up with the Ibo girl and now, I'm engaged to an Indian woman." Alo went on to tell Nwoke about his fiancée, Uma.

They talked about Alo's house in the village and all the vehicles he planned to ship. The new home was right next to Rev. Nwanta's but still uncompleted at the present time.

Fifty-five minutes after leaving the airport, Alo pulled into an underground parking garage of his condo in Towson. This was an upscale neighborhood located by the Towson mall and called 'The Penthouse'.

"So, this is where I was born?" Nwoke asked as he dragged his luggage to the elevator.

"In the area but, Saint Joseph hospital is down the road from here." Alo carried the small carryon for him.

They took the elevator to the 9th floor, got out and Nwoke dragged the luggage behind Alo who carried the carryon into the three bedroom luxury Condo. Alo showed Nwoke to the guest bedroom and placed the carryon on the floor.

"Help yourself with whatever. I gotta go, but I'll be right back." Alo left back out of the apartment condo.

Nwoke studied the lavishly furnished three bedroom condo and wondered what his uncle was really into. Even though he was only eighteen, he could still tell the difference between a fixed income living and a business income life-style. His uncle fit the latter and he hoped Alo was in the same business as Mary and Cynthia. Uncle Alo was beginning to remind Nwoke of Uzo's father; too much money without visible source. He liked his room with its private bathroom and the view of the mall. The Berber carpet and big screen TV's in all the rooms, including the dining and the living room. He got an ice-cream cone out of the Freezer and paced the living room floor then stopped by the telephone and picked up the cordless receiver and called Uzo. "They're on their way back to you. I'm at my uncle's apartment right now," he told Uzo after Uzo desperately answered the phone, thinking it was Cynthia calling. He then pressed the speaker button and walked over to the entertainment center to check out the CD's. He tried to find a CD that Uzo had never heard but, it was impossible as his thirty-one year old uncle had all the latest Rap tunes so he inserted the Chronic by Dr. Dre and walked over to the dining area where he thought he saw half a blunt of weed and started smoking while Uzo listened to the popular Hip-hop tune. When Nwoke got back on the phone, he coughed so much that Uzo asked him what the problem was. "The Chronic. My uncle is the man, you. I am really home at last," Nwoke said and continued to laugh and cough as the two friends laughed together and rapped to the familiar lyrics.

"I'm going to hang up and see if I can get some marijuana myself," Uzo said on the speaker phone.

"We call it weed here, yo. Do that and hit me back. You got the number to the house, right?"

"Yup. The same one you gave me here right?"

"Right." Nwoke hung up and walked back to the kitchen to start feeding the munchies that had now got a hold of him.

Alo returned three hours later at 3:10pm and smelled some weed. "I didn't think you smoke weed. Be careful and never smoke while you're doing anything serious only during pleasure, okay. Always smoke in the house and stay in the house if you have to drive. But, if somebody else wants to do the driving, let'm," Alo lectured and went straight to his bedroom with a small plastic bag in his hand. He came out ten minutes later and asked Nwoke if he was ready for a little sight-seeing and Nwoke said yes.

They took the elevator to the underground residential parking garage and got back in the BMW. Alo drove south of York road, past Towson State University.

"That's your father's school and the one he wants you to attend," Alo said and pointed at Towson State as he slowed down in the right lane. "Now, that's where you were born." Saint Joseph hospital was right next to Towson State.

"That's Saint Joseph's hospital?" Nwoke responded.

"That's just the entrance. Whenever you feel like it, you can go inside. I don't like hospitals." Alo continued north of the busy main road and into the city.

"Things are different down here. This is just like Aba and parts of Lagos. The people look just like us, too." Nwoke observed.

"Well, this is the city and mostly lower income blacks."

They reached the intersection of Treemount and North avenue and it was even more crowded than what they had seen earlier. The rush-hour was also beginning to set in.

"Why are those people standing around doing nothing?" Nwoke asked, referring to some addicts and homeless people scattered about the intersection.

"Some of those people are drug addicts and some are small time drug dealers. They make a lot of money," Alo answered and the light changed and he proceeded downtown.

Nwoke didn't ask any more questions as he went into deep thought and wondered if that was some of the heroin that Mary and Cynthia had delivered or, was his uncle involved with some of those helpless-looking people. They rode around the busy downtown area, including the Baltimore Inner Harbor and, due to the evening rush-hour, it took more time and Alo was able to show his nephew who had faint memory of the city he had last seen in 1985 at the age of nine.

The following day, which was a Wednesday, Alo drove Nwoke to Towson State and he took the SAT and also applied for admission with his GCE and High School certificates which the university was very familiar with and listed his major as Business Administration. After that Alo took him to the Motor Vehicle Administration and Nwoke applied for a license with his Nigerian International driver's license. He took a driving test and passed. The MVA gave him a driver's license for the State of Maryland.

"That's your father's church right there," Alo pointed at the Holy Trinity Anglican church on Allegheny avenue, Towson, around the corner from the Penthouse.

Nwoke could remember most of the land-mark around the all-white membership church that was not racist. "Do you ever go to church, uncle?"

"When your pop comes to preach. That's it. I just don't feel right in a church where I am the only colored person." Alo pulled the BMW into the designated parking spot and the uncle and nephew got out and went into the elevator. Alo pressed the ninth-floor button'.

"Now, that you got your license, here are the keys to the Celica," Alo announced as he came out of his bedroom.

"Thank you so much. I just can't believe how good things have been going for me. I told dad not to worry about me that I'll be alright," Nwoke lied, not knowing that the Reverend had remitted some money to Alo's account to cover his tuition and fees.

But, Alo really didn't need the money but he didn't want to send it back anyway since that would arouse suspicion from the man of God. "I'm just gonna get another economy car to run around in. It's never good to drive a luxury vehicle everywhere you go, especially when you're a black man in a white man's country.."

Nwoke saw a chance to find out what this man really did for a living. "Why not?"

"Well, it attracts the attention of of the police and that's the last problem you want."

"So. when do you feel the need to drive the Toyota Celica?" Nwoke avoided looking at his uncle as he focused on the TV.

"Business."

"Legal or illegal?"

"Both." He looked at the boy. "Okay, smarty. What are you getting at. I know you think I do something else for money, like your girlfriend, right?" Mary's jewelry came to Alo's mind.

Nwoke wondered how he knew.

CHAPTER TEN

The British Airways flight arrived at 9:00am London time which was 2:00pm Eastern U.S. time. Uzo met Cynthia and Mary at the airport in a taxi and took them back to his father's house

"We could have came to your house by ourselves, you know that," Cynthia said, happy to see Uzo again as they sat in the back of the taxi.

"I just couldn't wait to do this." Uzo engaged the twenty-three year old in a long tongue kiss as Mary watched.

Cynthia still didn't want to let Uzo in on the plan. She was considering Uzo's offer to live with him after resigning from her job. She had already made enough as a drug dealer since she and Mary got the jobs as flight attendants. They both had big homes in Liberia and some luxury vehicles to go with it. Mary and Cynthia has always considered going to college and majoring in Nursing.

Forty minutes later, the taxi pulled up in front of Uzo's house and Uzo paid the fare and carried the two luggage inside, one after another. Uzo and Cynthia immediately went up to the bedroom, leaving the luggage in the living room.

"Hey, darling Uzo, did you miss me like I missed you?" Cynthia asked, sitting down on the bed and removing her shoes.

"Of course, I did." Uzo helped her with her uniform skirt while she helped him with his jeans. The two hit the king-size bed and devoured each other like they had been apart for years.

After listening to all the noise Cynthia and Mary made in the next room, Mary decided to pick up the phone and call Nwoke. They spoke for about thirty minutes and Mary told him to approach Alo with the plan as soon as possible. Nwokeassured her he had made progress and that he would have a definite answer by the time she returned to the U.S. in one week after going to Afghanistan and Thailand.

"I hope this is my last trip then I'm going to come and live with you because I can no longer imagine my life without you. I love you and you have a good day," Mary concluded.

Nwoke told her that he was going to check on his SAT scores in his own car and that he looked forward to seeing her in one week.

Nwoke scored 100% on the SAT exam and was admitted to the school of Business Administration at Towson State University.

"This is wonderful. I have known anyone to get everything right in that tough exam. I went to Morgan myself and those students over there can't even get fifty percent of the required score right. If I give you a check for your tuition, will you pay it? 'Cause your dad sent some money to my account for that."

"Of course. All I have to do is give it to the admissions office, right?"

"Right, I tried to stop him since that ain't nothing to me but he didn't want to hear it. You see, money ain't nothing to me." Alo continued to watch the world News on CNN.

"Oh yeah, you know my girl has a very good connection in making money all around the world." Nwoke studied his uncle for immediate response which he hoped would be favorable.

Alo turned his face from the television and looked at his young nephew, suspiciously. "I knew that girl was up to something. What business are you talking about?"

"Heroin from Thailand or Afghanistan."

"Hey, don't say that too loud!" Alo raised the volume on the TV as the surround sound came through the Bose system. "Call it rice or something. You never know who's listening. The U.S. is a tough place to do illegal business and get away with it."

"Oh yeah?" Nwoke had no idea except for what the Lagos taxi driver told him and Uzo.

Alo moved closer to Nwoke, looking interested in the proposal. "When is she coming back?"

"In about five days"

"Good. She'll stay with us and I'll have a talk with her." Alo's Beeper went off and he excused himself and left the apartment.

Nwoke decided to take some classes so that he could graduate early. The classes began the same day that Mary and Cynthia were due back to the 'States, so he was unable to pick them up and they caught a cab from the airport.

Alo was waiting in front of the Penthouse Condos when the taxi arrived. "Welcome to Towson," Alo greeted. "I'm glad you came back." Alo paid the fare plus tip and helped the two women with their luggage into the lobby. They took the elevator to the apartment.

"Make yourselves comfortable." Alo said and showed Mary to the room where Nwoke was staying while Cynthia was shown the other empty bedroom.

Mary and Cynthia found Alo attractive at 6'1" and medium build.

Cynthia sat down in the comfortable leather sofa by the window. "So, where's your wife?" she boldly asked, looking at the handsome Alo, wondering why he wasn't married.

"Well, I'm not married but, I'm engaged." Alo thought about doing something with the pretty young thing, but since he preferred women in their late twenties and early thirties, he dismissed the idea. Besides, that was Nwoke's childhood friend's girlfriend and he wasn't going to lose his respect to the young adults.

Mary knew that Cynthia would never cheat on Uzo, so she decided to change the subject. "Where's my Nwoke?"

"He should be back shortly from school. He wants to accumulate as many credits as possible so that he can graduate at least a year early. I don't know what he's in a hurry for."

Mary smiled as she figured why the young Nwoke was probably in a hurry to get his degree.

Even if the temptation were to persist, Alo understood that one of the most important rules in the game was to never mix business with pleasure. But, since Mary and Nwoke planned to be partners, that rule may not apply to them.

Nwoke walked into the apartment and immediately rushed to Mary like a little boy who had just come home from school and expected some treat from his mother. "Hello everybody!" He dropped his back-pack on the floor and kissed Mary who immediately stood up and kissed him back. "Hi, Cynthia. I'm sorry I didn't see you in time."

"I'm sure you didn't. I see how much you missed her," Cynthia said and smiled, admiring the couple.

Uma, Alo's fiancée came over and prepared dinner later that day and that was Nwoke's first time of seeing her since it was always Alo that went to her place. She was about 5'6", slender and beautiful with a dot on her forehead. She had a Nursing degree from Towson State and was now a Registered Nurse at GBMC hospital. She still had a deep Indian accent since she had only been in the U.S for as long as it took her to obtain her degree, which was five years. "I am so happy to meet all of you. Nwoke, I hear that you're going to my former school. Good choice, but how do you feel about the majority being white?"

"It doesn't make a difference to me. I was the only black in my Elementary school, Cromwell Valley, down the road."

"Oh, yeah. That's where you went? I live in those apartments by the school."

After Uma left, Alo had a meeting with Cynthia and Mary in which details of the illegal business proposal was discussed. The sooner Mary and Cynthia would supply, the sooner Alo was ready to begin. Alo didn't want to bring his nephew into it since he wanted him to focus on his studies, but Nwoke didn't want to listen as he figured he could do it as a full time student. To make it hard for

Nwoke, Alo told him he had to find his own distributors since he wanted to be hard-headed.

Mary and Cynthia had one kilogram each but, they didn't want to let Alo know just yet. They were going to drop it off before coming to the apartment, but since Alo was waiting and lived close to the hotel they normally met the customer at when he didn't drive to the airport, they suspended the idea. With Alo in the picture now, they wanted to try him out with some of what they got but, they needed permission from the big boss.

"Nwoke, I need to call Nigeria," Mary said, standing up but hoping that Alo would be the one to respond.

"You can use this phone," Nwoke suggested.

Alo cut in immediately like Nwoke had said something wrong. "Oh, not a good idea if it's the kind of call I think it is. Is it?" Alo studied Mary.

Mary understood his meaning, "Yes it is."

"Then, I'll take you to the phone. And,' Nwoke please pay close attention to these little things if you really wanna get in the game later in your life. Right now, you're just a minor in America." Alo turned and faced his new partner. "Come with me you all."

Cynthia didn't want to leave the carryon unattended, even though he trusted Nwoke. "That's okay, I think I'll stay and watch TV..

Alo took Mary and Nwoke to a payphone at the mall that accepted credit cards since he had more than ten different cloned credit cards under different names, but none in his.

Mary was impressed at the sight of Nordstrom, Hechts and Victoria secret. "Wow, I gotta tell Cynthia about this. She loves Victoria secret."

"Oh, okay, there's the phone. You got the number?"Alo asked and pulled out his wallet from his hip pocket and took out a Visa-credit card.

Mary retrieved her boss's phone number from her pocket-book and dialed after Alo swiped the credit card. The international number started with 011234 and Alo knew it was a Nigerian number but, Nwoke wasn't paying attention. Mary spoke to her boss for about five minutes and hung up. She opened the phone booth and stepped out.

"You okay, now?" Alo asked.

"Thank you very much. You know how to cover your tracks." Mary smiled at Alo and followed him as they walked back to the Condo.

Nwoke tagged along, feeling somewhat left out. Five minutes later, they entered the apartment to see Cynthia still sitting in the same spot, but now she was on the phone talking to Uzo. "Hey, Mary and Nwoke, Uzo said hi."

"Tell'm we said hi, too," Nwoke responded, sitting down, looking like he wished he was a little older.

Cynthia related the message to Uzo over the international phone line and told Uzo she would call him back.

Mary invited Cynthia to Nwoke's room and told informed her about the change in plan. "I'll front him mine but, I'm only going to give him half to see how fast he can get rid of it, then go from there."Mary said.

"That sounds good What about Brian? Did he say it was okay to just give him one?" Cynthia asked. Brian was their only Towson distributor.

"yes, he said it was okay. Let's call him and tell'm to meet us at the mall by Nordstrom in about one hour."

"Oh, they have a Nordstrom here?"

"And a Victoria secret, girl. On second thought, we'll just call him from the mall and tell him where we are, then go shopping while we give him time to get there," Mary suggested.

"That sounds good because I think he'd always said he had to drive from Baltimore and that's not far from here."

"Plus, he had always said that BWI Airport was closer for him if we could help it." Mary added.

Mary walked over to her Carryon while Cynthia went to her room to retrieve the one kilogram for Brian. Mary took the carryon and placed it on the bed and opened it. Nwoke walked in and stood there quietly and watched. She then went into the carefully sewed compartment on the left side of the carryon and, using a pair of scissors she got from the bottom of the carryon, cut through the threads and extracted the entire one kilo of pure Thailand heroin wrapped in a see-through flat plastic bag. She put it on the reading table and turned around to leave when she saw Nwoke. "How long have you been standing there, boy?"

"The whole time and I saw everything."

"Well stay right here. I gotta get something from your uncle." Mary left the room and went to the living room where Alo was still watching TV and drinking beer. "Excuse me, Alo."

"Yes, Mary," Alo answered

"Do you have a scale that measures in grams?"

"Of course. I have whatever you need. Give me a minute." Alo stood up and went to the kitchen, opened the door that lead to the rear balcony, reached into a flower-pot and retrieved a small object wrapped in plastic and brought it to the dining table and unwrapped the plastic. "Here you go."

Mary walked into the kitchen and took the small scale from Alo, said thank you and went back to Nwoke's room where Nwoke was still waiting. "Watch this carefully, my student." Mary measured the entire one kee to confirm the weight and then split it in half and measured each half. Satisfied that each half was what it was supposed to be, she wrapped the other half of the pure beige heroin and put it back inside the carryon. She then retrieved a facial mask and a ziplock bag and put the facial mask on and asked Nwoke if he needed one but, he said no and quickly left the room as the odour was beginning to make him dizzy. Mary put the cut bag of little stone-like pieces of heroin in the ziplock bag and zipped it up. Cynthia was already waiting in the living room with Alo and Nwoke as she walked in."Here you are, Mr. Alo. Now, how long?" she asked as she removed the facial mask and headed for the bathroom to wash her hands.

"It all depends on how potent it is," Alo answered but Mary couldn't here him since she was already running the sink water, but Cynthia listened. He studied the little pieces of rock-like drug in the bag and unzipped it a little bit on one end smelled it. "Oh, my goodness!" he screamed. "This is got to be it! I have never smelled anything that strong. The Afghanistan product isn't half as strong as that."He zipped the bag back up as Mary walked back out from the bathroom.

"Well, I heard you. So, what do you think?" Mary asked, as Cynthia and Nwoke just listened.

"I'll let you know when I get back," Alo said and took the scale from the dining table and used a spoon to scoop what looked like three grams and tore a tiny piece of the original plastic bag the drug was wrapped in and poured the small quantity inside and wrapped it up, then put it in a one dollar bill, folding it tight. He took the scale and replaced it inside the flower-pot. "Bye," he said and exited the Condo. Five minutes later, Alo was at the phone booth in the mall. He made one phone call and the person on the other end answered in two rings. "Yo, what up?" He had to speak 'yo' slang since he was now dealing with one of the toughest Ghetto drug dealers in West Baltimorecity.

On the other end of the line was one of his workers named Risky. "Chillin and waiting on you, my nigger."

Alo told him he needed to see himASAP and they agreed to meet at the same spot they met last. The spot was at the Baltimore Memorial stadium where the Orioles played baseball. Alo went back to the Condo and got in the Camry he had just bought after giving Nwoke the Celica and drove to the Stadium on 33rd street in North-east Baltimore. Since he got there first, he just sat in the Toyota Camry, a few yards from the empty stadium and waited. Five minutes later, a gold colored 1993 Acura Legend Coupe pulled up behind Alo's white Toyota and Alo recognized the vehicle through his rearview mirror and got out. The six-feet-two dark-skinned slim figure of the handsome Risky, wearing a red baseball cap and a fat gold chain over his black oversize T-shirt, strolled to the Toyota and Alo stepped out with the folded dollar bill and shook Risky's hand. They walked back to the intersection of Lochraven blvd and then back, pretending to be two friends just taking a walk. This was normal around the stadium. They parted ways and as Alo was driving back up north of York Road, he heard a commercial on the radio about cellularphones and immediately stopped at the Radio Shack about a mile from Towson and bought one with one of the cloned credit cards. Using the new cell phone, Alo called his apartment to see if Nwoke and co. were still there but, when he didn't get an answer, he knew the young adults were gone.

After graduating with a B.A. in Social Work from Morgan State, Alo was pretty well versed on how society functioned. A friend of his is serving ten years in a Federal prison for not properly covering his tracks and Alo had learned from his friend's mistakes. A few minutes after he got home, his pager vibrated and he immediately called back the unfamiliar number from the cell phone. Risky answered in one ring and from the background noise. Alo could tell he was calling from a phone booth on the street.

"Yo. it's a go....I mean fire is burning," Risky said on the other end of the line, sounding happy and excited. "We got one down, you feel me?" Risky referred to an overdose of a Junkie testing the powerful heroin.

"Word?"

"That's my word."

"Okay, I got five Heinekens left. Hit you when on my way." Alo referred to five hundred grams as five Heinekens, eventhough it was really 497 grams, minus the three g. tester.

"I'll drink all when you're ready."

Alo then told him about the cell phone and Risky said that he would get one and they hung up.

Alo sat there and waited for Mary and Cynthia to return from the mall. He wondered how many kilos the two young adults were able to supply weekly and at what price. He had a lot of projects in the village that needed completion. He had to figure out a way to make the best of what seemed like a gold mine and he had to do it before the female hustlers came back from wherever they went.

Meanwhile, Brian met Cynthia and Mary at the mall in front of Nordstrom while Nwoke waited, playing security guard. Cynthia handed the mixed breed hustler the one kee and he gave them seventy thousand dollar cash in a blue plastic bag and left.

"You wanna finish shopping or go drop the money off first?" Nwoke asked the two women as they came back.

"It's not safe to be walking around the mall with this much cash," Mary said and looked at Cynthia.

The trio quickly walked back to the apartment, stopping shopping for the day. The minute they walked in, Cynthia went straight to her room and safely put away the seventy grand in the carryon's hidden compartment. She rejoined the crew in the living-room.

"Okay, I need to have a word with you guys. How much per kee?"

"Seventy thousand." Mary answered.

"That means you want thirty five thousand for the five hundred, right?"

"I would think so." Mary continued to take charge of the conversation as Cynthia and Nwoke listened.

"That's fine. I'll pay you tomorrow unless you want it now."

"No that's fine tomorrow is just fine."

Alo sat up and took his cell phone into his bedroom and dialed Risky's number and Risky answered in one ring as if he had been waiting by the phone for the call. "Yo, I'm gonna see you tomorrow at the GSF and N." Alo said in code words referring to the gas station on Falls rd. and Northern pkwy. he did no business transactions after 9:00pm. The clock on the wall showed the time as 9:20pm. Alo rolled a blunt and told his company he would see them the next day and drove to Uma's apartment for the night.

Alo and Risky met at the agreed location at 11:00am the next morning to discuss price. While Alo was on one side pumping gas, Risky was on the opposite side of the same pump as they discussed, in code words, the price.

"I'm gonna need at least one hundred dollars per case." Alo meant grams.

Risky knew he could make well over $200.00 per gram with 99% pure heroin on the street after cutting it. "It's a deal, yo," Risky responded as he finished pumping the fuelinto the Infiniti Q45.

Alo told him that he would have it delivered in one hour at a spot of his choice by the regular delivery man. He finished pumping gas into the BMW and headed back home while Risky did the same.

One hour later, the delivery man made the delivery to Risky in West Baltimore's Security Square mall. After that, Alo dipped into his own money and paid the bill, satisfied the profit was enough for a start.

"Oh my goodness! This is the fastest transaction I've ever seen from a client that wasn't purchasing,"Mary exclaimed in total shock and looked at Cynthia. The two nodded approvingly.

"We got another one for you." Mary went to the bedroom and retrieved the other half and gave it Alo as Nwoke walked in from school.

"Hey girls, what's up with you'll?" Nwoke asked as he took his back pack and put it on the coffee table and kissed Cynthia, then took the back pack to the bedroom and came back to the living-room. "What's up, unc?"

"How are you young man?" Alo responded and took the bag Mary had just given him and left the apartment.

"Hey baby, your uncle is the man. We wish we had met'm when we first got started, we'd probably be retired by now." Mary liked the outfit Nwoke had on that made him look like anAmerican High school kid.

Nwoke had on a blue NY Yankees baseball cap on, a black Malcolm X t-shirt and some white Air Jordans with a fat gold chain. The saggy blue jeans gave him the look of an aspiring Rapper. "I wish you didn't have to leave tomorrow," he said as he sat next to Mary.

"That's all good and well but, I just couldn't stay another day without Uzo," Cynthia cut in and stood up and went to the kitchen.

"I'll be back sooner than you think,"Mary said. Her mind was busy thinking about how much they were going to be making with Alo, especially after they establish their own source, instead of working for the man.

Alo came back after putting the product away in his stash at a local storage facility. He planned to give the second half of the one kee to his partner in East Baltimore named Cnote. But he wanted to know exactly how many grams of cut the heroin was able to stand per gram. "I'll see you guys later," he said and left. He went to his stash and retrieved three grams of the uncut product and drove to East Baltimore to see Cnote. Cnote to one of his apartments and they sat down.

"So, what's up?"the average height and stocky Cnote asked. He was very health conscious and didn't smoke nor drink. Strictly about business and getting money.

"I got this I wanna check out." Alo put the product on the table, well wrapped in plastic and folded in one dollar bill.

"Okay, son. Is it different?"

Alo played dumb. "I don't know. That's why I wanna check it out."

Cnote went into the bedroom and brought a mixture in a ziplock bag. He then wiped the glass cable with a Kleenex tissue and went to the kitchen and put the tissue in the trash can. He took a teaspoon and a small scale from one of the cabinets and came back to the dining table. Opening the dollar bill, Cnote scooped up one gram of the raw heroin and measured it on the scale to confirm. Then, he scooped up ten grams of the mixture and dumped it into the pure drug. The total weight on the digital scale was now 11 grams. He then emptied the mixed product on the clean dining table and crushed the heroin with the spoon, mixing it with the mixed substance. "Okay, we're done for now. Let's find out how good it is." He lead Alo out of the apartment and they went downstairs to his pick-up truck which he always drove when he was dirty. He Cnote drove to a female stripper's house who was also a heroin addict. Her name was Brown Sugar and she was also very clean for an addict.

"Hello, Cnote baby what's up with you and the stranger?" Brown Sugar asked as she let Cnote and Alo into the mid-class neighborhood apartment in North east Baltimore. She was also very pretty.

"Yes, this is my friend and we need you to try something for nothing. Where's your Roommate?"

"In her room. You want me to get her?"

"Please," Cnote responded.

Brown Sugar, who was brown complexioned, short and petite, slowly walked to one of the two bedrooms, switching her hips.

Alo looked at her and even found her very attractive for an addict. In her daisy duke shorts and tight t-shirt, you could not see any needle tracks. Alo wondered how she got high.

Two minutes later she came back out with her Roommate. Cnote gave her a twenty-dollar worth and she disappeared in the bathroom. Then he gave another twenty dollar worth to her white Roommate and she snorted it right in front of Cnote and Alo.

"Wow! This hits great!" the skinny white woman exclaimed as she sniffed multiple times and waited for the heroin to take effect. Five minutes later, her speech was dragging and she walked over to the big sofa and sat down. "Whereeeee diiiiiid youuuuuu geeeet this," she mumbled under her breath and nodded then dosed off.

But Brown Sugar· was still in the bathroom and this gave Cnote a little concern after seeing what just happened to Brown Sugar's Roommate.

"Let's see what's taking Browny so long," Cnote knocked on the bathroom door but got no response as Alo watched the delirious Roommate wake up and then dosed back off. Cnote opened the door to find Brown Sugar laying down on the floor with the needle stuck to her neck. "Hey!Call 911!" he yelled out to Cnote.

Alo went to the phone on the kitchen wall and dialed 911. "Let's get out of here, please." He dashed out of the door.

Cnote shook Brown Sugar's roommate and then followed Alo out of the apartment. He caught up with him on the parking lot and sighed in relief. "You gave them the address, right?"

"Of course," Alo responded as Cnote pulled off.

"Yo, that's the shit! How much?" Cnote knew if that happened on a 10 to 1 gram number, then he could put it on a 20 to 1 gram and make a killing.

"Give me $120.00 per gram and I got half a kee for you to start with right now," Alo said, knowing that Cnote would still make about $2000.00 per gram or even more.

Cnote agreed immediately and drove Alo to his Toyota which was parked at Cnote's apartment. Alo told him he would have it delivered by his delivery man within two hours and left.

Alo got home thirty minutes later and paid Cynthia and Mary the thirty-five thousand from his own money.

The following day, on their way to Dulles InternationalAirport, Cynthia and Mary made the deposit of $100,000.00 through their boss's personal Banker in Washington DC and split the remaining forty thousand evenly between themselves. Theyflew back to London, spent two days with Uzo and then flew back to Murtala Muhammed International Airport in Lagos but, this time they didn't stay at the Marriot. They stayed at the mansion of their big boss, Gabriel Ogar.

Gabriel Ogar's mansion was located in Ikoyi, Victoria Island Lagos on a fifteen acre piece of land along the coast of the Atlantic ocean. It was constructed by an American company located in New York. The underground Bunker was built as a shelter in the event of an external invasion by a foreign government. The twenty-bedroom Villa had Italian marble floors throughout the entire house; pool house that included all modern fitness equipments and a Waterfall in the back of the big back-yard.; 20,000 square feet bought from the government. The big time drug lord employed a security team from the Nigerian Army and police. He ran one of the world's largest international heroin smuggling and distribution network.

One of Ogar's drivers picked up Cynthia and Mary from the airport and drove them to the mansion. They were shown to their rooms and thereafter, met with the big boss in the reception lounge.

"Good day, master. We are here to tell you about the man we talked about on the phone." Mary said, sitting down opposite her boss.

"Very well, tell me about this man and how you have come to know him," the tall, bulky, dark-skinned Ogar with tribal marks across both cheeks, responded as he studied the two female messengers before his eyes. He wondered if Cynthia and Mary were up to something.

"Well, you know how hard it is to find a Nigerian distributor that is also a friend. He is very fast and when we gave him what you authorized, he was done within twenty hours." Mary said as Cynthia listened.

The London educated man from the Yoruba tribe of Nigeria, wearing a gold-coloured Dashiki, stood up and walked over to the window and thought for a minute. "How long have you known this man?"

"Well, he is my boyfriend's uncle and I've known him for ten years but I didn't know what he did until now." Mary lied.

"So, how long do you two plan to work for the Airline?"

"We hope not for too much longer since we have saved enough money to further our education. We want to be Nurses.'"

The big black man now turned and faced the two women. "I guess she is also speaking for you, Cynthia."

"Yes sir," Cynthia responded.

"You see when I was introduced to you by John, I knew that this day would come, so I made arrangements for it. Both of you have brought millions to the organization and the least I can do is to make sure that you are happy.

What exactly are you suggesting?" Ogar was no longer suspicious of the two flight attendants.

Mary continued to speak. "Sir, if it is possible, we would like to stop carrying. Is there another means of getting to us in America and London. With the new man, I think we can, move any amount."

"I am sure that can be arranged. So, are you saying that you plan to reside overseas and distribute?"

"Exactly," Cynthia decided to respond, knowing that was her plan, but she wasn't sure of distributing for much longer since money wasn't an issue with Uzo.

"Are you one hundred percent sure because that can be very dangerous, especially in America?'"

"Yes we are," Mary responded, not fully aware of the extent of the dangers associated with the illegal business.

"Good I'll arrange for something as soon as possible. You may go to the: dining area for dinner and then retire to your rooms for the evening I'll see you in the morning."

Mary and Cynthia thought about calling Uzo and Nwoke to tell them the good news but decided it was best to surprise them, instead. But in their private rooms, before going to bed, they each called their teenage boyfriendsto tell them how much they missed them.

In the large breakfast room, the big screen television channel was always on either CNN International or BBC. CNN Int. was a subsidiary of CNN America but only carried headline international News events. It was established to compete with BBC (British Broadcasting Corporation. This morning, it was on CNN and the Newscaster had some breaking News.

"THERE'S BEEN A BIG HEROIN BUST IN BALTIMORE, MD. WITH LINKS TO AFGHANISTAN, A DEA SPOKESPERSON SAID TODAY," the red-headed female Newscaster announced. However she couldn't give out details of the bust since the investigation was ongoing to catch the perpetrators.

This news killed Mary's and Cynthia's appetite but when Maryrealized that their link was in Thailand and not Afghanistan, she relaxed a little. "Hey, Cynthia, I'm glad they got theirstuff from Afghanistan.

"We have dealt with Afghanistan, too. Let's just hope it had nothing to do with Alo and Brian," Cynthia responded.

One of the maids, who was standing there with two bottles of orange juice in hand for Cynthia and Mary, looked at the two visitors and noticed the concern in their eyes. "Those American government people are ruthless when it comes to drug dealers. My master has lost a lot of men and women over the years." The chubby young woman set the bottles of orange juice on the table and left, without saying another word.

Cynthia and Mary looked at each other, wondering if the maid was trying to give them a hint. Something cold went through the spines of the international drug dealers.

"We can't do this for long, Mary," Cynthia said.

"I know, that's why we must obtain our college degrees while we're still young and make something of ourselves," Mary responded.

"But how're we going to make a comfortable living working for wages?"

"I know, but who said we had to work? We can start a professional business related to our degrees like Uzo's father who studied Electrical Engineering," Mary concluded.

The two women didn't eat another slice of plantain or custard powder as they discussed their future. In the end,

Mary decided to make twenty million dollars and quit while Cynthia decided to call it quits after the next drop off in London.

"Uzo can petition for my visa to stay in London," Cynthia ended.

"So can Nwoke," Mary added.

Ogar's wife walked in and greeted the two guests and introduced herself as Cecelia. She was about 5'9", light-skinned and very beautiful. She was still in her night-gown. She had two children; a ten-year old boy and a twelve-year old girl. Ogar originally had three wives from three different countries at the age of thirty-seven but, he sent two of the foreign ones back to their countries to alleviate the headache that came with multiple female partners. He was now forty-two with only one wife.

The head of the security team, Santo, walked in to greet the guests. "Hello and welcome my beautiful friends," he said with a smile. He wasn't bad looking at six feet and medium built. He was a shade darker than Cynthia.

"Hello, Santo," Cecelia greeted, giving the chief of security an intimate look.

Mary and Cynthia looked at each other and wondered if there was something going on between the two. They also knew it would be very dangerous for any woman to cheat on the ruthless Gabriel Ogar.

Chapter Eleven

The Crossover

At 12:00pm, Mr. Gabriel Ogar called the two female partners into his conference room for a meeting before lunch. He had devised a new plan to flood the streets of the highly profitable Baltimore city region with 98%·pure heroin to help speed up his goal of reaching one billion.

There was always an air of fear whenever Gabriel Ogar spoke. "Good morning ladies,"Ogar greeted, sitting in his exclusive chair in the lavishly furnished conference room. The room was just like a conference room of a major corporation such as IBM or T-Rowe Price. It was located on the first floor of the Villa.

Cynthia and Mary responded by also saying good morning.

There were five heavy-set men in their mid thirties sitting opposite Cynthia and Mary.

"Okay, girls. These men are going to be your link between myself and you. I want you to look at their faces carefully because I will not tell you their names. It is your responsibility to recognize them when they arrive." He looked at Cynthia and Mary to make sure they were paying attention and they were. "I will give you their pictures numbered agents: 1,2,3,4and 5. That is it. These men must be picked up on arrival and driven to a convenient hotel but you don't have to worry about picking them up. However, you do have to be there with the pictures for your own safety and once they have exited peacefully, then you may leave and await further instructions by telephone."

Mary and Cynthia had no questions, so they took the pictures and went to their rooms to get ready. Mary called Nwoke to see how he was doing and tell him how much she missed him. Nwoke asked her where she was calling from in Lagos and when she told him her boss, Nwoke wasn't too happy.

"We're about to leave any way, baby. Don't worry, he is married and lives with his wife and also too old for me," Mary said.

"Is his house in Victoria Island?" Nwoke asked on the other end of the international line, remembering what the taxi driver from the Marriot had told him and Uzo about a dangerous drug dealer in Lagos.

"Yes, but that's all I can say. I'll see you in a couple of days." She hung up.

One hour later, Mary and Cynthia were driven to the airport, where they later boarded the flight back to London, performing their duties as flight attendants. Could this be their last flight from Lagos toLondon as employees?

Six hours after take-off from Murtala Muhammed Airport, the plane landed at Heathrow Airport, London. Cynthia got out and rejoined Uzo at Uzo's newapartment near King's college, London where he had now been admitted for the Fall semester. Cynthia later called her boss and told him she was resigning her position as flight attendant. Mary connected the next flight to Dulles International, maintaining her employee status.

Seven hours later Mary exited the plane after submitting aletter of resignation she had written on the flight. Nwoke picked her up in the Celica after school.

"Hey, baby. That was my last flight attendant duty. I just resigned."Mary informed Nwoke as she got in the car.

"Are you serious or are you joking?"

"No, seriously and I missed you so much." She kissed him."I plan to attend college and become a Registered Nurse. My mother is going to mail my High School transcript."

"So, you did this all for me or for money?" Nwoke asked and stepped harder on the Sports car as it raced up 95North.

"For us to be together, comfortably, even if we're poor." Tears formed in Mary's eyes and she looked down on her lap.

Nwoke was quiet for a minute, confused about what was happening to his young life. He also felt the same way about this woman beside him. He took his right hand and grabbed Mary's left hand and squeezed it. "I guess Cynthia did the same, too?"

"Yes. She's at Uzo's new apartment."

"Oh, I meant to ask you; is your boss's name, Gabriel Ogar?"

"'How do you know?" Mary was surprised.

"A taxi driver in Lagos showed his mansion and said he was the most dangerous drug dealer in Nigeria. Please be careful."

Mary thought about what her younger lover had just said and wondered if she had made the right decision in continuing the risky business and now, she had crossed over to even a more dangerous phase of drug dealing.

They got to Baltimore and then drove through the city to Towson as Nwoke showed Mary what his uncle had shown him when he first got to Towson. She enjoyed the lecture but, at the sametime felt sorry for the bad-looking addicts of the product she was distributing.

When they finally got home, Mary called her parents in Liberia and told them that she had quit her job and was about to attend college in the Fall. They were happy for her and promised to mail her High School transcript immediately. The following day, which was a Tuesday, Nwoke took Mary to Towson State University and she took the SAT and completed the application for admission. Two days later, she was admitted and paid her tuition and fees for one year, after which, the school gave her an I-20 for a student visa from Immigration. Alo accompanied her and Nwoke to the INS building downtown and she presented all supporting documents for the Student Visa. After waiting four hours, she was granted a four-year visa with a stamp on her Liberian passport.

"I don't know how to thank you guys. You have been so good and supportive of me and I appreciate it," Mary said as they walked out of the INS office.

"Don't even mention it. I can't even begin to tell you how happy I am to meet you," Alo responded with a smile as Nwoke tagged along.

They got in the car and drove through the city again, to Towson. When they got home, Mary now felt she was settled and ready to begin business. She picked up the phone, checked thetime to make sure that her boss was not asleep and called Ogar at 5:30pm U.S.E.S.T. (10:30pm) Nigerian time. Ogar answered the direct line and Mary told him that she was ready to entertain the five visitors and he told her to stand by. She then called Cynthia and told her to get ready but, Cynthiatold her she was going to call Ogar herself to confirm when.

Ogar was not happy about Mary and Cynthia not calling as soon as they got back to let him know they made it safely. It had now been five days and Mary and Cynthia knew that this was definitely a deviation of the rules. Ogar warned that this should not be allowed to happen againas penalties could be very severe. Mr. Ogar had people in Europe and America to enforce his strict guidelines when need be. He informed Mary and Cynthia that it would take two days to get the men ready and another day to put then on the plane since it took special arrangements to bypass the screening process at Murtala Muhammed Airport. The men would be onthesame flight but, two would get off in London while the other three would connect to the U.S. In U.S., the three men would have to be picked up by another team of workers and taken to the nearest hotel in Towson from where Mary and her people would pick up· the product.

Alo didn't mind Mary discussing the proposed venture as long as the conversation was general without specific details being mentioned. Anything specific would have to be at the phone booth.

"Alo, can you handle the three kees of the same quality?"Mary asked Alo as they sat in the living room, watching TV andplaying checkers.

"Piece of cake," Alo responded as he seemed more focused on the television news than the checker game Mary and Nwoke were playing.

"I guess they will never catch the organizers of that ill-fated smuggling attempt from Afghanistan, hah?" Mary was referring to the heroin bust she heard on the news on CNN when she was at Ogar's house.

In Summer school, Nwoke had taken notice of a particular student who drove a new Lexus to school and looked fresh daily. He hadn't seen him wear the same clothes twice either. Nwoke planned to meet the student and make his acquaintance so that he could start his own money-making operation if his instincts were right about the student. The more he thought about the kind of money Mary was making, the more Nwoke wanted to make his mark in the game and possibly upgrade the family's name beyond that of the popular Rev, Nwanta.

Three days after speaking to her boss, Mary sat by the TV, waiting for the right time to call Lagos for instructions. She knew the messengers must be on their way but, she wanted to wait until about 9:00pm Nigerian time to call if she didn't hear from the big boss. Alo and Nwoke were just as anxious as she was but they didn't get up extra early like Mary.

The house phone rang twice and stopped at about 9:00am and Mary recognized the signal and asked Nwoke to walk her to the pay-phone to make the call to Ogar and discuss the details. Alo gave her a one of the cloned credit cards and Nwoke accompanied her to the mall. She placed the call and wrote down the phone number to the mediators that Ogar gave her. Nwoke watched his older lover and admired her swag in the hustling game. This was a woman in control and Nwoke was turned on by this.

Mary hung up the pay-phone and stepped out of the booth. "Do you know where the Sheraton Hotel is?"

Nwoke was now familiar with the area around the mall. "I think that's the hotel down the road by Goucher college, but let's ask Alo just to be sure," Nwoke responded and turned and lead the way back to the apartment.

Mary asked Alo as soon as they walked in and Alo was shocked at the convenience of the arrangement and wondered how Mary's boss knew. Did the man also know where they lived?

"If your boss chose that hotel on his own, then he is very dangerous and cannot be played with. Do you understand? Everything we do must be right and no mistakes allowed,"Alo stressed.

This comment by the experienced Alo, sent chills up Nwoke's spine. He wondered if it was even safe to continue since Mary already had about half a million dollars saved in a U.S. Bank.

"We just have to be cautious. My boss is not that bad, unless you cross him or try to outsmart him. But, if you're honest with him, there is no problem."

Alo drove the Camry to the Sheraton hotel which was only about three minutes behind the Condo. Nwoke and Mary got out while Alo waited in the car since he decided to park in front of the five-star hotel. Alo took the number from Mary and dialed the mediators for the room number while Mary and Nwoke stood beside the car. When somebody answered, he handed the cell phone to Mary. Mary spoke in broken English and made a mental note of the suite number and gave Alo back the small cellular phone.

"Okay, come on Nwoke, let's go," Mary said and Nwoke followed behind.

They went to room 503 and knocked once as instructed by one of the mediators. One minute later, the knob turned and the door opened.

"Please come in," a heavy-set black man with a heavy Nigerian accent invited.

Nwoke and Mary entered and Mary recognized the man as one of the five men that Ogar had shown her and Mary in Lagos.

"Welcome. So, there's a change in plans because I thought we were supposed to watch for you at the JFK airport but, I'm happy you guys made it this far,"Mary said as she and Nwoke stood by the door.

The man studied Nwoke as if he was only expecting the female. "Yes, the boss changes plans all the time as a precaution." The man turned and walked into one of the three rooms of the Executive suite. Two-minutes later, he came out, followed by two of the men Mary also recognized and gave Mary a black plastic bag. Mary said thank you and left the hotel suite with Nwoke.

They were back at the condo in five minutes and Mary immediately asked Alo for the scale. Alo gave her the scale and she weighed the content kilo by kilo and got a total of three kilograms.

"At least, it's all there," Nwoke said, studying the egg-shaped little balls of heroin. "Why do they look like that?"

"I think I know why and I don't think you wanna hear it," Alo said, looking at Mary.

"Me, too and I think it's better you don't know, Nwoke. You just might lose your appetite." The thought of the process of ingesting and then excreting the little balls of the deadly substance made Mary lose her appetite for food.

Nwoke accepted the experienced people's recommendation and dismissed the thought of how the drug got into the U.S. He picked up one of the balls and weighed it by itself and it weighed 20grams. That meant that each of the Messengers carried fifty balls which would equal 1000 grams.

Mary thought about how much each of the men received for going through the inhumane procedure. Then her thoughts wandered over to Brian and she decided to call him and update him since she had nothing for him. She asked Alo if she could use his cell phone and he gave it to her. Brian answered in two rings."Hello Brian. This is Mary and I'm just calling to tell you that something came up, so, we'll be seeing you next week, okay?"

Brian didn't seem to have any problems with the news. Hethanked Mary for calling and hung up the phone.

"Okay, Mr. Alo. The balls are in your hands." Mary gave Alo the bag of three kees.

Alo thanked her, got the cell phone back from her and left for the storage facility. He returned fifteen minutes later without the bag.

"I know you didn't get rid of all that so fast," Nwoke said and smiled at his uncle as he continued to learn something new everyday.

"Of course not. That's one of the most important rules; never leave weight where you rest at."

Nwoke made a mental note as he also tried to figure out a way to get closer to that student at his school. Since Nigerians were getting popular in the drug game, maybe he should just introduce himself. No, that didn't seem right. Should he send Mary when the Fall semester starts in an undercover capacity? After weighing his options, Nwoke concluded he would send Mary initially and then come in later.

Meanwhile in London, Cynthia didn't want to tell Uzo what she really did since Uzo would probably not allow her to continue. Since she had already obligated herself to this deal which she planned to make her last one, there wasn't any need to upset Ogar unnecessarily. She had close to half a million saved in different banks around the world and that made her feel financially secure. The two messengers from Ogar had contacted her on the number she gave her boss while Uzo was at his father's house discussing something with his father who had arrived the day before. She studied the pictures of agents 4 and 5 for the last time after they asked her to meet them at a hotel near Kings college, then she called a taxi and asked the driver to take her to the hotel. She collected the two kilos and left. Still dealing with Ogar's clients, Cynthia took another taxi back home and went to a phone booth and called the telephone number she was given for the regular customer. The client asked her to meet him at the parking garage of the Buckingham mall in east London. Cynthia took another taxi to the agreed venue and waited in the busy parking garage while the taxi driver left the meter running. Five minutes later, a red Jeep Grand Cherokee, fitting the description the client had given her, swung around the corner and pulled up beside the taxi. A man resembling Uzo's father looked through the passenger side window and motioned for the taxi to follow him.

Cynthia's heart dropped and she told the taxi driver to follow the Jeep. "Well, what do you know? it is Uzo's father. I wonder if Uzo knows about this?" she asked herself under her breath. She thought what would happen if she and Uzo were to get married. Since she'd never met Uzo's father in person, they would probably have to meet as in-laws. She may have to keep a secret for the rest of her life. What if Uzo already knew? What would be the reaction of Mr. Otu the first time he learned that his daughter in law was former partner?" All these thoughts ran through Cynthia's head as the taxi made a left and a quick right then pulled into a small parking lot of a seafood restaurant. Mr. Otu waved at Cynthia to come to the Jeep. With two kees of heroin in a back plastic bag, Cynthia stepped out of the taxi and walked to the Jeep, opened the passenger side door and jumped in the vehicle. She looked around the parking lot to make sure there was no one watching and, after seeing only three empty vehicles, she gave the bag to Mr. Otu and he gave her a similar coloured plastic bag and she exited the Jeep Grand Cherokee. Cynthia was so nervous after coming in close contact with her lover's father that she forgot to tell the taxi driver where to go.

"Where are we going, miss?" the chubby white cab driver asked, startling Cynthia who was busy watching the Jeep pull off.

"Oh, I'm sorry. Back to where you picked me up." Cynthia responded, knowing deep inside that was her last drug transaction.

Alo and Brian were able to move a total of ten kilos weekly throughout the rest of the Summer and when Fall came, it was also time to start school with Mary.

On the first day of school, the campus was busy as students attempted to find their class-rooms and different buildings. The predominantly white University was also known for its reputable Nursing program which Mary was now enrolled in. With the well-dressed Mary sitting beside him in the brand new Mercedes 190E, the freshly dressed Nwoke drove into the parking garage and found a space on the third level. The couple got out and headed for their classes since they had already pre-registered for their different classes. But, on their way to the main building, Nwoke spotted the Lexus SC400 that was white in color and detailed from top to bottom, including what looked like Armorall on the four tires. The clean car was headed towards them as they had just walked out of the garage.

"Hey, that's him," Nwoke said, looking at the on-coming vehicle.

"Who? What are you talking about?"

"Right here," Nwoke didn't want to point at the Lexus that was now about to enter the garage. "The Lex. Remember the guy I told you we were gonna try and meet?"

"Oh, yeah."

Nwoke came up with a plan. "You walk past him and say hi, then ask for directions to Newman Hall and if he only tells you where it is, ask him to please show you in a sexy heavy Nigerian accent," Nwoke instructed, looking at his pretty girlfriend, hoping that nobody was ever going to take her away from him. "You know, play your role as a female when you see a guy you like."

Mary smiled. "Okay."

Nwoke left Mary standing close to the entrance of the student parking garage. Mary took her mirror out of her Gucci pocket-book and, with her back turned to the garage entrance, pretended to be fixing her make-up while, at the same time, checking through the mirror to see where the targetted student was. within three minutes, the handsome male student appeared in the mirror behind her and she quickly put it back in her pocket-book and started walking with swaggering strides, knowing that he would walk past her and he did. But, the light-complexioned student didn't even notice the African beauty as he increased his pace as if he was running late for class. This gave Mary concern and she wondered if she had lost her charm from being so caught up in the younger Nwoke. Mary took the small mirror from her pocketbook once again and checked her face and hair, seriously and, satisfied with what she saw, she put the mirror back in the expensive pocketbook and ran after the student. "Hey! Hello! she yelled for his attention as other students looked in her direction.

He finally turned to see who was yelling as Mary had now reached where he was. "Are you okay?" he asked the panting Mary.

"Yes. I just wanted to ask you a question. My name is Mary and I am an international student from Nigeria." Mary looked at the handsome light-skinned student who looked to be about her age. He was about six feet tall and very fresh and clean. The Gucci link around his neck told Mary he wasn't your average college student.

"What's the question?" the student asked, looking Mary deep in the eyes as if he didn't trust her.

Mary smiled and wondered why he hadn't introduced himself to her also. "Can you show me where Newman Hall is?" Mary noticed the Rolex on his left wrist. His muscular figure attracted her.

"Sure, come on. By the way my name Derrick." He turned and continued to walk in the same direction.

Nwoke was watching the two from a distance and appeared to be enjoying every bit of it.

Mary walked beside Derrick and now they looked like couples.

"What accent is that? You look like you might be Ethiopian.'"

Mary almost said Liberia but, remembered that Nigeria was more popular, especially in the kind of business they were in."Nigeria."

Derrick's face lit up at the mention of Nigeria. "Oh, yeah? So, how long you've been here?"

"About four months and this is my first day attending classes and a friend of mine wanted me to meet her at the Newman dorm."

"You like it so far?" he asked.

"So far, so good. I'll be glad when I become a Registered Nurse."

"Is that your major?"

"Yes."

They continued to talk and walk and Derrick seemed to be more interested. He told her she was cute and she blushed and asked him what his major was and he said Business. Mary now wanted to lure the young man into the intended area of conversation.

"I can't wait to see this my friend for the business," Mary commented to see what kind of feed-back she was going to get.

Derrick stopped and faced the pretty african student. "What kind of business. I know you Nigerians are always upto something."

"I'm sorry but I can't tell you just yet." Mary avoided eye contact.

"This is Newman, you want me to wait for you or walk in there with you?"

Mary looked around to see if she could spot Nwoke but evidently, Nwoke was still hiding. "No, that's okay. This is something I have to handle myself."

"Can I get your phone number? I wanna learn more about your people."

"I'll take yours because my boyfriend can get very jealous at times."

From a covert position, Nwoke saw the stranger take out a piece of paper out of his back-pack and scribble something down and hand it to Mary. He was now very concerned and jealous after seeing the smile that followed on Mary's face.

Mary and Derrick parted ways and she felt the plan was halfway accomplished with the contact phone number and the interest she was able to place in Derrick's mind.

The minute Derrick left, Nwoke emerged from nowhere like a stalker. "So, what did you all talk about?"

"'Nothing, really. Just introduction, at least I got his number and also told him that I had a jealous boyfriend so that he will not get his hopes up," Mary explained.

"Great. So, you like him?"Nwoke seemed to exhibit a sprinkle of jealousy in his voice and Mary noticed.

"You're jealous aren't you?" she asked as they stood still in front of the dorm. She enjoyed knowing that the man she loved was jealous of her. She now felt much more valuable and this gave her a sense of security, knowing that all the pretty girls walking around the campus posed no serious threat to her relationship. "If it makes you feel any better, here's his number and his name." Mary gave Nwoke the piece of paper with Derrick's number and name.

Nwoke left for his class and Mary stood there for about five minutes before she started looking for her own classroom or shall we say, lecture hall.

Mary got out of one of her general requirement courses before Nwoke and the agreement was that they would always meet in the Library. That's where Mary was when Derrick walked in with his back-pack and when he took it off and placed it on the table Mary was in, she noticed it was a Gucci back-pack.

"So, where's your boyfriend?"Derrick asked, leaning over the table, looking Mary in the eyes and smiling.

"In class. He should be here shortly. "Where's your girlfriend?"

"Don't have one but, I got some baby mamas."

"Baby mamas? What's that?"

Derrick now became even more interested since he had never met a girl or woman that didn't know what baby mama was. "Can you tell me more about your people 'cause I think that's where my ancestors are from?"

At that moment, Nwoke walked in and came straight to where Mary and Derrick were seated on the first floor of the three-floor library. He kissed Mary on the lips and asked her who Derrick was. Derrick cut in and introduced himself and shook Nwoke's hand. They all left the library and went to the Dunkin donuts on York road.

"Hey Nwoke, Derrick here tells me he has children at the age of twenty one. Can you believe it?"

"My dad told me that's possible." Nwoke didn't know how life was in the ghettos since he'd never been around it before he left for Nigeria at the age of eleven and since he's been back for the few months.

"Are you guys telling me that you don't have babies out of wedlock in Nigeria?"

"I'm sorry, my friend but that's unheard of in our culture. The woman would never get married in her life and very much ruined."

Derrick was shocked. "I think that's why you guys are so disciplined. I must visit there at least once in my life."

They finished having donuts and hot chocolate and left, only to meet again.

The following day at school, the trio went through similar routine but this time Nwoke decided to go straight to the point since he felt he had already wasted enough time playing around. This time they ended up at Ruby Tuesdays also on York road, not far from the school. Some big burgers were on the table for lunch.

"So, Derrick. What do you do for money? You seem to be very rich?" Nwoke asked as he took a bite of the delicious burger.

Derrick wondered where this was going? Could the couple be undercover federal agents? Not foreigners, but then you never know with the feds. All these thoughts raced through the mind of Derrick as he sat there and observed the two international students. "I have a real estate business."

"At your age? is it yours or one of the family members?" Nwoke asked.

"Family," Derrick lied. He actually planned to start one after graduating.

Nwoke asked him if he could move some heroin and Derrick said that he knew somebody that could and that he would be in touch after he asked that person. They finished lunch and Nwoke gave him the number to his cell phone and they parted ways, to meet at another time.

That evening, Derrick called Nwoke and asked him to meet at the Towson mall at 7:30pm. Nwoke and Mary decided to walk to the mall where they met Derrick at a food stand on the second floor.

"He wants to see a sample," Derrick said as they sat at a table on a pizza stand.

They ordered a large pizza and shared the slices since they already had dinner.

"Okay, if you wait here, I'll go get it," Mary said and went bact to the apartment while Nwoke stayed with Derrick.

"So, why does your friend deal drugs?" Nwoke asked, knowing that Derrick was probably the one.

"I don't know. I guess you'd have to ask him."

Mary returned twenty minutes later with three grams of the sample and gave it to Derrick. Derrick left the slice of pizza he was eating and quickly left the mall, like somebody who just hit the lotto and was in a hurry to claim the prize.

"Wow. He must be in a hurry," Mary remarked as they watched the clean college student take off.

"I think he's the real dealer but, I'm not gonna say anything. We're just gonna play along with whatever he wants us to think."

"I didn't even think like that. You're good, little Nwoke,"Mary said and kissed her boyfriend.

They finished the rest of the pizza, paid the bill and walked back to the apartment.

Mary decided to stay out of the picture and just allow Nwoke to deal with Derrick. One hour later, Nwoke's cell phone rang and he answered. Derrick was calling to tell him that his friend said the product was a 'go'.

"What do you mean by that?" Nwoke didn't know what the term meant.

"It's good."

The following day after classes, they met at the football field and discussed the details and the more Nwoke heard, the less he wanted to get involved. Nwoke now came to terms with himself that he just hadn't learned enough to be dealing the illegal substance. After the meeting, Nwoke went back home and told Mary that it would be better for the two of them to just go ahead and get their degrees and let the experienced Alo expand the market with the new client.

"Well, how much commission are we going to get from each kee. I need to be making some money, too, that was the whole purpose of the plan." Mary wasn't too happy about the idea, even though it was a good one.

"Okay, we'll just ask uncle when he gets back," Nwoke said as they continued to do their home-work in the bedroom.

Alo didn't get back till the next morning as he had been spending a lot of time at his fiancée's residence since Mary moved in. The following morning before they left for school, Mary presented Alo with the new addition to the distribution network.

"Where and how did you meet this guy?" Alo asked as he ate plantains and drank some tea for breakfast at the diningtable. "I'm very cautious when it comes to who I deal with in this dangerous business. Sometimes undercover federal agents can pretend to be customers and set you up for a very long prison sentence."

Nwoke thought about what he'd just heard and then looked at Mary and saw a scared face. They both looked back at Alo as Mary cut in.

"Well, he's a student at the school, so you think he might have two jobs?"

"No. Are you sure he is a student at Towson?" Alo asked.

"Yup and I've been seeing him since I went to Summer school." Nwoke intervened.

Alo stood up and walked over to the living room with the cup of tea in his right hand. His face now lit up. "Is he paying up front?"

"He said he would if he had to. He also claims it's a friend of his and I didn't care to ask but, I know it's him."

"Well, that's what they all say when they first stopped dealing with you. Your guess is probably right that he's the one. Okay, I'll start by making him pay up front, then go from there."

Alo finished his tea and went to his room to take a shower while Mary and Nwoke went to school. After school, Nwoke met Derrick at the library and they went outside and discussed some more details. They called Alo and met with him at the Baltimore Inner Harbor and Alo disclosed the terms to Derrick.

"My friend is gonna need about one hundred grams to start," Derrick told Alo.

Alo immediately knew that was not on the same level as he. They found a bench by the Science Center and sat down in the mild Fall weather.

"Okay, that's fine. It's one hundred and twenty dollars per gram, so one hundred grams is twelve thousand,"

Alo explained with the hope that the young adult could bring his weight up after a couple of days if he were a real hustler.

Nwoke, Alo and Derrick, now looking like partners, went their separate ways. Derrick called two hours later and said he was ready and Alo met him at Mondawmin with his delivery man and had the delivery man give Derrick the 100 grams. Alo, then collected the money from Derrick.

When Alo came back, Mary asked what percentage was she going to get.

"Since you guys made the contact, you can get all the profit he brings, plus what you've been getting from me. Is that good?"

Mary almost jumped up and hugged Alo but, she thought Nwoke might get jealous. "Thank you very much, Alo. You are the best at the game."

Nwoke just stood there in the middle of the living room and smiled. "Thanks unc. I knew you were the best and that's why I wanted you to handle it."

After two weeks of consistency, Derrick was now buying half a kilo at a time and coming back in two days. He sold strictly on the street and no longer kept it hidden from his Nigerian suppliers. This lead to an increase in shipments from Ogar and now, between Derrick, Cnote, Brian and Risky, Alo was moving at least twenty kilos per week as the purity of the heroin brought customers from all over the country. The workers now sold both weight and twenty dollar capsules. Business was booming and Alo handled it well. Nwoke and Mary continued to attend school full time, hoping to have millions by the time they graduated. Nwoke would graduate a year before Mary due to the Summer courses he took.

One day after the campus closed for the Spring break, Alo decided to take the young adult for a ride into the hood where Derrick had his strip in West Baltimore.

"Let's go for a ride, you all," Alo said·

"Why?" Mary asked, wondering why the big unc wanted to take them for a ride all of a sudden.

"I just thought maybe you all wanna see how the workers work in the ghetto," Alo responded but, he had another thing in mind.

Nwoke got himself together and Mary followed suit. They left the apartment in ten minutes and went down to the underground garage.

"Here's the key, Mary. You drive." Alo gave the key of the brand new Range rover to Mary.

Mary walked toward the BMW but when she pressed the keyless entry unit, the white Range's headlights blinked twice.

"Over there," Alo pointed since the two lovers had no idea that Alo had bought a Range rover earlier that day."

"Wow! Uncle Alo, this is nice. We're gonna get one of these," Nwoke said as they studied the white luxury SUV.

Alo hit the keyless entry and the doors opened. Mary jumped into the driver's seat and felt the soft beige leather seats and the wooden panel. Nwoke played with the CD player.

"That's ninety-four grand, kids." Alo said as he sat down in the back seat.

"Where to, big unc?" Mary asked as she adjusted all necessary options for a comfortable driving.

"Just go straight down York Road and make a right on Northern Parkway." Alo responded.

Mary followed the directions and twenty minutes later, they were at the intersection of Park Heights and Cold Spring.

"Just pull into the McDonald's parking lot,"Alo said and Mary did so.

They let the windows down halfway on each side so they could hear what was going on outside. The crowd of street-level dealers and heroin addicts scattered about as they tried to fulfill their needs.

"Earthquake! Earthquake!" shouted a teenage-looking male dealer as he pulled up his sagging over-size jeans.

"Where Boogie at?" asked a skinny black female junkie who looked like she was malnourished.

The boy looked at her. "They on hold right now. Your ass better get what you can before you get sick."

The junkie ignored the dealer and walked away.

"I wonder where 'Boogie' is?" Nwoke asked as they continued to watch the crowd.

"That must be the name of the good heroin," Alo replied. "Call Derrick and let'm know we're here."

Nwoke picked up the car phone from its cradle and called Derrick but got no answer. Five minutes later Derrick showed up on the front passenger door window.

"What up, yo?" Derrick said, startling Nwoke.

"Hey, what's up?" Nwoke responded as Alo and Mary looked on.

"Nothing that I can't fix," Derrick said smiling at the trio. "Hey, this is nice. Might just grab something like this." He looked the shiny Range-rover over.

"Who is Boogie? They're getting a lot of business," Alo asked.

"That's me. We just came back on and, look at that crowd! It's like a Fourth of July out there!" Derrick pointed at the crowd.

He was right as Mary, Alo and Nwoke turned their heads and noticed the sudden rush of addicts to an alley just on the other side of Cold Spring. A line had formed, stretching out along the sidewalk parallel to Cold Spring Lane. There were three young males positioned in three corners to look out for police cars or uniformed officers on foot. But they were not always able to spot undercover narcotics detectives.

All of a sudden, the crowd broke out running in all directions. Mary and Nwoke didn't understand why until they saw three plain clothes white males jump out of a green Cavalier, guns drawn at no one in particular as all the junkies and small-time dealers had practically disappeared.

"Okay, get down on the ground," ordered a voice behind Derrick.

Derrick complied as three more undercover Baltimore City narcotics detectives surrounded the SUV and ordered everyone out of the car.

Mary's heart was racing as she was the last one to step out of the Range.

"Okay, pretty girl, you come over here," the female undercover said to Mary.

Mary slowly walked around the vehicle and complied. "Please, let me go. I don't know what is happening. Please I'm just a student," Mary cried, tears now rolling down her cheeks. Her voice was so unsteady that the chubby white female detective showed signs of weakness for the young foreigner.

"That's okay, baby. I believe you but I have to make sure you're not part of this crowd," the woman said and started searching Mary as she leaned against the Range rover with her hands and legs spread apart.

The officers searched everyone and when they didn't find any contraband or drugs, the lead detective told them to get back in the car while Derrick was asked to leave the area.

"I don't know why you guys were parked here in this one hundred thousand dollar vehicle but one thing I can tell you is that if you got something to do with this crowd, it's gonna catch up with you on a larger scale and I mean much larger than local police. Now get out of here and don't come back," the lead detective said and turned around and joined his partners in the Cavalier.

Mary started the vehicle and pulled out of the parking lot. She made two right turns and drove back to Towson.

The shock of what had just happened kept the trio quiet until about five minutes after they got inside the apartment.

Alo went to the fridge and grabbed a cold bottle of Heineken while Mary and Nwoke just sat and watched the news.

"I want to quit, today!" Mary finally said out loud. "I cannot go to prison, please."

"Me too,"Nwoke supported.

Alo finished the Heineken in three gulps and burped. "Calm down kids. Just because we decided to see how they actually make the money for the first time since we started this business, doesn't mean that we will always be exposed to that kind of danger," Alo said as he looked at the two young adults. "All we have to do is keep doing what we've been doing and we don't have to worry about that kind of thing happening again, okay?"

Mary looked at him defiantly as she still had not fully recovered from the shock. "Didn't you hear what the police said to us? I want to go home before I go to jail, please listen to me."

Nwoke walked over to join Mary on the couch. "Hey, baby uncle is right, so just cool down. I think since Derrick seems to be doing pretty good for himself, we should increase supply and build two good mansions; one in Liberia and one in my village, ship some cars and then call it quits. Can you call your boss for that?"

Before Mary could answer, the phone rang and Alo answered.

"It is for you, Mary." Alo gave Mary the cordless phone and went to his room.

Mary spoke to Cynthia for about five minutes and hung up. "Cynthia is officially engaged." She looked at Nwoke, fixing her eyes steadily.

"No problem. We'll soon get married after college. Their marriage is a little premature, if you ask me," Nwoke responded, callously. "For now, just call your boss and let's see if we can increase the supply."

Mary made the call to Gabriel Ogar and he was happy to do so.

CHAPTER TWELVE

Post Graduation:
Beginning of an end

For the next three years, the trio had a consistent run until summer of 1997 when they agreed to make a final deal after Nwoke and Mary graduated from Towson State. The lavish graduation party was attended by Mary's parents from Liberia and Nwoke's parents from Nigeria. The two future parents-in-law took very kindly to each other, ignoring the age difference between the two lovers.

Alo met with his workers, Derrick, Risky and C-note at the lounge on Treemount to discuss the details of the plan ahead. However he did not want to tell them the truth abou this retirement from the dangerous business since that was a bad idea.

"You all, there will be a brief interruption after the next shipment you get. I'm gonna take my wife to Jamaica for about two weeks, then we'll resume," Alo informed the three partners as they sat in the VIP Section of the lounge, sipping Domperignon.

"Yo, that ain't no problem," C-note said and sipped from his glass.

The rest agreed and understood. Alo ordered two more bottles of the expensive drink and they drank for about two more hours and Alo checked his Rolex for time.

"Hey, it's almost seven. I gotta go." Alo stood up and when he saw that the tipsy partners weren't moving, turned and said goodbye and left.

One week after the meeting at the Treemount Lounge, on a hot Monday afternoon in July of 1997, Nwoke and Mary were informed by the Mediators that the Messengers were due sometime that weekend. The specifics of the carriers' trip were not disclosed for security reasons. The only information they had was that the carrier-messengers would arrive in two different flights over a two-day period due to the quantity of the heroin which amounted to twenty kilos. Alo, Mary and Nwoke anxiously waited so that they could get it over with.

Alo planned to go home with his family early for Christmas and spend at least one year. He had accumulated enough money to retire on.

Rev. and Mrs. Nwanta had just returned to Nigeria a few weeks before, after attending Nwoke's and Mary's college graduation ceremony at Towson State. The holy man regretted that Nwoke didn't follow his footsteps to become a minister and informed him of Theo's marriage to a princess.

Friday passed rather quickly and then Saturday came. Nwoke and Mary were having goat and oxtail barbecue in Alo's backyard. They discussed the details and, also wondered what day the messengers would arrive as they cheerfully consumed Heineken and Guiness. Suddenly the land phone rang and stopped after two rings. Alo immediately told Mary to run to the phone booth and call the Mediators since the ringing of the land line indicated a signal.

Mary left the crew in the backyard, drove to the Mall phone booth and called the Mediators. She returned fifteen minutes later. "They said the flight should arrive at BWI at about 7:30 pm tonight," she informed Alo and Nwoke as she sat down to finish her barbecue. She washed some of it down with a bottle of Heineken.

Two hours later, Alo consulted his watch by Cartier and it said 6:30pm."You got the pictures, Mary?" he asked.

"Yes, of course. It's in my pocketbook." Mary double checked by retrieving the pictures from her Coach pocketbook. The pictures were still in the original DHL envelope it was sent in a few days before.

The pictures were used to identify the messengers as they exit the international arrival area of the airport to make sure they were not being followed by a body attachment or an undercover customs agent.

Alo finished his beer, took the pictures from Mary and led the way. "Come on, let's go." He walked into the kitchen and gave Uma a kiss and left.

Mary drove the Range rover to BWI and, because the evening rush hour had almost died down on 895 and 695, they arrived at the airport in thirty-five minutes.

"If they make you move the vehicle, Mary, you know the Routine --just circle around and remain in the vehicle," Alo instructed and exited the SUV, followed by Nwoke. "Oh, one more thing, Mary if we're not out by 8:30 pm, leave the area please and go to my house and wait by the phone but don't put any fear in Uma."

Mary agreed and pulled off while Nwoke and Alo walked into the KLM-Northwest terminal. The time was now 7:10 pm and they positioned themselves and studied the pictures one last time.

"So Mary still has the pictures of the others that's supposed to arrive tomorrow, right?" Alo confirmed.

"Yes, but I think she was smart enough to leave them in the Benz," Nwoke responded.

Twenty-five minutes later, the announcement of the arrival of KLM flight 918 came over the intercom. They positioned themselves in two angular directions to get a clear view of the arrival passengers as they exited the revolving doorways of the international arrival section.

The five expected messenger-carriers, who were made up of three men and two women, were heavy-set in figure. The size of their stomach was necessary to contain a maximum of one thousand grams of pure heroin rolled in balls of 20 grams a piece, carefully wrapped in multi-layers of plastic and scotch tape.

Fifteen minutes later, the first passengers, who were mostly white tourists, walked through the revolving doors, followed by other mixed race of passengers. Alo and Nwoke continued to pay close attention. After about one hour of watching passengers exit the international arrival area of the airport, a Nigerian man dressed in expensive-looking Dashiki walked through the doors and Alo approached him, joined by Nwoke.

"Excuse me sir," Alo said as he stood in front of the dark-skinned man with tribal marks on both cheeks.

The man stopped dragging his suitcase and carryon. "Yes, can I help you?"

Nwoke stood beside Alo as the last of the passengers walked past them.

Alo showed the man three of the pictures. "I'm sure you're from Nigeria. Please have you seen any of these people?" he asked as he watched the man's expression.

"Oh yes. I think this woman here is the one that fainted on the plane and the ambulance just took her away after we landed. She seemed very sick."

Nwoke and Alo were shocked as the man looked through the rest of the pictures and then studied Nwoke and Alo.

"Are they your relatives? These two here were standing with some customs officers when I left."The man pointed at the other pictures.

"Are you sure?" Alo asked and looked around, sensing there was trouble.

"Yes. They are holding all the Nigerians but I managed to get by before they announced that all Nigerian passengers should stand apart from the rest. I think you should go inside and ask to see them. I must leave, please." The man hurried out of the airport entrance.

"Thank you!" Alo said and told Nwoke to put away the pictures as they quickly ran outside and jumped inside the waiting SUV.

"What's wrong?" Mary asked as she pulled off.

"We may have to forget about those messengers. I'm sure they are in trouble." Alo replied, looking paranoid as he studied the occupants of the cars beside them to make sure they weren't being followed.

"What are we gonna do now, uncle?" Nwoke asked, checking the side view mirror on the front passenger side for any tail. His heart was beating extremely fast and he wondered if it was going to explode.

"Oh my God! I hope I don't go to jail." Mary said out loud.

"Turn the radio on to the news station," Alo said. "The good thing is that the messengers did not have our info. We were supposed to meet them at the Hyatt if they made it; so that's a good thing. I'm glad we know they didn't." Alo leaned back and listened for any breaking news on the AM station, feeling safe and sound.

This reassurance from the experienced Alo, appeared to calm Mary down and decreased Nwoke's heart beats. Mary drove the luxury SUV, obeying the speed limit as they cruised to Alo's house.

"I guess we were just paranoid over nothing. The news station confirmed it by not mentioning anything about the bust," Alo said as they walked into the house. "You two are welcome to stay the night in the guest room."

The young couple, who were now scared of the situation at hand, accepted the offer and went down to the guest room in the basement. They were happy to have a shoulder to lean on. Nwoke turned on the television to the local news station and sat down in the comfortable bed while Mary sat next to him. They were hoping for any breaking news.

Alo came down briefly. "If you guys want anything, help yourselves." He stood on the bottom of the stairs and studied the inexperienced couple. "There is still some of that barbecue left upstairs in the dining."

But Nwoke and Mary had no appetite for late supper. The time was almost ten pm as their eyes were fixed on the television set.

"I have to go and call Mr. Ogar to let him know what's going on,"Mary said and stood up.

"Okay, I'll take you to the phone booth at the gas station down the road,"Alo offered,"are you ready?"

"Yes. Nwoke, are you coming?" Mary turned to look at Nwoke who seemed preoccupied with the current situation.

Nwoke didn't even move his face. "No. You two go ahead. I'm gonna sit here and keep an eye on the late news."

Alo drove Mary to the phone booth and Mary called her boss in Nigeria. Gabriel Ogar told her he already got the news and she should leave the area and exercise extreme caution. He also told her to forget about the other scheduled fifteen messengers. Before she could ask any questions, he had hung up.

At the Baltimore Washington International Airport, the U.S. Customs Authority agents were busy interviewing other Nigerians aboard the KLM flight. There were a total of fifteen Nigerian nationals on the plane since it was a connection flight from Amsterdam, Holland. They were transported to a local hospital for stomach x-rays but only five passengers tested positive for balls of the deadly drug. The first one who suffered from the corrosion of the drug was pronounced dead on arrival at the ER of the hospital. A second messenger died after the extraction of the 50 balls but three survived. The deceased were one male and one female.

It was determined by doctors at Saint Agnes Hospital that the delay in the connection flight probably caused the stomach acid to gradually corrode the plastic wrap around the substance.

The exposure of this unique drug smuggling operation caught the attention of investigators at the U.S. Customs Authority in Baltimore.

In the recovery room at the hospital, a tall bald-headed white male, wearing a white overall walked into the room where one of the surviving messengers lay in a hospital bed. "Hello, I'm Dr. Yarborough and I am one of the surgeons who extracted the balls of heroin in your digestive system," he said as he stood over the bed of one of the messengers.

The male messenger looked up at the white man, wondering where the police were since his legs and arms were chained and cuffed. "I am Ola," he responded as he looked around the big room.

There were two state police officers standing guard outside the door. There were also four more uniformed officers guarding the adjacent two rooms as the Special Customs agent-in-charge, had ordered the separation of the smugglers.

"You are from?" the doctor asked in a polite voice with a smile.

"I am from Nigeria," the chubby man who now looked exhausted responded, still looking at the white doctor.

"Do you do this often? It takes a lot of guts to ingest such delicately dangerous object into your digestive system." The doctor studied the man closely, wondering how much he was paid to risk his life in such a way.

"No, I don't. This is my first time," Ola lied.

Dr. Yarborough could tell he was lying but decided not to go any further and leave the Customs to do their job.

In the adjoining room, the female messenger was being very cooperative and somewhat truthful to a customs agent.

"Ma'am, do you know how close you came to dying?" the tall muscular Hispanic-looking agent asked. But when he didn't get any answer from the paranoid woman, he decided to give her time to think about it since she had been cooperative thus far.

After about two minutes, the woman whose name was Femi Odobela, responded. "No, I do not."She was a heavy-set dark-skinned woman who looked pregnant but wasn't.

"Well, the doctor said that you were about ten minutes from death."

The woman's eyes lit up and then closed as she began to pray in her native language.

After about two minutes of prayer, the agent asked her what she prayed about.

"I thanked the almighty Lord for saving my life. Thank you, sir and God bless you,"she said to the agent.

"Thank you, do you wanna tell me who put you up to this?"

The woman told him who her boss was and what they were supposed to do on arrival.

Agent Michael Spinard was in the third room with another male messenger after dismissing the other ten Nigerians who were negative to the x-ray. "Can you tell me what the arrangement was after you guys got through customs?"

The man who claimed to be the lead messenger-carrier, looked rather unhealthy due to his weight. He was brown-skinned and at least three hundred pounds of soft fat tissue. He appeared to be about 5'6" as he lay shackled and cuffed to the bed. "Well, I don't know who they are or what they look like," the man whose name was Bola Oluto as it appeared on his passport, responded.

"They were supposed to meet us at the Hyatt Regency hotel downtown Baltimore."

Spinard was disappointed as he realized how smart the organizers were. He could never find the recipients of the five kilos of heroin. It could be too late to get back and reenact the arrival to see if they would show up at the hotel. He picked up his cell phone from its holster and called Baltimore City police to sendan officer in plain clothes to the Hyatt and make some inquiries about any Nigerians who may have asked any questions in the past hour or reserved any rooms at the five-star hotel. He finished and closed the flip-phone and replaced it in its holster. "Now, you and your partners are in a world of trouble. You may be looking at twenty years unless you can tell us who organized all this and help us find them."

Bola now looked scared as sweat began to form on his forehead. "What do you mean?" he asked, looking like a victim of circumstance as he studied the tall, slim blond haired agent.

"What I said; twenty years in a U.S. federal prison, possibly maximum security."

"Why? It is not my own!"

"I know that, but you were carrying it so that means you are also responsible, sir."

A knock came on the door and one of the uniformed police officers who was guarding the door entered. "Sir, the agent next door wants to see you."

"You think about that and I'll be back." Spinard left the room and joined his partner in the next room.

"Hello, Spinard. I wanted you to be present while Ms. Femi tells us how she got lured into the business. Okay go ahead. Ma'am." Agent Levitz said.

Femi began spitting history, hoping this would spare her. She was thirty-three years old, married with one little boy. "I was contacted while working in a restaurant in Nigeria by three men who came to have lunch. They told me I was wasting my time cooking and serving food at my age and also said I could get up to ten thousand American dollars in one trip if I could swallow fifty rolled balls of heroin, which we call 'gbana'." She took a deep breath and tried to reposition her hands which were immobile in the cuffs. "That was more money than I could make in ten years working in the restaurant. Can you please remove the handcuffs?" she begged.

The two agents looked at each other.

"No, we cannot. I'm sorry but it is normal procedure," Spinard answered.

"So, I accepted the offer and resigned from the job and now, this."Tears filled her eyes and she began to cry.

"Who sent you, ma'am?"Spinard asked.

Femi sobbed and took about one minute before answering. "His name is Ogar, that's what they call him and he has a big house in Lagos, near your embassy."

Agent Spinard face lit up as he believed they were making progress. "And they didn't tell you the dangers involved in swallowing the deadly substance?"

"No, sir. They didn't. I saw the layers of plastic that were wrapped around it and thought it was safe,"she cried as she thought about the twenty years in prison. "Okay, I am sorry but can you please let me go? I have a four year old boy and a husband, please, please, please."

"Okay, I'm sorry, but the courts have to decide your fate. Now, what were you supposed to do on arrival?" The agent wanted to know if her story would correspond with the lead messenger, Bola.

"I am just following them but I think we were supposed to take taxi to a hotel and meet them," she replied.

Agent Spinard's cell phone vibrated and he answered. "Spinard."

"Sir, the only Nigerians here at the hotel are Yellow Cab drivers. The Bellboys have no information. I'm sorry," the uniformed city police who had been sent by the police chief said on the other end of the line.

"Thank you." Spinard hung up. As he opened the door to come back to Bola for some more questioning, he saw a couple of news reporters holding their microphones for the cameramen in the hallway.

"What can you tell us about the Nigerian heroin smugglers, sir?"a black female reporter asked.

Agent Spinard wondered how they got the information so fast. "Nothing. The investigation is on-going and there will be a press conference at the airport when we are ready." He brushed past them and disappeared into the next room.

"Is this why they don't allow direct flights from Nigeria to the U.S.?" a blond female CNN reporter asked as the door closed in her face.

Agent Spinard, along with his main partner, Levitz, finished arrangements with the Hyatt Regency hotel to continue the investigation. On the way out, Agent Spinard addressed the press one last time. He asked that they don't release any information about the bust until the following morning at which time the initial investigation must have been completed with or without success.

The agents, along with the three surviving messengers left for the Hyatt Regency hotel in downtown Baltimore with the hope of trapping the main recipients of the failed drug smuggling attempt.

They knew deep inside that the chances of the smugglers showing up were slim to none.

At Alo's house, the trio patiently waited for the eleven o'clock news. They were disappointed when the news ended without any mention of the bust.

Uma wondered why Alo was up so late and why Mary and Nwoke were spending the night since they had never done so before.

"I must tell you all that the Feds are also very tricky, so don't get it twisted." Alo informed the young adults as the news went off, succeeded by 'Jay Leno.' He stood up to leave the living room and join Uma in their bedroom. "I would not be surprised if they are at the hotel now waiting for us after telling the news crew to hold on."

Mary and Nwoke looked at him without a word. Alo left the living room and retired for the night.

Nwoke and Mary looked at each other and did the same, to the guestroom.

The agents sat in the lobby of the Hyatt Regency hotel and waited while the messengers were assigned specially wired and monitored room. After three hours without seeing any Nigerian around the premises inside and outside, they called it quits and took the messengers into custody.

Mary and Nwoke rose early to watch the news in the guestroom. They could here footsteps upstairs as Uma prepared breakfast and got the baby ready for daycare.

The six a.m. news on channel 11 came on promptly as Nwoke checked the digital clock built into the expensive headboard.

A beautiful red-headed white female newscaster began: "DEATH AT THE BALTIMORE WASHINGTON INTERNATIONAL AIRPORT WAS THE ATTRACTION YESTERDAY EVENING FOR PASSENGERS ABOARD A KLM FLIGHT OUT OF AMSTERDAM. EVIDENTLY, A NIGERIAN PASSENGER WHO CONNECTED THE FLIGHT IN AMSTERDAM HAD INGESTED 1000 GRAMS OF HEROIN WRAPPED IN SCOTCH TAPE WHICH DID NOT HOLD UP FOR THE DURATION OF THE FLIGHT," she paused as she turned the report over to a black male reporter live at BWI.

"VALERIE, THIS IS NOT YOUR REGULAR OVERDOSE. IMAGINE 1000 GRAMS OF PURE HEROIN DISSOLVING IN YOUR STOMACH."

The reporter elaborated on how the stomach acid had corroded the plastic wrap and caused the death of two of the carriers, leaving three survivals. He allowed Agent Spinard to make a plea to the community to help them find the rest of the perpetrators. ACCORDING TO DOCTORS AT SAINT AGNES HOSPITAL, THIS IS A VERY DANGEROUS WAY OF SMUGGLING DRUGS,"the reporter continued. "WHO WOULD HAVE THOUGHT SOME PEOPLE WOULD GO TO SUCH LENGTH TO MAKE MONEY. BACK TO YOU, VALERIE."

The news sent chills up Mary and Nwoke's spine as they sat up on the bed, dumbfounded and wondered how they had indulged in such a dangerous business. The two hearts concluded the same thing; it was time to do something else, somewhere else.

Footsteps descending the stairs took their attention from the news which had now gone into something else. "What are you two thinking? I just finished watching the news, too." Alo sat down in a sofa by the bed-side. "That's what comes with the drug game. In my ten years, I've seen many fall and many rise; it's a gamble. Right now, the prosecutor may inform the U.S. Consulate in Nigeria to arrest your boss if the messengers talk and I'm sure they already have," Alo continued, looking at the two young adults. "Unfortunately, the two countries have an extradition treaty."

"Oh, I don't think that will be possible. They will have to find him first and he could be anywhere in the world by now,"Mary said.

"I wonder what kind of information the living messengers gave them or plan to give them?" Nwoke asked.

"They'll probably tell all they know in order to get a reduced sentence and I'm afraid they don't know enough," Alo answered.

"What's going to happen to the dead messengers then?" Mary asked.

"Oh, if nobody claims them, they'll be buried or cremated by the government."

"What a waste of life. Just like that, I feel guilty." Mary said with a sad tone.

The phone rang and Alo answered. "Hello." Uzo was on the phone informing them of the news he heard and Nwoke congratulated him on his new-born but didn't admit he had anything to do with the failed attempt to smuggle the drug into the United States. Mary did not want to speak to Cynthia at the moment so, the call ended five minutes after it started.

They didn't have to worry about the second flight of five additional messengers since Ogar would immediately cancel it.

Later in the day at their office inside the BWI Airport, Agent Spinard and his chubby, balding partner, Agent Levitz booked the three messenger-carriers and transported them to the CentralBooking facility in Baltimore City. They had enough information on the big boss, Gabriel Ogar, for the prosecutor to execute an international arrest warrant.

At exactly seven p.m., Alo met with C-note and Risky at the Treemount Lounge. Alo began by telling them about the bust.

"You don't watch the News, yo?" Alo asked, shocked that his trusted partner wasn't aware of what had transpired.

"Ain't got no time for News, yo. Too busy watching the streets," Risky responded, drinking a 40oz Steel Reserved beer as they sat at the bar inside the Treemount Lounge' with Cnote.

"I ain't heard nothing either, man. So, what are we gonna do now?" Cnote asked, drinking a 16 ounce bottle of orange juice. Cnote liked to stay fit and was very concerned about his health as he spent a lot of time at

'Bally's fitness club. He didn't drink alcohol and kept a clear mind at all times, so that he could focus on selling his product. He was more of a business man than a street hustler.

Alo related the entire incident to them and the trio finished their drinks and left the lounge.

CHAPTER THIRTEEN

Three months went by after the bust at BWI without any leads or development for the government. It was now the month of December and that meant that Christmas was just around the corner. The messengers had provided the Customs with enough information on their boss, to at least, go and search for Gabriel Ogar in Nigeria. As a result, the prosecutor recommended a reduced sentence of five years each which the Judge granted without hesitation. They were all now serving their sentences in Low security Federal prison. The government, under the recommendation of Assistant U.S. Attorney, James Cohen, included the hunt for Gabriel Ogar in the following year's budget.

"There's gotta be somebody out there who knows something. The drug was meant to be delivered to somebody or some people and not a ghost," Spinard analyzed, as he sat at a table inside the Dunkin donuts, not far from BWI, opposite his partner, Levitz. This was a routine most mornings before they went to the office.

"Maybe, we oughtta try and convince the government to offer a reward for any information leading to the arrest and conviction of the conspirators," agent Levitz suggested as he took a bite of the honey-glazed donut. "You think somebody might have seen the other guys who came to pick them up, before they ran?"

"C'mon, the chances of anybody noticing something as remote as that are not just slim but, nonexistent," Spinard disagreed, shaking his head as he took a second look at his chubby partner and wondered if he was serious. He drank his cup of coffee and gazed out the window. "The idea of the reward is a good one and I'm gonna suggest it to the boss and see what he says," he concluded and finished the cup of coffee and stood up to leave, leaving a tip on the table for the Indian Waitress/Cashier.

Levitz stuffed one whole donut in his mouth and followed his partner.

The government agreed to offer a reward of twenty thousand dollars for any information leading to the arrest and conviction of the suspects the drug was to be delivered to. The offer was announced on CNN and all the local radio and television News stations and Newspapers. Within eight hours of the announcement, the tip line at the Customs house in downtown Baltimore was lit with all kinds of callers with all kinds of misinformation and worthless information as they tried to get their hands on the twenty thousand-dollar reward money. Most of them tried to see how far they could get.

After about forty-eight hours of answering the tip line by the operators, a unique call came through. The man had a heavy accent and sounded black as he claimed to be on the same flight as the carriers. The operator placed him on hold while she spoke with Spinard's receptionist.

"Yes, put'm through," Spinard said to his receptionist on the speaker phone and waited for the man's voice to come on the line. "May I help you, sir?" He listened for a minute and then; "okay, I understand that, but what proof do you have to show us that you were on the same flight?" he asked the man, wondering why he wasn't at the hospital for x-ray as all Nigerian nationals were ordered to undergo.

"That is because I left the arrival station before your people made that decision," the man answered.

Spinard put him on hold and dialed the receptionist to get Levitz to come to his office immediately. Levitz walked into Spinard's office in two minutes. "Okay, sir, go ahead."

"I still have my ticket and my boarding pass," the man said.

"Great, when can you stop by at the office?" Spinard asked, looking at Levitz as the two exchanged looks, excitedly.

"I can stop by tomorrow after work and that is around 5:30 in the evening, since I get off at 4:00pm. This will allow me enough time to get there in the heavy rush-hour traffic."

"Very well, sir. I'm gonna transfer you back over to the receptionist so that she can take your information. Thanks for calling, Mr......what's your name again?"

"Bayo. Mr. Ade Bayo."

"Hold on for the receptionist, Mr. Bayo." Spinard pressed a button, listened for a few seconds and then pressed the off-button on the speaker phone. He looked at Levitz, who was still standing up. "I think we got something there. He might even be the man we're looking for. You just never know, with the loss of twenty kilos of some pure heroin, they just might be desperate enough for cash, so we got to keep a close eye on him." Spinard sat back in his chair and leaned back, staring at the wall, thoughtfully as Levitz was still standing up and followed the gaze of his boss as if there was really something out there.

Nwoke and Mary were now regulars at Alo's house as they search for answers. For the past couple of days, they've only gone home to sleep and spent the days at Alo's as Alo continued to educate them on the U.S. Criminal Justice system. They were sitting in the living-room, watching CNN to see it there were any new development on the case. They had seen and read about the reward that was offered by the Feds, but they didn't think there was anybody, other than their workers, who knew they were involved. Alo and Nwoke knew that snitching was not taken lightly by the workers and so, they didn't condone it either. They had confidence in the silence of their American partners.

"Hey, uncle. Do you think that the man we questioned that day at the Airport might try to claim that reward?" Nwoke asked.

"That was almost three months ago. I don't think he can possibly remember what we looked like, even if he tells them about us, they're gonna need more than that to give him anything," Alo answered, flipping through the pages of the Washington Post newspaper, while Mary was reading an article in the New York Times about some Nigerians who were indicted on some credit card fraud charges.

"Well, I guess he must have forgotten how we looked but, don't you think we should be going back home instead of hanging around to see what happens?" Nwoke continued.

"It's up to you. I know that I don't have any reason to run just yet and besides, Uma isn't gonna leave her job for nothing in this world; not for the money but, she loves taking care of people and the baby is just too young to be changing environments."

Mary finished reading the article and refocused on the television set. Since there was nothing interesting in the news, she decided to put her two cents into the conversation. "Do you guys know how they caught some guys in New York that I'd just finished reading about?"

"How?" Nwoke asked, getting curious.

"Well, listen to this; by fingerprints on the credit cards they were using. Each time they presented it to clerk or a cashier, the fingerprints were taken off the card, without their knowledge." Mary looked at the two of them, holding the paper up to their faces to support her claim. "I think if they can do that, they can find us so, Nwoke, let's get out of this forsaken country!" she raised her voice loud enough to wake up the sleeping Glenn.

Alo got up and walked over to the baby's crib and picked up little Glenn, but then when Mary saw him, she joined Alo and took the baby, trying to play the motherly role since Uma was at work.

The expected informant was on time for his appointment with Spinard and Levitz at 5:30pm, the day after he made the phone call.

Spinard and Levitz were in the conference room with the man as he related the story of what happened on the fateful day in question. Spinard placed the documents the man had brought with him as proof of him being on that flight. He and Levitz studied the documents as the man spoke. The two agents looked for any signs of deceit on Mr. Ade Bayo's expression.

"So, tell me, what happened on the plane, again?" Spinard asked for the second time to see if there were any inconsistencies in Mr. Bayo's story but, there weren't any.

Mr. Bayo innocently recanted what happened on the plane on that fateful day for the second time, sensing that the agents didn't trust him. He also volunteered his passport which had the Customs arrival stamp on it for that date. The ticket stub and boarding pass were authentic. The agents verified his employment while he was there and found out that Mr. Bayo worked for an engineering firm in Perryhall, Baltimore county. He had been employed there for ten years after getting his Green-card. After considering all the facts and the consistency in the man's story, Spinard and Levitz were convinced that Mr. Bayo was telling nothing but the truth.

"Levitz, please tell Martha to come in here for a second and when she does, tell her to get the FBI artist on the phone and see if he's available right away," Spinard ordered. He studied the responsible Nigerian, who had a Bachelor's degree in Engineering and had a good job but, was also willing to turn his own kind in. Maybe, there are some good Africans. "You're not in a hurry, are you, Mr. Bayo?"

"Not at all," the dark-skinned Bayo responded.

Martha came to the door and Levitz told her to get the FBI Artist on the phone and see if he's available that evening.

"That's good because we are now going into over-time," Spinard responded to Mr. Bayo's agreement to stay.

Martha returned to the conference room ten minutes later and informed them that the FBI master sketcher was not going to be able to make it until the following evening at 4:00pm.

"Well, Mr. Bayo. Is there anyway that you can get off work early tomorrow? We really need you to give a complete description of what those men looked like. Well, as much as you can recall so that the Artist can come up with an image to help us."

"Mr. Bayo hesitated for a few seconds. "Okay, I'll see what I can do. I'm sure if I explain to my boss, he will have no problem letting me get off at 3:00pm so that I can be here before 4:00."

"If you need me to talk to him, I will," Spinard assured.

"Good. But I do not think that will be necessary, sir," Bayo responded. "I guess I can go, then?"

"Sure. See you tomorrow. You know your way out?"

"The same way I came, right?"

"Right."

Spinard and Levitz shook Bayo's hand as he walked out of the conference room.

The following day, Mr. Ade Bayo, arrived at the office at exactly 3:35pm, beating the beltway rush-hour traffic. The FBI master sketcher arrived thirty minutes later and immediately took a seat next to the informant.

"How are you today, Mr. Bayo?" the Artist asked, looking at Bayo and studying him.

"I'm fine but, how do you know my name?" Bayo responded.

"Don't worry about that. I am the FBI, you know and I know a lot more about you than you think."

Mr. Bayo seemed a little surprised but didn't show any concern as a law-abiding citizen. He wore a navy-blue two-piece suit over a white shirt and navy-blue tie to match. He looked very professional to the Federal agents in the room.

Getting his pencil and other drawing utensils out of his brief-case, the FBI Artist, who didn't bother to introduce himself until now, started interviewing the informant.

"Please, can you tell me your name so that I can know who you are?"

"Oh, I'm sorry but my name is Mr. Alfred Burito and I am also an FBI special agent," the agent responded and continued to ask his questions.

Bayo willingly and cautiously provided Mr. Burito with details of the appearances of Nwoke and Alo as far as he could recall and the FBI special Artist filled in the blanks the as best as he could.

After about thirty-five minutes of listening and drawing and erasing, Mr. Burito was able to come up with a close likeness of both Nwoke and Alo. "Is this what the older one looked like?" he asked holding up the likeness of Alo and paying close attention to the tribal marks across both cheeks of Mr. Bayo. He also knew the marks indicated a certain tribe in Nigeria.

"Yes, that is very good. I am surprised you were able to do that based on what I just said or did you come here with the picture?" Bayo responded as Spinard and Levitz paid attention.

"Thanks for the joke but, this is what I was trained to do as a Special agent of the Federal Bureau of Investigation. Now, does this one look like the younger one that you also described?"

"Yes but, he might look older on the sketch than he looked in real life," Bayo responded, studying Nwoke's sketch a lot closer than that of Alo's.

"Okay, no problem, I think I can fix that right now," Burito said and placed the sketch back on the table and began erasing and drawing.

Spinard and Levitz looked at each other in excitement and optimism, feeling a sense of accomplishment.

After about five minutes of amending a few lines on Nwoke's sketch, Burito presented the image once again to Bayo and he said it was perfect.

Spinard and Levitz, who had sat in the room, quietly observing the session, finally stood up and sighed in relief, one after another.

"I guess that's it, then, Mr. Burito? What a great lead we got now," Spinard said, looking at Burito and Bayo and then shook the hand of Burito.

"Yes, I'm done," Burito said and put all his utensils back in his brief-case. "See you all again." He left the room.

"Here, Levitz," Spinard said as he studied the two sketches, nodding in approval.

Levitz joined him in studying the two sketches for about one minute and then the two agents looked at Bayo to see his expression but, his face didn't look too happy. Bayo looked like an employee who was waiting for his long overdue paycheck. Spinard noticed this and immediately spoke up.

"Mr. Bayo, thanks for the information but, you're free to go. We'll be back in touch with you if the images prove fruitful. Like the ad said; any information leading to the arrest and conviction of the conspirators and I'm sure you understand what that means. After all, you are a college graduate," Spinard informed Bayo as they watched him carefully.

Ade Bayo, now feeling defeated, gathered his documents and left the room, not looking too happy about the delay in his reward.

"Okay, partner, lets's get to work," Spinard said as he picked up the two papers with the sketches of Alo and Nwoke Nwanta on them and left the room, followed by Levitz.

The two happy agents left the room and went to Spinard's office. They started by giving Martha a list of News organizations they wanted her to fax the sketches to, including CNN. Next, they broke the good news to the prosecutor, James Cohen.

Alo's cell phone rang and he answered it in one ring as Nwoke and Mary were getting ready to leave for the night. It was Risky on the other end of the line.

"What's up, yo?" Risky asked on the other end of the line.

Alo stood up to see his nephew and his girlfriend to the door. "Nothing. What's up with you?" Alo talked and walked.

"Nothing, just called to holla at you and see where we was at, you know what I mean?"

Alo didn't want to talk too much on the phone. "Where you at?"

"Around the way."

"Let's meet at the last spot,"Alo suggested.

"Okay, when?"

"Thirty minutes is good," Alo said and hung up the phone, knowing that the last spot was at the Treemount Lounge. "Okay, you guys drive carefully and I'll see you tomorrow," he told Mary and Nwoke, who had now got inside their Benz E 320. Alo came back in the house and told Uma that he had to go somewhere real quick. He went outside and got in the Lexus LS 400 and headed for the Treemount Lounge to meet Risky. The time was now 7:30pm and Alo knew that the night crowd would soon start arriving at the Lounge, so he stepped on the gas pedal a little harder since he didn't plan on spending too much time at the bar. He got there at exactly 7:50pm and looked for Risky's car as he was parking but, when he didn't see any Range or a Lexus GS 300, he decided to call. He called and Risky told him he was already inside the bar. Alo parked, got out and went inside, realizing thatwhen you had the cash, you could drive anything at any given time.

"What's up with your peoples, yo?" Risky asked Alo as he found him in the VIP section, where he was sitting, for some privacy.

"What do you mean? I told you what happened or did you think I was lying?" Alo answered, sitting down in the comfortable soft leather seating.

"So, you ain't got no other connect, son?"

Alo looked at him like he had had a little too much to drink as he noticed the empty bottle of Moet sitting on the table, next to the full bottle. "Yo, when you start drinking?"

"What are you talking about, man. I always drink, it's Cnote that don't drink. You sure you okay?"

Alo realized he wasn't quite himself and remembered it was Cnote who didn't drink and lived in the gym most of the time. At that moment, he decided he needed a drink himself. He saw the extra glass and took one and poured himself a full glass of Moet and quickly drank it and then poured another one and drank half. "Hey, pretty waitress!

Can you get us a couple more bottles of Moet, please?" he yelled to the waitress through the half empty Bar-lounge.

"Now, listen, yo. We can't let that one fall keep us down forever. I mean, I could re-up with something else but, I have a reputation now and I must maintain it to keep myrespect in the streets," Risky said as he drank another cup of Moet like it was Spring water.

The waitress brought the two bottles of Moet and left.

The alcohol was beginning to have some effect on Alo as he studied Risky and thought he was crazy for making the comment he'd just made. He was now determined to lecture the uninformed and ignorant worker. "Hey, listen to what I have to say. The heat is on. Do you understand what I mean by that?" he picked the filled glass and emptied half of its content into his stomach and continued. "To be honest, we're not even safe right now, right here, man. Those Feds are on to us and, if you still haven't seen the amount of reward they're offering for me, you'd better go check out the Baltimore Sun paper."

"Word?"

"Yes, that's my word!"

Even though he was tipsy, Risky was now beginning to get a little scared as he heard the word 'Feds'. He knew, from his friends doing time in the Feds, that a heroin conspiracy charge was not a joking matter, especially when it's that pure shit. He had two uncles and three former partners who were serving twenty to thirty years in the Federal prison system. He did not want to grow old in prison and have all the younger offenders calling him Old G. He thought about his girlfriend, Sherrie and couldn't bear the thought of another man sleeping with her and that was bound to happen if he went to prison.

"I'm sorry, yo. I didn't know it was that deep. How much is the reward?"

"Twenty thousand dollars for information on me and my people. Now, you know that's very serious but I don't think they got anything 'cause I only deal with Riders, right, my nig?"

"You already know what it is."

The two hustlers drank some more Moet and talked about the chances of the Feds getting at them until about 9:00pm when the crowd began to stagger in. They noticed the few casually dressed couples that came into the bar area and got up, leaving hal a bottle of Moet and two hundred and fifty dollars for the waitress. When the waitress saw them leaving she stopped what she was doing and rushed to the VIP room to retrieve her all-too-familiar big tip.

Feeling very tipsy now but, still with their senses, Alo and Risky walked out of the Lounge.

"So, what are you driving now?" Alo asked as they stopped outside the door of the Lounge so that he could answer his cell phone that was ringing.

"Oh, I copped an Escalade the other day, yo," Risky answered.

"Hello," Alo responded to the phone call, ignoring the answer from Risky.

"Uncle, did you hear or see the special News report just now?" Nwoke asked on the other end of the line, sounding hysterical and paranoid.

Alo froze in his tracks, trying to gather his thoughts. "What are you talking about? The News doesn't come on till 11:00pm."

"This was a special report, interrupting the regular program."

Alo's heart rate increased pace but, the effects of the alcohol kept him in control as he feared the worst. "A special report about us?"

"Yes, they showed our sketches on TV and they looked like us."

Alo was quiet for about two minutes as Risky paid attention to Alo's end of the conversation. "So, when was this?"

"About five minutes ago. Not only the sketched pictures of our faces but, they also had the ages almost perfect. They were only off by a year or so. What do you want us to do, uncle? Mary and I aren't gonna hang around all these white neighbors."

Alo looked at Risky, who now had his eyes fixed on him, listening intensely as he could tell from what he heard that things were looking pretty bad for his partner. "Okay, you two can go ahead but, avoid Airports and public places in the area. Drive to New York and, please·obey the speed limit. Let Mary drive and I'll meet you guys later. I gotta talk to Uma and straighten out a few things before leaving." He paused for about thirty seconds and continued. "On second thought, why don't you just take Uma and Glenn with you and I'll call her right now and tell her to start packing her stuff." He hung up the cell phone and looked at Risky, then surveyed the street to see if there was anything unusual or anyone that didn't belong in the all-black neighborhood. Then he flipped the phone open again and called Uma and told her to start packing, that Nwoke and Mary where on their way to pick her up. Uma argued but, he told her what the consequences could be if she didn't go with Mary and Nwoke. She agreed reluctantly and started getting her things together.

"What was that all about, yo?" Risky asked, getting a little scared himself and wondering what he had gotten himself into with the Nigerian.

"Like I tried to tell you earlier, this isn't a joking matter. Now, the Feds got me and my nephew's sketched pictures," Alo explained to the tipsy Risky, studying him and expecting some kind of solution, but nothing came out of Risky's mouth but a second question.

"How the fuck did they do that?"

"You tell me, 'cause I have no idea."

Risky looked up and down the street and focused on his brand new Cadillac Escalade and noticed a dark blue Chevy Caprice with pitch black tinted windows that was only legal for the Feds, sitting on top of the street by the traffic light on the opposite side of his SUV. He then moved closer· to the side-walk so that he could see directly through the wind-shield and that's when he saw the two white men inside the Caprice with their eyes fixed on where he and Alo were standing. "Yo, I think we're being followed," he said, looking way from the Caprice.

"Where and how do you Know?" A paranoid Alo asked, looking straight ahead, so as not to arouse any suspicion by anyone.

"The Caprice on top of the street on the other side wasn't there when I parked my truck and there are two white dudes sitting inside, watching us, but don't look."

"How can you tell they're watching us?"

"Because when I walked up to the side-walk, I could see much better since the side windows are tinted."

Alo wasn't sure what to do. How could they have found him that fast? Are they God or what? He concluded Risky must have had a little too much Moet. "I'll be right back, yo. Stay right here." Alo walked up to the main street and headed for the top of the busy street to see for himself. He walked past the tinted window Caprice, without paying it any attention but, somehow he could feel the two men staring at him so he branched off to the store that was right beside it and bought a lottery ticket. As he was coming back outside, he took a quick look at the men and their eyes met but he continued back to where Risky was. He concluded they must be following Risky or somebody else.

"yo, you see what I mean, now?" Risky asked as Alo stopped in front of him.

"Maybe so. Why don't you just go straight to your truck and I'll go to my car and, please act like you don't see them 'cause we can't just continue to sit here."

"Okay, then. I'll see you later," Risky said as the two drug dealers parted ways.

Risky had no idea that he had been under surveillance for about two weeks, now, after visiting an old connect in the Bronx, New York city to see if he had anything good. Unfortunately for him, the old connect was under surveillance by the DEA.

Alo was now in the worst situation of his life because of this. The two DEA agents who were sitting in the Caprice, noticed Alo's face when he walked past them and into the corner store. They were able to snap two quick shots of Alo's face. The polaroid camera produced the picture of Alo in minutes and the agents cross-checked it with the most recent Federal suspect photos and found it resembled the last one they had just received from the Customs Authority. One of the agents notified their partners on North avenue and Treemount avenue, with a description of Alo's car and tag number.

255

Risky pulled off in the Escalade and checked his rear-view mirror to see if the Caprice was following and it was, about three car-lengths behind. He slowed down to see if they would pass and, to his surprise, it did. But, what he didn't know, was that a second surveillance team in white Chevy cavalier, was up the street, waiting just in case Risky did something like that. His mind became at ease once again and he thought he might've just had a little too much to drink and needed to go home and sleep it off or take it out on Sherrie in the bed room. He carefully pulled back out onto the main road, onlyto be followed by the white cavalier, unnoticed.

Alo checked his rearview mirror in the Lexus and saw no tail but, a couple of vehicles and the one immediately behind him, was a yellow cab. His mind also became peaceful and he, too, wondered if the Moet had something to do with his paranoia. Since he was parked the opposite direction, he made a left on Eager street and, one minute later, made another left on Aisquith street. He drove for another two minutes before making a third left on North avenue. Three minutes later, he came to a complete stop at the traffic light on the intersection of Treemount and North. After about five seconds he proceeded to turn right on red, which was allowed after 7:00pm. The second Chevy Cavalier got behind Alo while a third surveillance team followed Risky in a green Cavalier.

The white Cavalier with the two DEA agents stayed on the tail of the Lexus LS 400 until it reached where Treemount ave became York road, then a red Cavalier took over while the white one stayed behind, slowly. Alo still had no idea he was being followed. The Caprice had parked ahead on the corner of Coldspring lane and York road, since the agent-in-charge, Thomas Johnson and his partner, agent Billard, were waiting for Customs agent Michael Spinard to call them back to advise them on what to do.

After agent Spinard got the message, he immediately called back. It was actually the operator who delayed it for a few minutes.

"Agent Johnson, DEA, can I help you," Johnson answered as he sat in the Caprice with Billard.

"This is agent Spinard from Customs and I'm returning your call. Now, can you please tell me which one of suspects you have?"

"Well, sir, it was from a sketched picture that was distributed earlier today," Johnson could hear the sound of a small child in the background, telling him that Spinard was off duty and on duty. "The older Nigerian of the two, I believe. It looked like him and his friend is under surveillance for the same reason, that's how we ran into him," Johnson explained on the government-issued Nextel cell phone.

"That's just great! Can you confirm if the individual is in fact the suspect?"

"Yes we can. But, we don't have him yet. We do have him under surveillance as we speak and we can just get the traffic police cruiser in the area to do a traffic stop. Now, if we do that, what information should we look for, sir?"

"We don't have a name for him so, just see if his name is foreign and do a quick profile before you make an arrest. To me, his association is good enough to bring him in for questioning."

"Okay, sir, we'll see what we can do." Johnson hung up. He then called the unit that had Alo under surveillance and told them to do a traffic stop through the local police that had jurisdiction over the area they were now in to get the identity of the individual driving the Lexus.

The unit following Alo was now in Baltimore county part of York road and they proceeded to do so by contacting the Baltimore county police headquarters in Towson, who immediately dispatched the information to the traffic patrol units in the area.

Just before Alo turned right on Joppa road, a Baltimore county police cruiser pulled him over while the DEA agents in the cavalier stopped behind the cruiser.

"May I see your license and registration, sir?" the white police officer asked as Alo pulled over on the right lane of the road, diverting traffic to the left lane.

Alo didn't understand why the officer stopped him since he wasn't speeding or driving erratically. "What is this all about, sir?" Alo asked as he handed the officer his license and registration.

"I'll let you know in a minute. What a name. Where are you from?" the officer asked, looking at the license.

"Nigeria but, I'm a U.S. citizen by Naturalization," Alo responded, nervously, wondering why the unusual question.

"I'll be back," the officer said and walked back to his cruiser to show the two DEA agents the license and also inform them of Alo's nationality.

The two DEA agents immediately followed the police officer to Alo's Lexus and arrested him after reading him his rights and telling him who wanted him for questioning. They later informed Johnson who informed Spinard. Spinard then obtained a search warrant for the residence of Alo Nwanta and sent another team to search the house.

Fortunately for Alo, Uma and Glenn were gone but, unfortunately, the feds found some incriminating photos and documents. All the vehicles were confiscated and the home acquired.

Alo was taken to the Central Bookings facility and booked.

Right about the same time, Risky was also picked up by the other unit after he tried to out-run the four-cylinder Cavalier. The City police was called to assist and Risky's brand new Cadillac SUV was totalled. Unfortunately for the feds, he had an out-of-state driver's license from the common wealth of Virginia and they couldn't determine his residence in order to execute a search warrant. The government would later find out through their Virginia counterpart that the address on Risky's driver's license was non-existent. A check of his fingerprint revealed his real name and his mother'saddress but, when the feds checked out the address they discovered that Ms. Jackson had been dead for years.

In his office at the BWI Airport, agent Spinard could not wait to tell his partner, Levitz about what had transpired the previous night while they were off.

"Hey, Jonathan, I almost worked twenty four hours yesterday 'cause the phone kept ringing till a little past midnight and I kept answering," Spinard said as he made his first call of the day by 8:05am, the morning after Alo and Risky's arrest

"What happened?" Levitz asked, curiously.

"Well, partner. We got one of the Nigerians on the sketch just that quick."

"Are you kidding me?" Levitz sounded very surprised at the speed with which the sketches yielded result.

"I kid you not. Where are you anyway?"

"Just getting in. I'll see you in a few."

"Okay, hurry. We gotta go to the Central Bookings and see what we can get out of this guy....he just might lead us to the rest of them." Spinard dropped the phone and waited for Levitz so that he could give him the complete story as they ride to the Bookings.

Martha walked into Spinard's office right after he hung up the phone. "Mr. Bayo is on the phone for his reward. He claims he heard about the arrest of one of his sketches. You wanna talk to him?"

"I think we got enough information to give him the reward so, go ahead and start the process."

Martha left the office and Levitz walked in with a donut and a cup of coffee in his hands.

"Are you ready?" Levitz asked and took a bite of the donut.

"I know that's not all you got. Where's the box?"

"In my office. Let's go," Levitz said and lead the way.

Together, the two agents walked out of the office.

They arrived at the Central Bookings Facility thirty minutes later. They signed in at the security cage and surrendered their weapons.

The two agents came back out from the Central Bookings Facility ten minutes later after Alo told them he wouldn't speak to any law enforcement agent without the presence of his private attorney. They were disappointed to the fullest.

"I think we might have a fight on our hands," Spinard lamented as they walked toward the parking lot.

"You find out what kind of evidence we got on this guy, yet?" Levitz asked as he took the van keys out of his pocket and let himself in on the driver side.

Spinard jumped in on the passenger side after Levitz let him in. "I don't know yet. C'mon, let's go see Mr. Cohen. There might be something in those documents seized last night by the search team or maybe his American accomplice might be willing to talk." Spinard said and picked up his cell phone and called DEA agent Johnson.

Agent Johnson told him that Dante Jackson, aka, Risky had also told them the same thing. "It's looking more like a tough case. I think we might have those so-called gangsters on our hands."

"What do you mean?"

"They're not gonna snitch on anyone and that makes the case very, very difficult."

Levitz made a right on Lombard street and two minutes later, he made a left and a quick right into the underground garage of the U.S. Federal Courthouse, where James Cohen was waiting.

CHAPTER FOURTEEN

The ride to New York was rather slow, due to the constant disturbance of the little boy and the obedience of the speed limit by Mary. There was constant change of diapers and feeding since Glenn was not used to travelling at night in the absence of his crib. As a result, Mary had to keep stopping in rest areas before Nwoke insisted they check into a Motel in New Jersey, right off of I-95.

After a few hours at the Motel, the trio with the baby, started back out very early in the morning, now refreshed from the rest. They were now almost at the Lincoln tunnel and none of them knew where to go, so Nwoke decided to ask the attendant at the Toll-booth.

"Then, on second thought, Mary, you ask'm," Nwoke suggested when he realized that he could be recognized by the attendant.

Mary agreed and pulled up to the booth and paid the fee. "Excuse me, maam, can you tell us how to get to the nearest five-star hotel in New York?"

The white female cashier studied Mary momentarily and glanced at her company in the luxury SUV. She also heard the heavy accent and figured that Mary must be lost. "Well, just keep to your right as you get off the tunnel and then go straight into downtown Manhattan, you'll see signs leading to the Marriot." She smiled as Mary eased of the accelerator

"Okay, thank you and enjoy the rest of your day," Mary said as she was pulling off. She stayed to her right as the woman had directed.

Uma checked her Rolex and it told her that the time was 7:43am as the Range rover arrived into the city of Manhattan. "Oh, my God, Glenn is gonna be sick. He hasn't had enough sleep. I'm so scared. How did you all get yourselves into this mess that made me leave my house so suddenly? I have been on my job for more than ten years and I love helping people. I hope we come back soon 'cause I didn't even give them a notice." Uma was a registered nurse at GBMC hospital.

"Well. I don't know about coming back soon but, I do know that uncle will soon join us." Nwoke responded as he looked for signs to the Marriot.

"How come we don't see any signs?" Mary asked, moving her eyes from left to right.

"I don't know but just pull over right there let's ask the man at the hot-dog stand," Nwoke suggested.

The Korean-looking man with a heavy accent told them to go up to 42nd street and turn right and look for Radio City Music Hall. The Marriot Marquis was about two or three blocks from the Music Hall.

"Uma, I take it you've never been to Nigeria?" Nwoke asked Uma as the SUV turned right on 42nd.

"Yeah. Once on our honeymoon, remember? But, we only stayed a week. The weather is just like Indian weather."

"Yeah, I remember hearing about it but I didn't see you."Nwoke responded as Mary drove past Radio Music Hall. "We're yet to go there."

"You'd never liked New York, at least that's what you told me," Mary commented.

"Too congested; look at all these cabs and people everywhere. Oh, okay I think that's it over there," Nwoke pointed at the Marriot Marquis Hotel.

Mary pulled up in front of the five-star Hotel and one of the Bell-boys came rushing to the Range rover.

"Tell'm to give us a second, Mary," Nwoke said and turned his head to Uma. "Now, we're gonna need you to check us in, Uma. Get two suites. You got your id with your maidenname on it?"

"Yes, my work id before I met Alo."

"Good. How about credit card under the same name?"

"Yes. Nwoke, what is really going on. Alo told me a little but, I think he left out some things. Are we in serious danger because I can just take Glenn with me to India?"

"No, we're not. I'll explain later. Just go get the suites so that Glenn can get some sleep. It's gonna be all right."

Uma really didn't know the extent of the problems facing her husband and inlaw. She'd never known anybody to experience any problems with the law, especially in the U.S. The more she thought about it, the less she wanted to go with them as the situation was beginning to look more like something out of a movie scene. She decided to confront Alo when he joined them. As she was exiting the SUV, Nwoke's cell phone rang, interrupting her thought process.

"Wait a second, Uma. You okay with getting the suites?" Nwoke asked as Uma attempted to step off the SUV.

"Yes. I'll be right back," Uma answered and left the vehicle, followed by the Bell-boy who was tired of standing by the door waiting for them to get out of the SUV.

"Hello," Nwoke answered the cell phone.

Derrick was on the other end of the line. "What's up, my man?"

"Nothing. What's up with you?" Nwoke wondered why Derrick was calling. Could it be that the Feds got him too and told him to call and find out where he was? He thought.

"You need to jet, like, right now, yo."

Nwoke thought that Derrick must've just heard and saw the sketches or maybe pictures on the News. "Why would I jet? Something wrong?"

"You aint been watching the News this morning? Your sketch and your uncle's been all over the network. Well, the most recent update said that they got your uncle but, that you were still at large," Derrick said, sounding paranoid himself on the phone line.

"Nwoke's heart dropped and he looked at Mary but, she was busy watching the scene outside as people that looked like tourists and celebrities came in and out of the five-star Hotel. "Are you sure about that?"

"What do you mean am I sure? Anyway, where are you? In the car somewhere, already running, since you can't get to a TV?"

Nwoke was quiet for about a minute or two, not knowing whether to cry or what. He looked at Glenn who was now sound asleep and wondered when the baby was gonna see his father again. "Thank you, let me call you back, later," he said and hung up and looked at Mary who was now staring at him.

"What's the problem?"

"They got Alo."

"Oh! Mine. I told you we should've left when we did. Now, see that?"

Nwoke didn't respond to Mary's comment. For the first time since he left his father's house at the church compound, Nwoke bent his head on the dash-board and started praying.

Ten minutes later, Uma came out of the revolving doors and went straight to the back door and opened it. "Okay, I'm done. The lobby is actually on the 13th floor, Can you ᴊ believe that?" Uma said as she unstrapped Glenn's car-seat.

"Well, don't you need some money to put back on your credit card?" Mary asked, feeling sorry for the woman who may be temporarily out of a husband, maybe for a long time.

"That's okay. It was only three thousand dollars for the two suites. There's no limit on the card, so we can straight en it out later." Uma explained and took little Glenn out of the back seat and waited for Mary and Nwoke to come out of the SUV.

Nwoke and Mary came out and two Bell-boys helped with the luggage and they all went up to the 23rd floor of the Marriot Marquis. Their rooms were next to each other; Nwoke and Mary were in suite 2305 while Uma and the baby checked into suite 2306.

In their suite, Mary immediately turned on the television set to CNN. "This is almost like our apartment in Towson," she said and sat down in the living room of the suite with the remote control in her hand.

Nwoke didn't respond as he was too pre-occupied with the thought of his uncle going away to a Federal prison for a long time. After about ten minutes of watching for any information on the News channel, Nwoke relaxed. "I guess we missed it, hah. Derrick said it was earlier this morning and it's already 9:50am so it might come on later."

The couple sat there and wondered what their next move was going to be. Nwoke looked around the suite for the first time since he walked in. The suite was big and elegantly furnished. It had two bedrooms and two full baths at the good price of fifteen hundred per night. The windows over-looked the city of Manhattan. The ringing of Nwoke's cell phone startled Mary, even though the voice of the Newscaster on CNN was loud and pretty much filled the room.

"Hello," Nwoke answered on the second ring, not recognizing the number on the LCD.

Derrick was on the phone again. "Yo, it's me again. I just had to get another phone. I'm just as scared as you."

"Smart move. Now, did they say how he was caught?"

"You know the people ain't gonna say the details. But, they did say it was the DEA that made the arrest after getting a copy of the sketches which included yours. The Customs have him now but, his man is under the DEA custody."

"What man? You didn't say anything about his man."

"I think his name is Dante Jackson, but I'm not sure so don't quote me on that."

Nwoke couldn't think of anyone named Dante Jackson but, he remembered that the last time he spoke to Alo, he told him he was going to meet Risky. He concluded

Risky's real name must be Dante Jackson. "That must be Risky, yo."

"Oh, you know'm?"

"Kind of. But, please get'm a good Lawyer so that he can make bail. Keep this phone for at least a couple of days. I might even change number myself, so if you call and get what ever message, don't be discouraged. I'm gonna have to go now and thanks for the information and assistance." Nwoke pressed the off-button and just sat there. Mary tapped him on the shoulder.

"What's next? I heard some of the conversation," she said, trying to look at Nwoke's face which was facing the floor. "So, are you gonna tell me how Derrick said they found Alo?"

Nwoke told her what Derrick told him. "I still don't know how they got our sketches," Nwoke said and then looked up at

"They probably have the real pictures by now if they went to the address on Alo's license. That's what they do in the movies, you know. Anyone could've given them your description, right?"

"Wrong. It would have to be somebody who knew we knew the messengers and I can only think of one person."

"Who's that?"

"The Nigerian man we asked at the Airport about the people that got caught."

"Oh yeah?"

"Yeah."

"So, that means if they get somebody like Brian. He could give them a description of me and Cynthia?"

"If he's a snitch or in need of money. Yes. But, I don't think that'll ever happen. If Brian saw what Derrick saw, he probably already left town and changed his phone numbers," Nwoke said and stood up and walked over to the window that over-looked the city that never sleeps. He thought about his twenty-second birthday that was coming up on the 23rd of December. He had planned to have his wedding on his birthday in the village and continue the celebration through Christmas and New year in the new mansion he and Mary had built. Nwoke now wondered if all that plan had gone down the drain or if the almighty God can perform some miracles. He thought about calling his father to pray for him but, quickly discarded the idea. "Alright, Mary dear. I think you should be the one tobreak the News to Uma, woman to woman. I don't think I can do it after telling her that Alo was gonna join us."

Mary agreed and left the suite to face the already depressed Uma.

In his 12 by 9 cell at at the maximum security Federal detention center, not far from downtown Baltimore, where Alo had been transferred to from the Central Bookings facility across the street, he was restless and wondered if Nwoke and Uma had heard about the ordeal and made arrangements for a Lawyer to get him out of jail. He was sure it was national News, so even if they were in New York, they should have heard something or read something. He thought about calling the cell phone number but, decided against it since all calls going out of the detention center were monitored by the Feds. He then took a closer look at the small window with iron bars and knew there was no other way possible to get out. Alo now felt that the whole world had descended upon him.

The heavy iron door slid open and he was looking at an out of shape white correctional officer who must have weighed at least two hundred and ninety pounds. "Dinner?" the C.O. asked

Alo shook his head in disgust at the bologna sandwich, without saying a word. The C.O. pulled the door to slamming closure and continued his evening meal service as an inmate worker pushed the food-wagon to the next cell.

Alo had not eaten nor drank anything for the two days he'd been at the detention center. The wing Officer-in-charge was now getting concerned and wondered if Alo was on hunger strike or just faking so that they would feel sorry for him. Alo thought about his young son who may now, be without a father for some years. All his hope now rested on somebody getting him a good criminal defense attorney. The government offered him a court-appointed lawyer but he refused. His bond hearing was coming up the next day and he could hear the Muslim inmate praying next door and, all of a sudden, Alo decided to join him, silently and spiritually.

Derrick contacted a high-priced attorney in Rockville at the initial cost of twenty thousand dollars, which would increase as the case progressed. The attorney's name was John Guilick and he specialized in Federal drug conspiracy cases. Since Alo was a naturalized U.S. citizen, he was eligible for bond. He was going to represent Alo at the bond hearing.

Derrick picked up his new pre-paid cell phone and called Nwoke on the old number but the operator told him that the number was no longer in service. He remembered that Nwoke had told him he was going to get another phone. He deleted the old number from his cell and waited for Nwoke to call him. Ten minutes later, still sitting in his office, Derrick's new cell phone rang and he answered in one ring.

Nwoke was on the other end of the line. "This is my new cell, yo. I just got it."

"I just tried the old number a few minutes ago and I'm glad you called when you did. Anyhow, I got your unc a good lawyer and he's gonna represent'm at the bond hearing tomorrow morning."

"That's great!" Nwoke exclaimed on the other end of the line.

"Now, hold up, my man. The lawyer said there's no guarantee that the judge will grant him bond due to the seriousness of the charges on the criminal complaint," Derrick paused for a few seconds and continued as Nwoke listened on the other end of the line. "Mr. Guilick also said that the government considered Alo a flight risk and, if at all they do grant bond it would be extremely high and may involve property, which cannot belong to the defendant. He charged me twenty thousand but it's gonna go up."

"Well, don't worry about the money. I gotchu. Just stay on top it to see he does what he's supposed to do to get my uncle out of jail. You will be rewarded and thank you." The line died.

Derrick got up off his chair and walked over to the window and gazed down the busy intersection of Pennsylvania avenue and North avenue through the blinds. He looked for anything or anyone that didn't belong but, the streets were too busy to tell.

Uma Nwanta had taken the News from Mary with a devastating blow. She was now feeling a little better after Nwoke told her there was hope at the Bond hearing. Nwoke thought about calling his father for prayers but then changed his mind as he thought the News might give his mother a heart attack. If his mother heard that her smartest son, who ran to the U.S. to attend college and become a respectable citizen, had now become a fugitive, he may never see her again. Nwoke sat there in the parlour of the suite, wondering how things would have been if only he had listened to his Godly parents and remained in Nigeria after High school. He definitely would not be on the run right now, but he wouldn't have built a mansion either and shipped all those vehicles. He had millions in the banks in Nigeria and Switzerland with his lovely wife, Mary. Then, what good are those things if you can't enjoy them? Would he even be married by now? Maybe to Helen but, he doubted the possibility of early marriage under the watchful eyes of Rev. and Mrs. Nwanta. He would have still been in the Medical School. Either way, nothin is more precious than one's freedom, Nwoke concluded in his young mind.

"What are our plans, Nwoke? How in the world are we gonna get through the Airport with you and I being wanted by the Feds?" Mary asked as she sat in the sofa opposite Nwoke and realizing that it was just a matter of time before the Feds tied her into the mix. There were more than enough documents at Alo's and their apartment to incriminate her. Her real pictures were also available to the investigators so they didn't need a sketched image of her. The last thing on her mind at the moment, was sex.

"We're gonna have to wait and see what happens with unc., tomorrow. First of all, we're gonna need new Nigerian passports and I trust you can handle that through your former coworkers, right?"

Mary hesitated for about one minute and agreed with a nod. "I guess I just have to make some calls but, why do I have to wait to get started?"

"You don't. I'm just not gonna leave the country without my uncle; it just wouldn't feel right."

"So, you love your uncle more than me?" Mary was jealous and she showed it by standing up and staring at Nwoke, waiting for a response that would determine if she was going to have to leave him in the Hotel suite by himself or not.

"Of course not. That's a different kind of love and you know it. You're twenty seven years old, Mary." Nwoke responded as his eyes met hers.

After about thirty seconds, Mary sat back down, realizing that her younger lover was right.

The loud knock on the door brought Nwoke and Mary to their feet. Nwoke slowly tip-toed to the door and peeped through the security peephole, while Mary stood still by the sofa. He saw a serious-looking Uma, standing on the other side of the door with her young son. He turned the door-knob and let her in as his heart rate returned to normal.

"Hi, Nwoke and Mary. May I sit down?"Uma said as she sat down with little Glenn sitting next to her.

Nwoke acknowledged her and closed the door. "Hi."He didn't want to upset the already angry looking Indian beauty.

"Can you please explain to me what's going on? Glenn asked about his Daddy and I didn't know what to tell him so, I brought him over here so that you can tell him," She broke down and started crying.

Mary walked walked over to where she was to console her. "It's okay. Hey, little Glenn, daddy will come tomorrow," she said to the little boy and picked him up from the sofa.

"Daddy! Daddy! Daddy!" Glenn muttered, hitting his right hand against Mary's neck and looking at her.

This touched Nwoke and he quickly walked over to where Mary was and took his nephew from her. "Daddy will be here very soon," he assured the innocent little boy, not wanting to be specific.

Dante Jackson, aka, Risky, was being held in the same detention center as Alo but, in a separate Wing. Neither of them knew the other was there since there was no means for them to contact each other. The government had given both cases to the same prosecutor, Assistant U.S. attorney, James Cohen. James Cohen was known for his dislike of Africans and African Americans. Cohen planned to make the two defendants co-defendants as he uncovered more evidence linking the two. Mary was also beginning to come into the picture as Cohen continued to analyze all documents from both residences.

Since there were no wire-taps or any other direct evidence linking the two suspects, the government would have to depend soully on the testimony of either one of them. Cnote was lucky to escape it all and the agents knew nothing about Derrick or Brian, yet. In their effort to build a strong case, the agents were asking all inmates with drug cases if they ever dealt with any of the defendants. Any useful information would get the inmate a two-point reduction.

The word had reached Cnote through one of his workers who was locked up in a state facility and Cnote immediately disappeared from the streets of Baltimore.

The lead investigator in the case for the Baltimore branch of the DEA, agent Thomas Johnson, decided to visit Risky since the Customs was not having any luck with Alo in obtaining some kind of information to, at least, give them an idea of what's been going on and for how long. The incarcerated carriers only had limited information.

Risky did not wake up for breakfast so, he was sound asleep when the iron door swung open at 6:05am and woke him up. "Breakfast and visit at 7:30 Dante Jackson," a female C.O. voice announced at the cell door.

The word visit made Risky wake up and eat the boiled eggs and drink the milk for the first time in almost three days. His bond hearing was not until 9:00am so, he hoped it was his attorney that Sherrie had retained. He finished the so-called breakfast and washed his face in cold water since the hot water at the Detention center didn't work unless you asked for permission to go to the main floor and take a shower. The chances of being allowed to take a shower that early in the morning were very remote. Showers were only allowed during recreation time.

Fifteen minutes later, Risky was in the special visitor's room, facing his worst enemies."Who are you? I know I don't have two lawyers."

"You're right. I am agent Johnson and this is my partner agent Billard. We're from the DEA and just have a few questions about the Nigerian you were seen with on the night of your arrest and the man you visited in New York before that," Johnson asked, keeping his eyes fixed on Risky as he waited for the initial response.

Risky didn't say a word as he remained silent to see if the men could tell him what they knew.

After no response from the defendant, Agent Johnson continued. "We've been watching you for a while now and you are in some pretty serious trouble and facing a lot of time, unless you can help us," Johnson informed Risky.

Risky still didn't say a word. He wanted to find out what else they had other than seeing him with Alo and the dude in the Bronx. To him, that really didn't amount to anything and if they had anything else, like wire-tap information, he did not recall saying anything incriminating on the phone. He figured since they didn't appear to have any prior knowledge of his dealings with Alo since the surveillance began after Alo took a break and he never did anything with the New York man from the Dominican Republic, only one visit to check out what he had and it wasn't top quality like he was known for, so he cut him loose. Risky concluded that the men were just fishing for information and decided to keep his mouth shut.

"Thanks for listening, Mr. Jackson, now what can you tell us to help yourself and your family?" Johnson ended, eyes still fixed on the suspect, soon to be defendant in a federal court.

"I appreciate your willingness to help me, but you see, I'm waiting for my attorney and I think you should be talking to him and not me," Risky informed the two detectives in a kind voice that told them they might have a fight on their hands.

The two federal agents got up to leave and Johnson had to give Mr. Jackson food for thought. "I remind you that you're facing up to fifty years, Mr. Dante Jackson," he lied to see if that would make Risky give in but silence followed and they proceeded to the door and called out to the correctional officer to let them out.

Risky thought about how true the last statement by the agent was and decided not to give it any credit since he was just too experienced in the game to buy something like that. Then, after the C.O. let the agents out, he gave it another thought and tried to assume it was true. He was now thirty years old and a fifty year sentence would put him at around seventy something with good time, when he would be finally released. The thought of this made him chuckle a loud laughter as the C.O. returned to take him back to his cell before Bond hearing.

Back in his cell, he had about another hour to rest and think about a way out of this dilemma and violating the code of the streets by snitching, was not going to be a part of it.

Thirty minutes later, Risky was let out of his cell to join the rest of the inmates going to court in the holding cell. Fifteen minutes later he was cuffed and shackled, along with the other inmates and transported to the Federal courthouse in downtown Baltimore.

The ride was only about ten minutes long. The only good news that Risky has had since he was arrested, came as soon as he sat down in the holding cell at the courthouse.

"Mr. Jackson, your attorney is waiting for you in the booth," one of the white male Marshall told him and opened the door to let him out.

Dante Jackson was cuffed once again but without the leg iron. He was uncuffed before entering the secured booth to face Mr. Warren Goldberg, who was a well known criminal defense attorney in the country. He knew then that Sherrie had done what she was taught to do in situations like this.

Alo was transported in a separate van by the U.S. Marshalls along with four other inmates also scheduled for court. Alo was kept in the next holding cell from the one that Risky was in. He also met with his attorney in the booth before court to discuss important details about the case against him.

During the meeting, Mr. John Guilick informed Alo that all his vehicles, home and U.S. Bank accounts had been frozen due to incriminating documents obtained during the raid of his residences on Epsom road and the Pent-house Condo on Allegheny avenue. Included were family pictures and Nwoke's and Mary's pictures with their names on the back. British Airways uniforms with Mary's name on them. Alo didn't know whether to commit suicide or live through the nightmare. He wasn't so much concerned about the values he had lost since he still had millions in India, Nigeria and Switzerland. Mr. Guilick was determined to make the best of the bond hearing to maintain his reputation from the publicity of the case and attract more clients.

The bald-headed lawyer, wearing an Armani suit and versace-framed glasses, looked very clean and classy as he glanced at his Rolex to check the time. The Rolex told him it was time to head upstairs to the courtroom. "See you in a few minutes in court," Guilick said and got up and motioned for the Marshall to let him out.

It took almost an hour before Alo was called by the Marshalls and escorted to the courtroom. The hearing lasted about fifteen minutes with both sides presenting their arguments in support of their claims. The prosecution contended that Alo was a flight risk since he was born in Nigeria and just had dual citizenship but, the defense countered by saying that Alo Nwanta was entitled to the same rights as any other citizen of the United States, regardless of where he was born. The Judge listened to both sides and set bail at one million dollars cash.

Risky was called two hours later and his bail was set at half a million dollars cash and collateral. The two defendants would be required to wear electronic Ankle bracelets in a home approved by the government.

Derrick, who had been paying close attention to the proceedings in the courtroom, quietly got up and left the courtroom and then exited the building to his car in the paid parking garage. He immediately picked up his cell phone and called Nwoke. Nwoke answered the phone in one ring like he was waiting for the call. "Yo, your uncle got lucky."

"You mean he's out of jail?" An excited and happy. Nwoke asked on the other end of the cell line.

"No. At least not yet but he has a chance. His bond was set at one mill, cash."

"We can handle that, can't we?"

"Of course, but we just have to figure out how because, sometimes they wait for you to post such an enormous amount of bail and then put a trace on the source, which can include a constant surveillance on the person who pa-id it," Derrick explained to his inexperienced friend.

"Oh, really? Those Feds are nothing to play with, hah?"

"Sheeeeet we've been playing with them all these years so, they can't be all that. Don't worry, I'll figure something out 'cause you guys have helped me out a lot. I gotta go now. I'm gonna let you know what I come up with."Derrick hung up the phone and started the Mercedez·420S and pulled up to the parking attendant and paid his ticket.

Nwoke was still in his pajamas when he spoke to Derrick and, after hanging up the cell phone, he got up and went to the living-room where Mary was sitting, glued to the television set which had been on CNN since their arrival in the big apple. "Hey! Uncle made bail," he said, excitedly to Mary.

"What? That's great! So, does that mean he's on his way here?" Mary asked, getting a· little excited herself.

"I'm afraid not. Derrick gotta finda way to payone million dollars in cash to the courthouse before he can be released to an approved home."

"What? That sounds complicated," Mary responded not paying attention to the television anymore.

"Not only that. He also has to wear an electronic monitor on his ankle."

"Should I tell Uma about this or not?"Mary asked, sounding disappointed at the conditions set forth for the release of Alo.

"I guess you can tell her, at least it's a step in the right direction."

Mary thought about calling Uma but then decided it was better to just walk over next door and watch her reaction.

"Uma, your husband may join us sooner than we thought," Mary told Uma as Uma opened the door and. let her in.

Uma was elated and immediately jumped up in her nightgown and gave Mary a big hug, forgetting to close the door. The two women held each other like two sisters who had just hit the lotto for thirty million."Let me close the door," Uma said and let go off the hug and. as she got to the door, a Chinese man from room service was standing, facing her in front of the open door.

"Room service. Did you order breakfast, maam?" the short Chinese man asked with a big leather insulated bag in his hand.

"Yes, I did. I'm sorry to leave you standing their. Thank you," Uma said and accepted the food the man brought out of the bag in a smaller plastic bag. She gave him a fifty dollar bill and told the man to keep the change.

"Well, let me let you eat your breakfast and feed Glenn and I'll see you later," Mary said and left the suite.

Thirty minutes later, Uma knocked on the door and Mary let her in. "Hello, Glenn," Mary said to the little boy as he walked beside her mother.

"I wanna speak to Alo and Glenn also wanna say hi," Uma said in a happy tone of voice.

Nwoke had to think fast. "Aaaaah....he doesn't have a phone yet. My friend who went to the court hearing just told me a few minutes ago."

"Oh, okay. Just let me know when he gets a phone." Uma agreed and then related the message to Glenn.

For the first time since they arrived in the city that never sleeps, Uma and Mary decided to leave the Hotel and do some shopping and sight-seeing., while Nwoke, whose picture was all over the national and world News, decided to remain at the suite for his own safety.

Forty-five minutes later, the two rich women were cleaned up and freshened up for the big apple with the little boy.

"We'll see you later, then," Mary said as they walked out of the door.

"Okay. You all be careful now, and don't forget to call me if you notice anything unusual or suspicious around," Nwoke said as Mary closed the door behind her.

Nwoke had to think fast, now. It was time for him to apply his exceptional intelligence to the current situation at hand He turned down the volume on the television set. After about thirty-five minutes of meditation, which included some prayers he'd learned from his father, the almost-twenty-two- year-old Nwoke decided to go to the lobby on the thirteenth floor and use the pay phone. He was surprised there were no pay phones at the five-star luxury Hotel. He wanted to call Uzo. He consulted his watch and the time was 1:00pm and that meant 6:00pm in London. He wondered what kind of chance he would take if he just walked outside and used a pay phone on the street or just buy some refill cards and used thepre-paid phone. He decided the chances of anyone recognizing him were too slim so, he walked briskly to the elevator and took it to the ground level and when he saw the same Bell- boy that parked the "Range rover, an idea came to his head. "Hey, buddy," he said as the black male who sounded like a Jamaican immigrant came to him.

"Yes, my good friend. What is up with you, man?" the young man asked with a smile.

Nwoke told him he wanted him to go and get him some refill cards for the brand of phone he had. The man agreed and Nwoke gave him a one hundred-dollar bill and told him to buy eighty dollar worth and bring it to his suite. The man returned fifteen minutes later and gave the cards to Nwoke who had decided to wait in front of the Hotel for him.

In his suite, Nwoke called Uzo and asked him to help him obtain four Nigerian passports under any names he chose, that matched the ages of Uma, Glenn, Mary and himself. Uzo was aware of what had transpired through the BBC network but he didn't think it had come to the point of running and he didn't ask any questions. Nwoke thought about including Alo but, something told him to wait until Derrick got him out. Uzo told him to be strong and that he would get back to him after speaking to a friend of his and Cynthia, who knew more about that kind of stuff than he did. At the mention of Cynthia, Nwoke wondered if he should have just waited for Mary to come back from shopping and sight-seeing. He gave Uzo his new cell phone number and hung up. Nwoke knew that if this could be accomplished, they would be one step ahead of the U.S. Federal agents who had now taken over the hunt for them.

Sunday came rather fast and Derrick decided to call Nwoke and tell him that the best possible means of getting the bail money to the courthouse without any trail, was to wire it to the lawyer's account from a foreign Bank account. Mr. Guilick had been rumoured to accept under-the-table large amount of money for bail when it was necessary, for a fee. Derrick decided to pay a visit to Alo at the Federal Detention center to see what he had to say. He told Alo what the plans were and Alo approved immediately without given it much thought since he was now desperate and willing to do anything that spelled freedom for him. Alo told him to find out what Risky's status was through the lawyer since he didn'tknow his real name.

"Give the girlfriend a call and find out what they are doing about his bail. If they're not doing anything, then tell Nwoke that we cannot afford to leave Risky in jail. He is the only proof that the government has against me," Alo informed. Derrick in the private visiting booth that was used by all the inmates. He also knew it wasn't bugged. He checked the small booth for bug but, saw none and Derrick did the same.

Derrick nodded that it was clear as far as he was concerned. "We probably couldn't tell even if it was. But, I. heard what you said.

"Alo thought about what Derrick had just said and expressed concern but, he knew it was too late to stop talking. "So, the lawyer said it was okay to wire the funds to his account?"

"Yes... well, he did it for a friend of mine and I don't see why he wouldn't do it for anybody else that can afford the fee," Derrick responded and studied the burgundy jumpsuit that Alo was wearing. He thanked the Lord he was on the visitor's side of the glass that divided them.

"Thanks a lot, man. Get in touch with Mr. Guilick as soon as you can and take care of that through Nwoke."

Derrick nodded in agreement as he avoided saying anything through the receiver mouth-piece.

"Okay, you have a safe trip, back home and, please always watch your back. I wish I did." Alo hung up the receiver and Derrick left. The C.O. later came and escorted him back to his cell.

Derrick got in his car and called Mr. John Guilick from his car phone to make an appointment to discuss the details of the money transfer. Mr. Guilick told him to come to his Baltimore office in downtown, Baltimore where he would be all day Monday.

Early monday morning, by 9:00am, Derrick was in John Guilick's office. First, he asked for Risky's real name and status and Guilick gave it to him and also informed him that Alo and Risky were now co-defendants based on mitigating circumstances. The high-priced attorney then told him the total amount of the remittance would have to be the dollar equivalence of one million and thirty thousand dollars. Derrick had no choice but to agree to the terms set by the attorney since there was no other means feasible. He took the account number and Risky's information and left the office.

It only took Derrick fifteen minutes to get to Sherrie's house in East Baltimore after speaking to her on the phone. Sherrie told him that they had made arrangements for Risky's bond.

"Can you please have him give me a call when he does get out?" Risky asked Sherrie as he was leaving the house.

"Of course and thank you," Sherrie agreed and closed the door behind Derrick.

After accomplishing all that he wanted to, Derrick found Nwoke's latest pre-paid phone number and tried to reach him with the good news since there was no other means as fast. He updated Nwoke on the status of everything and gave him the Bank account information with the total amount to be transferred that included the 3% fee of 30,000.00 for the temporary release of Alo Nwanta.

In London, at the newly purchased one million pound home, the new-born baby was crying for some similac which her mother, Cynthia, quickly attended to. Uzo had made several calls to people he knew in high places to see if there was a faster way of getting the passports but, in the end, he resorted to his wife, Cynthia. Uzo had tried to avoid getting Cynthia involved as she had now turned over a new leaf from the life of crime and became a born-again Christian. Giving birth to a bouncing baby girl played a big in Cynthia's repentance. But, at the same time, she was ready to ask for forgiveness if it involved helping her best friend with whom she'd been through so much with.

"Well, my ex-boyfriend still works for British Airways and I'm sure he still has some very good connections all over, including some people at Nigeria Airways," Cynthia told Uzo as she fed the baby her bottle.

"Your ex-boyfriend?" Uzo wasn't too happy about that as he responded with a jealous tone to his voice.

Cynthia looked at him, surprised at his sudden expression "I know you can't be jealous after all those girls you told me about in Aba, including the twins," she said as her eyes waited for the expression on Uzo's face to change.

"Yeah, that's right. I told you about my ex's but you never told me about your former co-worker, so where's he now?"

"I just told you. He still works there."

"How do you know? So, you must still talk' to him."

Cynthia placed the baby in her crib as she had fallen asleep. "Uzo, can you please stop? Don't forget that I still talk to my female friends who are still employed there and they tell me what's going on with who and, he just so happens to be dating one of them, if you care to know. Now, does that make you happy?" She walked up to Uzo who was sitting down on the couch and face, up close, staring into his eyes which now showed defeat.

Uzo dropped the subject and refocused on getting his best friend out of the U.S., safely and he knew he wasn't going to achieve it by arguing about his wife's past."Can you find out how to get Nigerian passports in different names, under the table, ASAP?" he asked, without looking at her.

Cynthia decided to sit next to her jealous husband. "For who?"

"Nwoke, Mary and some others. They need to get out of the U.S. as soon as possible but, without using their names."

"Oh, my God. Let me make a call real quick. Is Mary okay? She can also do this, unless she lost the numbers," Cynthia said and got up to get the phone.

"I really don't think she's in a position to do so right now for one reason or another, but I didn't ask. Just make the call and ask questions later," Uzo said, firmly, turning his head to look at Cynthia to make sure she did what she was supposed to do.

Cynthia took the cordless phone and went to the bedroom and retrieved her small telephone book. She found the number she needed and dialed, putting the cordless phone on speaker so that Uzo won't think otherwise. The man answered and she blushed with a smile and Uzo noticed this but didn't say a word. Cynthia told the man what she was calling for without much chit-chatting and he put her on hold. The man came back on the phone two minutes later and told her he would have to call her back and Cynthia hung up and waited. She didn't want to go back to where Uzo was until she got an answer from the man. Ten minutes later the phone rang and Cynthia answered. "Hello."

"Hey, Cynthia. I can have that ready for you in three days since you're in London. I gotta go to Nigeria and get it."

"Great! Thanks."

"How's your husband and the new baby?"

"They're fine and how's your girlfriend?"

"What girlfriend?"

"You don't think I know. But, anyway, try to do that for me as soon as you can and I'll talk to you later." Cynthia cut the conversation short, since Uzo was listening and she didn't want him to get jealous again for no reason.

"That's great. I heard," Uzo responded.

The phone rang again and Cynthia answered in one ring. "Hello."

"Yes, it's me again. I forgot to tell you. How soon can you have the pictures? You hung up so fast that I didn't get a chance to finish."

"Probably in a day or two," Cynthia answered, looking at Uzo to see if he had any input but none came.

"The sooner the better." The man hung up.

"I gotta call Uzo and see if they can send the pictures today," Uzo said and took the phone from Cynthia. He consulted the Wall-clock and it showed 6:55pm, which meant about 1:55pm in Eastern part of the U.S., where he hoped Nwoke and co, were. He called Nwoke but the prepaid phone was no longer in. service, so he hung up. He wondered what happened to his childhood friend. He then turned to Cynthia."Nwoke's cell phone is off, but I'm sure he's gonna call. While we're waiting, can you call the man back and ask him if the passports can be delivered directly to JFK or any Airport in the U.S.?"

"That sounds like a good idea," Cynthia agreed and took the phone from Uzo to make the call.

The time in New York city was 7:55pm and Nwoke realized that he'd given Uzo enough time to make the inquiry on the passports, so he got up and walked to the dining table and picked his new pre-paid phone and called

Uzo. Uzo told him to send the pictures as soon as possible and. that it would take three days thereafter.

"Okay, I'll get them together and take some pictures. How much is that gonna cost total?" Nwoke asked on the international line.

"Well, don't worry about that. Just get the passport photographs to us the fastest way you can," Uzo responded.

"Thanks, buddy. I'll let you know when it's on the way. Your address is still the same right?"

"You mean the new place we just bought a few months ago?"

"Yes. Not the apartment or your father's house."

"Yes, use that address. I didn't even think you had it." Nwoke said goodbye and hung up the phone. He told Mary to get Uma and the bay ready so that they could go and take a professional passport photograph.

Thirty minutes later, they were ready and Nwoke was a little hesitant about being seen in public but, since he hadn't shaved in a few days, he figured he could just put on a New York Yankees baseball cap and take it off when he takes the picture. The plan worked and they followed the direction of the Jamaican Bell-boy and went to the camera shop two blocks from the Hotel and took the pictures.

When they returned, Mary went straight to her bedroom, now feeling like things were getting better. Nwoke sat in the living-room, watching CNN. When Mary didn't come out in ten minutes, he wondered if she was angry at something so, he decided to find out. He got up and walked into Mary's room and as he moved closer to the bed, he saw her clothes laying on the floor and his heart skipped a beat. He wondered what had happened as she was nowhere to be found. Nwoke, slowly moved toward the open bathroom door and as he got closer, he could hear the shower running and his mind became at ease when he saw her shadow through the showerscreen. She appeared to be playing with her breasts and Nwoke immediately thought about joining her since they had not made love in a few days but something told him not to. His manhood kept telling him the opposite as he watched his beautiful girlfriend play with the important organs of her female body. He ripped his clothes off and opened the shower door and stepped inside the steaming hot water.

"I was wondering how long it was gonna take you to come in and go inside me," Mary said and kissed her younger lover and husband-to-be. Nwoke kissed her back with a burning desire for more as she surrendered her yearning body to his thirsty mouth.

After about thirty minutes in the shower, they finally came out and dried their exhausted bodies.

"I wonder if you could have handled all this," Nwoke commented as they came back into the living-room.

"Of course, if all that Cynthia did was call some of our former co-workers but you never asked me. Anyway, what's the difference, perhaps it's safer that way."

"Oh yeah, come to think of it....maybe it is. You think you can get the pictures to them faster through the flight?"

"Now, let me see." Mary thought for a few seconds. "I think I could. Let me make a call first." Mary walked over to the phone after figuring it was safe to call British Airways without giving out any incriminating information. She dialed the 1-800 number and asked for the JFK office. She spent about ten minutes on the phone before finally connecting to someone she was familiar with. Mary avoided going into detail about anything. She used Cynthia's name as a former employee since the feds may have contacted her former employer for information. She told them that she had some pictures to get to Heathrow rightaway. They told her that they had a flight leaving that night. "Thanks," Mary said and hung up.

"Sounds like good news to me," Nwoke said after overhearing the conversation.

"Yes. Call Cynthia and tell her I'm using her name to send the pictures through one of our co-workers from Ghana stationed at JFK."

"Okay," Nwoke said and called Uzo on the prepaid phone and handed the phone to Mary.

After speaking with Cynthia for about two minutes, she hung up.

"How are we gonna get to the Airport?" Mary asked.

"That's not a problem. We're not driving. The taxi is available and I'll aske my Jamaican connection downstairs. Are you ready my love?" The heated sex made Nwoke feel much better.

"Just give me a few minutes. youngin"Mary said with a seductive smile as she walked to her bedroom, feeling like things were getting back to normal. She came back out five minutes later wearing a Versace dress and a Gucci leather coat and boots. "We don't need Uma, do we?"

"Nah. You look good. I see you did some interesting shopping. We'll just tell Uma on our way out. Shall we go?" Nwoke took Mary's hand and walked out of the suite.

Mary told Uma at the door while Nwoke waited. After that, the couple went downstairs, Nwoke still wearing his baseball cap and now, some glasses with a Ralph Lauren frame. They told the Jamaican Bell-boy to get them a reliable yellow cab and he did so. They got in the back of the taxi and Nwoke told the driver he was gonna need a personal cab driver on call. The Dominican cab driver agreed and gave Nwoke his card.

The taxi pulled up to the British Airways terminal at JFK forty minutes later and Mary got out while Nwoke remained in the cab with the driver.

Mary quickly walked into the Airport and went straight to the British Airways check-in counter. There was no one in the line since the next flight wasn't till 11:00pm.

"Can I help you, maam?" the young man working behind the ticketing and check-in counter asked as he studied the expensive looking Mary, standing before him.

Mary explained who she was, giving him Cynthia's name and why she was there. She passed the envelope with the passport photos over the counter. The young white clerk studied the name on the envelope and as he did so, Mary reached inside her Coach pocket-book and placed a fifty dollar bill on the counter, studying the man who couldn't have been more than twenty-two years of age.

"Thank you so much," Mary said and then turned and headed for the door but, before she could take a few steps, the young man called her.

"Hey, maam!" the clerk yelled, coming from behind the counter.

Mary turned to see if he was calling for her. When she saw the young man almost standing right next to her, she answered. "Yes?"

"Please. take my card." the man said, obviously impressed by Mary's generosity.

Mary accepted the card and said thank you and turned and exited the building to meet Nwoke. Something told her that the white man liked black females. One minute later, she joined Nwoke in the cab with the meter still running. "Done." She said as she sat down, next to Nwoke.

"Wonderful, my beautiful one. Give me a kiss,"Nwoke said and kissed Mary on the lips and told the driver to take them back to the Hotel.

The happy cab driver obeyed his rich passenger and pulled the Chevy Caprice Yellow cab out of the curbside onto the main flow of Airport traffic.

The cab pulled up at the Hotel thirty-five minutes laterand Nwoke paid the two hundred and twenty dollar fare plus a fifty dollar tip to the driver and left the cab, followed by Mary. The two of them waved at the driver as he pulled off.

"If you want, you can go on up. I wanna call Uzo and dad from the phone booth," Nwoke said as they walked into the first floor of the hotel.

"That's okay, I'll wait, I want to talk to Cynthia, anyway."

Nwoke asked the Bell-boy where the closest phone booth was and he pointed down the street and they went there. There were five phone booths and a subway station at the same location so, Nwoke gave Mary one cloned credit card.

"Use this to call Cynthia while I call Uzo. It's not a good idea for you to just stand there while I use the phone," Nwoke said and stepped inside the booth with another cloned visa that Alo had given him. "Inside the booth, Nwoke dialed Uzo's number and waited. Five seconds later, Uzo answered the international call. "Hey, it's me and it's leaving tonight on the 11:00pm flight and since it's a six-hour flight, it should arrive Heathrow about 5:00am our time which is 10:00am London time, right?" Nwoke analyzed.

Uzo agreed on the other end of the international line and the two friends said goodbye and hung up.

Next, Nwoke swiped the credit card again and called Nigeria. The international phone line at Rev. Nwanta's church compound residence in Aba rang for about twenty seconds before a little boy's voice came on the line. The voice sounded like a mature little John, his younger brother who was now sixteen-years old.

"Hello, hello, hello," the voce said repeatedly.

"Hello, is this you, John?" Nwoke asked.

"Yes, Nwoke?"

"Yup and why do you sound so grown? How tall are you now?"

"Almost six feet. I'm sixteen."

"Yeah, right. Please get dad on the phone, little boy."

"How tall are, again? Have you grown since you went to the 'states?"

"I said get off the phone and put mom or dad on. I don't have time for games right now."

The seriousness in Nwoke'svoice sent little John running on the other end of the line. Rev. Nwanta's voice followed about two minutes later.

"How are you, my son?" the deep voice of the Holy man asked over the international line.

"I'm fine. How's everyone?"

"Good. Ada just got engaged and getting ready to get married but, no date has been set, yet."

That wasn't what Nwoke wanted to hear at the moment but, he wished his older sister luck. "Any news happening over there?" Nwoke wanted to know if the word had reached home and it had.

"You know there's news. Where are you right now? I know where Alo is and I'm very disappointed in him. He was supposed to be a role model...."

Nwoke cut the Rev. off. "Dad, I'm sorry. I should've listened to you and Mom but, it's too late now and I'm coming home."

"How? According to the Newspaper article, you're wanted by the U.S. Marshalls and their job is to find you. I'm just going to have to pray for you and who's the girl, Mary?"

Nwoke looked outside to see if Mary had finished talking to Cynthia but she hadn't. "I'll explain later. We're gonna get married and she has a degree in Nursing from my school."

"Okay, just be prayerful and have faith so that my prayers will work."

"Say hello to everybody and tell them I'll be home soon." Nwoke hung up the phone and just stood there inside the booth, wondering what Mary's reaction was going to be when she finds out that her picture was now in the News. He then wondered what kind of impact the unfortunate situation had created for the family. But, they'd been watching CNN since they got to New York so, when was the broadcast made? He figured that the Marshalls were probably targeting the country of origin first before the U.S. For the very first time since coming to America, Nwoke regretted travelling abroad.

The knocking on the booth glass broke his thought and he stepped out of the phone booth and joined the latest fugitive on the Marshall's most wanted list.

Ten minutes later in the living-room of the suite, Nwoke realized that this situation created by greed had become larger than it seemed. He continued to watch the

Mike Manley

News on CNN but, nothing so, he decided it was better not to let Mary know since her picture was only being shown in West Africa. But, then all of a sudden, breaking News on CNN as they paid attention.

"THE NEWS HAS JUST REACHED CNN THAT THERE IS A FOURTH SUSPECT ALSO AT LARGE WITH THE WANTED SUSPECTS. THIS IS A WOMAN AND POSSIBLE GIRLFRIEND OF THE WANTED MAN," they showed Mary's picture and her full name as it appeared on the flight attendant uniform.

Mary's heart dropped but, when she realized it was only a matter of time before the feds put it all together, she calmed down. She thought about the lavish life-style they had exhibited by building such expensive mansion in Nwoke's village within a short period of time and shipping all those luxury vehicles. Nwoke was probably the talk of the village and she was probably the talk of the town she came from in Liberia called Monrovia. To make matters worst, they even hired a German architectural company to construct the mansion in Nwoke's village which was named 'Nwoke's villa'. A caretaker was also employed to take care of the property while they were not there. At least Nwoke was able to disguise his looks by growing a beard and wearing reading glasses but, what was she gonna do to disguise her appearance? "Nwoke's voice interrupted her thoughts.

"What's for dinner, baby. Don't worry about them, you're gonna be just fine. We'll send Uma to get you a wig and some glasses tomorrow, okay? It won't be that much longer and we'll be out of here," Nwoke reassured her.

"Thanks but, I'd rather you do the ordering tonight," Mary responded. Dinner was the only thing that was ordered at least four hours in advance.

"Okay, no problem." Nwoke picked up the menu from the coffee table and started looking through it.

"Anyway, what did your father say?" Mary asked, trying to take her mind away from the current situation.

"Well, I'm the bad apple of the family, if you really wanna know."

"Is that what he said? Well, I know he had to ask about me."

"Drop the subject. He knows everything about all of us. The news got there before we saw it on CNN. Believe it or not."

"I think they might even have all the pictures at all the international Airports. Who'sgonna transfer the money to the lawyer's account tomorrow?"

"I'm gonna have Uzo handle that." Nwoke finished ordering dinner and called Uzo on the prepaid cell and gave him the lawyer's information and Bank account number.

The two fugitives sat there and wondered how much time they had before the U.S. Marshalls found them.

Risky's girlfriend, Sherrie, waited outside the Federal Detention Center on Madison street, near downtown Baltimore, with Jay-Z's 'You can't knock the hustler' blasting in the white Range rover. She was parked on the street since she had no need to go on the main parking lot. She'd been waiting for about twenty minutes and still there was no sign of Risky so, she decided to step out of the SUV and walk up to the front entrance of the Detention center and ask how much longer it before Dante Jackson was released. She turned the stereo off and stepped out of the expensive vehicle, Sherrie stood about 5'8", honey-coded complexion smooth skin and pretty face. She had just got her hair done at her salon and it looked very attractive over the diamond earrings. Her Coach pocket-book matched the color of her white boots. The temperature outside was about 30° on this cold Winter day and she wore a navy blue Gucci suit that fit her curvaceous body as she walked to the security booth of the maximum security Detention center. She asked about Dante Jackson and the Correctional officer inside the booth told her he couldn't be specific as to what time but, he would be in a van when he did come out under escort. Sherrie turned around, feeling disgusted as she walked back to the SUV.

Sherrie's mother, Ms. Washington, had posted bail the Saturday after the hearing, giving up the deed to her home and putting up additional one hundred and fifty thousand dollars to cover the half a million dollar bond since the value of her home was only three hundred and fifty thousand dollars. Money was not an issue as Risky had millions spread out all over the country in Sherrie's name and her mother's. Risky's mother died when he was only twelve years old and he never knew who his father was. Risky was the only child and he began hustling at the tender age of thirteen years. But, still he managed to complete High School and attend Morgan State University for three years before doing his first bid in the State system. He never went back to finish.

Two hours after Sherrie parked on Madison street to pick up her boy-friend, Risky, at exactly 1:10pm, a navy blue van with pitch-black tinted windows, pulled out of the side gated entrance of the Red-brick building, but Sherrie couldn't see the occupants until they turned and headed toward her, stopping beside the Range rover. The front windows came down and a white male who was driving, asked her to follow them and pulled off without giving her a chance to respond. She figured that Risky must have told them who she was. Sherrie couldn't understand why they were taking him to the house when she was there just to do that; if she'd known, she wouldn't have wasted her time coming. The van turned left on the next street and then about three more blocks, made another left and headed East on Monument street.

It only took about fifteen minutes to arrive at Ms Washington's home at 2021 Morgan street in East Baltimore. This was an upper-class neighborhood, consisting of Doctors, Lawyers and successful business tycoons. The houses were so far apart that the neighbors couldn't see what went on in the house next door. Since the Marshalls wore navy blue Polo shirts and khaki pants, one couldn't really tell they were members of the federal law enforcement community.

"You go ahead and open the door first, maam," one of the Marshalls said as the three of them stood by Risky on the porch of the big home.

Sherrie rushed past them, nervous and uncomfortable around the federal agents, not even looking at Risky and put the keys in the door-knob, decoded the alarm system and then turned and pushed the heavy Mahogany door open and entered the house. "You can all come in now," she said, holding the door and stepping back as the three U.S. Marshalls escorted Risky into the house.

Inside the very well furnished living-room, one of the Marshalls uncuffed Risky and ordered him to sit down while another one reached inside a black duffle bag that was obviously issued by the government and took out a round plastic object that could be an Ankle bracelet and told Risky to lift his left leg up. Risky did so and he put the bracelet around Risky's left ankle and then snapped it, after adjusting it to the size of his ankle. The Marshall then pressed a button to activate it and the object produced a beep-beep-beep sound. The third Marshall, then reached inside the same duffle bag and gave Sherrie a small booklet and also gave one to Risky. He then had both Risky and Sherrie's mother sign a two-page contract.

"This doesn't implicate me in anyway does it?"Ms. Washington asked after signing the contract.

"Not if you do what it says, so take your time and read over it. That's why we tell you to read it before signing, maam." the third Marshall explained.

Ms. Washington took the paper and went back upstairs, knowing that the worst that can happen is for her to lose the home that her daughter and her boy-friend had bought her.

"We hope we don't have to see you before trial, sir," the Marshall who drove the van warned and lead the other two out of the house.

"Hey honey, I missed you," Risky said, happily as he put the 'Rules and Regulation' booklet down and stood up to hug his girlfriend.

"Oh, I missed you, too," she responded, passionately and kissed him back.

Uzo called Nwoke at 4:00am in the morning, Eastern U.S. standard time to get the Lawyer's LLC name as requested by the Bank in London. Nwoke went to his room and got the information from his Carryon and read it to Uzo over the international line.

"Okay, let me go back inside and try again," Uzo said and hung up.

Nwoke knew then that Uzo must have been calling from the Bank. He laid back down and went back to sleep.

Thirty minutes later, Nwoke'scell phone rang again and it was Uzo calling to confirm the remittance of the 1.3 million dollars to Mr. John Guilick's law firm account. He also informed Nwoke that the Bank manager said that the funds would be available in the U.S. within forty-eight hours. The conversation lasted about three minutes and Uzo wished him luck and hung up the phone. Nwoke laid back again and tried to go back to sleep, hoping that was the end of the early morning conversation.

Nwoke and Mary slept until about 9:30am, even though, Nwoke had a hard time going back to sleep after the back-to-back calls from Uzo.

"Uzo called last night....well, I mean early this morning to tell me he had remitted the money to the Lawyer's account," Nwoke informed Mary as they lay there, looking at the ceiling. This was the second time they slept in the same bed since they checked into the hotel.

"So, we just have to write him a check on the London account."

"Well, that's in your name so, whenever you get a chance.

"And how much is gonna be left when the check clears?" Mary asked the Business major.

Nwoke thought for about thirty five seconds. "About three million pounds, which is approximately six million dollars."

"You think he'll be out sometime today?"

"Nah, it takes about forty-eight hours for the money to reflect on the U.S. account. So, I'm thinking maybe sometime tomorrow or even Thursday; but no later than Friday. Give and take," Uzo explained.

The ringing of the cell phone interrupted the conversation between the two lovers on the run from the law.

"Hello," Nwoke answered in a deep, early morning voice, just like somebody who just woke up.

Derrick was on the other end of the cell phone line. "Hey, Risky's girlfriend just called me and I spoke to him. He was released yesterday afternoon on some kind of Home detention. Should I give him your number?"

"I don't think that's a good idea. Don't the feds have to monitor him till the trial?"

"Yes, I just asked, that's all. What else is happening?"

"The money should be in the lawyer's account tomorrow or next, but, do you think it might be possible to get him out before then?"

"couldn't speculate. I'd have to find out from the lawyer himself to see if he's willing to put up the money and then, just replace it when it finally shows up in his account. But, I seriously doubt that he will since Nigerians got so much up their sleeves. I wouldn't do it."

"Try, anyway. So, they're gonna monitor him just like Risky?"

"I think that's what Mr. Guilick said. The only difference is that they are at home, instead of jail."

With that last statement by Derrick, Nwoke wondered how in the world his uncle planned to escape the forces that be and join them in the big apple.

CHAPTER FIFTEEN

The 1.3 million dollars did not reflect on John Guilick's law firm account until Thursday morning, December the 22nd, one day before Nwoke's first day and three days before Christmas. Nwoke was depressed about having to spend Christmas and his twenty second birthday as a fugitive. Who said selling drugs was a good business?

Derrick was about to pick up the phone and call John Guilick when it rang. "Hello," he answered on the first ring.

"Hello, Mr. Richard and how are you this morning?" John Guilick asked on the other end of the line.

"I'm fine, Mr. Guilick. Can you hold on for a second please?" Derrick rushed to the door to kiss Rita and give her a goodbye hug as she left for the office. Then he returned to the phone. "Okay, I'm back. What's up?"

"The bond for your friend, Ale Nwanta has been posted. Since he's gonna be staying in your home till trial, the court requires that you go down to the courthouse and sign some papers. After that, it could take up to twenty-four hours before he's finally released to you."

Derrick's heart skipped a beat at the mention 'released to him'. He wondered if the whole arrangement was a good idea, after all. He didn't want to be responsible for a foreigner who may decide to skip town and the country at any time. "Does that mean I would be held accountable for his whereabouts?"

"It all depends on what you mean by that. You can't play security guard to the man but, you do have to provide the shelter he needs till court date. Besides, he will be wearing an electronic ankle monitoring device, if that makes you feel any better."

Derrick's mind became at ease at the mention of electronic monitoring device. "Okay, then sir. I'm on my way to the court house now and I'll let you know if I have any more questions," Derrick hung up the phone and called Nwoke immediately with the good news.

"Hello," Nwoke answered on the first ring as if he'd been expecting the call from the familiar number.

"Hey, I'm glad you haven't changed the phone yet. But, uuum I just got off the phone with Alo's lawyer and he said the bond has been secured."

"Thank you so much, Derrick. I'm so glad Mary and I took the initiative to meet you based on our instincts," Nwoke said on the other end of the long distance line, excitedly.

"I gotta go down to the courthouse and sign some papers and give them the· address of my house. I wonder why the lawyer didn't do that? But, anyhow. he said that Alo would be wearing an electronic monitoring system on his ankle just like I told you."

"Well, let me not hold you up. I wanna find out more about this device your talking about," Nwoke said and got off the phone.

Derrick decided to drive to his grand mother's house first before he going to the courthouse. He got there in about twenty five minutes and asked her if a friend of his could stay at her house until he went to court but, the old woman refused as she asked Derrick if he had lost his mind. Derrick thought about other ideas on his way to the courthouse but, nothing else seemed tangible so, he drove directly to the courthouse. He signed the papers and provided all the necessary information requested and went back home. The clerk told him that the U.S. Marshalls would be transporting Alo to the residence on file at the federal courthouse. They would be contacting Derrick before they left the Detention center.

On his way home, Derrick thought about the current situation and analyzed its implications and came to the conclusion that he really had nothing to be afraid of. He was a responsible citizen with a legitimate business that paid taxes. Most of all he wan't currently involved in anything that would jeopardize his freedom and Rita's. Half way home, he changed his mind and decided to go to the office instead and let Rita know what was about to happen. Rita was fine with the idea since it was just one person and more than enough space. The house was a seven hundred thousand dollar home in the Randallstown area of Baltimore county. It had seven bedrooms, a family room, living room, two kitchens and four bathrooms with a three-car garage and a big back-yard, all sitting on a five-acre piece of land.

Ten minutes after Derrick sat down in his office, his cellphone rang and he looked at the LCD but didn't recognize the number. He decided to answer it anyway since there was nothing to fear. "Hello."

Risky was on the line. "Yo, it's Risky, what's up?"

"Hey, what's been happening, my nig?I hope you're enjoying your freedom."

Risky asked him when he was going to stop by so they could talk. Risky wasn't too comfortable talking on the phone. Derrick told him he would try and stop by in about twenty minutes since he wasn't doing anything. Risky said that was fine and hung up the phone.

Derrick drove to Sherrie mother's house in East Baltimore twenty five minutes after talking to Risky. He parked the Bentley on the street in front of 2021 Morgan street in East Baltimore and got out. He walked to the door, looking up and down the street to make sure he wasn't being followed. Satisfied there were nothing unusual in the upper-class neighborhood, he pressed the door-bell and waited. About three minutes later, the door opened and Sherrie stood in the doorway.

"You must be Derrick, come in," Sherrie said, studying the handsome young man before her.

Derrick went in. "Yes, I am and you must be Risky's girlfriend, Sherrie, right?"

"Yes." Sherrie looked at the Bentley and then stepped back inside and closed the door. "How are you?"

"Fine and yourself?"

"Good now that Risky is home. Let me get'm," Sherrie said and disappeared in the back of the elegantly furnished home of Ms. Washington.

Derrick got comfortable and walked over to the window and surveyed the street once more to make sure nothing pulled up after he came inside. He then went to the back window and looked out at the big back-yard.

He saw four luxury vehicles parked that looked like they hadn't been driven in months as they were covered by ice. They included Mercedes CLK drop-top BMW 745, Jeep Grand Cherokee Limited and Infiniti Q45.

Risky emerged from the back in his shorts and Derrick noticed the black ankle bracelet on his left ankle. "What up Derrick?" Risky asked, startling Derrick who was still studying the object on Risky's ankle, wondering if it had a secret camera and microphone in it.

"I'm sorry. You're Risky, right?"

"Yes."

"I thought you were from Edmonson avenue on the West side." Derrick didn't want to give him the impression that he was also a drug dealer that just hadn't been caught, yet.

"Of course I am but, I also stay at my girlfriend's. This is her mother's house. My house is in Virginia," Risky lied.

"So, what did you want to talk to me about?"

"How long you've known Alo and when is he getting out?"

"Hey, sherrie, can I get a paper and pen?" Derrick no longer felt comfortable talking in the house so he wanted to start communicating by writing.

Risky looked at him, wondering what that was all about. Sherrie brought a paper and a pencil promptly. Derrick wrote something down and gave it to Risky. Risky read it and wrote something in response. They went back and forth a few times and Sherrie went upstairs and came down five minutes later and gave Derrick an envelope with his passport photograph in it.

Derrick learned that Risky had attended Morgan State University with Alo and that was how they met. During that time Risky dated a few Nigerian women and fell in love with the country. He now felt this was the time to go there and learn more about his motherland.

"It was nice knowing you all and I'll see you two later," Derrick said and left.

Sherrie approved of the idea if at all Alo was thinking the same thing. She wrote that she would rather know that Risky was in another country than serving a twenty or thirty year sentence in a Federal prison. After that, Risky and Sherrie started talking again, making sure they only discussed normal things that were not incriminating.

Derrick drove off slowly, glancing at the high priced homes on the street, making sure there was nothing unusual going on with the neighbors since the feds were known to use neighbors to plant certain surveillance equipments. About one mile into the main road, which lead to North avenue., Derrick checked his rear view mirror once again for any tail and when he saw no steady tail of a vehicle, he stepped on the gas pedal of the Bentley and joined I-83 ramp which would take him to I-695 West since he hadn't planned on returning to the office.

Nwoke's birthday passed without any celebration except a happy birthday wish from Mary when they woke up. They continued to anticipate the release of Alo from detention and Uma was beginning to get impatient as Mary felt Alo was holding her up. The couple argued back and forth, but not too seriously. Mary wanted to leave as soon as the passports were ready while Nwoke and Uma insisted on waiting for Alo. Their debate was interrupted by the ringing of Nwoke's cell phone.

Derrick called and told him that Risky gave him his passport photograph so that he could follow them to Nigeria if that was the plan.

"Did you tell him that was the plan?" Derrick asked, wondering how in the world Risky knew.

"No. He came up with the idea. I guess he knew. I don't know about that. Alo isn't gonna leave me with trouble from the feds, is he?"

"Of course not. Look, you talk to him when he gets out but, hold on to the picture till then. Talk to you later." Nwoke hung up the phone. Before he could tell Mary what was happening, the cell phone rang again and he answered in one ring. "Hello."

Uzo was on the international line. He told Nwoke that the passports arrived the night before through a different Airline but that the envelope was still delivered to the same connection at British Airways. Uzo told them to go and pick up the envelope the same way Mary delivered the pictures. Nwoke asked him if he got the check and Uzo said yes and the two friends hung up the phones, avoiding long conversation.

Nwoke called Uma in the next room and asked her to go and get Mary a wig and glasses and Uma agreed. Nwoke came back into the bedroom and tapped Mary on the shoulder to wake up.

"What's the problem?" Mary asked, still sleepy.

"Uzo said the passports are here so we gotta go get it. Get ready because Uma is gonna get your wig and glasses."

Mary immediately got up and went to her room to get ready while Nwoke did the same.

They were both dressed and ready in thirty minutes and were now waiting for Uma to return with the wig and glasses. Uma knocked on the door fifteen minutes later and gave Mary the disguise materials. Mary put them on right there in the living room of the suite.

"So, what do think, Glenn?" Mary asked, looking down at little Glenn who had no idea of what she was talking about.

"You could have fooled me," Uma commented, approving the disguised Mary.

Nwoke nodded and said: "let's go. We've wasted enough time already."

The two disguised fugitives left the hotel suite, feeling very confident of themselves while Uma returned to her room with her baby. While they were in the elevator, Nwoke tried to call the Dominican cab driver that took them to the Airport but he couldn't get any reception so, he waited till he was downstairs. When they got to the front of the building, Nwoke asked the Jamaican Bell-boy to get him the Dominican cabbie and the Bell boy did so. The cabbie arrived fifteen minutes later and they got in and left for the Airport.

As they sat in the back of the cab, Mary remembered that the clerk at the British Airways had given her a card. She went into her pocket-book and retrieved the card and called him. As she waited for someone to answer the phone, Mary noticed that the cab driver was looking at her strangely. This made her more comfortable, knowing that the disguise must have worked.

"Hello, is this David?" Mary asked as the operator sounded like the young white male who'd given her the card.

"No. it's not, maam but, if you'll hold on, I'll transfer you to him." The line was quiet for about one minute and then David's voice came on the line.

"David Thompson, can I help you?"

"Yes, David. This is Mary, remember I gave you an envelope a few days ago?"

"Oh, yeah. How are you? I didn't think you would ever call," the B.A. clerk said, obviously misunderstanding Mary's purpose for calling.

Mary wanted to be nice, even though Nwoke was listening and probably wondering what in the world was going on between her and the attendant. "Yes my dear. Can you check to see if I have any envelopes waiting from the same person you gave mine to."

The clerk placed her on hold for about four minutes and then told her he had the envelope in his hand.

"Thank you, I'll be there to pick it up, see you in a few, sweetie." Mary hung up and told Nwoke to keep quiet before he even uttered a word.

Nwoke obediently agreed and faced the road ahead, looking at the cabbie to make sure he wasn't paying them any attention. "What's up, my man?" he asked the cabbie.

"Nothing. I see you have a new girl,,, hah?"

Nwoke thought for about one minute and looked at Mary, smiled and then agreed with the cabbie.

The ride to JFK lasted about forty minutes from the hotel. The cab pulled up in front of the British Airways terminal sign and Mary got out while Nwoke decided to wait in the cab with the meter running.

"See you in a few, sweetie," Mary said as she walked away, turning her swagger on to make things a little easier on the nice clerk who obviously had a crush on her. She walked into the Airport and straight to the counter with only two customers in line. David was attending to one of the customers while a female clerk was attending to the other. Five minutes later, her turn came and she approached the familiar clerk with a smile. "Hello, my dear David."

David looked up at her and returned the smile. "How may I help you today, maam?" he asked, not recognizing Mary.

Mary just stared at the young adult who was probably Nwoke's age. "Yes, I'm Cynthia and I came for the envelope, remember?"

"Oh, mine! You've changed overnight. I mean...you look very different from the last time I saw you."

"Yeah, that's because I got a new hair-style and I need my glasses to read what's in that envelope."

"Wow, you still look so beautiful but, more professional," David commented and reached behind the counter and gave Mary the envelope.

Mary took the envelope and said thank you. She then reached inside her pocket-book and handed him another fifty dollar bill and smiled. "Be good now and give me a call sometime, okay?"

"Okay, Cynthia. You can bet on that," David said and continued to watch Mary as she walked away.

Just before she got to the revolving doors, Mary opened the manila envelope and looked inside to make sure the passports were there and they were. Three minutes later, she was in the cab. "Got it," she said to Nwoke.

Nwoke's face lit up with a smile. "Let me see." Nwoke took the envelope and looked inside, then reached inside and took the passports and studied each one of them. "Driver, you can take us back to the hotel," Nwoke said and nodded to Mary with satisfaction for a job well done.

"Now, what do you think?" Mary asked, turning to look at Nwoke as she felt very important for her achievement.

"Good job and I love you, that's why you're gonna be my wife in a couple of weeks. I'm gonna call dad and tell him to start making arrangements for the wedding in a couple of weeks or even less. Nwoke kissed her on the lips and noticed the cab driver was looking through the rearview mirror.

The Dominican cab driver smiled at the rich couple as his eyes met Nwoke's and then quickly turned his head back to face the busy road ahead as he pressed a notch harder on the gas pedal.

Derrick didn't see the need to go to the Detention Center since the Marshalls were doing the transporting, instead, he decided to stay on the phone with Risky. Risky was lecturing him on how the entire process worked. The two criminals avoided discussing any incriminating topics over the phone line that could be tapped. Derrick kept checking the digital clock next to the TV set, while at the same time looking out the front window to see if there was any navy blue van outside. To his disappointment, there was nothing but the neighbor's cars and trucks. Still on the phone with Risky, he came back to the couch in the living room and sat back down when he noticed that only two minutes had passed since he last looked at the digital clock."so, what time did they finally get to your house, yo?" Derrick asked Risky.

"Oh, I can't even remember exactly but I know it was sometime in the afternoon, 'cause Sherrie waited a long time outside the joint," Risky responded on the other end of the line.

Derrick checked the clock again and it showed 1:59pm. "Yo, it's already 2. You think they're still coming?"

"Guaranteed. Them feds ain't like that. They would've let you know by now."

It wasn't until 3:35pm when the dark blue van with pitch-black tinted windows pulled up in front of Derrick's house. Derrick wondered how they found his house without calling to ask for directions like everybody else who visited him for the first time. But, when he realized who he was dealing with and the type of technology they had, he stopped wondering and quickly walked to the Mahogany door and opened it without waiting for the agents to ring the doorbell.

Alo was leading the three agents as they directed him to the house he'd never been to. He was cuffed to the back with leg-irons to hold his legs. He looked like he'd lost at least six pounds.

"Yes, please come in," Derrick said as they got to the vestibule. He stepped back inside the house to allow Alo and the three Marshalls inside.

"Where's the living-room, sir?" the Marshall directly behind Alo asked in an authoritative voice as he looked Derrick over.

Derrick closed the door after they all entered. "Please follow me." Derrick lead them to the huge livingroom.

The tall, bulky bald-headed white Marshall ordered Alo to sit down on the couch in the living-room and went through the same process as they did at Risky's house. The Marshalls finished by handing out the rules and regulations booklet to Derrick and Alo. Alo then signed some papers as well as Derrick and they left.

"Hey, welcome home, my friend. I know what you've been through. I was once in the county Detention center for the weekend and I almost died in that hell-hole," Derrick told Alo who looked relieved.

Alo got up and walked to the window to make sure that the Marshalls were really gone."Hell ain't the word. Fire is more like it. So, what's up, man? I know you've been talking to your buddy." Alo tried to avoid mentioning Nwoke's name since he didn't know if the ankle bracelet was bugged.

Derrick understood and nodded. "Yeah, he's alright. Those dudes must have had a long day, coming so late."

"Yeah, I was the last one they dropped off because you live so far out."

"All right, my man. What can I serve you? I know you haven't had a good meal in....what, say a little over a week?"

"Yeah, I think so, maybe a week," Alo said and came back to the couch, focused on the television news station. He felt his ankle and the electronic monitoring object and wondered what else was in it to stop him from taking it off. Was there some kind of explosive planted inside the device? All kinds of thoughts went through Alo's head as freedom and his family were a priority for him at the moment. He remembered the lead Marshall telling him if he goes outside the restricted perimeter, he would be in violation. He picked up the hand-book again and began reading it thoroughly. "Just order a pizza with everything on but, no anchovies. Thanks."

"My girlfriend has already prepared a delicious meal for you, sir," Derrick informed him.

"Good. I'll just eat that later but, right now, I would like a large pizza with everything but anchovies on it," Alo reiterated as he continued to study the rules and regulation governing the federal home detention program.

"Your wish is my command. I gotchu, big boss." Derrick walked over to the kitchen and picked up the cordless phone by the wall next to the refrigerator and called the pizza place and ordered the large price destroyer. He then got his prepaid cell phone and called Nwoke with the good news. Nwoke answered on the first ring, changing his voice. "Hey, wut up? Hold on for your uncle, son." Derrick gave the phone to Alo, interrupting his reading.

"Yes."Alo said into the mouth-piece. "How are Uma and Glenn?"

Nwoke was happy to tell him that his wife and baby were fine and worried about him. Alo thought about getting the number to the suite that Uma was in but changed his mind. They made sure that no names were mentioned on the phone so that if it was tapped, the feds wouldn't be able to trace anything. They spoke for about twenty minutes and, as soon as they hung up, Dominoes pizza rang the doorbell with the order.

Derrick answered the door, took the pizza and paid the delivery man. He set the large pizza on the dining table for Alo. Alo quickly went over to the dining room and devoured the large pizza with everything on it like a hungry lion who hadn't eaten in days.

After Alo ate the pizza, Derrick showed him the passport photograph that Risky had given him and then wrote something on a piece of paper, telling Alo that his partner in crime wanted to go to Nigeria and become a citizen. Alo replied in writing, telling Derrick to take a picture of him just like the one that Risky gave. Nwoke had already requested the photograph when he spoke to him on the phone, using code words. Derrick went to his room, got his camera and did as Alo asked. Alo asked him by writing, how long it was gonna take to process the pictures and Derrick responded by informing him of the latest technology at Ritz camerashop on Liberty road that did it in one hour. Alo then replied by telling Derrick to send the two pictures to his wife Uma with the hotel address by overnight mail. Alo was now feeling in control of things again after the long break in the hustling game.

Derrick stepped outside with the prepaid phone to get the address to the hotel but, before he could call Nwoke, something told him not to and he went back inside the house. He decided to wait until he got to the camera shop. He might even get another phone after talking to Nwoke on the current one. He told Alo that he would be back shortly and left the house to process the photograph. Ten minutes later, Derrick was at the camera shop. He submitted the cartridge and went next door to the Radio Shack and bought another prepaid phone and filled it up with one hundred dollars worth of minutes and called Nwoke for their address. Nwoke told him they had relocated to the Hilton and gave him that address and Uma's room number. He wrote it down on a piece of paper which he would later dispose of after sending the pictures by overnight express.

At the U.S. Customs office inside the Baltimore Washington International Airport, agents Michael Spinard and Jonathan Levitz continued to review documents that the DEA had provided them about the record of Dante Jackson and his possible link to Alo Nwanta. But, the puzzle wasn't fitting well so the two agents decided to divert their attention to documents from their co-workers who searched the two residences belonging to Alo Nwanta.

"We know now that the girl had something to do with all this but, to what extent?" Spinard asked as he scanned through some of the papers on the table.

"Well, she did do a lot of travelling but then, that was part of her job as a flight attendant. So far we have nothing showing us that she may have brought some drugs on some of those trips or did she?" Levitz attempted to analyze without success.

"Mr. Cohen got her on money laundering because of these deposit slips with her name and her boyfriend's name on them. That maybe all we have for now and if something else turns up later then, we'll pursue it."

"Okay, here's a picture with Mr. Derrick Richard. What do you make of it?" Levitz asked, looking at a college picture that Mary, Derrick and Nwoke had taken at a basketball game.

"Nothing, really. They were college buddies, that's all that says. Even if there's more to it, we don't know yet."

"Now, Mr. Cohen already went through the documents and got whatever he got. I guess we're suppose to see what we can gather, right?"

"To help our investigation and help the Marshalls find them. They ran for a reason and as soon as we find them, they just might tell us but, until that happens, we gotta do what we have to," Spinard concluded.

"Let's not forget that we have an appointment with Mr. Cohen," Levitz reminded Spinard.

"You're right and we only got twenty minutes to get there. Let's get out of here."

The two agents arrived at James Cohen's office fifteen minutes later. Cohen was known for going out of his way to put away colored offenders, especially when they were from Africa, specifically, Nigeria.

"Do we have anything in those documents that can give us a lead on where those two are?" Cohen asked as he sat in the conference room with the agents.

"No, we don't. But, we intend to ask the big brother who is in our custody to see if he can feed us any information." Spinard responded.

"Didn't you already try that? Don't do it, he has an attorney by the name of John Guilick and I'll see what kind of deal he's willing to get for his client," the prosecutor countered.

"Okay, then. How about the carriers?" Levitz asked.

"Nah, I think they told us all that they know. See, the big boss in Nigeria used different carriers for each trip and these ones in custody never met the people they were delivering to," Spinard answered while Levitz listened. They wondered if the prosecutor was satisfied with their efforts.

"Smart guy....hah. we're definitely gonna try and get his black ass. At least we know where he is in Nigeria, right?" Cohen said.

"Yes we do. We just hope he's still there."

"Okay, gentlemen, I guess that's it for now. Keep looking over the documents; sometimes you can miss things that you find later and I'll also do the same here. We got enough copies to go around the world if need be," the prosecutor looked at both agents and continued. "I want you to interact with the arresting DEA officers, Johnson and Billard for· their input regarding that Dante Jackson 'cause I believe he played a major part in all of this. Next, I want the phones at the residence where Mr. Jackson is staying tapped and placed under constant surveillance to see if there's any contact between the conspirators," Cohen finished and dismissed the agents.

"Okay sir, we'll be in touch," Spinard said as he and Levitz left the office. Three minutes later, they were at the underground parking garage for the courthouse where they had parked the van. They got in and left for their office at BWI.

Christmas was depressing for Uma, Glenn, Nwoke and Mary. Uma managed to get Glenn some toys which made the innocent little boy happy. Nwoke and Mary were preoccupied with getting out of the country so that they could be free and live like normal people. They were tired of looking over their shoulders constantly. But, the passports for Risky and Alo still had to be processed.

Derrick kept to his promise and processed the pictures on time and sent them by overnight mail and Uma received them by the following day, which was Friday and handed them over to Nwoke just as she'd been instructed to do. Mary took the pictures and did the same thing she did previously.

Nwoke wondered what the. Feds knew thus far. Due to the way they left Baltimore, he wondered just how much incriminating evidence they left behind. He then realized that the investigators had a lot of information to work with and that was how they figured that Mary was also involved. His mind just kept revolving around the same things and this bothered him as he didn't know if it was paranoia or nightmare. He picked up the newly purchased prepaid cell phone and called Derrick on his new cell. The phone rang several times and, just as he was getting ready to hang up, Derrick answered.

"Hello," Derick voice said on the other end of the line.

"It's me what's up?"

"Nothing. Did you get the pics?"

"This morning, thanks and I appreciate all you've been doing."

"Anytime. Hold on a second, I think your unc wanna speak to you." There was a two-second pause and Alo's voice came on the line.

Alo asked if Nwoke had sent the info out and when he was expecting a response. Nwoke didn't want to be specific so, he told Alo that the info would be back shortly. The code·worded conversation, mixed with Nigerian broken English ended in four minutes.

Nwoke's mind wandered over to the Rangrover that had been parked in the Hilton's garage for about a day now, since they had the Jamaican Bell-boy from the Marriot Marquis drive to the Hilton. He wondered if the registration on the tags could be a lead for the Marshalls if they just happened to get that close. An idea suddenly popped in his head and he picked up the cell again and called Derrick back so that he could ask Alo for the shipping agent's phone number but, the line was busy so he hung up. He got up and walked to his bedroom to check in his Carryon from previous receipts. He found the number and called the shipping agent to come and pick up the Range from the garage at the. Hilton. He also gave them the name and number of the Jamaican Bell-boy. After that, Nwoke called the trusted bell-boy to relate the information and he agreed to meet the shipping company tow-truck outside the hotel when scheduled. The man was more than happy as this meant more money in his pocket. The luxury SUV would be on its way to Lagos Nigeria in two weeks.

"So, you think they're gonna find them?" Derrick asked as he was getting ready to walk out the door and got to the office.

"If they don't play their cards right. It's already all over the world that they are wanted."

Derrick stepped away from the door and moved toward Alo, who was standing in the middle of the living-room. "Just what kind of trouble am I gonna be in if you skip?" Derrick now appeared to be having second thoughts about moving along with the plan.

"From what I've read and what the lawyer said, no trouble since you're not a security guard assigned to guard me. They would keep the entire bond, though and that's a lot of money."

"Oh, yeah. I think I saw something like that in that handbook, too." Derrick came back inside and placed his briefcase on the dining table and picked up the hand-book and started reading again, this time, more thoroughly.

Alo got up and got the new cell phone from Derrick, who was still reading the material from the Marshalls about the implication of violating any of the rules in the booklet. He called Risky and Sherrie answered the phone in two rings. "Hello."

"What's up, girl? Where is your husband?" Alo asked.

"I wish we were married. Is this Alo?"

"Yes, of course. I'm out." Alo tried to keep the conversation discreet with coded language so that if the house was bugged, the listeners wouldn't be able to comprehend the meaning of the it.

"I know, I heard about it. How's your family?"

Alo didn't remember Sherrie ever meeting Uma and the baby so he had to be cautious about the answer to that question. Have you seen them by any chance?"

"Nah. You don't know where they are?"

"No. She probably heard about me and took off. Let me speak to him."

"You mean......"

Alo didn't let her finish as he didn't want any names mentioned on the phone. "Yes....him."

"Hold on. I think he's down the basement."

After about three minutes, Risky came on the line. "Yo, what up?"

"Hey, I got an idea and somebody'll be right there with the message." He hung up the phone before Risky got too curious. He then went over to the dining table and got a piece of paper and pen and scribbled something down and gave it to Derrick. "As soon as you're done reading," Alo said.

Derrick finished reading the booklet five minute later and read the note for Risky. "Okay. Be right back." Derrick now felt comfortable after reading the booklet for the second time. As far as he was concerned now, Alo could go to heaven if he wanted. Derrick drove to his office and asked the secretary to call a taxi. The taxi arrived in ten minutes and he gave the driver the note in an envelope with the address on it and a fifty dollar bill. The Russian cab driver smiled and took the envelope from him.

Twenty minutes later, Nwoke called Sherrie to confirm the receipt of the message and Sherrie acknowledged. She told him that a response was underway from Risky through another cab driver. Fifteen minutes latera black cab driver walked into the office and gave the secretary an envelope. The secretary gave the envelope to Derrick and he put the envelope on the table and called Alo. Alo told him to open it and see what the response was. Nwoke did so but avoided telling him what it was over the phone line but, he did tell Alo it was favorable.

Derrick did not get back to the house until 12:30 pm. He gave Alo the note and, after reading it, Alo responded in writing, telling him to go outside with the prepaid phone and call him a taxi and go back to the office. He didn't want Derrick anywhere around when he did what he had to do.

Derrick thought about calling the Marshalls at that moment but decided against it as he didn't want to be labelled a 'Snitch' by the streets. He was a gangster and he wanted to die a gangster. Besides, from what he read in the booklet, there was nothing too damaging about Alo fleeing. The worst thing was that he would never be able to co-sign nor house anyone on bail again for the rest of his life. After hesitating for about five minutes and thinking the whole plan through, Derric went outside and called a taxi for Alo and then got in his Jeep Grand Cherokee and left for his office.

The county cab service arrived twenty five minutes after Derrick called. Alo cut the ankle device for home detention and got in the taxi. "Mondawmin please," he told the cabbie. Five minutes later while they were on Liberty road, Alo asked the Indian-looking cabbie to use his cell phone and he agreed for an additional fee of 20 dollars. He called Risky and asked him where he was and Risky said he would be at the Mondawmin mall cab stand in fifteen minutes. Alo hung up and gave the cabbie one hundred dollars and told him to step on it as he was running late for an appointment.

Since the Customs Authority did not have the man-power to conduct twenty four hour surveillance on suspects, the monitoring of Derrick Richard's residence and whereabouts, was turned over to the DEA. Agents

Thomas Johnson and Donald Billard of the DEA arrived at the Customs house in downtown Baltimore at exactly 1:35pm to pick up the warrant for wiretap and surveillance of Derrick Richard's residence and office. The Judge approved it the day before. After obtaining the warrant, the agents headed for Derrick's home in Randallstown. Half way to Randallstown, they received an emergency call from the U.S. Marshalls Home Detention monitoring unit.

"Are you serious, sir?" Johnson asked on the Nextel cell phone.

The Marshall told him to hurry up and that they were on their way to both addresses that included Ms. Jackson's residence, where Dante Jackson had also destroyed his ankle device.

"What happened; partner?" Billard asked after hearing Johnson's reaction to the phone call.

"Step on it. They might be gone." Johnson answered and called Spinard to let him know. Spinard told him that he and Levitz would meet them there.

Billard turned the siren on in the Chevy van and placed it on the dashboard since it wasn't equipped with one. He stepped down hard on the accelerator, sending the family looking vehicle down liberty road as other vehicles cleared the way. "So, who else is with him?"

"That goddamm Dante Jackson, supposedly."

"Well, I know they got enough money to go anywhere in the world. One thing about being a fugitive is, if you have money it makes it a lot easier for you and a lot harder for the law to catch up with you," Billard commented as the van raced through the traffic.

Ten minutes later, the DEA agents were in front of Derrick's home at 1012 Carriottsville road in Randallstown, Baltimore county.

"We can't wait for the others, let's go find out who's left in the house," Johnson said and rushed out of the van and to the house, followed by Billard.

They rang the doorbell repeatedly and when they couldn't get an answer, they decided to go back in the van and wait for their back-up to arrive.

"I didn't think there was anyone there anyway. Spinard and the Marshalls should be here soon.

Fifteen minutes later, the Marshalls pulled up in a high-powered Chevy Caprice with siren, followed by Spinard and Levitz, in a Chey van.

Upon seeing them, Johnson and Billard stepped out of the van and approached the others.

"We don't think there's anyone left in the house. Should we kick it in or what?" Johnson asked Spinard, who was really in charge of the case.

"Nah, if you're not in a hurry, I'd say we wait for someone to come home and see what they do. We may have an Aiding and Abetting charge with this situation," Spinard responded.

"Sounds good, then." Johson responded. "Since we already have the warrant for wire-tap. Maybe we should have it done now before they get in,"Billard suggested.

"Great, but we're gonna have to make sure they don't walk in on us. That means someone is gonna have to go to their office and keep a tab on'm," Johnson added.

"We can send the Marshalls to do that. That's not that hard. They just have to let us know when the couple leaves the office but, if we're done by then, they can just go about their business of hunting for the fugitives,"

Spinard suggested, looking at the two Marshalls who were standing behind Spinard and Levitz.

Johnson then placed a call to the office of the DEA and requested the technical team to come to the residence and tap the phones and plant a bug in the house. The team arrived about one hour later in a Gas and Electric utility truck and immediately went to work. They deactivated the sophisticated alarm system and went inside the house. They tapped the land-line and installed a microphone to pick up all the sounds in the house.

"Yup, he must've cut it with a Butcher knife," Johnson said as he picked up the ankle-sized electronic monitoring device off the kitchen floor.

"Well, I'll be damned," Spinard responded as he walked over to the kitchen and looked at the destroyed device. "These folks are really bold." He took the device and held up to the light and studied it.

Billard and Levitz joined them in the kitchen.

"Sometimes you wonder whose side the law is on. Why do they even have the bond system?" Levitz commented as he put the small electronic device in a sandwich bag as evidence.

"Okay, thanks you guys. You can go on back to the office," Johnson told the technical team members and they left.

Satisfied there was no one else in the house, the agents locked the door and waited outside for the occupants to come home. After two hours of waiting outside in the vehicles, Johnson's cell phone rang and he answered. One of the U.S. Marshalls watching Derrick's real estate office told him that Derrick and his girlfriend had just left the office in two separate vehicles. The time was now 4pm.

Twenty-five minutes later, through heavy rush-hour traffic, Derrick pulled around the corner and stopped the Grand Cherokee in front of his house, followed by Rita in a BMW 535 but, she pressed the remote to the garage and pulled inside while Derrick parked on the street. The agents had decided to wait it out by listening to the conversation in the house through the electronic device installed by the technicians. But, unfortunately for them, Derrick had already schooled Rita on how to react to the absence of Alo in the house.

"We've been listening for about twenty minutes now and I'm yet to hear anything telling us that they knew about the escape," Spinard remarked as they sat about one block from the house, in the van with Johnson and Billard parked right behind them.

Spinard got out of the passenger side of the van and walked back to the van behind them and told Johnson that they should go inside and do some fishing. Johnson and Billard agreed and, together the agents drove the two vans one block forward to 1012 Carriottsville rd. They all got out and walked to the door. Spinard rang the doorbell and Derrick didn't waste anytime answering as he opened the door like he was expecting some company.

"Yes, can I help you?" Derrick asked the plain clothes agents.

"Mr. Richard, I'm agent Michael Spinard and behind me is my partner, agent Jonathan Levitz and we're from the U.S. Customs Authority. Behind us are agents Johnson and Billard from the DEA and we're investigating the alarm signal that went off earlier today from your residence. I believe Mr. Alo Nwanta was on Home detention here and you are the responsible party?"

"Yes, please come in. I just got home from work and have no idea what you're talking about. You might wanna ask him yourself," Derrick responded and closed the door behind the agents.

"Is Mr. Alo Nwanta in the house, sir?" Spinard asked as all the agents watched Derrick's reaction.

"I'm sure he is. Hey, Rita! Can you see if Alo is up there and tell him he has company?" Derrick yelled out to Rita who was upstairs. He then went downstairs to check the basement. When he came back upstairs three minutes later, Rita was already standing in the living-room with the agents. "Well, I don't see'm. Did you see him upstairs, baby?"

"No. He wasn't in his room," Rita responded.

Derrick looked at the agents one by one. "What happened again?" he asked, innocently.

"Our Home Detention unit received a signal today from your residence indicating that the monitoring device had been destroyed or tampered with. What can you tell us about that, sir?" Spinard asked.

"Like I told you, we just got home from work. I thought he was here like always. We have no idea where Mr. Nwanta is. Can't you just try to find him through the device, evidently he's still wearing it since it's not here."

"You mind if we take a look ourselves?" Johnson asked to throw Derrick off and make him think they hadn't already been inside.

"Sure, help yourself."

Derrick followed Johnson and Billard while Rita tagged along behind Spinard and Levitz. The agents went through the entire home in about ten minutes and reassembled upstairs. Spinard looked at the other three agents and then, back at the couple. "Okay, Mr. Richard, if you hear from him, let us know or you might be in some very big trouble," he lied to intimidate Derrick.

"Okay," Derrick responded.

Johnson and Spinard gave Rita and Derrick their cards and left the house.

Inside the Diamond Cab, Risky and Alo sat in the back seat, discussing the journey ahead as the cab was now on the New Jersey Turnpike. It took them about forty five minutes before they finally found a taxi on the Mondawmin cab-stand to take them to New York. Most of the cab drivers were scared for their lives since they'd never known anyone to catch a cab all the way to New York. They spoke low so that the driver couldn't hear them through the bullet-proof shield that separated passengers from the driver. The shield provided an uncertain security for the drivers.

"You think this thing will make it all the way to New York?"Alo asked the cabbie, who hadn't said a word since they left Baltimore. When he didn't get a response, he knocked on the shield.

The driver heard the loud knock over the radio and turned the radio down."yes, what is the problem, sir?"

"I said; do you think we're gonna make it to New York in your taxi?"

Risky cracked a smile.

"Yes sir. This baby will make it anywhere in the United States of America. This is a former police car and it was built for riding everywhere," the driver responded, studying Alo through the rear-view mirror as he noticed a slight accent

"What brand of vehicle is this?"

"Chevy Caprice."

Risky and Alo heard the foreign accent but didn't comment. They just looked at each other and then at the driver, who also checked Risky out through the rearview mirror as he drove.

"It's kind of a good thing that he can't go any faster so, we don't have to worry about getting pulled over by the popo," Risky said.

"Are you guys going to tip me good for my struggle?" the dark-skinned cabbie asked, checking the rearview mirror for a response from the two hustlers. He could tell they were up to something because he had never had a fare go to New York in his thirteen years of driving taxi in Baltimore city. He figured Alo was probably Jamaican since too many Africans don't hang tight with Americans.

"If you get us there safely, I'm sure we will," Risky responded as Alo decided to keep the conversation with his 'home boy' limited. "Where are you from, my friend?"

"Nigeria and where is your friend from?" the driver asked.

"Nigeria," Alo responded. "Are you Yoruba?"

"Yes. I take it you're Ibo?"

"Yep."

"So, what the fuck am I then?" Risky intervened.

"You're gonna be Ibo after I get finished with you," Alo responded with a smile.

"That's very funny...hah ha...ha..ha," the driver cut in, laughing. He attempted to increase the speed on the old Caprice by stepping harder on the gas-pedal but, the loud engine produced no immediate effect as the car remained steady at 60 mph.

Risky turned his head to face his partner-in-crime once again. "You think the Marshalls and the DEA are at my house?" he asked Alo.

Alo didn't want the driver to over-hear the conversation so, he asked the driver to turn the radio up. Since most music stations didn't pay attention to the news, they had nothing to worry about. "I'm sure they were there minutes after you cut it and probably still there, questioning Sherrie and her mother. Did you tell her to go back home?"

"Not right away but, she's probably there by now."

"Well, they ain't got nothing to worry about as long as they do what they're supposed to do and not admit to knowing anything."

'Moneyain't nothing but a thing' by Jay-Z came on the radio station and the two fugitives sat back in the seat to listen and enjoy the song.

"Can you turn that up, please?" Alo yelled on top of his voice over the already loud music.

The song ended four minutes later and the Nigerian cabbie asked for half of the fare up front, after reducing the volume of the radio. They were now at the end of the Turnpike and preparing to pay the toll. Risky and Alo looked at each other and laughed.

"How much was it again?" Risky asked.

"Five hundred dollars, have you forgotten?" the driver responded.

Risky reached in his hip pocket and brought out several stacks of one hundred dollar bills, wrapped with rubber bands. He then peeled out five hundred dollars and placed it inside the small cash compartment built into the bullet-proof shield. "You can turn the radio back up, now."

"Thank you very much, my friend," the driver said as he took the money out of the compartment with his right hand, checked it and put it in his shirt pocket. He then reached under the steering wheel with his left hand while holding the steering with his right and pressed a button, letting the shield down. He now felt safer and more comfortable with the two rich passengers that God had sent him. That was probably what he earned for the entire week.

"Thanks for letting that thing down. I can breathe a lot better now. That oughtta cover the entire fare, right?" Risky asked.

"Yes, of course but, we drivers also accept generosity, if you know what I mean," the cabbie said and smiled, check the two passengers out through the rearview mirror as the cab approached the toll booth before the Lincoln tunnel.

The following morning, the hunt for the fugitives continued as the case had now been turned over to the U.S. Marshalls officially. Assistant U.S. attorney, James Cohen told them to make a priority to find the four conspirators. Warrants for wire-tapping had been obtained for Sherrie's land-line phone since her mother had now moved in after surrendering the deed to her home. Sherrie's cell phone was also tapped and she was placed under constant surveillance, just like Derrick. I The DEA requested past phone records of Sherrie's land-line and cell to see where most of the calls were going and coming in order to trace the whereabouts of Risky. The government began proceedings to confiscate the home of Ms. Washington and all vehicles registered in the name of Dante Jackson which were none. Risky made sure that nothing of value was in his name.

Unfortunately for the agents and the surveillance teams, no calls nor contacts by mail had been made since Alo and Risky took off. Not even to their nearest relatives. The government wondered if the phone lines at the homes were even working. The prosecuting attorney had now included escape in the charges against Alo and Risky. There was still no sign of Cnote or anything linking him to the defendants.

The two criminal defense attorneys representing Alo and Risky, namely John Guilick and Warren Goldberg, respectively, had asked Derrick and Sherrie to tell the fugitives to turn themselves in ASAP or forfeit all the cash deposit for the bonds.

Risky and Alo were staying at a Holiday Inn which the cab driver had agreed to check them into. It was located on the outskirts of New York city while Nwoke and co were now at the Hyatt Regency in downtown Manhattan after staying at the Hilton for a few days. Alo was able to get in touch with Nwoke by asking the cab driver if he could use his cell phone after checking into the Inn. They planned to remain at the Holiday Inn until their passports were ready by the 29th of December. Even though they had separate rooms, Alo and Risky still spent the days together in one room. Right now they were in Alo's room, eating a pizza.

"You think I can survive in Nigeria?" Risky asked as he took a bite of a slice of pizza, watching CNN.

"'Alo took a slice and stood up and walked over to the window as he took a bite. He carefully pulled the curtains to the side to see if there was anything out of the ordinary on the parking lot but, there was nothing but parked vehicles belonging to the guests of the Inn. "If you can survive in this cold weather, you can survive in Nigeria, the black man's nation. In fact, you just might not remember anything about the U.S. for real."

"You're joking, right? What about the Lions and Tigers?"

"Who told you that? I haven't even seen any since I was born. Did any of those Nigerian girls you dated in college tell you that fairytale?" Alo responded and walked back over to the bed and sat down opposite Risky with the coffee table between them. The pizza was in the box on top of the table.

"Nah, yo. I see it all the time on television."

"That's the white man's way of trying to deceive you and turn you against your heritage."

Risky thought for a minute as he swallowed hard on the delicious pizza with everything on it but anchovies. "If that's the case, then, I just might have to make it my home, permanently. You know I can't come back here and neither can you. Sherrie can join me later but, I think I need her here to keep an eye on things and send money when I need it."

"I figure we get the passports on Monday and leave on the next available flight. This will put us in the village for the New year's celebration so that you can see how a real New year is celebrated."

At exactly 6:35pm on Monday, the 29th of December, the British Airways flight carrying the Nigerian passports of Risky and Alo, landed at JFK. Cynthia had called Mary on Nwoke's prepaid cell to let her know. Mary called David Thompson to confirm and he told her there was an envelope at the counter for her.

Nwoke and Mary rushed down to the Airport with the same cab driver to pick the envelope up.

"I think we should send the cab driver to go inside. You wait here while I go with him; don't worry, I'll be out of sight. With the recent turn of events, I think it would be best this way," Nwoke suggested as he and Mary sat in the back of the cab.

"okay," Mary agreed.

Nwoke asked the Dominican cab driver for the favor and he agreed with no reservations, knowing he would be well rewarded by the rich couple.

"If we're not back in ten minutes, jet," Nwoke advised Mary and stepped out of the cab, followed by the cab driver.

"Wait!" Mary shouted as Nwoke was almost at the entrance.

Nwoke came back quickly to the cab to see what the problem was. "Yes, what's wrong?"

"Why are you talking like that? You better come back. I love you. Give me a kiss. I'm gonna call and let David know that my brother is coming to pick it up for me."

Nwoke kissed her and rushed back to meet the cab driver, who was already inside.

"I hope I don't get a ticket," the driver said as Nwoke caught up with him.

Nwoke stayed about twenty feet away as the cab driver approached the clerk at the counter and got the envelope.

"Tell your sister to give me a call ASAP. It's very important," David said, believing the cab driver was really Mary's brother.

"Okay, I sure will," the cabbie responded and turned and left, followed by Nwoke.

"Wow, I'm glad you two came back quick. He almost got a two hundred dollar ticket for parking in front of the terminal and leaving the cab unattended but, I told the officer· that you just went to get my luggage from the door," Mary gladly said as Nwoke sat down beside her.

"Oh, he wants you to call him ASAP, maam," the cabbie told Mary and started the engine, turning the hazard lights off.

Mary looked at Nwoke and then asked him for his cell phone. He hesitated for few seconds and gave it to her.

"What's the problem? He just might have something important to say," Mary told the jealous Nwoke who was looking at her like she might be hiding something.

Mary called David Thompson and he told her that her picture was on the screen saver of all the computer terminals in the Airport.

"Since when and are you sure it's me?" A paranoid Mary asked.

"Well, yeah but before you got the new hair-style and the glasses I saw you with last time. Is that why you did what you did? Are you okay....you don't seem like a bad person or a drug dealer," David responded on the other end of the phone.

"Can you please pull off. Nwoke give him some money, he was a great help," Mary told the cabbie and Nwoke. "I'm sorry, David....umm that's not why I looked like that. As a matter of fact, they got the wrong information. I'll talk to you later. Thanks a lot and you will be hearing from me." Mary didn't wait for a response before hanging up the cell phone.

"What happened? They got our pictures or something? Nwoke asked, studying his fiancée who looked more nervous than ever.

"My picture. Oh, I didn't ask'm if yours was also on the screen saver."

"Well, can you call'm back, please." Nwoke gave her the phone back.

Mary called David back and he told her there were other men under the same warrant.

"How many?"

David told her there were three other men and she hung up the phone.

"Probably you, Risky and Alo are the other three men he was talking about," Mary said as the driver joined the main highway back to the hotel.

Forty minutes later when they got to the hotel, Mary gave the cabbie another three hundred dollars in addition to the two hundred Nwoke had given him. The couple got out and went to their suite at the Hyatt.

"What are we gonna do now?" Mary asked as she sat down in the parlour of the suite, watching the big screen TV that was tuned to CNN. They made it a habit not to turn the TV off.

"I'll think of something, don't worry. At least we got their passports and now, we just gotta find a way out of the country," Nwoke responded.

"I don't think I'm gonna stick around to find out. I've wasted enough time already."

"Where are you gonna go?" Nwoke asked as Mary got up and headed for her room like she was going to start packing her things.

"Canada. You can come or you can wait for those 'hot' fugitives and get very 'hot' yourself."

"Hold on now I'm not gonna let you get yourself in some more trouble. The Airports are sealed but I'll bet you my uncle got an idea. Besides, the borders are just as sealed as the Airports so, you can forget it," Nwoke said and moved toward Mary who was at the door of her room. "Come on, you know how much I love you and wouldn't let anything bad happen to you," he said and put his arms around her.

"Well, let's get out of here and go back to the Hilton."

"For what? We can't be trailing back. What if the Marshalls' have already been there, we'll just be walking into their trap."

Mary hugged him back, surrendering to Nwoke's sense of reasoning.

Nwoke's cell phone rang and he answered. Alo called to tell him that they should all come to the Holiday Inn with everything until they figure out something. Alo wanted to stay out of the crowded city for the time being and, since the Holiday Inn was on the outskirts of town, he felt it was more of a hiding spot than big Hotels in big cities. Nwoke didn't agree but he went along with the plan, anyway.

Thirty minutes later, Uma checked them out and they got the Dominican cab driver to take them to the Holiday Inn. When the cab finally pulled up at the Holiday Inn forty five minutes later, Nwoke asked the dedicated cabbie, who was now making more money than he'd ever made in his life, to check them in. The driver did so and Nwoke gave him five hundred dollars and Mary gave him three hundred.

"Thank you very much you two. God will bless you in whatever you do. You never told me your names, I'm Fernando Martinez," the cabbie finally introduced himself and smiled.

"Oh, we are Mr. and Mrs Joshua and we are from Kenya,"

Nwoke lied with a straight face as Mary looked the handsome cabbie over and gave him a goodbye smile.

Uma and Glenn went to Alo's room and Alo was elated to see them. Risky remained in his room while Nwoke and Mary shared one of the rooms rented by the cabbie that dropped them off. Alo later joined Uma in her room for a little privacy without the little one.

One hour and twenty-five minutes later, they all assembled in Alo's room for a meeting.

"I want you all to meet my long time partner, Risky. he claims his family-tree goes back to Nigeria but, he doesn't know which tribe," Alo introduced Risky to Mary and Uma since Nwoke already knew who he was. Glenn continued to scream daddy! Daddy! Dadd! As Alo held him. He showed signs of missing his child.

"Nice to meet you all," Risky acknowledged everybody in the room.

Mary, who had been standing by the door, not feeling too happy about the backward trip, walked over to the chair by the desk and took a seat, admiring the family of her in-law-to-be. Uma placed her right arm around Alo and Glenn, further emphasizing the unity between them. The more Nwoke and Mary observed this, the more they wanted to get married and have their own child. But, the next words by Alo quickly reminded them of their fugitive status and they had to get lose from the feds, first.

"God will not allow no man to break us up, okay?" Alo said and kissed Uma on the lips and then looked at her for a few seconds and let out a sigh of relief like a man who'd just rescued his family from a hostage situation.

Nwoke looked around the room with two big pizza boxes and couldn't believe how his uncle was living. If somebody told him that his uncle would even consider spending one hour in a place like the room at Holiday Inn, he would've told them they were crazy.

"We're gonna make it out of the country, trust me you all. Just be patient and bear with me as I think through this,"Alo continued. He had no idea about the Airports being sealed off.

"Uncle, why don't we just go back to Midtown Manhattan and get you all a comfortable hotel suite so that you can celebrate properly," Nwoke suggested while Risky looked like he agreed with the idea.

"Celebrate what? We still have a long way to go. Now, where're the passports?"

Nwoke said excuse me and went to his room and got the envelope with the passports in it: He gave the envelope to Alo and Alo opened it and brought out two Nigerian passports of Risky and himself. He studied them and nodded.

"This is why I love my country. You can do anything with money. Hey, Risky, I like your new name, brother," Alo said and handed Risky his own passport.

"Word? What's the name?" Risky asked as he got up to get the passport. He looked at the name and his picture in shock.

"What the....I can say the first name....David.."

"Okeke....Okay...kay. Say it just like that...ok kay," Alo assisted his friend in pronouncing the Ibo last name.

"Okaykay...David okkay. Got it. I know that Ima need to know how to say that to do whatever we gotta do to get to the motherland. I'm now officially a Nigerian, yo" Risky looked around the room, smiling at the crew wondered if he was okay.

"It's only a passport, man. It is what we do with it that matters, you dig?" Alo said as he was still thinking about Nwoke's suggestion, but he wanted to stay as far away from the big city as he could. "Nah, Nwoke. I think we better stay here for now. Freedom and safety are more important than comfort and I just spent about a week in a jail cell so, right now, this is comfortable to me until further notice."

"Okay, one more thing, unc. The Airports are sealed and our pictures are on the screen-savers at all the terminals counter and who knows where else," Nwoke informed.

"What? I didn't know that. When did you find out and why didn't you tell me?" Uma exploded, feeling betrayed and upset. She withdrew her hand from the shoulder of her husband and stood up.

"I'm sorry Uma. I didn't have the time. We just found out when we went back to the Airport for the passports," Nwoke explained as Risky listened.

Alo put Glenn on the bed and started pacing the floor. He walked over to the window and pulled the curtains and peeked out on the parking lot to see if there were any white· men sitting in any of the vehicles. "So, how did you get the passports then?"

Nwoke looked at Mary for a response, followed by Alo's eyes and Uma's and Risky's.

Mary felt like a victim of circumstance. "Okay, my friend at the British Airways counter said so. We had to send the cab driver to get the passports. All the terminals do have our pictures and real names on them, well, except for Uma and Glenn."

Risky, who hadn't said a word so far, just couldn't keep quiet any longer. "Mine, too?"

"I'd guess you're the fourth one since he said there were four wanted fugitives who may be attempting to flee through the International Airports," Mary responded.

Risky now showed a sign of confusion, since he had never travelled outside the country. He couldn't think of any idea other than the Mexican border. "How about the Mexican border, yo?"

"I'm afraid that's probably as bad as the airports. They work hand-in-hand," Alo explained to his American friend who looked hopeless. "Okay, there's gotta be a way out. At least, we've achieved the first part which was to get the passports in different names and, now we just go to figure out a way to use it to our advantage," Alo analyzed, coming back to the bed and sitting back down on the foot of the bed while risky and Nwoke continued to stand.

After hearing all this, Uma began to feel sorry for her husband so, she moved closer to the foot of the bed and put her right arm around him again while Glenn lay in the middle of the bed and watched. "C'mon, honey, let's go to a more comfortable place. I need you more." She looked him deep in the eyes, seductively as Glenn stared blankly while everybody else in the room watched.

Alo wondered if his wife really knew the degree of the dangers they faced. They'd already made love when she· first got to the Inn and to him, that was enough for the moment. He looked at Glenn and then back at his wife and the look in her eyes gave him an instant erection that would only be worthwhile in a comfortable hotel suite. "Do you really miss me, baby?" he asked as his eyes met hers.

"Yes, I really do. I was scared that I might lose you; a man like you is hard to replace," Uma said, knowing that most rich men were taken. Alo Nwanta gave her everything she wanted and more. Alo bent his head down for about three minutes while everybody in the room kept quiet. "Okay, you guys win. I don't have much to pack and it's already 6:34pm. Risky, go tell that nice receptionist to get us three clean Limos."

Risky agreed and left the room to handle his business with the pretty receptionist he thought he was going to hit at least once.

That's a great idea, uncle 'cause they all have tintedwindows and dividers. Wherever they drop us off at, is not where we're gonna stay," Nwoke added, appreciating his uncle's solutions to problems.

Everybody went to their respective rooms and got their things which weren't much since most of the luggage hadn't even been unpacked. Risky returned about ten minutes later and told them the Limos were on the way.

"If her relief gets here in time, she just might be riding with me and I hope you all don't mind. It's only just for the night," Risky said as he came back to the room with his small carryon that looked more like a leather duffle bag.

"Now, hold on, my brother. That's a no no," Alo said and stood up. We can't get too comfortable to the point of taking strangers with us. Anything could happen. What if she notices your picture all of a sudden? That could happen and that can cause a lot of problems, you know." Alo was now standing in front of Risky.

"Yo, I didn't think about all that. You're right. I just hope her relief doesn't get here before we leave."

Thirty minutes later, the Limos lined up in front of the Inn and, fortunately for Risky, the receptionist's relief worker had not made it in time.

Derrick decided to leave the office early and come home to make sure that everything was okay. He noticed the mail-lady who should have been a mail-man, walking away from his house. He wondered if the regular guy was sick or just off duty. "Hi dear," he greeted the middle aged white female who looked like she spent a lot of time at Bally's health club.

"Hi," the mail-woman responded as she continued to the next house that was about half a block down the street, not really paying attention to Derrick or, at least, pretending not to.

Derrick looked up and down the street, wondering where the mail truck was as something told him the lady was an imposter. He was able to spot what looked like a mail-truck about half a mile up the street. He opened the door and went inside, placed his briefcase on the dining table and thought for a minute and decided to go back outside and conduct a brief surveillance of his own. He looked down the street to see how far the lady had gotten but, she had disappeared but the U.S. mail truck was still where he thought he spotted it. Derrick became confused, so he got back in the Grand-Cherokee and drove slowly down the street and, to his surprise, when he reached the mail-truck, he saw the regular mail-man walking up to the truck. He scanned the street one more time but, the physically-fit lady was nowhere to be seen.

"What's he doing?" Agent Spinard asked the white male undercover from the DEA, who had now joined forces with the Customs authority to investigate the international drug smuggling operation and locate those responsible.

"I don't know. He must suspect something," the man who was sitting on the driver's side of the Gas and Electric van, responded. "You see how he slowed down by the truck?"

"All he got was junk-mail and there was nobody in the house when I rang the door-bell. I didn't hear anything either." the woman who played the role of the mail-lady said sitting in the back of the van.

Levitz and another DEA agent were sitting next to the woman in the back seat. The DEA agents were also responsible for the monitoring of the land-line phone in Derrick's home.

Derrick came back around to his house and parked on the street. He went inside as the agents watched.

"Is he making any calls?" Spinard asked the DEA agent with the gadgets in his ears.

"Not yet. He might be too smart to make any incrinating phone calls from that house after what we just saw him do," the Hispanic-looking man responded as he listened for any audio sound from the house.

After one hour of waiting without hearing anything but the News on CNN, Spinard and levitz decided to leave the agents to continue their duty.

"Okay, thanks again, you guys,". Spinard said since he couldn't remember the names of the other DEA agents who included the lady so, he and Levitz nodded to them and exited the van. They walked behind it to their Chevy cavalier and left the neighborhood.

"Smart kid," Levitz remarked as they rode up liberty rd.

"Well, from what we know, he has a Bachelor's degree from Towson State, I believe, in aahh. Business Admin. if my memory serves me right. I don't even think he's involved in all this."

"But he knew the guy some kind of way to let him stay in his house. Plus, he seems to have too much money for somebody who just has a real estate company that hasn't recorded any profit since it started," Levitz countered.

"That's what Mr. Cohen said right?"

"Yup. The company hasn't made any money since it started." Levitz drove up the I-695 ramp that would take them back to the office at BWI.

Derrick was now convinced he was under surveillance after the scene with the fake mail-lady. He was now extra cautious and vigilant. He planned to write a note to Rita to only hold normal conversations in the house and the office. The ringing of the house phone interrupted his thoughts. "Hello."

John Guilick was on the other end of the line. "Good afternoon, Mr. Richards and how are you on this cold day and happy holidays."

The confusion that the fake mail-lady had created in Derrick's mind, made him wonder if he should even be talking to the caucasian lawyer. After a brief hesitation, he responded. "Yes, Mr. Guilick. Happy holidays to you and how may I help you?"

"If you can get in touch with your friend, tell him that we have a pre-trial hearing coming up in a few days and it would be in his best interest to turn himself in. The last thing he needs right now is a failure to appear in a federal court. The government is willing to offer a good plea deal at the moment." Mr. Guilick's voice sounded colder than it was outside.

The criminal defense attorney's voice sent chills up Derrick's spine and he decided to walk over to the front window and cracked it a bit to breathe in some fresh air and also make sure it was snowing. "I heard what you said, sir, but I have no idea where Mr. Nwanta is or how to contact him," he answered and surveyed the street.

After a three-minute hesitation, Mr. Guilick responded. "All right, then, when and if you do, relate the message to him," the high-priced attorney said and hung up the phone.

Derrick switched off the cordless phone and returned it to its cradle. He sat back down and continued to watch CNN to see if there were any updates on the fugitives but, nothing. He sat there and considered his options. He knew the feds had nothing on him. Derrick now wondered if it was even a good idea to even keep in touch with the fugitives since he had already sacrificed enough. He concluded that it was best to just cut them off.

Sherrie sat in her living-room with her mother, watching the News on CNN for any updates. "Hey, ma. Do you think he's gonna make it to Africa and become one of them?" Sherrie asked.

The pretty Ms. Washington, who looked good for her age of fifty-one, had always believed that all black people were from Africa but, it was the white man that caused the separation amongst them, "he's already one of them so, I don't see why not," she answered and looked at her daughter through the versace-framed glasses. She always dressed exquisite and expensive like she was born into money.

Outside, in a black tinted-window Chevy caravan, sat two DEA agents conducting surveillance on Sherrie and monitoring her phones and mail. The agents sat about two blocks up the street.

Sherrie had a Beauty salon at Mondawmin mall and her head Beautician had been in charge since the arrest of

Derrick but, she'd been stopping by to check on it. She was now considering returning to work since things seemed to have calmed down. "I wish him luck, but I wonder how he's gonna let us know he made it."

"Why can't he just call or write?"

"C'mon ma, you know the feds probably got this phone tapped and just waiting for him to either write a letter or call."

"Oh, I ain't know all that. They got that kind of time?"

"Maa. They got all the time in the world and all the money, too. If he hadn't been messing with those Nigerians, they might've left'm alone but, now......"

"When are you two getting married?" Ms. Washington asked, fixing her gaze on her daughter, whom she'd always wanted to be married before having any children, unlike herself who still can't track down Sherrie's father.

"I don't know mom but he thinks it's gonna be sometime this year and I'm ready."Sherrie really didn't care for marriage since all her girlfriends who got married are either divorced or separated and all under the age of thirty. She was now twenty-nine and she knew that once they tie the knot, they'll start having problems, just like the rest of the couples she knew.

"Sherrie, please get married before you turn thirty, that's the only thing that will make me happy. I loved the house and the Town-car but, you can't buy marriage. It makes the relationship complete."

"Mom, even if we do get married tomorrow, what difference do you really think it's gonna make?"

"It's gonna make a big difference in the children's lives when you do have one, okay?"

Sherrie thought for about one minute. "Are you ready to go wherever he might be, 'cause that's where the marriage 'll be?"

"I'd love to witness that kind of marriage in the motherland, just like in the Eddie Murphy movie.... ahh...'Coming to America'. That would be just wonderful." Ms. Washington smiled as she looked at her beautiful daughter and wondered if a royal wedding could actually happen between her daughter and Risky.

But, with the two undercover agents sitting outside in the van, the reality of an African wedding between two African-Americans running for their lives became somewhat, a dream.

"Where would you go if you were Mr. Nwanta?" Levitz asked Spinard as they sat in Spinard's office, trying to put the puzzles together for the Marshalls who were already in full force, nation-wide.

"Home."

"Where's home?"

"Nigeria."

"Do you think he's there already?"

"Not a chance in the world. We got all the borders covered including all the international Airports and I just can't see them making through so fast. The Marshalls are pretty good, you know."

"Even with all that cash, you don't think they just might be able to squeeze through some kind of way?"

"We'll get'm or at least get one of them. They can't be that slick," Spinard contended.

"We checked with the DEA surveillance teams and they have yet to hear anything that could give us a lead in the right direction?"

"I'm afraid nothing. No calls have come into the homes or go out of the homes. I can't believe it myself; these Nigerians are pretty smart and I think they're doing this intentionally. Remember they've probably got relatives and friends that's been through it all."

"You're right. I hadn't thought about that. It's almost like we're dealing with foreign intelligence."

"I wouldn't go that far but you gotta give'm credit in some of the crimes they've committed."

"Are we at a dead-end?" Levitz asked pessimistically, getting up and walking to the window and looking at the cold wind that swept through, shaking some of the trees in the distance as if a Winter storm was underway.

"We just might be," Spinard agreed and joined his partner in observing the biting wind outside.

After getting out of the Limousines, the four fugitives along with Uma and Glenn, took three yellow cabs to the W. Hotel in Times square in an effort to eliminate any traces that may have been established by any of the Limo drivers. Nwoke paid two of the cab drivers to check him and Risky into a suite and Risky, into a separate one. Uma checked her family in. They were able to avoid detection due to the class of people they came in contact with; people who had money and minded their own business. Nine out of ten criminals will not stay in five-star hotels. You find them in Motels and Inns.

In their private executive suite, Nwoke asked Mary to use her former co-worker who'd been helping them all along, to see if he could get them through the Airport for a fee. Or, get Cynthia involved and he'll see what Uzo can do with other Airlines since Nigeria Airways had been banned from flying to the U.S.

Alo and Uma were having a time of their lives, trying to catch up on the love-making they missed while he was in confinement. Glenn was kept in the second room where he played with the toys his mother had bought him for Christmas.

"I still think we'd been better off at the Holiday Inn outside the city. The less eyes you come in contact with, the less the chances of someone recognizing you," Alo said as he cuddled up under the satin sheets, next to his wife.

"I disagree with you, honey. I think the busier it is, the less people have time to recognize or remember things 'cause they're busy. But, in a sparsely populated area, everybody knows everybody and they could recognize you and pay close attention from miles away, you know what I mean?"Uma countered as Alo looked at her like she was right.

Risky was in his lonely suite, debating whether he shouldgo out to strip club or not. He flipped through the menu for room-service and ordered a lobster tail. Then he used theremote control unit to find a movie on the movie-channel ofthe cabe network and waited for his dinner as he focused ona triple x-rated porno flick. He decided to stay out of the way by staying indoors.

Chapter Sixteen

Mary hung up the phone and sighed in relief. "My girlfriend in Liberia who's a flight attendant with the Nigeria Airways, suggested we drive to across the border to Canada and take a Nigeria Airways flight out of Toronto to Abuja," she said to Nwoke who had just got off the phone with Uzo.

"C'mon, I already thought about that. The border is even worse cause it's less busy. They have all day to check you out including asking for your social security number. Now, if we could swim or pay somebody on the boat, we might end up in the woods but, who do you know that can risk picking us up?" Forget that," Nwoke conclusively analyzed.

"Do you think we can get a U.S. passport?"

"Why not but it probably won't be in three days. I would not wanna risk it, though." Nwoke started pacing the floor of the living-room.

"What are you thinking about? I wanna go home, Nwoke." Mary stretched across the comfortable sofa in the spacious parlour of the W. Hotel suite.

"Nothing really. Just options we might have to risk if this doesn't materialize soon."

The couple just sat there and waited for Uzo or Cynthia to call back and tell them what they got. Five minutes later, the prepaid cell rang and Nwoke answered.

Uzo was on the international line. He told Nwoke that Cynthia had made contact with her ex-boyfriend again, the same one that arranged for the passports. Uzo said it would cost a total of fifty thousand dollars to get them through JFK to Germany on Lufthansa German Airlines and then connect to another flight to Lagos or Abuja.

"Thanks my good buddy. Let me check with the crew and hit you back," Nwoke said and hung up. He walked over to the sofa and stood above Mary, smiling. "Well, I think they just did it again and we just might be on our way," Nwoke told Mary.

"That was Uzo?" she responded and sat up in jubilation.

"Yup and he said it's gonna cost just fifty grand. The same connection as the passports. let me go tell uncle and see what he thinks. I'll be right back."

"I'll be in bed when you get back. It's getting late," Mary said, knowing that they would make love to celebrate the latest goodnews.

Nwoke went to Alo's suite which was on the same floor and gently tapped on the door.

"Coming:"Uma's voice yelled from inside the suite. A few seconds later, the door opened and Nwoke stepped inside.

Uma had on her nightgown, looking rather exhausted from what was probably a rough work out in the bedroom with the deprived Alo. "What's up, Nwoke? You look like a poor person who just hit the lotto for a couple of million or maybe a billion."

"Yes, I did. Where's uncle?"Nwoke asked, trying to avoid looking at the beautiful sister-in-law whose hard nipples were showing through the silk nightgown.

"Sit down. I'll get'm, he's in the bedroom." She went to the bedroom and told Alo that his nephew was there.

Three minutes later, Alo emerged, looking like he'd been in fight and got knocked out in the fifth round. He had on his pajamas, supplied by the hotel and no shoes. "What's up?"he asked as he sat down next to Nwoke.

"I think our best chance just came through."

"What's that?"

Nwoke told him what Uzo said and the price and Alo agreed without any hesitation.

"For that type of money, it's gotta be legit. But, what about Germany? You know these European countries are tied to the U.S. and really the U.S. is just an extension of England."

"What do mean?"

"Just call him back and ask him what kind of screening are we gonna encounter in Germany and is that also paid for. If he has an answer and knows what he's talking about, then just tell Uzo to pay him and I'll do the reimbursement," Alo finally instructed the young nephew and went to bed.

Nwoke got up and left the suite. Seconds later, he joined Mary in the bedroom. He would wait till the morning to call Uzo back.

The following morning, Nwoke got up early and called Uzo with the questions. Uzo told him that the man said everything was included and, as long as they had a Nigerian passport, it was easy to get on board. But, they had also made arrangements for one of the Airport security employee to walk them through if at all there was any problem, which he seriously doubted.

In his office at the BWI Airport, agents Spinard and Levitz, had just received recent phone records of the only cell phone registered in Derrick's name. Derrick had gotten rid of the cell phone after Alo escaped. But, unfortunately for the government, there were no strange numbers that could provide a lead as to where the fugitives may be. As they were looking the lists over, the phone rang and it was the secretary. Spinard put her on speaker.

"What is It Martha?"Spinard asked.

"The operator says there's a man with a heavy accent who claims he drove the two escapees to New York. Do you wanna talk to him?"

"Please put him through," Spinard and Levitz looked at each other in shock, thinking things couldn't get no better.

"Hello," the man said.

"Hello. This is agent Spinard and how may I help you?"

"Sir, I am calling about the reward because I have the information you need," the man said.

"And what information is that?"Spinard asked as Levitz listened.

"I drove the two people you are looking for to New York."

To Spinard and Levitz, the man sounded like Mr. Bayo."Where are you from, sir and what is your name?"

"My name is Jedu Oshu and I am from Nigeria."

"When was that that you drove them to New York?"

"Two days ago in my taxi. Now how do I get the ten thousand dollars?"

"Sir, we have to make sure you're telling us the truth and then we have to actually find them based on your tip. That's why we said any information that leads to the arrest and conviction of the suspects or fugitives and, in your case, information that will lead us to the fugitives. Do you understand?" Spinard informed.

"Yes, please go to the Holiday Inn on the outskirks of the city and pick them up."

Spinard looked at his partner in disbelief and joy then, continued. "Sir, where are you and when can you come in so we can discuss the details of what you just told us?"

Mr. Oshu told the agents that he was driving around all day and everyday and whenever they wanted, he could just drive to the Airport and stop by the office. Spinard asked if he was available right away and he said yes so, they told him to stop by. Two hours later, Mr. Jedu walked into the office and the agents escorted him to the conference room where they had interviewed Mr. Bayo a few weeks before. Jedu related the entire information to the agents, including the location of the Holiday Inn and Spinard told him he would get the reward once the Marshalls picked the fugitives up. Jedu wasn't too happy about that and he let them know.

"Can I get some part of the money now and the rest, later?" Jedu asked, looking the two white men in the eyes like he didn't trust them.

"I'm afraid it doesn't work like that, sir. Trust me, you've provided us with valuable information and the government will be more than glad to reward you."

The last assurance by Spinard gave the taxi driver more hope that he was going to get his money. He just hoped the two men where still where he dropped them off at. Jedu got up and left, hoping to pick up a good fare from the Airport.

Spinard called the head of the U.S. Marshalls in New York and related the message immediately. "I think we got'm."

"I never thought it was gonna be that easy but, it's looking like that, buddy," Levitz responded as the hopeful agents smiled at each other and waited.

One hour later, the lead U.S. Marshall for the state of New York called Spinard and told him that the fugitives had checked out of the Holiday Inn the same day they checked in.

On December 30th, at exactly 5:45pm, Nwoke's one-day old prepaid cell phone rang and he answered. Uzo called to give him specific instructions on the next Lufthansa flight leaving from JFK to Munich, Western Germany at 10:00pm. Since the organizer was in the city of New York, Nwoke was to pay the fifty thousand into a bank account at one of the Banks in New York city. He decided to call his favorite Bell-boy at the Marriott Marquise Hotel to assist him since his face couldn't be under Bank scrutiny. The man happily agreed as that meant more money for him just like when he handled the shipment of the Range rover. Nwoke got the cash from Mary and Risky and called his favorite cab driver who took him to the Airport twice. By the time the cab got to the W.Hotel in Times Square it was already 6:01pm and the designated Bank closed in half an hour. The driver drove like a typical New York city yellow cab driver as the yellow Chevy caprice maneuvered its way through the busy traffic. They got to the Bank at 6:20pm and Nwoke sat in the cab while the Bell-boy went inside and made the deposit to the account as Nwoke watched. He showed

Nwoke the receipt and Nwoke compared it to the account number he had and it matched.

"Thank you very much. It's not easy to trust someone to do what you just did, my friend and I'm gonna reward you and this nice cab driver," Nwoke said and gave the Bell-boy one thousand dollars and gave the driver 700.00. "there may be a lot more coming. Take me back to the Hotel."

Nwoke walked into Alo's suite to find Risky sitting in the sofa, watching the News. Uma closed the door and took a seat next to her husband.

"So, what's up?" Alo asked.

"It's done," Nwoke answered, still standing in the middle of the parlour.

"What's done?" Alo asked, wondering what his nephew was talking about.

Nwoke had been so busy to get the money to the Bank before closing that he'd forgotten to tell Alo. The last time he let Alo know anything was when Uzo told him the amount of money needed. "Oh, I'm sorry I didn't tell you but, I just deposited the fifty grand into an account at a bank after talking to Uzo and we're supposed to leave tonight."

"What? I'm so glad, yo. I was just telling your uncle about what the bitch at the Holiday Inn told me," Risky said.

"What?" Nwoke asked, looking at Risky, curiously.

"The Marshalls were just there a couple of hour ago," Risky answered.

"How in the world did they trace us there?" Nwoke now moved closer to Risky and sat down next to him.

"It's gotta be the cabbie that dropped us off. He probably wanted that reward just like the other 'home boy' that gave them our description. Us against us, that's all we're good for and you thought the white man was our problem; we are our own problem," Alo lectured.

"You see, I'm glad we left when we did. That's God's work, right there, you all. I'm gone to pack my shit. The flight is at 10pm." Nwoke got up and left, followed by Risky.

Before Nwoke could tell Mary what Risky had just told him, his cell phone rang as soon as he walked into their suite. "Hello."

John, the Bell-boy was on the phone to tell him that the U.S. Marshalls were at the Hilton Hotel, asking questions with their pictures. "But, the receptionist told them that you guys checked out days ago," John told him on the line.

"You're sure about that?"

"I'm sorry but it's true and I didn't think you were in any kind of trouble."

"Thanks." Nwoke hung up, heart racing.

"I think we better get out of here right now. I don't know they're doing it but, they are too close for comfort," Nwoke told Mary who was sitting down, watching the News.

"They're probably gonna check all the hotels in New York city but, how do they know that we're in new York?" Mary asked looking confused and scared.

"Well, Risky had just told me he talked to the girl at the Days Inn and she told him that the Marshalls were there," Nwoke responded and went straight to the bedroom. Mary walked right behind him. "I don't know how uncle got to the Inn but, I think whoever took them there, told the Marshalls." Nwoke went into the walk-in closet, gathered a few things and threw them in the luggage. "Don't just stand there and cry, go get your stuff ready."

Mary went to the other room where she kept her belongings and did the same. The couple were packed and ready in ten minutes. They went to Alo's suite where Risky was already packed and ready.

"Uma, you go downstairs with Glenn and check us out. Give her your keys, too, Mary and Risky," Alo instructed as he stood in the middle of the living-room floor like he was commanding an orchestra. "I told you guys about these people, you can never underestimate them. My guess is that someone at the Holiday Inn recognized us and told or, it could've been the Nigerian cab driver that drove us from Baltimore. But, this isn't the time to figure out who told who. We're gonna leave one by one while Uma goes to drop off the keys. Nwoke, you call that same cab driver and tell him to bring another cab with him ASAP."

Nwoke looked at Mary and Risky. "Now, we do have enough money left for whatever that may come, right?"

Mary said they had more than enough while Risky just nodded in agreement. Uma left the suite to drop the keys off at the check-in counter. Nwoke called the cab driver and the cabbie told him that he would be there in ten minutes since he just around the corner. They all gathered their luggage and met Uma on the ground floor. Five minutes later, the Dominican cabbie and another cab pulled up. The Bell-boys helped the crew with their luggage and they tipped them and left the W. Hotel for what they hoped, was the last time.

At the Federal District Courthouse building in downtown Baltimore, Assistant U.S. Attorney, James Cohen, had succeeded in getting a sealed indictment against the absent Nwoke and Mary and now, just waited for the eventual apprehension. The testimony of Mr. Bayo and supporting documents obtained from Alo's home on Epsom road and the condo on Allegheny avenue, assisted the government in convincing the Grand Jury to hand down the indictment.

"So, what we have now is that they were last spotted in the city of New York, according to the Marshalls, is that right?" Cohen asked Spinard, who was in the office of the prosecutor on this pre-New year's eve.

"Yes, sir. But the Holiday Inn is on the outskirts of Manhattan and I passed on the information immediately and the Marshalls said the attendant told them they had checked out as soon as they got there. They are right now checking all the hotels, motels and Inns in and around the city," Spinard responded while Levitz listened.

"How long did it take them to get there, do you know?"

"Well, it took them a couple of hours to call us back and tell us that the fugitives had checked out," Spinard responded

"That would mean they're probably still in the vicinity since they appear to be too smart to travel in their names."

"I believe so sir. I don't even know how they've been able to check in and out of hotels without somebody recognizing one of them," Levitz added.

"You know how most of us are. We rarely pay attention, unless it directly concerns us."

"They might have changed their appearances," Spinard said.

"If that was the case, the Holiday Inn wouldn't have recognized them." Cohen walked over to his drawer and retrieved a file.

"If only we can arrest somebody who knows what their next plan is, maybe, we could give the person a deal for info., you know what I mean?"

Cohen placed the file on the table and sat back down in his chair, facing the two agents who were sitting opposite. He began flipping through the pages. "Well, I think we already have somebody and his name is Derrick Richards."

"But, he's not talking on the phone about anything we wanna hear. He only talks about business or family stuff. He hasn't even mentioned their names since the investigation began. Truthfully, you might even think he doesn't know who the fugitives are," Spinard added.

"They're not stupid, now. I think that's all in their plans. They'll find some other way to communicate sooner or later. We're still checking the mail, right?"

"Yes, we are."

Cohen lifted his face up from the file and stared at the wall as if he'd seen something that didn't belong. "One thing about those Nigerians is that they always get their college degrees first before committing any crimes and this makes them very evasive. I'm gonna make sure these ones are brought to justice. Okay, you guys, let's call it a day. It's almost 8:00pm and you've had enough overtime." Cohen got up and lead the way out of the office and the empty building.

The fugitives were supposed to meet a Nigerian, who was the mastermind behind the exit plan. the man supposedly worked for Lufthansa Airlines. The meeting place was about thirty-five minutes from the W.Hotel. They were now only ten minutes from it.

"'Why do some of these meters tick faster than others?" Nwoke asked the cab driver who was a stranger to him. The Dominican cabbie had Mary and Nwoke in his cab.

The cabbie tried to laugh it off. "I'm sorry, I forgot the meter was still on from the last fare." He turned the meter off to avoid any problems.

"You still didn't answer my question, my friend. I just wanna know," Nwoke continued.

Mary bumped him to give him a signal to forget about the fast meter and spare the cabbie trying to make an honest living.

"It is a mechanical and electrical fault, sir. I really don't know. Are you from Public Service Commission?" the nervous driver asked.

"That's okay. Just forget it. Where are you from?" Nwoke asked the mulato-looking young man.

"I am from the Virgin Islands and you?"

"Kenya," Nwoke lied.

The cab pulled up in front of the Nigerian restaurant five minutes later.

"I think there's more to it than what you just told me but, I know you gotta live, too," Nwoke said and gave the cabbie two hundred and fifty dollars for what was probably a seventy dollar ride.

The cabbie was very happy as he got out and brought out the luggage. "Thank you very much and here's my card, just in case you need another cab another day."

"Yo, I'm scared to death. You sure this is gonna work?" Risky said as he got out of the front seat and stretched.

The friendly Dominican cab driver, pulled up right behind them and Alo, Uma and Glenn got out while the cabbie brought their luggage out of the trunk. Uma gave him three hundred dollars and he thanked them and also gave them his card. The two cab drivers pulled off when they saw the Nigerian-looking woman come out of the restaurant and headed toward the crew.

"Hello, you must be the honorable guests that I'm expecting. I am Alice and welcome," the chubby, but healthy looking woman introduced. She then looked at the restaurant and motioned two young boys that were looking out of the window to come and take the luggage inside.

Alo introduced himself and allowed everybody else to follow suit by saying the names on the new passports and they did.

"Thanks for the kindness," Mary said to the woman as they followed her to the restaurant.

The young helpers took the luggage inside and set them in the back.

The smell of cooked Nigerian meal greeted the crew inside the mid-size restaurant. All the tables were covered with white cotton-covers. The restaurant was well furnished and one could tell it wasn't meant for the poor. The smell of delicious African dishes brought back a lot memories for Alo, Mary and Nwoke.

"I feel we're already home," Nwoke commented as they sat at a table of their choice.

"I think we should get closer to the window," Nwoke suggested, looking at Alo for approval.

"Agreed," Alo said and got up and moved to a table closest to the window facing the street, followed by the rest of the crew. "Now, that's much better. At least, we can see them coming."

"Yo, you don't think they're coming here, too, do you?" Risky asked Alo.

"You never know with them. I don't put nothing past those federal agents."

"Good. Are you all comfortable, now!" the woman asked as she walked over to the table where the crew had occupied.

"Yes, we are and thank you for the hospitality," Alo responded for the crew.

"I hope you are all hungry so that you can taste some delicious Nigerian cooking," Alice said with a smile that almost lightened up her dark-skinned complexion.

Risky wondered why the restaurant was empty and the food smelled so good. "That smell makes me hungry. What is it, Alo?"

"Fufu soup with stockfish, at least that's what it smells like. I'm sure you will enjoy it," Alo answered.

"I might as well get used to it," Risky looked around the big table at his company and then studied the white-cotton material that covered the table and smiled. He was greeted with a befitting welcome to the African culture.

Alice brought the menu and they all ordered. Risky wasn't sure what to order so, Alo ordered some rice and stu with goat meat and oxtail and pepper-soup on the side.

Alice brought the tray with the orders twenty minutes later and placed it on the big table. Another prettier and younger waitress who also looked African, brought a second tray with the side orders and also placed it on the table.

"Please enjoy your meal?" Alice said and left, followed by the other waitress, who was dressed in all-white uniform.

They finished eating the delicious meal thirty minutes later to everyone's satisfaction.

"That was the best meal I've had in my thirty-year life. I love that soup. I think I'm gonna love it in Nigeria, especially if the girls look like the last waitress that brought the food," Risky said and smiled at everyone. "Yo, why is it empty in here, anyway?"

Alo was busy studying his wife and son, making sure that Glenn was satisfied with the custard powder he just had. The happy face of the little boy gave him the answer he was looking for. "You got a point there. Then again, they might've just closed early but, I'm gonna find out."

Alice brought another tray full of assorted drinks that included a gallon of the traditional African alcoholic beverage, Palm wine.

"Why isn't there anyone here but us, Alice?" Alo asked as he studied the woman and looked out the window to see if it was a set up for the Marshalls to get them.

"That is because my master told me to close it down for you and your people. I thought you saw the sign outside."

"Oh, I guess we weren't paying much attention. Okay, thank you for the drinks," Alo responded and looked outside for the sign but, he didn't notice anything. "hey, Risky, you see anything?"

Everybody looked through the big window but saw nothing indicating closure.

"You want me to double-check, uncle?" Nwoke asked and stoodup.

"Yes," Alo answered.

Nwoke got up and walked through the reception area before the closed door. He opened the heavy mahogany door and walked out into the cold weather without a coat. As he turned around and faced the building, he saw a small sheet of paper that said the restaurant was closed early for cleaning and that it would reopen on the 3rd of January. He came back inside and told the crew. "This is big if he closed the restaurant just for us."

"But think about the amount of money we paid. That's a lot of cash for the average person," Mary added and looked out the window. "Oh, there goes a crew that just turned back when they got to the door. The sign is on the window, right?"

"Yeah, Nwoke responded and took a bottle of Palm-wine from the tray. "Yo, Risky, you might wanna try this. All natural."Risky did as Nwoke suggested and poured himself some of the African Palm-wine. "C'mon, now. This can't be all natural."

"Trust me it is and I'm gonna show you the tree it comes from and how they tap it when we get home," Alo intervened as he also took one of the Palm wine bottles.

Uma and Mary complained and Alo called Alice once again to return the other drinks and bring some more Palm wine.

One hour had now passed since they got to the restaurant and Alo didn't want to get carried away with the hospitality they'd received so he brought it to the attention of the nice woman. He called Alice again and this time, she was only about five feet from them on another table.

"Thank you so much for everything. I haven't had Palm-wine since I came to this country and that was a big surprise. How much is the bill and where is your master?"

"He said not to charge you but, you can tip if you want," Alice answered with a smile that didn't seem to have and end.

They all realized that the fifty grand was all part of the hospitality and relaxed. Alo told Uma to tip the woman and her partner. Uma gave her fifty dollars and when she tried to call for the other waitress, Risky intervened.

"I'll go take care of her," Risky said and got up, smiling at Alice."Where is she?"

"Okay, sir. I'll get her." Alice went back to the inner room of the restaurant and one minute later, the pretty, young waitress came out and Risky met her half way and gave her one hundred dollars. He then said something to her and she smiled and took a pen from one of the tables and wrote something down on a piece of paper and handed it to Risky. Risky returned to the table, smiling and forgetting why he was there.

Five minutes later. Alice came out of the back room with a bag and called them to join her in the back. The crew all stood up and went to the back with the little Glenn. Alice placed the duffle bag on a table in the room while everybody gathered around the table. Alice opened the bag and removed what looked like a pile of Lufthansa flight-attendant uniforms

"My master wants all of you to try them on because they were made in different sizes," Alice explained and then turned and pointed to a door she said was the changing room."please let me know when you are finished." Alice left the crew alone.

The five adults took turns changing into the flight-attendant uniforms, while little Glenn watched. It took them about twenty-five minutes to change and put away their regular clothes into their respective luggage. The time was now 8:03pm and the flight was due to depart at 10:00pm.

Uma checked herself in the mirror last."Do you think I really need this uniform, honey?" she asked Alo who was dressed and ready. "What flight attendant have you known to bring a little boy on the plane?"

Alo hesitated as he thought about it. Nwoke and Mary were also wondering along the same line after hearing the question.

"I was a flight attendant and I've never seen it happen but, you never know what the man's plan is so, let's just do what he said for now," Mary intervened, relieving Alo of the burden of answering the question.

Alo called Alice to let her know they were ready. Alice, who was already waiting, came back to the room within seconds. She checked the crew and, satisfied with what she observed, asked them to follow her as she lead the way.

"What about our luggage?" Alo asked.

"Don't worry, somebody will bring them, just follow me."

"Yo, this is some slick-ass shit. You heard?" Risky said as they walked out of the restaurant.

Outside, in front of the restaurant, were two Limousines.

"Those are for your safe journey, my friends and good luck. My master will meet you at the Airport," Alice said and smiled

Alo told Nwoke to give her another hundred and Nwoke reached in his pocket and found a one hundred dollar bill and gave to the kind lady. The same two young boys that brought the luggage inside from the taxi, brought the luggage out again and put them in the open trunk of the Limos, without asking what luggage goes where. Uma gave them twenty dollars each and they thanked her and went back inside the restaurant. The crew got in the Limos and headed for the JFK International Airport which was only about twenty five minutes from the restaurant.

It took the slow-driving Limos thirty-five minutes to get to the busy Airport. The two Limos pulled up in front of the Lufthansa German Airlines terminal but, before the crew could think about what to do next, the door opened in the first Limo with Alo, Uma and little Glenn inside and a Nigerian man got in as the diver came down. The very dark-skinned man, who sat in the middle seat, turned around and introduced himself.

"I am Mr. Umadi Mbutu and I will be guiding you out of the country tonight," the man said and then turned back to face the driver. "Please take us around to the back like the last time and also notify the other driver."

The driver did as instructed while the second Limo followed suit. They drove around to an empty spot behind the Airport and parked. Mr. Mbutu got out and told Alo and his wife to get out.

"What is happening?" Alo asked, frightened.

"Don't worry. You are in good hands. I've been doing this for too long. Do you think that your London friend would mislead you?" Mr. Mbutu reassured the couple and their young son.

Alo believed him and stepped out of the Limo. He looked back and saw Risky, Mary and Nwoke walking toward them from the second Limo. They stopped when they got where Alo and the big bossman were standing.

"Please, I need to inspect the passports you have," Mbutu told them while the drivers remained inside the vehicles

They all did as told and he took time inspecting the green passports. Nwoke watched Mbutu closely to make sure he was for real. Mbutu had on an Armani two-piece suit and some Stacy Adams. The collar of the white shirt Nwoke that the man was no joke and any doubts he had in mind, was immediately erased.

"For those of you who just joined these two here, my name is Umadi Mbutu and I am the flight-attendant manager of Lufthansa- German Airlines. I will be taking you across security and into the plane. Now, if you want complete privacy and comfort then you will be boarding the first-class unit and that will mean additional money." He looked at the crew for a response but got none so, he continued. "And, since the first-class seats are 7500 dollars each, I'm gonna need only thirty more thousand from you now."

Alo looked at Nwoke and Risky. They nodded and continued to listen to the business-man's lecture.

Mbutu then focused on Uma and Risky. "Where are you from, sir?" he asked Risky.

"Nigeria, but I was born here," Risky lied with a straight face.

"Okay, I figured that. You are still one of us, right?" Mbutu smiled.

"Yes, of course," Risky responded.

"How about you?" Mbutu asked Uma.

"India but, I'm married to him so I became a naturalized Nigerian citizen," Uma responded with a smile.

"Very well, then. Since you're all Nigerians, you don't need a visa to go home. I hope you haven't killed anyone because I don't help killers. Go and get the money so that we can go. The first-class tickets have already been reserved," Mbutu smiled, knowing that rich people only fly first-class for their convenience."

Risky, Nwoke and Uma brought ten-thousand dollars cash, each and gave it to Mbutu and the Limos pulled back around to the front.

"Your friend in London said that you broke the law by dealing drugs so, the U.S. government is trying to give you a lot of time in prison. If that's the case then, I'll be willing to do my best because I break the law everyday."

Mbutu then bent his head down a little and looked at Glenn." You ever been to Africa, little one?"

Glenn took one look at the intimidating Mbutu and hugged his father, burying his face in his shirt. The Limo came to a stop.

"Now, all you have to do is follow me. Everything else has been taken care of. Remember you're flight attendants and don't worry about what they think about the little boy; we've had them as passengers in our care till another adult picks them up at the other end after signing some papers and presenting an identification. So, that's not a problem." Mbutu finished and got out.

The crew met in front of the Lufthansa terminal and Mbutu checked his Rolex and it said 9:00pm.

"okay, you guys. The U.S. part of the check-point is the hardest but, since you all have foreign passports and going to that country in front of the passport, you should be okay," Mbutu advised and lead the way inside. He motioned to two TSA employees and they came out and took the luggage and disappeared inside, leaving the crew with their carryons.

The crew then followed Mbutu to the special check-in counter for employees of the Airline. He said something to the white female clerk and gave her an envelope. She smiled and stepped aside while Mbutu moved over. The clerk took all the passports, pretended to be inspecting them as she stamped all six passports and gave them back. The crew then followed Mbutu to the boarding gate where they also had to go through secondary inspection. One by one, they put their carryons through the metal detector conveyor belt and also walked through as they presented their passports. Mbutu did not have to go through the process since he wasn't travelling. When the Customs inspecting officer noticed the number of flight attendants, he became inquisitive as he had already seen quite enough flight attendants for Lufthansa pass through.

"I could've sworn I saw enough of you guys go through not that long ago," the tall, skinny, balding white male Customs inspector remarked as he looked at the familiar face of Mr. Mbutu.

Mbutu smiled, exposing his very white teeth. "Oh, I'm sure you did. These ones are in training and they are with me. How is your day?" Mbutu attempted to distract the attention of the focused inspector.

"Let me see the passports," the inspector demanded and took the six passports and started studying them one after another. "Lufthansa must be hiring a lot Nigerian flight attendants. I wonder why?" he commented, still inspecting the passports and not bothering to check the pictures at the computer terminal next to him.

"Well, they pay them less. You know everyone is trying to save some money these days," Mbutu said and checked the growing line of passengers behind them.

The inspector followed him in looking at the impatient flyers. "Some of you can go on the other line, you know," he said to the passengers and then hurriedly gave back the passports to the crew. "I wish you all luck on your new jobs," he said and allowed them to proceed without further examination.

The sweat that had formed on Alo's forehead, quickly dried up as they all walked briskly to gate F which was for the departing Lufthansa Airline.

"Make sure you all change your clothes before sitting down. Remember that was all just to get through. You can now finish the journey as regular first-class passengers, and it was nice doing business with you," Mbutu advised and decided to wait until the crew changed their clothes and got on the plane.

Alo, Nwoke, Risky, Uma and Mary, all went to the rest-rooms and changed into regular clothes. Since first-class passengers were given priority boarding, the crew by-passed the waiting economy-class passengers and went straight to the first-class section of the Boeing 747 under the escort of the flight attendant manager, Mbutu and got comfortable in their respective seats.

"You guys have a safe journey and please keep in touch," Mbutu said in the empty first-class section and left.

Risky had never travelled out of the United States and he was excited about the entire adventure of out-smarting the U.S. Federal government for a change. "We got all these to ourselves?" he asked Nwoke, who was seated to his immediate right.

"I don't think so. We're just the first ones on board but, you never know. Money can change a lot of things. With eighty grand, we just might, but I seriously doubt it. Yo, I liked that answer you gave Mr. Mbutu about being a Nigerian that was born here. That was smart thinking," Nwoke said with a smile.

"I know,"Mary added and leaned forward so she couldsee past Nwoke who sat between her and Risky. Risky blushed as she smiled at him.

Risky took his wallet out of his hip-pocket and opened it to make sure there was nothing tracing him to his past. He saw nothing but a few fifty dollar bills so, he put it back and took out the Nigerian passport from his other hip-pocket and studied it. "So, this is who I am, now....hah?"

Nwoke nodded. "And that's an Ibo name since you look like an Ibo man." Nwoke smiled as he took a glance at the passport.

Alo, Uma and Glenn were seated a few feet in front of Risky, Mary and Nwoke. The family of three had their own small compartment that appeared to be more spacious than the rest.

"I like your new name, yo," Alo turned his head around and said.

"It's more like me than Dante Jackson. That's the white man's name, my nig...ha..ah..ah," Risky responded, raising his voice a little.

Six more passengers joined the fugitives in the first-class section and thirty-five minutes later at 9:59pm, the announcement for take-off was made over the intercom. Everybody, including the flight attendants went to their seats and fastened their seatbelts. Five minutes later, the plane was on the run-way.

Fifteen minutes later, two blonde-hair pretty German women walked down the aisle and introduced themselves as the duty flight attendants for the first-class unit. The women instructed the passengers to study the menus and check their orders for dinner and preferred alcoholic beverages.

"I wish we'd gotten this flight before Christmas," Mary said as she picked up the menu and pressed the small movie screen in front of her. The screen popped out and the movie schedule flashed across it.

"C'mon, you know that's impossible during that busy period without, at least, a three month advance booking. Besides, look what we went through and now, it's looking like you're finally gonna be my wife," Nwoke responded, flipping through the food and beverage menu. "I think I'll have a Moet."

"Are you sure you want to marry me, little man?" Mary teased, smiling at her fiancé.

Nwoke leaned over and kissed her. "Of course I am. I love you."

Risky, who was sitting to the right of Nwoke, overheard the conversation and smiled at the couple. Uma turned their head and smiled.

The drinks were served shortly and they all took their time drinking slowly as they appreciated the freedom. Minutes later the entire section was quiet as the passengers began paying attention to the different movies they had chosen on their personal screens. The Boeing 747 reached its highest altitude with the GPS pointed to Western Germany.

The DEA surveillance on Derrick and Sherrie continued but, was not getting anywhere. The two hadn't communicated with each other since Alo and Risky were on Home Detention.

"Do you really think she was a major part of the conspiracy?" Johnson asked his partner, agent Billard as they sat in the lunch room of the DEA building near downtown Baltimore, eating a tuna sandwich that wasn't tasting too good.

"She could've been by flying back and forth but, right now all we got on her is money laundering. Anyway she's just as guilty as the rest of them so it doesn't matter whether she was pushing the heroin or not," Billard responded.

"I know but, right now they are under the direction of the King-pin and, trust me, when these folks are on their P's and Q's, they can be very difficult to find. I've caught'm with birth certificates and different passports and driver's licenses from all over the world. It's gonna be a fight." Johnson took a bite of the tuna sandwich. He chewed and swallowed rather quickly to avoid the taste.

"I think I better call the Customs and see if they stumbled on anything."

"When are you gonna do that?" Billard drank his soda.

"As soon as I get through eating," Johnson said and took a third bite of the sandwich and swallowed without chewing so that he could feel it going down his throat.

Ten minutes later, the agents finished lunch and Johnson took his government -issued Nextel cell phone and dialed agent Spinard's Nextel. Agent Spinard didn't answer as the line went straight to recording saying that the Customs agents were not available and that, if it was an emergency to leave a message. Since it wasn't an emergency, he didn't leave a message before hanging up. Johnson looked at his partner, feeling sorry for both of them as he realized the day was the first day of 1998 and most normal families were home, celebrating.

The day after the New year, January the 2nd, 1998, agent Spinard and Levitz arrived work rather early to continue where they left off. They now had phone records of Nwoke's land-line at the condo. They were busy studying it when the Nextel cell phone rang, interrupting the process.

"Hello," Spinard answered.

DEA agent, Thomas Johnson was on the line after working through the holidays with his partner, Billard. "Good morning agent Spinard. How was your New Year celebration?" his voice asked over the speaker of the Nextel.

Spinard wondered why the DEA agent was calling so early."It was fine and how was yours?"

"Well, I was here with my partner, trying to figure out how those two made bail in the first place. Who knows where they are right now. I wish Judge Mcmicken had presided over that bond hearing."

"Oh, yeah, maybe that was why it was so high. I didn't think they had that kind of money."

"Anyhow, you got any idea where they might be from those phone records?"

"The last we heard from the Marshalls, they were at the Hilton in Manhattan but, that was before the New year, who knows where they are now," Spinard informed Johnson as he tried to refocus his attention on the numerous international calls that were before his eyes on the list of phone records. "So, how is the Jackson case coming along?"

"Gosh. They still have money left after that bond they lost? You know they are all together so, I would assume Jackson is also in New York, right?"

"Well, I meant the case against him. Is the New york guy talking at all? Year but he's saying it'd been a while since they did any business together. He also said that Jackson had cut him off after he found a better connect whom we think is the Nigerian."

"Great lead." Spinard's attention was now focused on several international calls to London England. "I gotta take care of something right now and call you later if anything comes up on my end. Bye." He then turned to his partner. "Hey, Levitz, what's the number on those men watching Mr. Richard?"

Levitz got the number out of his small phone book and called DEA agent Patterson, who was with Lorenzo, parked not far from Derrick's office. "What do you want me to ask them?"

"Ask them if they got anything."

Levitz did as Spinard told him and Patterson said they had nothing. He also told Levitz that the man was a working-class citizen who didn't appear to be doing anything illegal so far.

"I'm afraid nothing," Levitz responded.

"Okay, they are trying to be smart. What do you think about all these calls to London?" Spinard asked, still studying the list.

Levitz walked over and looked at the page his partner was referring to and nodded.

"You think they ran there already? But, how? I thought we had the Airports sealed with their pictures on the computer terminals."

"Don't put nothing past those Nigerians. I'm gonna get Martha to check these numbers out and, if they belong to a Nigerian, then that's where they are or plan to go."

"I see what you mean. Twenty calls in one month, I wonder if he's got something to do with the 20 kees."

"We won't know until we get the London police to check the individual out." Spinard then buzzed his secretary and she came into the office within two minutes and he gave her the international number with the country code of 44 which is England. He told Martha to go through AT&T to see if they can get the name of the individual the number is registered to in London. Martha took the page with the number on it and went back to her office.

"I wonder why we don't see any call to the big boss in Lagos," Levitz asked.

"Do you really think that the bossman, Mr. Ogar, would give his workers his direct line?"

"I guess not and even if he did, these folks would never call him from their house phone. I think sometimes I forget who we're dealing with here. I'm sorry. I guess

I must be underestimating them, hah?" Levitz lamented and sighed.

"Underestimate is not even the word. But, don't get me wrong now. They ain't no Jesus Christ, we're gonna get'm. One thing about smart criminals is that sooner or later, they get over confident and underestimate us," Spinard concluded and lifted his face from the phone record list, knowing deep inside they had a very long way to go in the search for the fugitives.

The eighteen-hour travel time for the fugitives, landed them at the Murtala Muhammed International Airport in Lagos at exactly 9:00pm on the day after New year. Other than the five-hour lay-over in Munich, there were no problems with the German Department of Customs Inspection (GDCI). They maintained their first-class status throughout the entire travel. The International Dateline (IDL), put them ahead by five hours.

Alo glanced at his watch and it said 5:05pm but, when he looked outside through the Plane's small window, it was already dark. He remembered that Nigeria was five hours ahead of U.S. Eastern Standard Time and immediately adjusted his rolex. The five bottles of Rose consumed by the crew was still having some effects but not to the extent of intoxication. They kept their regular clothes on since they didn't need to impersonate flight attendants. The flight attendants from Germany were mainly Africans who cater for their own kind. The plane stopped and all the passengers got out and proceeded to the International arrival section of the Airport. First-class passengers were given priority at check out so, the crew were the first in line.

"Everybody okay?" Alo asked and turned and looked behind to check on his crew. Since Alo was the first in line, he was confronted by a chubby Customs woman who looked like she had been eating too much rice and fufu.

"Passport, please," the chubby light-skinned Customs woman demanded, looking at Alo.

Alo gave her the passport and also Uma's and Glenn's. She inspected them and stamped them one at a time.

"So, how long were you in the U.S.? Where's the passport you travelled with?" the Nigerian Customs officer asked as she gave the passports back to Alo.

"I lost it when I got my Green-card," Alo responded.

The female Customs officer looked at Alo and then at the Indian-looking Uma and her son and told them to go ahead.

Risky was next with a virgin Nigerian passport that only had one stamp from JFK and a second stamp in Germany.

"Are you all together?" the woman asked, studying Risky.

"Yes," Risky answered, getting a little nervous at the intimidating deep Nigerian accent of the chubby officer.

In Nigeria, the Customs were called officers and not agents. The inspector looked at Risky and then over at Alo, who was standing by waiting for the rest of the crew to get through so they could go to baggage claim and get their luggage from the conveyor belt. "Can you wait there with them?" she said as she pointed at Alo and family. She then pressed a button and, minutes later as she was inspecting Nwoke's passport, her supervisor showed up.

Nwoke and Mary were now sweating on their foreheads, wondering if the U.S. Customs had informed the Nigerian Customs to look out for them. The woman just ordered Nwoke and Mary to join Alo, Uma, Glenn and Risky. The supervisor studied the crew as the Customs woman continued to screen other passengers from the same flight. There were three other lines formed at three other inspection counters.

"What is the problem?" the tall, slim dark-skinned Customs supervisor asked, looking at Alo and the rest but then, he stopped and focused on Mary. "Hey, where do I know you from?" he asked Mary.

"I'm a flight attendant with British Airways and I probably saw you during one of my stops here. Anyway, I'm now employed by Lufthansa and my uniform is in my luggage," Mary answered, hoping that this was their way out of the mess.

"And who are they?"

"They are my family and they are with me," Mary responded, now looking a little relieved.

The supervisor asked them to follow him and the crew did so.

"Let me handle this. I think I have more than enough money in my pocket-book," Mary whispered to Nwoke as they walked behind the Customs supervisor. She knew that all the Nigerian Customs employees wanted was money.

The man lead them to his private office and told them to sit down. The office looked like a holding-cell in the U.S. with four wooden benches.

"Excuse me, sir. May I have a word with you, please?" Asked Mary in a kind tone.

The supervisor looked at the pretty young woman and wondered what she could possibly want to talk about in private. "Okay, come along, my dear," he responded and lead her out of the office door and closed the door.

Mary opened her pocket-book and brought out a stack of one hundred dollar bills that totalled one thousand dollars and gave it to the man and turned her back to him. She closed the pocket-book and turned to face the happy-looking man. "I' think that should take care of me and my people, right. I have a wedding coming up this week, so please let us go. We are in a hurry," Mary pleaded with confident eyes and added; maybe I'll see you again when I pass through under a better situation, you know what I mean?"

The man wondered what kind of trouble Mary and her crew were in to give him one thousand American dollars. He had never received that much in bribery for simple immigration violation. He concluded that since they didn't kill the president, they were okay with him. The very last sentence made the man smile as he sensed that he just might get lucky with the pretty flight attendant. He also wished he was twenty years younger. "Okay, take your people and go to baggage-claim and I look forward to seeing you soon," the man said and stuffed the cash into his pocket, looking to his left and right to make sure nobody saw what just went on.

Mary and crew left the Customs supervisor office and proceeded to the baggage-claim area of the busy airport. They claimed their luggage and checked out through secondary inspection where they had to declare the content of their luggage and open them if asked to. This was to ensure there were no contraband being brought into the country.

Outside the airport, they all gathered and hugged each other simultaneously as Nwoke lead them in prayer that lasted about five minutes.

"That's very good, Mr. Nwanta, well I mean Rev. Nwanta junior," Mary commended her fiancé as other's laughed. That was her first time ever seeing Nwoke lead a prayer anywhere.

"Hey, Risky. This is safe haven. You should be okay, now because we do things different here in the motherland, yo," Alo told Risky, who was busy studying the very busy environment and the almost all-black travellers.

"Oh, yeah? So, this is Africa, hah?" Risky responded as he continued to observe the cultural difference and the different shades of the black skin. "I believe my ancestors are from here. Just look at these folks; other than the Asians and Arabs and the few white people, these folks look just like the people you see in Baltimore city. If somebody told me this was the Africa that I'd been hearing about, I wouldn't have believed it."

The others just smiled as they listened and watched Risky's expression and reaction to the strange city. Little Glenn, who was almost two years of age, didn't say a word but one could tell he knew there was something different about the place.

Nigeria had a tropical climate which meant hot weather all year round. The average temperature was about one hundred degrees Fahrenheit and the seasons were: Rainy season, which began around June and lasted till September, followed by the dry season which went on from September through December when it briefly changes to Hamattan which is extremely dry with cool winds and an average temperature of about 70° Fahrenheit for the months of December and January. It changes back over to the extremely dry and hot temperature without humidity. It is the most populous country in Africa with a population of about 134,935,000. Abuja is the administrative capital while Lagos is the commercial capital. The major ethnic groups are: Hausa and Fulani who make up about 29%, Yoruba 21%, Ibo 18%, Ijaw 10% and Kanuri 4%. English is the official language, spoken by all, then there are about 250 ethnic and linguistic groups. The current system of government is Democracy with an election of the President, Senate, House of Representatives and House of Assembly every four years, similar to that of the U.S.

"Don't they make their own cars? All I see are Japanese and European," Risky observed as they stood by the taxi-stand. "You know what, I may keep my new African name."

"Well, I'm glad you said that, at least you can now tell Sherrie and the rest of the non-believers to join the bandwagon," Alo said as an available taxi pulled up at the busy taxi-stand.

Nwoke remembered what his father told his family in 1985 when they first arrived at the same airport and quickly intervened when Alo was trying to approach the empty taxi. "No, uncle. Let's wait for marked taxi. They usually park on the other side," he pointed at another taxi-stand with an Airport security guard standing at the entrance but no taxis.

"Oh yeah, I forgot, let's go. Everybody hold on to your luggage and carryons," Alo instructed and lead the way, followed by the rest.

Before the crew got to the taxi stand, two taxis pulled up with their dome-lights on.

"Oh, I see what you mean, now. So, what were those?" Mary asked.

"Private ones and they are cheaper but could be very dangerous, too," Nwoke responded as they stopped by the two empty taxis.

"You think I spoke too soon, yo? We ain't got that kind of problem at the U.S. Airports," Risky said.

"Yes you do. Those Gypsy cabs do the same thing. You can take your chance with those guys, all of them ain't armed robbers, you know," Nwoke countered.

Alo and his family got in the first taxi while Nwoke, Risky and Mary hopped in the second one. The drivers got out, wearing their white uniforms and put the luggage in the trunks

"You know what, I like that flight attendant," Risky said as he sat in the front seat with the driver.

"Please, sir. Can you tell me where you are going?" the brown skinned driver asked with a heavy Nigerian accent and Yoruba dialect.

"Oh, I'm sorry. Please blow your horn so that I can find out from my uncle. I think it's the Marriot but let me make sure," Nwoke said and got out of the taxi and rushed to the first taxi with Alo and family inside. He asked Alo through the open back window on the passenger side.

"Federal Palace," Alo answered.

But, Nwoke wanted to go back to the Marriot in Ikeja town for lost memories. "Why not the Marriot in Ikeja?"

Alo thought about it for a minute, looking at Uma, who nodded. "Okay. Driver, please take us to the Marriot in Ikeja. please." Alo had never been to the Marriot since he avoided foreign investors in his country.

Nwoke came back to the second taxi and told the driver to take them to the Marriot International.

Mary looked at him and smiled. "I know why you insist on going there.

Nwoke returned the smile."Just for old time sake, baby."

Risky turned around with a smile of his own as he overheard the soon-to-be married couple. "That's cool, yo. I think that's where Nnngooozi, well I mean the flight attendant said she was gonna stay at," Risky said, having a hard time pronouncing the name of the flight attendant he met on the connection flight from Munich.

"You mean, Ngozi, yo. That's gonna be close to the same way I met Mary almost five years ago," Nwoke said as the cab pulled off behind the first cab. Three more Airport cabs occupied the spaces left by the two cabs.

"You can't be for real, my man. Word?"

"That's my word. You can ask her, right now," Nwoke looked at Mary.

"You don't have to ask, Risky. I was also a flight attendant with the British Airways at the time but, Nwoke and his friend were leaving the country instead,"Mary intervened.

"And now, you guys are getting ready to be married, hah? You know what, I think I'm gonna like it here in Nigeria. That girl got Sherrie by a little bit, sorry to say," Risky commented as he watched the busy city under the illumination of the street lights.

"I can't believe you're saying that about your live-in girlfriend, Risky," Mary added.

"I don't think he said anything wrong, Mary. C'mon now,"Nwoke joined the conversation in support of his male counterpart.

"Fine, I'm out of it. I see I can't win against you two," Mary said, giving up on the argument.

Nwoke looked at the taxi driver and remembered the driver that had lectured him and Uzo the last time they were at the Marriot as young adults. "Hey, Oga wetin de happen?"Nwoke asked the taxi driver in broken english.

"Nothing.... I just de manage. How you de?" the skinny, middle aged driver responded in the same kind of english as he studied Nwoke through the rearview mirror. "So, where Una de come from?" the driver continued as Risky and Mary listened

Mary could understand some of the words but Risky only could only pick up the english words.

"I de fine and we just de land from America," Nwoke answered and looked at Risky who seemed to be very attentive. "Risky, if you're wondering, I asked him: 'what's happening?'And he said; nothing and that he's just managing' Then I answered that we're just landing from America," Nwoke interpreted for Risky and smiled.

"Yo, I'm gonna have Ngozi teach me that shit. I like that!"

Mary laughed as the Mercedes station wagon taxi came to a complete stop at a traffic light. There weren't that many pedestrians at that time of night as it was almost 10:00pm. Even the traffic wasn't as heavy as it was during the day time.

"I guess everybody is in the village for the New Year celebration," Nwoke said as he observed the light pedestrian and automobile traffic, unlike the last time he was there.

They continued to trail the first taxi with Alo and family for another fifteen minutes before they finally pulled up in front of the five-star International Hotel chain. The same Bell-boys who worked at the hotel five years prior, were still there and immediately recognized Nwoke and Mary, who hadn't changed much as they helped with the luggage.

"My friend, you look like a man, now," one of the Bell-boys said as he picked up one of the luggage by himself, followed by his co-workers as all four Bell-boys on night duty gathered around the rich kid's luggage, including his company and took them inside the lobby.

The Bell-boys then waited for the crew to check in.

"Well, at least we don't have to look over our shoulders anymore. I'm gonna handle the check in this time," Alo said, knowing that the employees of the hotel were not paying any attention to U.S. news and even if they did, they weren't going to give there own kind up without any benefits. He pulled out his green passport and confidently walked up to the check-in counter and presented his passport. "We need three suites, please," Alo told the pretty British receptionist.

The receptionist didn't even cross check the picture on the passport. "And how long are you staying?" the petite, blonde hair beauty asked with a heavy British accent as she typed several keys on the key-board of the computer.

Alo turned to Nwoke. "We'll be leaving tomorrow morning so that we can plan the wedding, right?"

"Right," Nwoke responded, holding Mary and looking at the Bell-boys who were waiting to take the luggage to the suites.

The check-in was completed in ten minutes. Alo got the cash from Uma and paid the bill in dollars. They got their keys and gave the Bell-boys the go-ahead to take the luggage up to the suites which were on the same floor of the half-empty hotel.

Risky tipped the Bell-boys after all the luggage were in the respective suites. He went into his private suite and called the number that Ngozi had given him. He was glad to learn that it was an international cell phone that worked all over the world on roaming, furnished by Lufthansa.

In their suite, Nwoke tried to use the prepaid cell phone to no avail since the network was different in Nigeria. He would have to buy a local cell phone in order to get any service. But, he wasn't gonna worry about that just yet.

"You don't think the U.S. feds just might send the info to these people?" Mary asked as she was undressing to get in the tub.

"Nah, they probably think we're still in New York. Let me see what they got on CNN international." Nwoke picked up the remote and turned the station to CNN international. "Even if they do, people ain't paying no attention to that type of stuff unless they start offering big rewards, then we might have problems."

"You gonna take a bath with me, baby husband?" Mary asked and dropped the last piece of clothing on the floor and walked into the bathroom, switching seductively.

Nwoke dropped the remote and quickly undressed, following behind his soon-to-be-wife.

Ngozi came up to Risky's room twenty minutes after he called her and had no plans of returning to her Lufthansa- employee reserved room on the ground level.

Uma and Alo were still trying to catch up on missed loving as they ordered room-service late supper.

"Are you sure that we are completely safe, now?" Uma asked as she tried to feed Glenn some jealoff rice.

"I should hope so but nothing is one hundred percent guaranteed. I know it's gonna be a lot harder finding us here than in any of those European countries,"Alo responded as he drank some Guinness to get ready for the night ahead.

Uzo and Cynthia were already in the village after celebrating both New Year and Christmas in their newly erected villa. Uzo's father was surprised at the sight of the daughter-in-law but, neither one said a word to the other. Mr. Otu didn't want his son involved in drugs like he was and also didn't like the fact that his son's wife was older and wiser. Mr. Otu was caught between a rock and a hard place. He knew that the wise Cynthia could easily blackmail him since no one in his family had no idea how he really acquired his wealth. There tired drug dealer decided it was best to keep quiet and leave things the way they are.

"Have you heard from your friend, Uzo?" Mr. Otu asked as they had spent New Year at Uzo's villa in the village.

"Not yet, dad but, he has a wedding coming up with Cynthia's friend and former co-worker.

"Oh really? When?" Mrs. Otu intervened, sipping on a glass of Domperignon.

"He wanted to have it before Christmas but then, I don't know what happened," Uzo said and forked a piece of barbequed goat meat to avoid any further questions from his father, who really didn't pay much attention to world News. He chewed the delicious meat and swallowed hard.

Mr. Otu remembered Cynthia's co-worker that he had come in contact with and wondered if she was the one Nwoke was going to marry. He also decided to keep quiet and remain out of the way.

"You're gonna be the Best-man, right?" Mr. Otu asked as he looked outside in the big party garden at the numerous guests who were dancing to the band's music.

"That's what he said," Uzo answered, not even sure Nwoke and co made it out of the U.S. with the passports he'd arranged for.

"Can I be one of the Brass maids or Flower girls?"Ije, who wasn't too happy about Nwoke getting married to somebody else intervened. She remembered her brief encounter and thought Uzowould have kept in touch but he didn't. Ije had a new and better looking boyfriend in college and didn't really care.

"Ije, you'd have to ask him. I'm sure he wouldn't mind," Cynthia cut in. She glanced at Mr. Otu and wondered if he had really stopped dealing drugs.

Nwogu had just graduated High school and was busy watching American music videos in the family room with other teenage guests. He was going to attend Oxford University during the Spring semester. He received the admission letter one week before Christmas.

"Son, how's business been?" Mr. Otu asked, wondering if his son was involved in illegal drug trade with Cynthia. He had learned about Nwoke's plight from his father, Rev. Nwanta but didn't want to let Uzo know he knew. He wanted to hear it from Uzo. How could he advise his son about something he was a part of? The more he thought about it, the more he wanted to confront Uzo but, he couldn't, because of Cynthia's knowledge of his past. He had to keep things the way they were, at least, for now.

The time now was 10:45pm and that was late in the village but, not in the town.

"I think I'll put Patience to bed," Cynthia said and got up to pick up the sleeping little girl from her Crib and take her to bed.

Uzo sat there, with a bottle of Heineken in his hand, wondering if Nwoke had tried to reach his father's house and got no answer since he didn't have the number to the village villa the last time he spoke to him. He remembered the satellite phone that was introduced to him by one of his Japanese suppliers and wondered why he didn't order it before leaving for Nigeria. How was Nwoke supposed to reach him in Nigeria? The answer to that question remained on Uzo's mind until he went to bed.

The fugitives slept well and peacefully for the first time since they had been on the run. The following morning which was January 2nd, 1998, they checked out of the Marriot and took two taxis to the local Airport. They boarded a flight to Owerri local Airport which was built after Uzo, Alo and Nwoke had left the country. The airport was much closer than the previously used Port-Harcourt local airport, which had now been upgraded to International Airport. But, it only catered to flights from France and other African countries on the international level.

"Yo, you think those motherfuckers might just decide to come this far?" Risky asked Alo as they sat in the arrival area of the Owerri national airport.

"They've done it before and I believe the charges are serious enough for them to come here," Alo responded, looking around for a taxi.

"What charges, dope? That ain't shit."

"When there's a dead body involved, it is. They might even file murder charges against Mr. Ogar."

"What are you talking about, yo?" Risky asked, not aware of the carrier who died on the plane because of the busted ball of heroin.

Alo took a few minutes and told him what happened on the fateful day, according to the News media. Risky was now less comfortable about the so-called 'safe haven'.

'I ain't know all that. Goddaamn, yo. You really think we alright over here?"

Alo looked at his friend and partner in crime, then looked at the rest of the crew. "For now, we should be. There goes two station wagon taxis. Let's get out of here you all."

The thought of the U.S. federal agents coming after him and then, transporting him on the plane in hand-cuffs and leg-irons, made Risky look over his shoulder, wondering if one of the white men behind them, was a federal agent from the U.S. but, when he took a second look and noticed the 'Shell Oil' on the man's yellow shirt, he relaxed and walked quickly behind the crew.

"They ain't coming this soon, yo," Alo said after noticing the paranoia in Risky's movement and expression. "By the time they figure out where we are, we'll be gone and, trust me, this is not the U.S. where they have all that high-tech network. We can buy our freedom here even if they happen to locate us," Alo reassured the American friend.

The last statement by Alo made Risky feel a whole lot better. "You are my peeps, yo. You all something else, if I'd got jammed up with one my hood brothers, I don't know where we'd be, right now.

Glenn bumped Alo to show him another mixed little boy who was looking at him. Alo and his family got into the first taxi as the little boy waved at Glenn like he knew him.

Nwoke, Mary and Risky got in the second one and the crew left for Ubakala Umuahia.

The U.S. Marshalls office in New York city, headed by Robert Davidson, a tall slim build bald-headed white male in his mid forties, had ordered his Marshalls to check all the Hotels and Inns in the state of New York. He also requested the assistance of the local police. All law enforcement officers concerned, had copies of the fugitives' pictures as they embarked on the venture. This lasted till the third of January without yielding any favourable result or lead.

In the end, Davidson ordered a few men to stake out in the five-star hotels the fugitives had been spotted in previous days. "These goddaaamn Nigerians just make me so sick to my stomach that I could just shoot one of them on sight!" Davidson said in a loud angry voice to his partner, Donald Spencer as they stood outside the Trump International hotel. The long Winter Trench coat he was wearing made him look more like a private detective than a U.S. Marshall.

The clouds were beginning to form at 3:25pm and the heavy winds that swept through the city made the two Marshalls shift side-ways to avoid a direct hit as light snow flurries began to fall, sending them running to their Ford Explorer

At the Federal Courthouse in downtown Baltimore, Assistant U.S. Attorney, James Cohen, had a meeting with the lead investigators of the case from the DEA and Customs; agents Johnson and Billard of the DEA and Spinard and Levitz from the Customs, respectively. They all sat around the conference table in the special room for prosecutors to hold private sessions. The agents paid close attention to the man who was in charge of prosecuting the fugitives and their big boss, Gabriel Ogar.

"Gentlemen, I've added another charge to Mr. Gabriel Ogar's indictment and that is the charge of murder one. This comes as a result of the passenger who died on the plane from the heroin he gave her," Cohen informed the attentive federal agents. "Now, Spinard, you said we should contact the British police for a follow up on the Nigerian two of the fugitives were calling, right?"

"Yes sir. AT&T has confirmed the name on the number and it is a Nigerian name. I just think they might even be at the residence as we speak," Spinard responded as the others listened.

"I'm in support of the idea, sir, since Mr. Jackson is presumed to be in their company," Johnson added.

"And if we get any tangible information, we pass it on to INTERPOL and if they don't want to cooperate to our satisfaction, then we'd have to make arrangements to go to the ally nation since we have an extradition treaty with United Kingdom," Cohen explained conclusively.

The agents agreed with a nod.

"We still have the surveillance on those two, Ms. Washington and Derrick Richard, correct?"

"Yes, we do," Johnson answered.

"Any connection to the London number by Ms. Washington or Mr. Richards?

"Not to our knowledge, at least nothing from the phone records indicate such," Spinard responded.

"So, you've already confirmed with the FBI that the name on the phone in London is in fact a Nigerian name, right?"

"Not only that, we also checked with Mr. Bayo and the carriers just to make sure," Spinard added.

"Good job. I'm gonna fax a request for the release of information on both individuals who are probably married and, with the Judge's approval and an attachment of the indictment, we should be able to get something done without having to physically go there. Any other ideas or questions?" When Cohen got no response, he dismissed the agents.

The time was 4:00pm in Ubakala Umuahia and, at the lavish estate of young Nwoke Nwanta, celebration and preparation for the 'Golden Wedding', was in full effect. All the married women from the village of Ubakala were busy rehearsing in dance groups under the guidance of Nwoke's aunt. Nwoke had asked his mother to start making preparation for the traditional wedding and the Rev. Nwanta was in charge of the church wedding. the traditional wedding was scheduled for the same night the bride and groom arrived home. Nwoke wasted no time in sending his driver to Otu's mansion in Aba to get Uzo and family but, unfortunately Uzo had gone to his village with his family. The village of Mbaino was in the same state as Ubakala. The caretaker told Uzo's driver that that Uzo's entire family went to the village for the holidays. He gave Uzo's driver directions to Mbaino and the driver went to Uzo's village and delivered the message. Uzo said to tell Nwoke that they would be at the traditional wedding later on that night.

The lavishly planned wedding was scheduled to begin at 10:00pm and last till morning while the church wedding would start at 4:00pm the following day followed by reception at both Saint Thomas Cathedral church and the Anglican Church in Ubakala village.

Uzo's driver came back a little later than he was supposed to due to the double trip he had to make. He parked the Toyota in the big car-park on the side of the building and got out. "Oga, he said that they will be arriving later on and that he is very happy at the News and also for the two of you," the short, stocky young man said as he walked into the huge compound and saw Uzo standing next to his aunt, observing the wedding preparation.

"Obi, thank you very much," Nwoke said and dismissed the hired help. Oga means: master in english.

Risky walked over to Nwoke and asked if he could use the land-line phone.

"Go ahead, it's in the Reception room on the first floor of the general area," Nwoke directed and pointed Risky in the right direction as he continued to listen to his aunt's lecture on how the traditional wedding goes.

Risky looked at the beautiful building, supposedly built by a German company and became confused. The villa was sitting on six acres of land with at least ten luxury vehicles parked in the 'Car-park, which was isolated from the main building. The color of the entire building was beige outside and white inside, shining like it had wax on it but it was really water and dirt-resistant paint. Risky stopped in his tracks and came back to where Nwoke was standing. "Main man, can you get somebody to show me where it's at? I'm lost in this mutherfucker."

Nwoke and his aunt laughed at the American gangster.

"Yo, please don't use curse-words around older people like my aunt. It's disrespectful in my culture. But, hold on a second, let me see this dance and I'll take you to the phone"

"Oh, I apologize, maam," Risky said and stood there and watched the pretty women shake there behind to the traditional African music which he couldn't understand the words.

There were about five different dance groups doing different dances. The live bands would arrive later. Most of the women were from different parts of the country but, came home for the holidays. This was a tradition in the Ibo culture; most indigenes travelled to the village of their birth to spend the Christmas holidays.

"Yo, this shit sounds like go-go music," Risky commented, shaking his head to the drum beat with eyes fixed on a woman who had the most protruding behind under the all-lace wrapper. "And that food smells so good that I'm already hungry. Is that the same thing we had in New York?"

"Yup. But, these are paid Chefs that my mom hired so it just might taste a little better," Nwoke responded as his aunt looked at him and wondered if he would cheat on his wife with one of the women dancing.

Nwoke and Risky watched the dances for about another ten minutes and then, Nwoke decided to walk his foreign friend to the Reception area of the villa to use the phone. Risky called Ngozi and invited her to the village for the wedding and the flight attendant told him she would request an emergency leave from her boss. Ngozi promised to be there if her boss granted her the leave. She took the name and address and hung up so she could ask her boss before the next scheduled flight departing at the same time as the traditional wedding was to begin.

"Yo, is that the flight attendant?" Nwoke asked.

"Yes, I think I'm in love, my nig."

"All these pretty bitches out here with no kids and no stretch-marks, dancing for you and you gonna come in here just to call a flight attendant that's five hundred miles away?"

"What's wrong with that? You and your man married one."

Nwoke paused for a minute, almost forgetting that the scheduled wedding was with a former flight attendant. "Maybe they have a way with men wanting to marry them after the first night, I don't know,"he admitted.

"Maybe so. Now, I'm gonna go watch some more and maybe make my choice for tonight if Ngozi doesn't show up till tomorrow," Risky said and smiled as they left the now empty reception room.

About twenty minutes later, Alo and his family walked over from Alo's mansion which was half a block away.

"This is really nice and where is Mary?" Uma asked, looking at the selected pretty women dancing intensely.

"Well, she can't be seen until the actual traditional wedding starts at 10pm," Nwoke answered, eyes fixed on the female dancers.

"Oh, really? I see why you're out here. You better be good, young man," Uma said and then turned to Alo. "And you, too.I wish I could dance like that, I would definitely join them." Uma started shaking her behind a little. After about two minutes, some of the women dancing, noticed and stopped and started looking the pretty Indian woman and smiled.

"They can teach you if you care to learn," Alo said so that Uma can get away for a few minutes and give him breathing space.

Uma hesitated and thought about it for a few seconds and decided to stay close to her husband before one of the women takes him away from her.

Thirty-five minutes later at 5:15pm, Theo and his wife, along with the rest of Nwoke's family, walked through the big iron gates of the villa from the Nwanta's mansion, which was right next door. The Reverend and Mrs. Nwanta, who arranged the wedding and then turned it over to one of Nwoke's aunt who was vacationing from London, disregarded the News of their son being a fugitive for the moment. They didn't want the so-called mistake by the smartest child in the family to ruin their happiness for him. Nwoke's physical presence killed any dubious perception of him and Alo by the villagers or anybody else who heard about the situation. The kind of attention created by fugitives in the U.S. was quite the opposite in Nigeria. Nigerians cared less about somebody running from a foreign government as long as they didn't commit murder.

The Reverend Nwanta and his first son, Theo, had planned a second wedding reception in the church compound at Aba for the soul reason of confusing the American federal agents should attempt to disrupt their son's Holy matrimony.

Two hours later, at 7:25pm, Uzo, Cynthia and Ije arrived in what looked like a brand new Rolls-Royce and one of the caretakers directed Uzo's driver on where to park since they planned to spend the night and maybe even stay longer. Uzo's driver was then shown to a room in the 'boys' quarters where Nwoke's caretakers and drivers stayed. Mr. and Mrs. Otu, who followed their son in a Ford Expedition, got out of the SUV and allowed the driver to park the over-sized truck next to the Rolls-Royce and do as Uzo's driver did. The rich couple found Nwoke's parents and joined them to honor their special invitation.

Cynthia managed to find Mary in the special isolation room in the main building. "Oh mine! I'm so glad you made it out of that country!" She exclaimed as she hugged her longtime friend she hadn't seen in years. She planned to remain in the room with Mary until the traditional occasion began in a couple of hours.

"Oh, Cynthia, if you only knew how relieved I was when we got on that plane, you would have rejoiced with me. I hope my parents had enough time to make it here in time for the church wedding tomorrow."

"They're not coming tonight?"

"I'm afraid not. It was just too short a notice for them to fly all the way from Liberia but, I'm sure they'll be here tomorrow," Mary answered, dressed in a gold and diamond lace wrapper and blouse with a head-tie to match. Mrs. Nwanta paid about ten thousand American dollars. Mary looked like a million bucks with the extra long diamond and gold earrings, pearl necklace and gold bracelet. There were two young females dressing her as Cynthia watched. "Can you all excuse us for a minute, please?" Mary asked the women so that she and Cynthia could have some privacy.

"You look like the Queen of Africa. I wish Uzo and I had a wedding like this," Cynthia said after the women left. She studied her girlfriend once again from head to toe, admiring her.

After spending about twenty minutes having girl-to-girl talk, Mary called one of the caretakers to show Cynthia to her room which was next to her's. Since the little girl, Patience was with her grand parents, Cynthia went to the special guest room, dropped her stuff and went in search of her husband in the busy compound.

Uzo wasn't worried about the occasion and the fugitive status of his best friend as they stood outside and watched the traditional dancers, talking about old times.

"I heard Helen and Deborah just graduated," Uzo informed Nwoke.

"Oh, really? You know what they majored in?" Nwoke responded.

"Nah, but it was a degree from the University of Port-Harcourt. I still think about her, man. I really liked her and her mother."

"Me, too. Helen was supposed to be my wife but I guess I was just too young but, this Mary did something to me, boy," Nwoke said and they both laughed out loud, still focused on the dancers.

"I wonder what's so funny?"Cynthia intervened as she found her husband. "Hello Nwoke. I can see why he's out here with you. C'mon, let me show you our room and you can come back and watch all you want." Cynthia took Uzo's hand and lead him away from the pretty female dancers that looked like their butts were carved like a statue. Uzo couldn't return until the traditional wedding began as Cynthia decided to make him forget about the women.

Everybody from all over the village and some parts of the state, assembled in the middle of the huge compound as police security forces guarded the estate. There weren't too many juveniles since it wasn't an appropriate environment for them. The time was now 9:47pm and anticipation was growing for the rich bride and groom who had received so much publicity. Even though there wasn't enough time for the invited guests to make it on time, most of them still did since they were already home for the holidays. This was the main reason why such occasions were scheduled during the Christmas holidays.

Mr. and Mrs. Otu, Rev. and Mrs. Nwanta, sat at the top of the wooden stage that had been put together earlier in the day. Patience sat between Uzo's parents while her parents sat opposite in a lower part of the stage but, still had a perfect view.

At exactly 10:00pm, the bride and groom, dressed in traditional outfits that matched, came dancing out of the main building in carefully selected steps that weren't too complicated to learn. The live band was playing to the beat of the foot steps as the two danced toward the stage in the middle of the compound with all eyes on them. The camera man provided extra lighting on top of the powerful fluorescent lights that lit the entire compound. Personal cameras were also flashing. The 'Golden Wedding' was indeed looking like the 'Royal Wedding' of England. From the three-foot stage, Nwoke and Mary danced their way down and started circling the spectators who watched with unparalled passion. Red roses poured out from the crowd, followed by a bunch of ten-naira bills but, Uzo and Cynthia were the only ones throwing ten-pound notes. Three of Nwoke's many aunts were responsible for picking up all the money from the ground. They danced their way back to the stage and then, the selected female and three male dancers joined them. Ten minutes later, the speaker and conductor took the stage with the mic as the live band stopped playing. The bride and groom were introduced and the purpose of the occasion was announced, disregarding anything else, like the couples fugitive status which some of the attendants knew.

Even though Ije had a boyfriend, she still had a desire for Nwoke. She stood alone and watched him as he danced with his new brideand thought about their passionate encounter together almost five years ago. The dancers that surrounded the bride and groom, shielded her from catching a complete view of the bride. She was able to see Nwoke from where she was, far in the back, isolated from the regular crowd. Ije moved a little to the left and saw Mary from head to toe. She didn't think that Mary looked better than her. She thought Mary was too old for the twenty-three year old Nwoke. She was glad she didn't invite her boyfriend and, now she just might have a chance to bring back some lost memories. Would Nwoke cheat on his new bride on the night of their wedding? She thought to herself and figured the only way to find out was to try but, not tonight.

Risky who was busy watching the women and not praying too much attention to the main attraction, looked to his left and saw a sexy young girl standing by herself and decided to join her. He walked over to where Ije was standing and stood beside her. "Hello, pretty. What's up with you?" Risky said in a loud voice over the music. "I mean wetin de happen?"Risky recited what Nwoke taught him in the cab from the airport to the Marriot in Lagos. The broken-English didn't sound too good but, Ije seemed to understand what he was trying to say.

Ije immediately recognized Risky was an American from the way he pronounced the broken-English words and his real accent. She turned to see who it was, trying to learn broken English. She cracked a smile at the tall, brown-skinned handsome figure, whose age she couldn't quite make out. "Who are you?" she asked looking him over.

"My name is David Okeke and I am Nwoke's guest of honor," Risky answered, trying to look serious.

Ije studied him for a few seconds and wondered if he was Nigerian born in the 'States or a real American. "Is that your real name?"

"Yeah. David Okeke."

"So, where are you from in the U.S.?"

Risky was surprised at the instinct or knowledge of the young girl with a slight British accent. He decided to just be himself. "Okay, you win. I'm Risky from Baltimore and I travelled with those two getting married over there," he pointed at the stage. "I'm probably going back after the wedding," Risky lied.

Ije realized the man beside her might just be lying about everything to impress her. "You're gonna go back where?"

Risky drank another cup of Palm wine from the tray one of the female servers was passing around. "This is good stuff. I wish I could take some back to Baltimore. "Oh, I'm going back to Baltimore."

"How are you gonna do that when your real name and face are all over the world?" Ije countered and waited boldly for a response.

"How old are you and how long have you lived abroad?" Risky asked, studying the age of the teenage-looking girl.

"I'm Ije and I'm Uzo's sister." Ije didn't want to say her age.

"You mean the dude from London?"

"Yes, Cynthia's husband and, I'm twenty. How old are you?"

"Ten years older than you. I think I'll go dance with some women," Risky responded, trying to avoid the young girl as the alcohol in the all-natural Palm wine was beginning to have effect. He started dancing his way through the thick crowd to the selected group of female dancers.

The dancers noticed the stranger as they were dancing and some wondered where he was from, dancing out of tune and out of dress code. Risky had one of his Air Jordans, a white T-shirt, baggy jeans and a New York Yankees baseball cap. His Gucci link glittered under the light. Regardless of his style, the female dancers welcomed the different-looking man and some actually got closer, with interest as Risky mixed into the crowd of dancers.

After about fifteen minutes of dancing, Risky drank some more and just stood aside and waited like a hunting Lion. He thought about Ije but decided that her parents would probably want to know where she was gonna spend the night. Two and half hours later, one of the female dancers who was obviously tired of dancing, approached him and he didn't have to do much talking to know what she wanted. He took her to his room for a night of village pleasure.

The celebration of the traditional wedding lasted till about 4:30am and the traditional Ruler of the village walked in with his body guards and took the stage with the microphone. He was dressed in a gold and silver Dashiki with a rope gold necklace around his neck. He was well known for his ownership of one thousand cows and three thousand goats. The village Ruler had four wives and twenty children. He pronounced Nwoke and Mary man and wife in the silence of the early morning as everyone kept quiet. The live-band and crowd came back alive as everyone mixed in with each other in a final celebration of the occasion.

The bride and groom slept until about 10:00am when they were greeted by one of the female caretakers.

"Good afternoon, sir. You have a visitor in the reception," the maid said as Nwoke opened the door.

"Who is it?"

"I haven't seen her before but, I think she may be from overseas because of the way she spoke."

Nwoke couldn't figure out who it was at the moment. "Okay, thanks, I'll be right down." Nwoke went to the bathroom, washed his face and brushed his teeth and got ready by putting on a pair of shorts and a tank-top with some slippers to cover his feet. "I'll be back Mary. Somebody wants to see me downstairs," he told his new wife who was still laying in bed. He descended the Oriental-rugged stairwell and walked across to the reception room which was past several guest rooms and the living room that was connected to the parlour in the main building. Nwoke walked into the reception room to face Ije Otu who was sitting there by herself as most guests and family members were still sleeping.

"Hello, long time no see and no hear," she said, looking at Nwoke's muscular thighs and slowly stopping in his eyes with a smile. She wore a tight T-shirt and a loosely fitted skirt that made one wonder what was underneath.

"Hi, Ije. I had no idea you were here. Why didn't you join the dancers on stage?" Nwoke said, not really paying the young woman much attention.

"Well, you know now." Ije stood up so that Nwoke could see her completely as she wore no bra.

"Well, you've grown into a very pretty woman," Nwoke noticed the hard nipples and he immediately remembered what happened years before.

"Can I get a hug, please," Ije moved toward Nwoke and he hugged her and she held him tight, squeezing her breast against his hard chest. Her platted hair smelled like fresh roses and Nwoke was tempted.

Nwoke quickly came to his senses when he realized that Mary just might decide to see who his company was. He pulled away from Ije abruptly. "I'm sorry but I can't do this. It might bring me bad luck," Nwoke said as he stepped back.

Ije retreated and then went into her pocketbook and took out a card and gave it to Nwoke, feeling somewhat rejected. "Bye, married man and I'll see you some other time. I'm gonna go back to my room, next to Risky's," she said, attempting to make Nwoke jealous but had no success. She brushed past Nwoke and exited the reception room as one of the maids walked in to clean it.

On the way back upstairs, Nwoke wondered if thirty-one year old Risky would sleep with a twenty year old. But, when he remembered how Risky was acting under the effect of the alcohol while he danced at the traditional wedding, he believed anything was possible whenever alcohol was involved.

Four hours later, at exactly 2:00pm, the two newly weds who had dosed back off, were once again awakened by another maid, knocking on the door. Nwoke got up off the bed and answered the door.

"Good afternoon, sir. There is a woman here to see somebody named Risky or David Okeke," the dark skinned maid said.

"That's the American who was dancing with the ladies last night and he is in guest room 132 on the first floor." Nwoke went back to the bed and checked the digital clock on the night-stand and noticed it was time to start preparing for the church wedding. He tapped Mary on the shoulder to remind her it was about that time for the final ceremony.

"Who was that?" Mary asked, turning over under the sheets.

The central air conditioning system was quite efficient as the temperature in the huge room was about 65°.

"Somebody looking for Risky. We'll find out later, it might be that flight attendant he invited yesterday. I'm going in the hot-tub."

It took Nwoke and Mary one hour to get ready in the bedroom but, Mary still had to go through the ritual of being dressed by a selected number of Seamtresses. While Mary was in the special dressing room, Nwoke went to Risky's room and knocked on the door. Risky opened the door and told him to come in. He saw Ngozi for the second time and she looked more beautiful than when she was in the flight-attendant uniform.

"Hi, Ngozi and we're glad you could make it. Risky has told us so much about you," Nwoke said and walked over to the sofa and shook Ngozi's hand. She stood about 5'7", light-skinned and slim with wide hips that fit her tight jeans perfectly.

"You must be the groom of the wedding David told me about," Ngozi said as she shook Nwoke's hand. She then sat back down and studied the young groom and wondered how old he was. "How old are you, if I may ask?"

"Twenty three. Why?" Nwoke responded, knowing full well what the answer was going to be.

"Nothing. I just thought you might be too young to be getting married, that's all. Happy wedlock."

Nwoke could tell Ngozi didn't want to go further on the subject so he said bye and turned and left the room. On his way out, he remembered they didn't have enough cash at the house so he decided to go to the bank in downtown Umuahia but first, he had to let his wife know. He sent a message through one of the maids to let Mary know. With the special security force hired by his father through the police commissioner, Nwoke went to the bank and withdrew ten million naira which was the equivalence of one hundred thousand dollars. He returned within forty minutes and put the large amount of cash in the specially constructed safe that only he and Mary had the code to. After doing so, he went back down to the reception area to wait for Mary to finish getting dressed. Two minutes after sitting down, Mary's parents, Mr. and Mrs. Austin walked into the reception room, surprisingly and Nwoke couldn't really place who they were, right away.

"Good-afternoon, sir and Maddam," Nwoke greeted as he stood up, obediently.

"Hello, son. What is your name and where is Mary Austin?" Mr. Austin asked, looking the young man over.

"She is getting ready for the wedding, sir. May I ask who you are, please?" Nwoke asked respectfully, looking at both Mr. and Mrs. Austin, wondering if they were Mary's parents.

"We are Mr. and Mrs. Austin from Liberia. The bride's parents," the tall masculine Mr. Austin answered and extended his right hand for a shake. He was dressed in a traditional African Dashiki and matching trousers with a hat that looked like a cowboy hat. His complexion was similar to Mary's and he had a deep voice. One could tell that they were spending a lot of Mary's money.

"Nice to meet you, too, Mrs. Austin," Nwoke shook Mary's mother's hand and introduced himself. She was a little lighter than Mary and her father but, had the same facial features as Mary. Standing about 5'6", Mrs. Austin looked very pretty for her age. "I see where Mary gets her good look from," Nwoke said and smiled, kissing her hand.

"Thank you very much, my dear. So, you want to take my daughter's hand in marriage, hah?" Mrs Austin asked and smiled.

"How old are you, son?" Mr. Austin asked, looking Nwoke over without a smile on his face.

"Twenty three, but you know that age is nothing but a number and I love your daughter," Nwoke said and sat down.

Mr. and Mrs. Austin sat down, too. "And can you tell me how you plan to be faithful at that age. You should be dating all kinds of girls your age right now. I know I was when I was your age," Mr. Austin said and watched Nwoke suspiciously, wondering what the young adult was up to.

The intimidating voice of Mr. Austin didn't shake Nwoke at all as he looked his father-in-law in the eyes, boldly. "I love your daughter very much sir and she has taught me a lot."

The response from Nwoke seemed to touch Mr. and Mrs. Austin and Mr. Austin responded accordingly. "Do not treat my daughter like your average girlfriend. Do you understand that?"

Mr. Austin said in a much more kinder and friendly tone.

Nwoke excused himself and went back upstairs to call his parents so they could meet Mary's parents. Shortly thereafter, Rev. and Mrs. Nwanta walked over from their mansion and to the reception room of Nwoke's villa, but the visitors were no longer there as one of the caretakers had moved them to the main living-room.

"I wonder where they are. Let me check the living-room," the Rev. Nwanta suggested and walked over to the living room, followed by his wife.

They met Mr. and Mrs. Austin and the two parents-in-laws of the Mr. and Mrs. Nwoke Nwanta hugged each other in good spirits and also welcomed each other without any reservations. The Rev. and Mrs. Nwanta decided to take the strangers with them, along with Mr. and Mrs. Otu to the church.

"But, please, I am yet to see my daughter. Can you tell your son to ask her to come down please?" Mr. Austin said as they were getting ready to leave for the church.

"Okay, I'm sorry. I thought you'd already seen her. I'll send one of the helpers to deliver the message. Meanwhile my wife and I are gonna get the other visitors at my house and come back," Rev. Nwanta said and called one of the maids as he and Mrs. Nwanta got outside.

Mary came down to the living-room in her long wedding gown ten minutes later and joined her parents in the living-room. Mary's mother broke down, crying tears of joy after seeing her little girl in the extra long and very expensive wedding gown. Mother and daughter hugged each other for about three minutes while Mr. Austin watched and then hugged his daughter.

"We will see you at the ceremony. we are now going with your husband's parents and Cynthia's parents-in-law to the church. Rev. Nwanta wants to make sure everything is in order before you two get there. I assume he is the presiding minister right?" Mrs. Austin said.

"Yes, he is," Mary answered.

Mary went back upstairs while her parents went outside to wait for Rev. and Mrs. Nwanta.

"This is some building, isn't it, dear?" Mrs. Austin asked her husband as she observed the lavish villa.

"Yes, it is. Maybe they were meant to be together after all. That business must be very good and I am happy for them." Mr. and Mrs. Austin hadn't heard about the warrant for their daughter and her husband since the U.S. feds didn't think the fugitives were in Liberia. Mary had told them that she was involved in an import and export business with her boyfriend and they believed her. Mary and Cynthia had also built big homes for their families in Liberia but, they weren't as extravagant as Nwoke's villa.

Rev. and Mrs. Nwanta, accompanied by Mr. and Mrs. Otu with Ije and Patience, pulled up at the gate in a Mercedes S500 and Chevy Suburban driven by Rev. Nwanta's drivers. One of the drivers got out and called the Austins to join the entourage and they did.

The Rev. avoided the News media that was following them since he really had no answers for them. He and his wife wondered how much Mary's parents knew about the activities of their daughter but decided not to discuss it at the moment. They also wondered if the young adults knew exactly what they were doing by having a lavish wedding as fugitives. The current life-style of their son and his wife had given the Holy man great concern and also the villagers who had never witnessed such a young person with so much money. The Rev. had run out of excuses for his son's lavish life-style. But, when the national Newspapers carried the story, he avoided answering any questions entirely. It wasn't uncommon for young men from Nigeria to travel to the Western world, especially U.S. for college and end up rich over night. This brought a whole new meaning to the word, college degree. They were looked upon as successful instead of criminals. Mrs Nwanta was disturbed about the fact that they gave Nwoke all he wanted in life without the family lacking anything but, now it all seemed to be to no avail. They didn't consider wealth a success unlike the public's perception of money. The Rev. and his wife felt that Nwoke had damaged the family name and image but, prayers could fix things. But, at the moment, the first step would be to preside over the wedding and bless the young couple so that they could have a happy wedlock at least.

At exactly 3:45pm on this 3rd day of January, Nwoke and his beautiful bride, Mary Austin, came downstairs, looking like princess Dee and Prince Charles at the 'Royal wedding' of 1981 Even Mary had no idea how much the lace-wedding-gown cost since the Rev. and his wife paid for both the gown and the tuxedo.

The 'Golden wedding'ceremony took place at exactly 4:20pm presided over by Rev. Nwanta himself and attended by dignitaries, including the governor of the state. The extra long and expensive white wedding gown worn by Mary and the custom made Tuxedo worn by Nwoke, provided an air of arrogance for the attendants and Camera crew. Mary and Nwoke walked down the aisle of Ubakala Anglican Church in Abia state of Nigeria in total harmony as the wedding gown dragged upto thirty feet behind.

The extensive and expensive reception at both Saint Thomas cathedral church in Aba and Ubakala Anglican church, attracted people from all walks of life as both the rich and poor came to eat and drink for free. It looked more like a party with live-bands and music of all kinds. It was estimated that over one hundred and fifty thousand people were present.

CHAPTER SEVENTEEN

The International Criminal Police Organization (INTERPOL), in cooperation with the London Police Drug Enforcement Unit, ran a credit check and a criminal history profile of Uzo and Cynthia Otu to whom the London calls were made. This had been ordered by the prosecutor, James Cohen and approved by a Federal District Judge. The London police only saw ownership of the multimillion dollar electronic importation and distribution founded by Uzo's father Mr. Otu as a means of cleaning up the illegal drug money he had earned over the years, They concluded that the couple were respectable citizens of the United Kingdom and paid large amount of taxes. This information was passed on to James Cohen and he felt like the investigation and the effort to find the fugitives had taken two steps backwards. He immediately called a meeting.

"Gentlemen, here's what we have," Cohen slid the two sheets of paper across the table to Spinard and his partner, Levitz.

The two Customs agents reviewed the information and nodded in disappointment.

"Secondly, the guy isn't even in London, right now. According to Heathrow Airport records, he travelled home, possibly for Christmas and I think our guys just might be there with him, in Nigeria," Cohen added.

"I guess that'll do it for us on that angle," Spinard said, staring at the wall for answers.

"No other leads, right?" Cohen asked.

"Not for now. We just have to sit back and wait. They won't be the first nor the last," Spinard added.

Levitz looked at him. "So how much longer will the surveillance go on?" he switched his focus to the prosecutor.

"For as long as it takes and trust me, I've been in this business for so long that I know sooner or later, we're gonna get a break," Cohen said and moved closer to the window overlooking the Baltimore Convention center. "They have to contact one of those two under surveillance sooner or later and, when they do we'll be right there," he concluded, smiling and gazing out the window at the cold new year traffic.

Sherrie and her mother, sat there in the spacious family room of the big home, watching CNN and flipping through the pages of the Baltimore Sun and Washington Post. They were hoping they would hear something about Risky either on the News or by telephone or mail. Mrs Washington wasn't too happy about the absence of grand children to buy Christmas presents for. She looked at the Christmas tree that was now by itself after they had unwrapped their gifts to each other.

Sherrie was beginning to miss Risky and she understood why he hadn't called but hoped he would find an untraceable means to communicate soon. They weren't even sure if Risky was alive or dead.

"Ma, you think he's okay?.....I mean if he gets caught, we'll hear about it, right?" Sherrie asked her mother.

"I would think so. I think he would call to ask for a lawyer if he gets re-arrested so, yes, he should be fine and may already be out of the country," Mrs. Washington thoughtfully said to her only child.

Sherrie looked at her mother and cut her eyes. "Ma, he's probably not even thinking about me right now. That's kind of hard when you're on the run for your freedom."

"If he's not thinking about you when he's on the run, then he doesn't love you. He should be wondering what you're gonna do and if the police have been here and locked you up. He has to be concerned about your welfare, child." Mrs. Washington tried to sound like a Social worker.

On that note from the experienced Mrs. Washington, Sherrie decided to pick up the phone and call Derrick. The phone rang twice and Derrick answered. "Hello."

"Yes, who's this?" Derrick's voice asked on the other end of the phone line.

"Derrick, this is Sherrie, Risky's girlfriend and how are you?" Sherrie asked as the agents outside listened.

"Oh, I'm just fine and you?"

"I guess I'm okay. Have you heard anything yet?"

"No. If you wanna stop by my office or something, just call and let me know, okay?" I gotta go now," Derrick hung up as if he was in a hurry.

Sherrie looked at the phone after hearing the dial-tone and wondered why Derrick had cut her off like that. But, then she figured he was afraid the Feds might have been listening and wanted to talk in person. The two could be charged with Aiding and Abetting if the government found out they assisted the defendants in the escape.

"Are you okay?" Mrs. Washington asked, noticing the surprise-look in her daughter's eyes.

"Yes. I might go have a talk with Derrick," she answered and put the phone back on its cradle. She then resumed her previous seat next to her mother's. "If he knew something, he wouldn't tell me on the phone. I don't even know why I asked that dumb question."

"Yes, you should've known better."

"Well ma, I gotta go to the shop and check on something real quick and I just might stop by his office."

Mrs. Washington studied her attractive daughter as she stood up. "Okay, watch yourself now. He is a nice looking young man," she warned with a smile.

Sherrie found her brand-new pocketbook her mother gave her for Christmas and walked over to the dining table and took her keys and exited the house.

Five minutes later after the Mercedes CLK had warmed up, she put the transmission in Reverse and slowly backed out of the driveway onto the street. Watching the rearview mirror for safety, Sherrie stopped and put the shifter in the 'D' position and pulled off.

About two blocks from the house, a dark-blue Dodge caravan followed behind her, unnoticed by the unsuspecting and inexperienced Sherrie Washington.

Alo, Ngozi and Risky were having a time of their lives in Umuahia township market, where they had gone shopping for some traditional African wears. On this 4th day of 1998, the market wasn't that busy so, they didn't have to spend too much time buying or looking for what they wanted.

"Is that the same thing as a shopping center in the 'States?" Risky asked as they headed back to the village under the police escort. There was a police car in front and behind the Chevy Suburban which was also driven by a police officer.

"Yeah, you can say that, except for the open market Vendors and Hawkers," Alo responded. He and Uma were sitting in the last row of the three-rows. Uma wasn't having that much fun because of the fugitive status of her husband. She only went for the ride to relieve boredom.

Alo told the driver to pull over and get them a couple of national newspapers that some teenage Hawkers were selling on the side of the road. The police driver did so and bought four Newspapers.

"Look at those happy couple," Ngozi said as she took one of 'The Daily Times' paper with Nwoke and Mary's picture on the front page, showing them walking down the aisle in the church.

"Let me see that," Risky said, looking over at Ngozi's paper as the SUV moved. They were in the middle seat. 'The National Tracker' Newspaper that Risky had didn't have the wedding as a headline.

Three out of the four papers had the Golden wedding on the front page. This made Alo and Risky uncomfortable and made Uma want to leave immediately. This was not good for people who were supposed to be in hiding but, they never thought of the publicity the wedding would bring.

"How far do these Newspapers go?" Risky asked, not feeling very comfortable about even being out-and-about in the town.

Alo looked at him and then at Ngozi, wondering if she knew anything about the fugitive status of her new boyfriend. "I would think anywhere in the world they have Nigerians who read newspapers from their country and subscribe to them." Alo looked at him again, understanding why he asked the question.

"That's not good," Risky said, shaking his head and trying not to be specific because of Ngozi who knew nothing about their status.

The Suburban pulled up in front of Alo's house, but instead of going in, he told Uma to go ahead. He, Risky and Ngozi walked over to Nwoke's mansion while the driver parked the SUV. They told Nwoke and Mary what the situation was and gave them the papers to read.

"I think we'd better get out of the country or make some very serious security plans," Alo suggested as they sat in the reception area while Nwoke and Mary read the article.

"Agreed," Nwoke said, lifting his head from the paper and looking at Risky, Ngozi and Mary who nodded in agreement to the plan.

"So, how long has this been going on?" Ngozi asked, not sure why the crew wanted to skip town because of a wedding picture.

Risky called her to his room after excusing himself from the rest. He moved the scattered luggage and carryon to the side of the big guestroom and asked her to sit on the bed and she did. Risky told her the entire story and to his surprise, the flight attendant said she wished she was in Mary's position to make millions.

"Do you think you can connect me with some of your people in Baltimore?" Ngozi asked.

"Not right now. I want you to stay here with me; I'm falling in love with you, Ngozi," Risky said as he looked her deep in the eyes. He moved closer and kissed her and she was more than glad to kiss him back.

After reading the 'Daily Times' Newspaper, the director of operations for the U.S. Embassy in Lagos, Nigeria, Mr. Nick Sandal contacted the head of U.S. Marshalls service in Washington D.C. He had compared the wedding picture on the front page to the pictures of Mary and Nwoke he had in his office from the FBI's most wanted list and it matched. He then read the article and the names also matched, shedding some light on the 'rich and famous' life-style of the fugitives. The head of the U.S. Marshalls contacted Robert Davidson of the New York branch of the Marshalls and related the information.

"So, we've just been wasting our time?" Davidson asked.

"I guess so because they are no longer in the Apple," the head of U.S. Marshalls service answered over the phone line.

"Thanks for the information, sir." Davidson hung up and called James Cohen.

"Are you sure about this?" Cohen asked over the long distance phone line.

"Yes and the fax should be there by now," Davidson said after faxing a copy of the Newspaper front page story that he received from the Washington branch of the Marshalls service.

"Hold on. I think Sherry just got it," Cohen said over the speaker of the big office phone. He came back on the line seconds later. "Okay, I'm looking at it right now. I already have the approval for the funding of the overseas trip in this budget year. Four of my agents will accompany you guys and CIA to Nigeria ASAP. These fugitives are pretty good at figuring out a way out of any unfavourable situation."

"How in the world did they make it through those tight Airports and borders? From what I gather, according to this article, the wedding was a couple of days ago and no one knows where their Honeymoon is gonna be so, we must give instructions to the U.S. Consulate there in accordance with international laws."

"I doubt if they'll leave their country since that would mean taking too much chance. I don't even know how they got out of this country, to tell you the truth," Cohen reasoned.

"Okay, I guess the mission will be headed by the CIA. So, I'm gonna get my crew together while you do the same. I'll be in touch," Davidson said.

"I will have them ready and also notify the head of the CIA in Washington. You just don't know how happy I am about the News." Cohen hung up the phone.

Assistant U.S. attorney, James Cohen buzzed Sherry to come into his office, after getting off the phone with Robert Davidson of the New York branch of the U.S. Marshalls service.

Two minutes later, the pretty white woman walked into the prosecutor's office. "Yes."

"I need you to start an expenditure sheet based on that approval we got for this if we had to go overseas to get those Nigerians."

"Okay, sir," the secretary said and turned around and left the office.

Next, Mr. Cohen dialed Spinard's cell phone to relate the good News.

"Hello," Spinard answered in one ring as his voice filled the room from the speaker of the phone.

Standing up and pacing the floor, Mr. Cohen spoke with a sense of accomplishment. "Agent Spinard, this is James Cohen and I have some good news. Your guys just had a lavish wedding in Nigeria and check this out; the wedding had the title of 'The Golden Wedding' and I'm gonna fax you a copy of the Newspaper clipping."

"Are you kidding me? How in the world did they get over there? I thought we had all the angles covered," a shocked and jubilant Spinard asked.

"Didn't I tell you that you can't underestimate those Nigerians and when you have the kind of money they have, anything is possible. Since I was expecting this and already got the approval for the expenses, You and Levitz get ready. I'm gonna tell Johnson and Billard to do the same. You will all accompany the U.S. Marshalls and a couple of CIA agents to that country and we can't waste too much time."

Spinard hesitated on the line for about twenty seconds like he wasn't sure if he wanted to travel to Africa in search of some fugitives. "Okay, sir. I'll tell Levitz and I hope my wife and kids understand," Spinard responded, lowering his voice as he must have realized the risks involved in the task ahead.

James Cohen knew that the approval of the agent's family was not even a factor since it was written in all federal law enforcement agencies job description so, he cared less. "I'm gonna need to meet with you all around 4:00pm today before you leave work so that I can further explain the international procedure governing the capture and extradition fo foreign fugitives, okay?" He hung up and dialed the DEA for agent Johnson to tell him the same thing.

Three hours later in the Prosecutor's conference room, the four agents sat around the big table and listened like college students in a lecture classroom, as the prosecuting attorney enlightened them on international law from a CIA manual.

"Gentlemen, we have a treaty with that country which allows us to bring fugitives back to the U.S. if they've committed a serious felony here in the United States, and this is to our advantage," he studied the faces of the agents to make sure they were following and they were so, he continued. "I have already instructed the U.S. Marshalls to proceed with the arrest through the Nigerian government police in cooperation with INTERPOL. Your expenses will be covered one hundred percent. Are there any questions?"

Johnson raised his right hand: "So, is it my understanding that we don't actually take part in the hunt for them since the Nigerian police will do so?"

"Yes and no. But, you may be required to give an input if needed and also play a minor role in the field while they are being sought after. I don't know what the circumstances will be when you get there but, I sure hope they will already be in custody. Just do the best you can," Cohen finished and looked around at the faces that didn't look too confident to fight the pending battle.

Nwoke sat on the west balcony of his villa, looking at the numerous luxury vehicles that were parked in the big car-port He thought deeply about what the United States Federal agents would do if they happen to come across the

Newspaper with their wedding picture on the front page, when his new wife interrupted his thoughts.

"Hey, look what Mr. Ogar sent us for our wedding," Mary said as she came out of their bedroom into the adjoining balcony with the gift in her right hand.

Nwoke took the small gift box and opened it. It was a His and Hers Rolex watch. Their names were engraved on the box. "Wow, this is nice. Where's he and how in the world did he find out about the wedding?"

Mary looked at the address on the DHL cardboard box. "it looks like he's in Morocco but, I doubt that's really where he is. Ogar is not the type that would let you know where he's hiding out. I think it's a front."

"Maybe not. Morocco is a country and he could be anywhere in it. Anyhow, wherever he is;if he can find us and send us a gift, so can those American manhunters. I think it's time to pack up and go," Nwoke took his Rolex out of the gift-box and put it on, then gave Mary hers with the box. He stood up and tried to go past Mary to the top of the steps that lead to the compound but, Mary stood in the way.

"What do you mean? Are we going to spend the rest our lives running? I don't like this one bit," Mary complained, looking Nwoke in the eyes.

"Would you rather spend your honeymoon in handcuffs and leg irons, cramped up in the plane gurded by racist white federal agents?" Nwoke asked as he stood in front of his pretty wife.

Mary thought about what her husband had just said and realized the extent of the danger they faced. She also knew that this was no time for honeymoon. She had to agree with her younger husband. She wondered if she should tell her parents why she's leaving the village all of a sudden. "We should first let our guests know we're leaving for our honeymoon, you know what I mean?"

"Sure, I'll let Uzo and Cynthia know and you go let your parents know. I'll also let my parents know," Nwoke said and descended the steps and walked across the compound through the gates to his parents mansion.

Mary went to the guest room where her parents were and told them and they expressed happiness for her.

After telling his parents and being croos-examined by the Rev. Joshua Nwanta, Nwoke went to seek Alo's opinion and it was no different from his. He returned to his compound and went to Risky's room and told him. After looking all over for Uzo and Cynthia, he finally found them on the east balcony, observing the surroundings and drinking some Palm wine.

"Yo, who built this?" Uzo asked Nwoke when he saw him walking up the stairs that connected the compound to the east balcony.

"It was constructed by a German company, you like it?" Nwoke responded as he stood in front of the couple who now faced him.

"Of course. If I'd known, I would have hired them to build mine. Anyway, the Nigerian company did a fair job on my property compared to this extravagant thing I'm looking at," Uzo responded, studying his best friend like he'd just met him "So, what kind of business are you into, again?"

"I never told you but, you can try and figure it out your self but, right now I just came to tell you that Mary and I are about to go on our honeymoon."

Uzo and Cynthia looked at each other and neither bothered to ask where the couple was going for their honeymoon. Even though Cynthia knew the nature of the business Nwoke and Mary were into, she never told her husband. And she planned to keep it that way.

Uzo wondered if he should even be in the presence of the criminals on the run from a sophisticated law enforcement agency. "I figured that was why you wanted the passports. Well I'm happy you're okay and safe. I think we're just gonna head on back to my place, right, honey?" Uzo looked at his wife and gave her a signal that was familiar to both of them and Cynthia agreed.

Nwoke noticed that the couple was not comfortable and decided to leave them alone. "I gotta go see my uncle for a minute," he lied and went back to the bedroom to start packing but he hadn't been in the room for two minutes when Alo tapped on the door and he answered,

Alo had walked over from his mansion to tell Nwoke that he thought the whole thing over and came up with a different plan. The plan was that they should remain in the village and just pay off the local police commissioner who would be the first to know about any foreign encroachment. The commissioner would then inform them ahead of time.

After hearing this, Nwoke thought about it briefly and agreed. He then wondered what was taking Mary so long to get back from her parents' guest room. At that instant, Mary walked up the stairs and came straight into the bedroom. Nwoke told her about the new plan and she was more than happy.

"I'm glad we don't have to leave. I'm starting to enjoy my newly-found royalty. They treat me like a Queen and I don't wanna give that up just yet," Mary said as she looked at Alo and her husband.

"Very well then, my dear wife. Why don't you go ahead and tell the others that we're not leaving right-away and I'm gonna go to the police head-quarters with unc and take care of that," Nwoke said and went to the special safe in the inner room and opened it and took enough cash to buy the police commissioner.

Alo and Nwoke left the bedroom and Nwoke got one of his drivers to take them to the commissioner's office, along with one of the police officers assigned to protect them by the commissioner.

It took them twenty minutes to pull up in front of the Umuahia police station. The officer in charge was a tall, skinny captain, who was happy to see the young millionaire at the station again. He welcomed Nwoke and Alo to his office which was hot and small with a noisy air-conditioner that seemed not to be blowing out cold air.

"How can I help you today, my good friend?" the OIC asked.

"Yes, sir I'm back and you already know me and I'm sure you know my uncle. We just need to see the commissioner," Nwoke said as he and Alo sat down on the wooden bench.

"No, problem. I'll let the commissioner know," the officer said and got up immediately to inform the commissioner, knowing that the rich young adult would break'm off before he left.

Five minutes later, the chubby commissioner, who looked like he ate better than the rest of the force, walked into the office, smiling. "Hello, my friends. Come on in," he said and motioned them to follow him.

Alo and Nwoke stood up and followed the commissioner through the small hallway and into a much bigger office that had two window air-conditioners on full blast. They sat down in the comfortable suede sofa, facing the commissioner.

"Good afternoon Mr. Ukandu. We were wondering if it's possible to get information ahead of time from your office or yourself," Alo said.

"What do you mean. I am not clear on what type of information you are referring to," Commissioner Ukandu responded.

"We are trying to avoid the American government because they want to put us in jail and they may try to come to the village," Alo clarified.

"Oh, I see." Ukandu thought for about one minute, looking at the beige wall. "Well, the last time such a thing happened, they went through me and then I sent my officers to go and arrest the man. So, to answer your question, yes but, you know it comes with a price," Ukandu said with a smile that told Nwoke and Alo they were covered if the money was right.

"You know that money is not a problem for us. How about two thousand American dollars if you can provide us with the information as soon as you get it?"

"That will be fine, my friends. Don't worry about the U.S government. They like to go to other countries and arrest people, but they will not allow other countries to come and arrest one of their own," the happy commissioner explained with a friendly smile.

The statement by the commissioner reassured Alo and Nwoke they were in good hands. Nwoke reached in the duffle bag he stashed some of the money he had taken out of the safe and counted two hundred thousand naira and gave it to the police commissioner.

The officer of the law stood up and walked over to his file cabinet, opened one of the drawers and put the cash in inside. He then returned to his chair behind the desk and picked up the desk phone and buzzed the OIC to come in his office.

The tall, skinny man came into the office three minutes later. "Yes sir."

"You know these two from their last visit. Well, I'm going to place you in charge of the new task-force I am forming to monitor any foreign police movement that may be forthcoming," the commissioner said.

"No, problem, sir. I will personally relate the messages to them," the OIC said and smiled at Nwoke and Alo.

Nwoke reached in his bag again and counted ten thousand naira ($100.00) and gave it to the OIC. They shook hands and Nwoke and Alo went to their waiting police escort, hopped in the Suburban and left the police station, feeling satisfied.

The U.S. Embassy director of operations, Mr. Nick Sandal, sat in his office in Victoria Island, Lagos and gazed out of the window, overlooking the blue waters of the Atlantic ocean. The phone rang and he turned and walked back to the table and pressed one of the buttons and then pressed another one for the speaker of the big office phone. "Yes, Mr. Sandal, here."

The deep voice of Robert Davidson filled the room. "This is Davidson from the New York branch of the U.S. Marshalls. You contacted me earlier about the fugitives that had the lavish wedding?"

"Yes Mr. Davidson, how may I help you?" Sandal checked the clock on the wall and it said 12:42pm so that meant 7:42am in New York. The day was January 5th in the two countries. He knew it had to be a very important call for the federal officer to be calling that early.

"Can you please proceed with the arrest through the Nigerian police immediately before they disappear once again?"

"We are preparing to and I was about to call and seek your office's authorization and a fax of the international warrant."

"Great, I'm faxing it now and some agents from the CIA, DEA and customs will be their for assistance to the Nigerian police."

"Good. Since we have an extradition treaty, there should not be much problems, if any. I will inform the Nigerian authorities immediately so they can pick him up through one of their precincts and I believe they are in one of the Eastern villages. The village is about one hour flight from Lagos."

"Very well then. I'm gonna have my secretary fax you the authorization and the warrant for all of them right now. If you need anything else, let us know. Have a good day." Davidson hung up.

Mr. Sandal informed the Ambassador, Paul Mason and then proceeded to follow the rules governing such international warrants, which he was very familiar with. He requested and emergency assistance from the president of the country. After receiving the fax from New York, Sandal then faxed it to the office of the president in Abuja and the national police chief. The response came one hour later with the Nigerian national police chief instructing the Umuahia police commissioner to make the arrest. Sandal took the fax from the police chief and went to the Ambassador's office. He then placed a call to the commissioner of police in Umuahia to confirm the information from the chief of police.

"I guess we're done for now?" Paul Mason asked after Sandal got off the phone.

"Yes, sir. We just have to wait for our agents to arrive and transport them back to the U.S.."

"Don't they also have to find the big boss when they get here?" Mason asked.

"Yes. I should hope they're not coming all the way here just to transport them back without the boss," Sandal responded, knowing full well that the big boss may not even be in the country.

After receiving the information from the national police chief and the director of operations for the U.S. Embassy, Commissioner of police for Umuahia branch, Mr. Ukandu, alerted his OIC who then personally went to the village and informed Alo and Nwoke.

"Thank you very much, my friend. I never did get your name," Alo responded after the OIC told him the news.

"You can call me Obi. Officer Obi."

"Okay officer Obi. we'll be in touch." Alo said as he and Nwoke bid their farewell to Captain Obi.

"Hey Obi, please do not tell them anything at all. They can take any information and turn it against you and you may just find yourself under a U.S. indictment," Alo informed the officer as he turned around to leave the compound.

Nwoke went back to his compound, and told Risky and Ngozi they were leaving right-away. He went up to the guest room where Uzo and Cynthia stayed, knocked on the door. Uzo answered and he told them that he and Mary were going on their honeymoon. Nwoke walked two doors to his room and told Mary to start packing.

"Why? They're not here yet, are they?" Mary asked, not really wanting to leave.

"No, but knowing them, they will be. They've already asked the Umuahia police to arrest us and I'm not gonna wait around for that to happen," Nwoke said as he opened his closet and started removing some clothes from the hangers.

"Then, if that's the case, I'm gonna tell ma that we're going back with them for our honeymoon," Mary suddenly changed her mind, now desperate to get out of the country. She started packing faster than Nwoke could see.

"They can go ahead. We're not going with them if you know how to get to your house by road. Remember, we're fugitives and we must try to avoid all airports as much as possible, for now." Nwoke suggested.

"You're right. I forgot the implications of flying, but we're in Africa, dear. We blend in well with the majority." Mary countered.

"Good point but, this is no time to be taking chances. We are now one and I want you to start acting like one."

"So, we're driving across two countries?" Mary said and stopped packing as she stood up with her hands on her hips, looking at her husband.

"Yes, we are driving and that's the end of the discussion." Nwoke ended and refocused on packing his stuff.

Thirty minutes later, everybody gathered at Nwoke's compound and Alo addressed them about the mission to safety and they all agreed with every word he said.

The sixth of January was a Friday and the assistant U.S. attorney, James Cohen, was about forty minutes late for work due to heavy traffic in the snowy weather.

He parked the Ford Explorer and walked briskly to the elevator and pressed the button for the fifth floor. Three minutes later, he was in his office. "Hey, Sherry, any messages?" he asked as he put his briefcase on his desk.

"Yes, one international fax from Nigeria," the secretary said as she walked into the bigger office with the paper in her hand. "I think it's from Nr. Sandal." She gave him the paper and went back to her office.

Cohen read it and his expression changed instantly. "What an incompetent group of police," he said and slammed the paper on the table.

Seconds later, Sherry came back in the office with another piece of paper. "Oh, yeah, I forgot to give you this, too."

The second paper was the cost of the trip for the four agents, excluding the U.S. Marshalls and the CIA. Cohen ignored it and refocused on the missing fugitives he thought they had in custody. After about ten minutes of deep thinking, he decided to get on the phone.

"Hello," agent Spinard's voice said on the speaker phone.

"How are you, Mr. Spinard? They missed our men. We should have just gone over there ourselves and surprised them."

"That's a corrupt government, too, isn't it?"

"Of course. We should've never trusted them to arrest a bunch of rich guys. I just got the message from the Embassy. That's why he didn't wanna call me on the phone and tell me that bull-crab because he knows I'll probably insult him with words."

"It's not their fault is it?" Spinard asked.

"I guess not. I'm just pissed. Those guys are probably in another country by now."

"You don't think they're still there and just paid the police off to keep quiet?"

"That's possible. I haven't talked to Davidson yet. I just wanted to let you know that now you guys are gonna have to actually help hunt them down when you get there."

The phone was silent for about three minutes. "Do you know when we are leaving?"

"I will, as soon as I check with the CIA. The sooner, the better."

"Thank you, sir." Spinard said and hung up the phone.

Cohen made another call to the CIA office in Washington and they expressed their disappointment in the way the warrant was handled and promised it wouldn't happen again. After listening to the CIA who now hastened the mission, Cohen decided to call Robert Davidson. He spoke to Robert Davidson about devising a much more secure strategy before they leave for the West African nation.

Mary's parents flew back to Liberia on the 7th day of January but, Mary did not let her parents know the venue of her honeymoon. She would rather surprise them than put fear in their hearts. By 10:00am, the fugitives packed up and said goodbye to Cynthia and Uzo in Uzo's villa as they were leaving. They had left Ubakala village after the visit from the commissioner's front man. Uzo recommended they go to his place first and they agreed. Cynthia and Uzo promised to join them shortly.

"You all be doing some serious shit over here, yo. This is how a black man should live," Risky said and shook Uzo's hand before getting in the Ford Expedition that was waiting.

"Thanks a lot you guys! Have a safe journey and be careful! See you all soon!" Cynthia yelled out to her departing visitors as the three-vehicle entourage pulled off.

"One day we're gonna have something like that, baby," Risky told Ngozi as he sat next to her in the SUV.

"Oh, yeah?" Ngozi responded and smiled.

"Yes, and it won't be long if the cost of labour is as cheap as they say it is. Piece of cake," Risky said as the police driver pulled off the full-size SUV designed for the rough roads ahead. Since they were headed west, Risky gave Ngozi enough money to rent an apartment in Lagos and wait for him. "I'll be back. I like this country a lot."

"Why don't you just stay instead of going with them?" Ngozi responded in a pleading tone.

"Because I wanna see what my partners do first. They know the system better than I do. Trust me, I will return," Risky said as he tried to speak Kings English.

Ngozi smiled at him and then leaned over and kissed him on the lips. She told the driver to take her to the next transportation park which was in the town of Umuahia. The police officer flashed the headlights at Nwoke's Suburban and they stopped on the side of the road. The driver got out and ran to the two vehicles in front and told them what the plan was and they agreed. Together, all three vehicles went to the taxi park in Umuahia township and Ngozi took a private taxi to Owerri airport.

Under the six -police officer escort provided by the commissioner; three driving and three riding in the back seats, the entourage headed for the Republic of Benin border. They drove for eight hours before stopping at a hotel a few miles from the border. Alo recommended they spend the night there and continue the next day and they all agreed while the well-paid police officers guarded the vehicles.

The fugitives continued the journey the following morning which was the 8th day of January.

"So, you guys ever been to Liberia?" Alo asked the police officer who was driving the Mercedes ML 320 SUV which was in the middle, behind Nwoke and Mary.

"One time before when we had to escort a political refugee from our state," the dark-skinned officer answered, without turning his head.

"Oh yeah? So, you guys just do escort when needed?" Alo continued, looking back to see if Risky and the other two officers were trailing behind and they were.

"Yes, you can say so," the officer answered and stepped on the gas-pedal to catch up with the V-8 Suburban that appeared to be pulling away on the deserted road.

Armed with a license and border permit for West African coast, issued by the OAU(Organization for African Unity), the Nigerian police officers had no problem getting the fugitives across the Republic of Benin border. After that, they drove another nine hours and checked in at a hotel that wasn't far from the next border which was Togo. The following morning which was the 9th of January, they crossed the Togo border without any problem. The unplanned journey continued through the border of Ghana and then Ivory coast which was the last border before their destination of Liberia. They finally got to Liberia on the 12th of January.

"I'm so glad we are finally home," Mary said and let out a sigh of relief, keeping her eyes on the road as the dirty-looking Chevy Suburban drove into Liberia.

"Were you born here?" the light-skinned officer asked, depending on Mary's direction to lead the entourage. He checked the rearview mirror to make sure that the Expedition and the Benz ML 320 were behind.

"Yes, I was born in Monrovia and that's where you'll stop us."

Nwoke looked at her. "So, this is home, hah?"

"For now, while they still think we're in Nigeria," Mary happily answered.

"Can you please direct the driver?" Nwoke asked, feeling a little jealous of his excited wife.

"This is a highway and when it's time to get off, then I'll let him know," Mary responded with a teasing smile.

The country of Liberia became fully republic with a constitution much like that of the United States in 1847. The American Firestone company, which ran the rubber plantations, was especially influential. It has a population of approximately 3,348,000 over a 43,000 sq miles in land mass. Mary's family lived in Monrovia, which is the capital. Ethnic groups include: Kpelle 19%, Basa 14%, Grebo 19%, Gio 8%, Kru 7%, and Mano 7%. The major language is English. Mande, Mel and Kwa are also predominant languages. Religions are; Christianity 40%, Islam 20%, traditional beliefs and others 40%. The currency for trading is the Liberian dollar. (Oxford Atlas of the world-eleventh edition, 2003.)

After about eleven hours of driving and through several states, the crew finally arrived in the capital city of Monrovia.

Turn the next left on George Washington road,"Mary directed as the SUV exited off the highway.

The driver followed the direction, checking the rearview mirror to make sure the others weren't far behind. They drove for about another ten minutes and made two turns through the busy town with congested brick buildings scattered about. The SUV came to a rather big home that was fenced and looked different from others on the same street.

"Wait right here while I get the gateman to let us in," Mary instructed and got out of the vehicle like a little child that just got home on the last day of school. The other two vehicles parked behind on the side of the residential street Five minutes later, Mary was on the balcony of the second floor of the big house, motioning to the drivers to pull into the open gates. She then disappeared and reappeared in the huge back-yard as the three SUV's parked in different spots.

Everybody got out and looked around the large well planned compound in approval. The home wasn't as extravagant as Alo's and Nwoke's but, it was still above average.

"What are we gonna do with these vehicles, now?" Alo asked Nwoke but then looked at Mary for answers and suggestions.

"I know what you mean. I don't trust them to drive those vehicles back to Nigeria. So, what's up Mary? Remember, this is your home like you said," Nwoke implied.

Mary thought for about one minute. "We can park them here and put them on the plane back to Owerri or Port-Harcourt," Mary suggested firmly as if she already had the answer.

As the crew stood there, wondering what to do next, Mary's relatives gradually surrounded them, removing the luggage from the SUV's and putting them on the cemented ground until further instructions from Mary. Mary's parents, who were already home, came out with a surprised look in their eyes.

"Have you already finished your honeymoon, my dear?" Mrs. Austin asked and hugged her daughter and her husband.

"Yes ma. We just decided to visit you all," Mary lied as she let loose of her mother's hands.

"Very well then. I'll assign them the rooms. The officers are staying the night?" Mary's mother asked as her husband looked on, wondering what the crew was really up to.

"Oh, no. Just Alo and family, Risky Nwoke and myself," Mary responded as her mother ordered the relatives and maids to follow her with the boxes.

Mary's mother assigned different rooms to the guests while Mary and her husband went to Mary's room. She then sent her drivers to drop the police officers off at the Airport after Mary gave each of them two thousand Liberian dollars which was the equivalence of about five hundred American dollars.

"I need to use the phone and call the village. I just remembered something."Nwoke excused himself from the crowd of relatives who occupied the huge home that Mary built for her family.

Mary escorted her husband through the fifteen bedroom house, into her private floor, with five guest rooms. She showed Nwoke to the livingroom where the land-line phone was. Nwoke called the chief caretaker of his villa and told him to go into his study-room and look in the top left drawer of the desk and get the 'Bill of Laden' for the Range rover he shipped from New York and travel to Lagos and call him when he got there.

"I can't believe that I almost forgot about that Range, baby," Nwoke said.

"I can," Mary responded with a smile. For some reason, she felt more comfortable and much safer in her own house. "Now, let me call Cynthia and let her know that I'm home." She dialed the number that Cynthia had given her to their house in Mbaino village.

"Are you serious?" Cynthia asked, surprised at the calmness of her friend after driving through four countries.

"Yes, as a matter of fact, my cousin, Josephine just told me that a couple of our high school mates had died,"Mary informed Cynthia on the international line. "Oh, my Gosh.....who?"

"Remember Labella and David; the perfect couple?""Oh yeah. I think they got married too, right?""Yeah, I think so. That's sad for such young people to leave so soon."

"Do you know what happened?" I know it wasn't a natural death."

"Car accident. I heard, after a night of drinking either by them or by the driver of the other car."

"Okay, we'll see you on our way back to London."

"Where's the baby? Still with the mother-in-law?""Yeah. She won't let her go for one second."

"Oh, that reminds me, I forgot to ask you what happened when you came face-to-face with your father in law for the third time," Mary asked for the second time since Cynthia didn't get a chance to tell her the entire story while they were in the village during the wedding.

Cynthia recounted the entire first time encounter with Mr. Otu.

After five minutes of listening, Mary imagined herself in the same situation and that made her more appreciative of her father in law."I tell you, I don't know what I would do if I were you. You are bold to stay in that tense environment,"

"That's my dilemma right now. I'll see you soon. Patience is crying. Bye." The line died.

Mary hung up the phone, wondering where the U.S. Marshalls were.

At the DEA office in downtown Baltimore, agents Johnson and his partner, Donald Billard, had spent most of the day, going over suspects and defendants from Nigeria, They were searching for Nigerians who may have had contact with Dante Jackson one way or another or those who had a similar case and faced a lot of time.

"All these defendants we have already interviewed and they'd never heard of none of these guys and these ones over here, have been deported," Johnson said as he shuffled three pieces of paper on the table.

"When was the first time we checked with the surveillance team?" Billard asked.

"I don't know. They were supposed to check in with us when something good came through."

'You mean this guy hasn't even called his girlfriend since he left?"

"I guess not. We assume he is in Nigeria with his partners.

Remember, they are under the guidance of a college educated Nigerian who probably has a lot of friends and relatives doing the same thing or been through the same thing."

"I think the best shot we had is gone. They probably got the word that the police were looking for them and took off," Billard said, taking his face off the three pieces of paper on the table.

"I thought we'd be in Nigeria by now. I already told my wife and she wants me to go and get it over with."

"It won't be that long. All I can say is that they can't hide forever and they won't be the last either," Billard added, conclusively, knowing that deep inside, the opposite of what he said could be possible, since it's a big world out there.

After repeated calls from the prosecuting attorney in the cases against the fugitives, Robert Davidson called his partner, Donald Spencer for discussion on the intended mission. The CIA felt that Davidson's office was the hold up.

"Okay, here's what we got," Davidson said, pointing at the map of Africa on the wall. "If they leave here,"he continued as his index finger pointed at Nigeria. "They can either go here, here or here, without going through any international airport." Davidson spoke with the experience of a man who has hunted fugitives all over the world. He had also taken special college courses in Geography. He showed Spencer all the surrounding countries that were drivable from Nigeria and when he realized how many there were his hope became even slimmer than before.

"I think we ought to just go there and do what we would do here to find a national fugitive. Evidently these guys are rich and famous in their country and that would make our 'reward' system work perfectly since people know them." Spencer responded, looking at his partner who seemed to agree with the idea.

Davidson picked up the phone and called James Cohen to tell him that they were ready, but little did he know that the CIA would be in charge of the mission to the sovereign nation.

CHAPTER EIGHTEEN

The Kingdom of Morocco lies in northwestern Africa. Its name comes from the Arabic Maghreb-el-Aksa, meaning 'the farthest west'. The Atlantic coast of Morocco is cooled by the canaries current. Inland, summers are hot and dry. The Winters are mild. In Winter, between October and April, southwesterly winds from the Atlantic ocean bring rainfall, and snow often falls on the high Atlas Mountains. The population is about 31,168,000 and the capital is Rabat. The government is constitutional monarchy. Ethnic groups are: Arabs 70%, Berber 30%. Arabic is the official language while Berber and French are also spoken. The currency used is the Moroccan Dirham=100 centimes. (Oxford Atlas of the world-eleventh edition, 2003).

America's most wanted, Mr. Gabriel Ogar, stood outside the rear balcony of his 3.5 million dollar mansion he had purchased from one of his partners who lived in the Moroccan capital of Rabat. He had been here since he got the news of his American messengers being under arrest, after the unexpected death of one of them. The ten-bedroom mansion, built from carved ancient Egyptian stones, was not as plush as the one in Lagos, but it was good enough to attract passers-by in the big city. He thought about his family back in Lagos and wondered how safe they were. The top security armed guards he employed from the Nigerian Army and his secret informant at the U.S. consulate, kept him abreast of any new development concerning him in the U.S. Ogar knew that since the U.S. federal agents were on the track of his U.S. partners, it was only a matter of time before they traced his whereabouts. But, he was determined to stay ahead of them at all costs. The drug lord did not feel too comfortable after the unusual silence, following the failed attempt to arrest his partners in the village after the much publicised wedding. This made him decide to call his lawyer in London who was well versed in international law. "Okay, that's enough for now," Ogar told the beautiful young Arabic woman who was giving him a massage. She got up and left as he walked inside and grabbed the cordless phone and dialed the international line to his lawyer in London. The English secretary answered in three rings. "Please, may I speak to Mr. Clinton?"

"May I ask who is calling," the voice of the secretary asked over the speaker of the phone.

Ogar hesitated for a few seconds before answering. "A client," he finally said.

"Hold on," there was silence on the phone as Ogar waited and about one minute passed by before a different voice came on the line.

"Yes, Alfred Collier here and who am I speaking to?"

"This is Gabriel Ogar from Nigeria and I have some pressing questions."

"I'll bet you do. A lot has been going on in Nigeria lately and I'm sure you can tell me all about it." Collier was referring to all the publicity about Nwoke and co., including the wedding.

"Yes, I heard. Now, my question is; does the U.S. have the right to do what they did through the Nigerian police when they tried to arrest the fugitives?"

"I'm sure they did or they wouldn't have done it. Unfortunately, your country signed a treaty with the American government that allows them to do so. Why do you ask?"

"Nothing. I just wondered because I know the people and I feel sorry for them. Thank you Mr. Collier." Ogar hung up the international call and took the cordless phone back inside the house and replaced it on its cradle. He then came back to the huge balcony, followed by the Arabian beauty, who was now half naked. Laying face down on the Chinese mat, Ogar ordered the woman to finish her duty and whatever else that was necessary to bring his body to a total relaxation, including his erect penis.

The woman began by saying something in Arabic which Ogar didn't understand but could sense what it was as she leaned over and removed his robe. She then pushed him over on his back and witnessed an erection that told her her duty was no where near completion. She smiled and slid her soft hands into the hot body oil and then began massaging the hard penis, sending her master into a world he had become very familiar with.

Ogar woke up two hours later and immediately picked up the and called his wife and told her to vacate the Victoria Island mansion and fly to Abuja immediately until further instructions. He thought about inviting her to Morocco but changed his mind since he didn't know exactly what the U.S. Marshalls'plans were. Maybe she could go back to Lagos later if the Americans don't show up. At age forty, Ogar had made millions dealing heroin since the age of thirty one. He studied Marketing and Finance at Sussex University in England and received a B.Sc. degree at the age of twenty five then got a job in the Greater Nigerian Bank as an accountant. After five years of working without anything to show for it, he turned to dealing drugs with a friend of his named John who was already big in the illegal business. Ogar didn't get married until the age of thirty after quitting his position at the Bank. He married his co-worker who was also a college graduate and a beauty queen. He didn't feel guilty cheating on his wife since she probably did the same thing when he wasn't around.

The home in Abuja was half underground but it didn't have a Bunker like the Lagos mansion. He considered it his hide-out spot but, this time the case seemed bigger than he had expected and required an out-of-the country escapade. The security in both residences were pretty much the same.

'Dinner is ready, master," the beautiful Ethiopian cook said as she walked out on the balcony from the livingroom.

Ogar stood up and followed her, hoping that his goal of reaching one billion dollars was still possible.

In the capital city of Liberia, the family of the newlywed, continued to entertain and show extreme hospitality to the foreign visitors whom most of them had no idea, were on the run from the most powerful government in the world. Uma had been complaining about the constant relocation and readjustments of her and her young child. She now wanted to go back to India with Glenn, but Alo wasn't ready to make that move just yet.

"Mary, this is really beautiful," Alo commented as Mary gave them a tour of the big home on their second day in the country.

"I think I'll go up to the room with Glenn. He seems restless," Uma said and turned around to go upstairs to the second floor where the guest rooms were.

They all turned around and looked at her and immediately noticed she was not happy about something.

"Okay, honey. I'll see you in a few." Alo said as his wife disappeared through the doors that lead to the stairwell Mary stood still and watched her sister-in-law and her little boy walk away, looking depressed. "What's wrong with her?" she asked Alo.

"I think she wants to go back to India," Alo asked.

"Well, let her go first and then, join her. In fact, I think that's a good idea," Nwoke encouraged, hoping that he and Mary can also go to India if things don't work out well in Liberia.

"Well, shall we continue?" Mary asked the crew who was standing still.

They agreed and Mary proceeded with the tour of her home.

Alo was right behind Nwoke as Risky and Mary were in the front. Alo continued to think about what Nwoke had just suggested. "Very well, we'll just take her to the airport tomorrow since she has nothing to fear," Alo concluded as they followed Mary.

"Now, these rooms over here are were all my cousins and aunts stay when they visit," Mary said as she pointed at the fleet of bedrooms on the other side of the compound, separate from the main building where the crew were staying."You can see why it's designed like a motel with the rooms numbered along the hall-way. The helpers also get their rooms here."

"Anybody in the rooms?" Risky asked.

"I believe so. I can't really say which rooms are occupied and which ones aren't. I can tell you that my relatives are always here, especially during the Christmas holidays."

"We're wasting money in the U.S. I wish I knew about all this here in the motherland, yo. I would've moved here a long time ago and built me a mansion like you guys," Risky commented.

Just then, a beautiful young woman came out of one of the rooms ahead of the crew and closed the door behind her and walked toward them.

"Who is that?" Risky asked, eyes fixed on the woman who looked to be about twenty seven, 5'6", light-skinned and permed hair that fell over her ears. She had high cheek bones and looked slim but fat in the right places. The tight jeans she wore revealed her wide hips while the sleeveless tank-top showed off her round cup-size breasts. Risky could feel love at first sight.

"Okay, are you guys ready now, Risky?" Mary asked, interrupting Risky's daydream and smile.

"Of course I'm ready but, can you introduce us to your relative?"

Alo just stood still, observing with interest as he folded his hands.

"Oh, that's my cousin, Josephine. Hello, Josephine. Have you met my guests?" Mary said as Josephine stopped in front of them, smiling.

"Earlier and how are you all doing?" Josephine responded, focusing on the attention she was getting

451

from Risky. She noticed his muscular arms and hard chest under the red blue T-shirt.

Risky stuck out his right hand for a shake. "My name is Risky but my African name is David Okeke. I am so happy to meet you." The two shook hands as others looked on with interest.

"Is that a name, Risky?" Josephine asked, still holding his hand.

"Yes it is."

"Oh. Do you like to take risks in life?"

"Only when it comes to making money," Risky answered and smiled and everybody else laughed out loud.

"Okay, that's enough. Can we go now?" Mary said and turned to walk forward.

"Of course. Josephine, can you please join us on the tour of the home?"

"No, that's okay. I've already seen the house a million times. I'll see you all at dinner. Enjoy your stay," Josephine said and walked away from the crew with swaggering strides.

"How much would I need to build something like this?" Risky asked, walking behind the crew, thinking about Josephine and why she brushed him off like that.

"Well, this only cost me about five hundred American dollars," Mary answered as she lead them into the spacious parlour with an indoor and outdoor space for extended comfort. "This here is what we call a parlour or living room."

"So, is this an extension of the living room here?" Risky asked pointing at the outdoor space.

"Yes, I know it looks like a balcony but it's not since it's covered all around.

The brief tour lasted about ten more minutes and they went to the dining area for dinner.

Dinner lasted about one hour and everybody retired to their rooms. Risky asked Josephine if she would stay and watch TV in the family room of the main building with him. Josephine agreed and put on a movie instead since there wasn't much on Liberian television. She lectured Risky on Liberian culture while Risky enlightened her on American culture which she was already familiar with.

"SO, do you rap. I enjoy rap music and the way the girls dance for Rappers on the videos," Josephine asked.

"Yes, I can rap if the music is available but, I'm not a Rap artist."

Josephine got up with the remote control which also controlled the the stereo system and walked over to the stereo set. She reached on top of the entertainment center and opened the CD case and flipping through the numerous CD's, she picked out a couple of CD's. "Can you rap to Jay-Z or Biggie Smalls?"

Risky was surprised that Josephine knew the Artists and had their CD's. "Of course, either one of them is good."

Josephine leaned over so that Risky could notice her behind as she picked up something off the carpet. "Okay, which song do you like the most on this 'Reasonable Doubt' CD?" she asked as she put the two CD's in the twelve-CD changer.

"Start with *You Can't Knock the Hussle*,"

Josephine pressed the skip button on the remote and Jay-Z's voice filled the room. Risky rapped to the familiar lyrics of the rap tune while Josephine watched and admired the foreigner. He made it seem like he was actually talking to her as she continued to blush and look away. Risky got the feeling that Josephine may be thinking that he is, in fact, Jay-Z. After the song and several other tunes from the Biggie Life after death' CD, they decided to call it a night as it had gotten dark outside. Darkness came around 7:00pm on the coast of West Africa.

Risky now felt that he had stolen the girls heart with his rapping so he made his move. "Why don't we get some drinks and go up to my room or your room?"

"I'm sorry but, I don't think that's a good idea. I just met you. Thanks for the rap. Good-night, Risky," she said and smiled as she turned off the stereo and the television, leaving Risky disappointed for the first time in a long time. Josephine then walked away slowly, switching her hips to further entice the already horny Risky.

Risky now felt a need for a blunt, which he didn't have. He planned to make sure he had some weed the following day to ease the stress that was now building.

The following morning, which was the 14th of January, the fugitives rode together in Mary's Toyota Land cruiser and the Mercedes ML 320 to drop Uma off at the airport. They waited till she boarded a flight to New Delhi India before heading back.

Nwoke and Alo realized that Uma was right in her decision to return home as they sat in the back seat of the Mercedes SUV, on the way back to Mary's house. They started thinking of a way to do the same thing as Uma and it would have to be soon.

"I think we should plan to go to India because I'm already missing my family," Alo said as they got out of the vehicles.

Mary and Nwoke looked at the lonely man and told him they agreed with him one hundred percent.

On the morning of January 15th, 1998, Chief CIA agent in Washington DC, Robert Davidson, accompanied by three other agents, headed for Baltimore to meet with James Cohen. At about the same time, Robert Davidson of the U.S. Marshalls service in New York, accompanied by three other Marshalls, flew to Baltimore to meet with the Assistant U.S. attorney. Customs agents; Michael Spinard, Jonathan Levitz, joined by DEA agents, Thomas Johnson and Donald Billard also headed downtown Baltimore for the special meeting in the prosecutor's office.

"Gentlemen, since you already know why we have gathered in this conference room today, I won't take much of your time in getting straight to the point.," Cohen studied the agents in the conference room for any signs of 'cold-feet' and saw confidence instead, so he continued. "We still wanna go after the main boss in Lagos since we're not sure where the partners may be at this time. Besides, he is really the murderer and the most wanted, right now," the prosecutor explained, standing at the top of the big table.

"Are we sure that's his real name?" CIA agent, Joseph Albertson asked.

Cohen hadn't thought about the possibility of Gabriel Ogar being an alias. He thought for about two minutes for an answer. "As far as we know, that's the name he goes by and since people know him by that name, we can find his house that the his messengers told us about in the big city."

The agents nodded in agreement-as they listened.

The assistant U.S. attorney continued and went on to explain the goal of the mission which was to send a message to the rest of the world. He cited past examples and the high rate of success. "Actually, it's even easier to cross international waters and bring a fugitive to justice than it is to hunt them down here in the U.S.," Cohen stressed.

CIA agent, Joseph Albertson decided to add: "the only time we encountered any serious resistance outside the country was in Colombia in the late eighties but, I doubt very seriously we'll meet such resistance in Nigeria."

"Oh, yes. I remember that situation in Colombia, but you still can't underestimate those Nigerians," Cohen countered.

"What would you say our success rate is in these missions?" Spinard asked.

"I would put it at about 90%," Cohen answered and looked around the table for reaction. "Are there any more questions?"

Silence followed as the agents looked at the prosecutor with nothing to say.

"Okay then, since there are no questions; goodluck." Cohen moved to the door and shook each agent's hand as they walked out of the conference room.

All the concerned agents went home to their families for the day. The following morning, the agents said goodbye to their families and headed for BWI Airport in Baltimore which was the meeting point before take-off. Joseph Albertson gave a final briefing for the twelve agents before they boarded the CIA Jet.

At exactly 10:00am on the morning of January 16th, 1998, The especially equipped CIA Jet, piloted by Joseph Albertson, took off from BWI and headed for the West African country of Nigeria. Equipped with laser-guided bombs, GPS, satellite phone and other sophisticated system of communication, the Jet flew at the recommended altitude with its nose pointed in the direction of Nigeria.

The temperature outside was 68 degrees Fahrenheit with south westerly winds blowing from the coast of the Atlantic ocean. Gabriel Ogar stood outside on the big balcony of his estate in Rabat and gazed into the massive land mass his mansion occupied. He'd been keeping in touch with his informants in the U.S. and Nigeria about the movement of the U.S. federal agents but still nothing. He decided to call his Lagos security chief for the latest information and the current state of things.

"Hello, who is this?" the security chief answered in one ring as if he had been expecting the call on the international phone which didn't ring that frequently.

"This is Gabriel. Is everything okay over there?"

"Yes, master. What happened? You haven't tried to call since you left. We thought that something happened."

"Has my wife left or is she still there?" Ogar asked, ignoring the question by his security chief.

"Yes, she has gone somewhere but I do not know where," the security chief said on the speaker phone.

"Good. Now, you know what my instructions are on what to do when there is an outside threat to my property."

"Yes sir. We are on stand by."

"Very well." The international call ended.

Ogar's chief of security was also employed by the Nigerian Army while the armed guards were from the police force in Lagos. Ogar paid the corrupt government close to fifty thousand American dollars annually. He wondered what the consequences would be if the U.S. federal agents showed up with the Nigerian police to arrest him and met serious resistance. On this thought, Ogar decided to call the Commander who provided him with the military part of the security team and find out how far they were willing to go to protect him.

The direct line to the Military commander in chief rang twice and he answered. "Hello."

"Commander, this is Gabriel Ogar."

"Hello, my good friend. How have you been?" the voice of the commander asked on the speaker of the cordless phone.

"I have been fine. I have a question, my friend."

"Yes. What is it?"

"If a foreign government invaded my home with the help of the Nigerian police, how far would your men go to protect me and my family?"

"As far as it would take, only if you're in immediate danger. That is what the orders are."

"Have a good day and thank you," Ogar said and hung up the phone. He then called the Lagos state police commissioner and asked the same question. The answer was also the same as long as the royalties were paid in full. After the two staunch confirmation by the two trusted officials, Gabriel Ogar told himself that any attempt by the U.S. government to encroach into his valuable property will be handled with the utmost resistance.

The thirteen-hour flight by the CIA Jet reached the Nigerian Air space at 2:00am U.S.E.S.T which was 7:00am Nigerian time. Albertson requested permission to land from the Nigerian Aviation service and immediately got clearance since they were being expected by the government.

All twelve agents checked their weapons to make sure they were intact before exiting the plane.

"Welcome to Nigeria, my friends," the short, stocky driver sent by the director of operations, Mr. Nick Sandal greeted.

"Thank you very much, sir and may I ask who you are?" Albertson responded after all the agents checked through the Nigerian Customs and declared their weapons and badges.

"Oh, my name is Bola and I work for your embassy. They sent us to come and drive you to your dwelling."

The agents studied the dark-skinned man and noticed his long sleeve oxford shirt with the Embassy's logo on the left pocket and followed him outside the busy Murtala Muhammad International Airport. There were two white Chevy Suburbans parked along the curbside of the airport with two police escorts in the front passenger seats. The agents took their seats, with six agents sitting in each SUV. Their personal luggage were placed in the trunks by the drivers.

The twelve agents were driven to the Embassy's living quarters which was very secured with military officers from the Nigerian Army. They were shown to their rooms where they rested until 10:00am. The Embassy living quarters was approximately five miles from Ogar's mansion and two miles from the Embassy. Spinard called James Cohen to let him know they arrived safely. About 11:30am, the same drivers drove the agents to No. 2 Eleke Crescent, the address of the American Embassy in Victoria Island, Lagos. They were then escorted to the conference room of the Embassy where they waited for about ten minutes before being lead to the lunch room.

The agents were joined by the Ambassador and the director of operations in the lunch room. They spent about one hour

"Welcome to Nigeria, gentlemen," the Ambassador said, standing up at the head of the big table. "I'm Paul Mason as most of you already know from the discussion in the lunch room and this is Nick Sandal. We will be attending to your needs and also oversea the mission." He looked at Nick Sandal to finish the briefing and Sandal stood up, next to him.

"I did some research myself and I'm glad to tell you that I have the address of Mr. Ogar and he's only about five miles from where you spent the morning." Sandal looked at all twelve agents before continuing. "His home is extremely fortified with police and military security forces so, it's not gonna be a cake-walk. Sorry we missed his four partners or workers, whatever you wanna call them. We should've been more prudent in the execution of the warrant. We learned our lesson; never trust the Nigerian police. That's the only way we figured he got the information before hand." He saw a raised hand and decided to pause for a question.

Agent Michael Spinard stood up like a student in a classroom session. "Have we confirmed they're out of the country and not still in the village or are we still going by what the police told us?"

"That's a good point and that's why you were sent here; to look at the situation from a law enforcement perspective. We are gonna have to make that confirmation, through a couple of you guys, then."

CIA agent, Joseph Albertson stood up to add his idea. "May I suggest we go undercover first to see what we can find out before applying force?"

"Good idea," Sandal agreed. "Any opposition to that?"

There was no opposition to the idea of going undercover in both the village and at Ogar's residence.

Albertson stressed the importance of their sophisticated weapon and the advantage they had over the security of Gabriel Ogar. The weapon they brought included MP-5's, AK-47's and some Gas-grenades. If it gets to tough, they would launch laser-guided bombs from the Jet.

The following day, which was the 17th of January, U.S. Marshalls' Robert Davidson and Donald Spencer accompanied by four Nigerian police officers from the Embassy's security force headed east for Ubakala village in Abia state. The eight-passenger Chevy Suburban was comfortable enough for the six crime fighters to travel in. The eight-hour journey on the rough and rugged roads was necessary for the arrest of the fugitives.

In the city of Monrovia, Mary was busy showing the crew around town during their first week in the busy city. The fugitives appeared to be getting very comfortable in the new environment. Alo had also started cheating on his absent wife as he started hanging out with the single Risky. Alo also hoped that Uma wasn't doing the same thing in India. The more he thought about this, the more jealous he became and the desire to join his wife grew. Alo tried to call Uma everyday but, due to the International Date Line which made about a five-hour difference in the time, he wasn't always able to reach her. he would still wake up at special times just to call and make sure Uma and the boy were okay.

Alo and Risky had just walked in after a night of drinking and dancing at a club that was walking distance from Mary's house.

"You guys know that you're so wrong," Mary said as Alo and Risky came into the family room, talking about the two beautiful models they'd just met who were aspiring to go to the 'States to further their modelling careers.

The two partners in crime appeared to be drunk since that kind of stuff was supposed to be a secret for a married man. Josephine, who had been playing hard to get appeared to be getting jealous. Another pretty girl just might take the rich handsome American from her. She would have to step up her game before it's too late.

"Why you say that? Yo, ask your wife why she said that." A drunk Risky said as he sat down.

"Hey, I ain't getting into it," Nwoke said and refocused on the television set."

"Because you go with my cousin, don't you?" Mary asked.

"Since when? She might be a virgin and I ain't got time to be breaking virgins with all these fine bitches floating around."

"Hold up, now, American Gigolo. They ain't no bitches. In my country men respect women, okay?" Mary corrected.

"That is correct," Josephine supported, studying the drunk Risky and imagining what she could do to him in bed since he thought she was a virgin.

"Okay, ladies, I'm sorry. Didn't mean to offend my sisters and please forgive me," Risky apologized and got up and walked over to Josephine, who was wearing a pair of dazy-dukes shorts to impress Risky. "What's up with you for tonight?"

"Sleep and it's even past my bed-time. I don't even know why I'm still awake," Josephine answered, looking away from Risky, sensing he was looking at her legs.

Alo got up and left, followed by Nwoke and Mary.

"I'm going to my room. It's already 12:00am and that is very late in my country. I know you Americans like to stay up all night." Josephine stood up and faced Risky who was standing right in front of her. Their eyes and faces met, followed by silence of the night. "Can you please move out of my way?"

"Why don't you like me?" Risky asked, looking at Josephine's lips and breathing down her neck.

Josephine looked around and saw there was nobody else around and decided it was time to stop pretending. "I do...I just want more than just sex." She looked at his lips, hungrily and he immediately kissed her. She locked her lips into his as their tongue sucked each other's.

Risky slowly laid her down on the carpet and pulled up her T-shirt to discover that Josephine had no bra on. He sucked on the hard nipples as she grabbed his crotch. Risky took his left hand and stuck it through the side of the dazy duke shorts to find that she had no underwear on either. He then took both hands and yanked her shorts down as she unzipped his fly-and pulled out the hard penis of the American bad boy.

"Spread your legs wide, please," Risky begged in a low, whispering voice, as Josephine responded by guiding the erect manhood into her wet womanhood.

The two made love in the family room for the first time. Afterwards, they went up to Risky's room and had sex till day break.

The final plan for the execution of the warrant for Gabriel Ogar was made at 9:00am on the 18th of January. After the meeting, Nick Sandal informed the agents who didn't go to the village, that Robert Davidson had called to tell them that there was no fugitive at the village villas of Nwoke Nwanta and Alo Nwanta.

The agents returned by plane while the police officers drove the SUV back to Lagos.

Nick Sandal requested five additional uniformed officers from the Nigerian police and the commissioner wasted no time in granting it. Sandal knew the request may have been denied if the police commissioner knew it was for the invasion of the highly respected Gabriel Ogar's mansion. So, to avoid this he claimed the additional officers was for beefed up security for their employees in the visa-issuing department after and angry Nigerian threatened a clerk for denying his visitor's visa application.

Upon the arrival of the five additional officers and the return of Davidson and Spencer from the village, Sandal and Albertson held a briefing. The briefing lasted about fifteen minutes before the federal agents and the accompanying Nigerian police officer took their positions in the three Chevy Suburbans. Armed with AK-47's and MP-5's, including some revolvers, the agents directed the drivers on where to go. The Nigerian officers felt honored to be part of an international fugitive arrest, even though they were not fully aware of the dangers that lay ahead.

"Nigeria isn't that bad, it's almost like home." Davidson commented, sitting next to Spencer in the second SUV.

"Yeah, I can see that. This is way different from the village we just left. I guess you could call this the Hollywood of Nigeria; look at all these buildings," Spencer reacted as he paid close attention to the sight they passed by full of beautiful mansions and corporate buildings.

"Me too," Levitz added as the second SUV made a left turn behind the first one and ahead of the third Suburban.

"Yup, this is definitely the rich and famous part of town, look at these cars and trucks," Spinard observed and looked back to make sure the third SUV with Albertson and his partners were following.

"Don't pull up in front of the house," Albertson advised on the radio to the first SUV with Billard and Johnson and several police officers.

"Okay," Johnson responded over the twelve-way radio they had brought with them.

Five minutes later, the twelve U.S. Federal agents and five Nigerian police officers arrived at the vicinity of Gabriel Ogar's mansion. They parked the three Suburbans about one block from the home of the most wanted man in America. CIA agent, Joseph Albertson stepped out of the third SUV and walked up to the second one where he asked Robertson and Spinard to join him. The rest remained in the vehicles while the five Nigerian officers guarded the three SUV's with their rifles drawn. Since there was no pedestrian traffic in the rich neighborhood, the passing automobiles thought it was just a routine police drill as they kept going.

"We're gonna have to use one of their own to go and ask questions so that we can get an idea of what kind of security we're dealing with, here," Albertson suggested.

The other two agents agreed and related the plan to the rest of the team. After informing the rest of the crew, Spinard and Davidson met Albertson by the first SUV.

"Are we all clear, now?" Albertson asked as he reached in his small back-pack and gave the designated police undercover a small electronic device that looked like a pager. He showed the Nigerian police officer a button to press if he was in danger.

The tall and bulky dark skinned officer who looked more like a body builder than an officer of the law, walked briskly up the deserted side-walk, staying under the palm trees and cashew trees for about one block and then made a right turn into the gateway that lead to the large front yard of Ogar's mansion as the sign said. Spinard and Davidson followed from a distance of about half a block while Albertson was watchful from about thirty feet. They pretended to be passers-by since they hadn't drawn any weapons and there were quite a good percentage of whites in the area. Spinard and Davidson got to the corner and hid behind some flowers as they kept an eye on the officer dressed in civilian clothes. They watched the undercover police officer stop at the gate and ask one of the police guards a question. Spinard and Davidson pressed their small transmitters so that they could hear what the undercover said through the pager-looking device they gave him. The audible conversation came in loud and clear on all the twelve-way radios as all twelve U.S. Federal agents listened.

"Is your master home, please?" the officer asked the guard who was wearing a shot-gun that looked like an Israeli Uzi.

The guard shook his head and studied the undercover. There were three uniformed police officers guarding the front gate. Spinard and Davidson peeked through the flowers and saw one of the guards approach the undercover, followed by the other two. The guard who responded to the question the undercover asked, opened the gate and walked past the undercover, eyes fixed at the main road.

"I think they suspect something," Davidson whispered to Spinard as Albertson joined them.

"Who wants to know where the master is?" the voice of the guard who was outside the gate asked.

"I'm looking for a job and I would like to apply now," the nervous voice of the undercover answered.

"Very well. Come inside," the guard invited and followed behind the undercover as he stepped inside the gate.

The other two guards frisked the man and reached in his front pant-pocket and brought out the transmitter. "What is this?" he asked, now looking directly at the flowers where the agents were hiding and then looking at his partners. He gave his partners a head signal and one of them went in the shack and made a phone call.

"Wait here, we will get you the application," the guard said as he came out of the booth.

"Oh, mine. The signal is dead," Spinard said as he pressed a button on the side of the radio without luck.

"C'mon, let's get out of here. It looks like those two are headed this way," Albertson said and turned around, walking away innocently, followed by Spinard and Davidson, pretending they were just casual observers.

After about one minute of walking toward where the SUV's were, they turned around to see if the guards were close by but, to their surprise, there was no one behind them so they stopped.

"Let's go back and see if he's okay," Spinard suggested while Albertson continued to walk back to the parked SUV's.

"Okay, c'mon," Davidson said and started walking back to the mansion.

The two agents got to the flowers and stopped to look and see what was happening but, the undercover had disappeared.

"What in the world happened to him?" Davidson asked as fear creeped up in his central nervous system.

"I have no idea but it's not looking too good. Let's go!" Spinard said and drew his revolver and stepped back. He looked back at the front gates and saw three more officers and one Army guard, bringing the total number of guards now to seven. He quickly put his revolver back in its holster and hastily headed toward the parked SUV's, followed by Davidson. "Hold up, now. Where the fuck are the trucks?"

"They probably moved them. Let's see," a paranoid Davidson said as the two agents quickly walked up the side-walk.

They got to the exact spot where the Suburbans were parked and looked around but, saw nothing that resembled American Chevy Suburbans, only a couple of isolated buildings and passing vehicles. The two foreign agents looked at each other and wondered what they had gotten themselves into. They drew their weapons once again but immediately realized -.there were no threats around and replaced them in their holsters.

"Hey, look over there," Spinard said as he looked behind a mango tree and saw three dead bodies of some white agents. Spinard drew his weapon again and got closer to the bodies, followed by Davidson.

"I can't believe this is happening," Davidson said as they stood over the lifeless bodies of the agents. His heartbeat now increased speed like it was about to burst out of his chest.

They didn't know whether to touch the bodies or what. They became confused and forgot what they learned in the academy. Blood was still oozing out of the bullet holes in the foreheads of the dead agents.

"How could this have happened?" Davidson asked himself, looking at the sky.

"I guess they got the best of us. A total of fourteen men, minus these three. How did they do that? We may have miscalculated this guy," Spinard lamented. For the first time since the arrest of the messengers, agent Michael Spinard wondered if the mission was even worth it. "These men probably had wives and kids, I reckon."

"Probably so," Davidson responded as he looked up and down the quiet road, looking for clue or at least, an agent that got away and survived. He saw nothing along that line. "We got to get out of here."

The two agents began running for their lives since they didn't know where the enemies were or what their next plan was. The dress shoes slowed them down as they ran aimlessly in the opposite direction, hoping to see a good Samaritan to give them a ride or a taxi that dropped somebody off in the upscale neighborhood. There were only five homes on the secluded avenue and the main road was at least three miles in the direction they were headed. The agents ran out of breath and stopped to catch some air from the atlantic ocean. Luckily for them, a taxi had just dropped somebody of at one of the houses and headed toward the main road which was the direction they were headed. The two tired and out-of-shape federal agents pulled themselves together and attempted to flag the taxi down but the driver kept going as if the agents looked out of place, since no one flagged a taxi off the street in the rich neighborhood. But-then, about ten yards past them, the driver hit the brakes and the reverse lights came on the back of the old Nissan taxi as the taxi backed up to where they were standing.

"Hello, Mr. Whiteman. What is the problem? Are you in danger?"

Spinard and Davidson looked at each other in relief and then at the light-skinned, balding driver.

"Yes, we are," the two agents responded in unison.

"Can you take us to the American Embassy at number 2 Eleke crescent please?"

The taxi driver studied the two white men. "Do you have dollars?" he asked.

"Of course, that's all we have," Davidson answered.

"Okay, hurry inside," the happy driver said, happy to make some American dollars.

Spinard and Davidson rushed to the back doors of the Nissan Stanza taxi and tried to open the doors but the doors were stuck.

"Can you let us in, please?" Davidson asked as he pulled repeatedly on the door.

"Oh. I'm sorry but you must first kick it," the driver informed the agents.

The agents kicked the two doors simultaneously and then pulled the handles again and the two doors opened. They jumped inside, happy to be out of the dangerous area as the taxi pulled off.

"How many of them do you have in captivity now?" Gabriel Ogar asked the head of his security team on the international line. He was sitting in the dining area of the Rabat mansion, sipping on a glass of Domperignon and watching CNN International via satellite.

"We have six of them and three that tried to resist, died during struggle, but one managed to getaway while two were just out of reach at the time," the chief of security informed his boss on the international line.

"That means they have gone for help. We must now arm the officers they brought with them since they helped us a lot.

You must also pay them handsomely for their brave work."

"Yes, sir. Do you think they will come back soon?"

"No, but I think they will find out what happened and when they learn that they have been betrayed, they will lose all trust in the Nigerian government and possibly get more assistance from home." He paused to think for about a minute and continued. "We cannot fight an all-out-war with the American government because they have too much technology. We will continue to use our heads. We must stall for time, so let me see what I can figure out but, in the mean time, get all the Israeli Uzi's ready along with the M-16's and the M-203 grenade-launchers."

The chief of security agreed and Ogar hung up the phone and started thinking about how to neutralize the threat of the U.S. armed forces.

The news of the missing American federal agents flashed across the BBC International News station as Alo, Nwoke, Risky and Mary watched in the family room of the main building of Mary's home in Monrovia. Nwoke had just got off the phone with his caretaker who went to Lagos to clear the Range rover. The caretaker told him he drove the SUV back and that it was now parked in the car-port of the compound. The total cost of clearing the luxury SUV was N800,000.00. The news of the missing American agents had made headline News all over the globe two days before but not anymore. The crew now wanted to see if there was any new development in the case. The president of the United States had promised to bring those responsible to justice, in a televised News conference. The U.S. government was now offering a fifty-thousand dollar reward for any information leading to the arrest and conviction of the perpetrators and one hundred thousand dollars for any information leading to the whereabouts and possible location of their leader, Gabriel Ogar and his fugitive partners.

"That reward is going to cause us some serious problems," Alo commented, looking down on the carpeted floor and shaking his head.

"Why is that?" Nwoke asked as they all turned and looked - at Alo for answers.

"Because our people are greedy and very corrupt. Those police officers that are missing with the American agents may have conspired with the security of Ogar's team against the U.S. federal agents. And don't be surprised if they're the same one to turn their boss in," Alo said.

"So, do you think they have enough information to do so??" Mary asked.

"Of course, they work for the man," Alo answered.

"You think he's even in the country, yo?" Risky asked, joining the dialogue.

"Of course not. We got a gift from him and we know he is no where near," Nwoke said.

"Slick-ass mutherfucker," Risky said, smiling at Alo.

"This is serious, yo. I told you all that the American government will go to any length to prosecute a black man, especially if he's from Nigeria," Alo said.

"I agree and it don't matter where you're from, as long as you're a black man, they'll smash your ass in that fake criminal justice system of theirs. I feel like I'm home now and I ain't never going back to that white man's country.

Yo, I'm ready to start my own house," Risky said and at that moment, Josephine walked in. "Hello, my beautiful one. Did you hear my last comment?"

"No, I didn't," Josephine responded and sat next to Risky, smiling like a woman who just found a new love.

"I said that I'm ready to start my own house," Risky said and kissed her on the cheek.

"That'll be great! Where? In Liberia or Nigeria?" an excited Josephine asked, hugging Risky on the sofa.

"Till we figure that one out tonight," Risky responded and squeezed her tight.

Nwoke stood up after a deep thought since he didn't pay any attention to what the discussion was all about. "Well, I think with all that reward money in U.S. dollars, they just might get a tip-off and find us."

"Yeah, you're right. You just can't trust the Nigerian police since they don't make that much," Mary contributed.

"Remember you all; we were dropped off here by three of them and they know exactly where we are," Nwoke concluded and walked over to the window that overlooked the busy road and pulled the drapes. He gazed out into the busy street full of pedestrians and wondered where the federal agents were at that moment.

CNN International started a segment on the corruption of the Nigerian government and how it is possible that the disappearance of the U.S. federal agents could be an inside job. "THE UNITED STATES GOVERNMENT WILL GET TO THE BOTTOM OF THIS. HOW CAN A PRIVATE CITIZEN EMPLOY, THE GOVERNMENT ARMED FORCES AND POLICE AS HIS" PERSONAL SECURITY TEAM? THE MURDERS OF THREE' AMERICAN FEDERAL AGENTS WERE BRUTAL AND UNCALLED FOR." the Anchor stated, leaving the listeners with the last question as they went to a commercial break.

"Goodness, Mary. I didn't know your boss was that wicked," Nwoke said.

"Do you think I know?" Mary quickly responded, wondering if she even knew the real Gabriel Ogar.

"I really don't think we should be hanging around. We made a mistake by having those officer drop us off here and now, the only way to solve that problem is to vacate the premises. Maybe we should go to a hotel or even go back to a different state in Nigeria since they would probably try to trace us here," Risky added.

"I'm gonna try to find a way to India. I miss my family. You guys should split up and when I get settled, I'll let you know and if you want to join me, you can," Alo said and looked around the big room for reaction but, everybody looked at him for a better idea.

"You leaving us, yo?" Risky asked, getting concerned about his long term friend and partner leaving him in the foreign land.

"It's not like that. I love you guys and I just think it's always good to spread out when there's a situation like this one. That's my experience and I've lived longer than all of you in this room.

"Okay then, I'm gonna need an apartment. Josephine can you arrange for one?" Risky asked Josephine who seemed more than happy to assist the rich handsome American.

"I sure can, baby," Josephine responded with a smile.

The sad and disappointing news of the murdered American federal agents had left Assistant U.S. attorney, James Cohen, speechless and very angry and desperate for a solution. He ordered additional agents on the surveillance of Derrick and Sherrie. In response to this, DEA special agents-in-charge, acting in place of Johnson and Billard, assigned three more surveillance teams in each of the two residences.

"You guys gotta step it up. Washington is on my neck over this and we still don't have a clue as to where the missing agents are and if they're alive," Cohen told DEA special agent-in-charge Raymond Martin over the phone line.

"We are doing our best, sir. I have three more vehicles in the areas of both suspects," Martin answered over the speaker of the desk phone.

"Okay, then. Keep it up," Cohen said and hung up the phone. He then called Washington to find out how much longer before they send the special envoy to Nigeria. The CIA chief told him it wouldn't be long. Cohen then called Nick Sandal in Lagos. "There's still no word on the whereabouts of the missing agents?"

"No, sir. But we're sure they are in the mansion or somewhere nearby," Sandal's voice responded over the speaker phone.

"How did you know that and why haven't you done anything about it. Even if we have to strike the mansion from the air, so be it."

"Well, sir, more lives may be lost if we did that. Besides I just assumed. We have nothing concrete. Anyhow the men are ready for whatever orders that Washington gives. They also thought it would be better to await the result of the reward offer."

"Okay. Keep me posted and ask Spinard to call me when he can. He did survive, didn't he?"

"Yes. Two of us got away from the scene while Albertson managed to make it to the Embassy later after escaping during the ambush. He's under medical observation but he should be okay."

"Keep me posted and I'll let you all know when the envoy leaves." Cohen hung up the phone and walked to the window. He looked at the blue sky for about one minute and then walked back to the file-cabinet, opened the top drawer and pulled out a file. He studied the file for about ten minutes and shook his head. Among the list of prosecutors in the federal system assigned to the Maryland district, he couldn't find any that went as far as he did to get a drug dealer. That was when James Cohen realized that his racist nature may have back-fired.

Sherrie and her mother were sitting in the living room listening and watching CNN as Ms. Washington went back and forth to the kitchen, preparing dinner. They still hadn't heard from Risky.

"Hey, mom! I can'tbelieve what they are saying about Risky on the News," Sherrie told her mother who was now in the kitchen which was connected to the dining and the living-room.

She was referring to a comment by CIA agent, injured Joseph Albertson about Dante Jackson's ability to kill at will, based on his juvenile record. But, according to Sherrie Risky only got in trouble one time for beating a classmate with a baseball bat, but the fifteen-year old victim survived.

"C'mon, Sherrie. You know that they're gonna tell all kinds of lies to paint them as black as possible so that the whole world will turn against them," Ms. Washington walked into the living-room from the kitchen with a kitchen knife in her right hand to see what her daughter was talking about.

"You and I know that Dante and his friends had nothing to do with the murders of those agents. They just need to look for the big boss....Mr. whatever his name is but I think they are scared," she finished and went back to the kitchen.

Sherrie followed her. "I just hope he's okay and that he can find some kind of way to send a message or call. I can't take it anymore and I don't wanna cheat on him." She grabbed an onion that was on the granite kitchen counter and took the mahogany-wood chopping-board laying beside it. With a sharp kitchen knife in her right hand, the lonely Sherrie helped her mother by chopping the big onion to small pieces.

The phone rang and Sherrie immediately dropped the knife to answer it.

"Hello," Sherrie answered.

Derrick was on the other end of the line. "Hi, Sherrie and how are you today?"

"I'm fine and you?" Sherrie wondered what Derrick wanted. Did he want her or something else?

Derrick was trying to apply reverse psychology on the agents who were listening. "I can't take this surveillance shit anymore. They must think I got something to with it. Look, they ain't even trying to hide. I can see them."

Sherrie wondered why Derrick was telling her all this but, whatever the reason was, she was gonna play right along. "Well, it don't matter to me as long as they're not harassing me and my mom."

Derrick continued along the same path. "I think they're just mad because they ran into the wrong guy in another country and got the short end of the stick...hah."

Agent Burr and Gomez, who were listening to the conversation outside Sherrie's house, disguised in a Gas and Electric utility truck, looked at each other and frowned in anger as Burr clenched his right fist.

"Sherrie realized what Derrick was trying to do and decided to end the call. "Okay, Derrick, I gotta go finish cooking but, you can always come see me whenever your girlfriend allows you to. My shop isn't that far from your office, right? Maybe we can have lunch since I know you can't sneak out for dinner. Bye." Sherrie hung up without waiting for a response from Derrick, leaving him thinking. She then switched her mind and wondered what Risky was doing at the moment and if he had cheated on her. Knowing the Risky that she knew, he probably got drunk after smoking some weed and forgot about Sherrie Washington. The more Sherrie thought about this, the more she wanted to have dinner, and not lunch, with the handsome Derrick.

Gabriel Ogar woke up and let out a big yawn in his spacious bedroom and walked over to the window and pulled the drapes and gazed out into the huge backyard of the Rabat mansion. He made it a point never to spend the night with any woman other than his wife. He felt a sense of accomplishment at what his security team had been able to accomplish against what he saw as a foreign invasion of his property. He kept thinking for about ten minutes and came up with an idea on how to keep the security guards happy and dedicated. He walked to the end table, still in his pajamas and picked up the cordless phone and dialed his mansion in Victoria Island, Lagos.

The chief of security answered the special international phone line in one ring, since he knew it had to be his master. "Hello, is this master?"

"Yes, Santo, it is I. Listen to what I have to say; I want you to send a note to the American Embassy, specifically, Mr. Paul mason, the Ambassador. Tell them if they try anything like force, the rest of the American agents would be sent to the Embassy in body bags. But, if they want peace, they should desist from any attack or invasion of my property and leave the country. They should also pay us one million American dollars if they want the agents alive. Try to convince them that I'm still there. Do you understand?" Ogar concluded.

"So, what do you want me to do with the money if they pay?"

"Keep one hundred thousand and divide the remainder among the security team, including the additional police they brought with them. Any other questions?"

"No, sir. Thank you and it will be done immediately."

Ogar hung up the phone. He then called his wife in Abuja to check on her. "How you de?" meaning how are you (broken English) His wife was happy to hear from him again and asked how he was and where he was. Ogar didn't think it was a good idea to say his present location over the phone line. Cecelia was aware of what had transpired and supported her husband's decision to defend their valuable property at all costs. "When are you coming back?"

"Very soon," Ogar lied. "Is there any news?"

"No, nothing. Everything in and around the house is still the same and all the workers are fine."

"How about the children?" Ogar had two kids, ages ten and twelve. A boy and a girl. He didn't want any more kids.

"Good. I will send for you soon. I love you and the children so take care." He hung up the phone and thought about the safety of his children and the safety of the Lagos mansion.

The five Nigerian police officers who accompanied the U.S. federal agents to Ogar's mansion had been paid twenty thousand naira a piece for the part they played in making the plan successful. But, now, they were going to receive more from the ransome if all goes well. The surviving agents, were now being held in the underground Bunker of the mansion. Aside from Ogar's well furnished bedroom in the Bunker, the rest of it was just an empty space with iron benches. It had been designed for bomb shelter.

The head of security of Ogar's mansion, Mr. Oba Santo, paced the floor of the spacious Bunker where all the captured agents were tied up and shackled. He had come down to the Bunker to interrogate the helpless agents after speaking to his boss. "So, how long are you and your people going to be in my country?" the tall, dark skinned muscular Santo asked as he stopped in front of DEA agent Billard. "I want you to answer the question."

"I'm sure as soon as you release us, we'll leave the country and never come back," Billard, who still had on the same clothes from two days before, lied.

"How many were you on this mission?" Santo continued, but now he moved over to U.S. Marshall Donald Spencer.

"We were twenty," the chubby Spencer, who hadn't eaten enough to satisfy his enormous appetite, lied, trying to intimidate Santo and his crew.

The Bunker was quite cool from the central air conditioning system while the temperature outside was almost one hundred degrees Fahrenheit.

Santo continued to question the agents as he studied all of them, suspiciously. "How long do you think it will take before your partners return for you?" he walked over to Levitz for the answer to the question.

The hungry-locking Levitz, who was now tired of eating rice, gathered his thoughts carefully before answering. "Once they call the president, they will waste no to me in attacking the estate from the sky."

Santo looked at him closely, getting a little scared but, then he figured he had to act quickly or use the agents as human shield. "If they attack, then you will all die with us and I am now going to send them a note." Santo left the Bunker.

The guard, who had been scrutinizing the federal agents since their capture three days prior, resumed his questioning. He repeated the same questions in an attempt to catch the agents in a lie but, the American-trained law enforcement officers stuck to their stories and so far, it seemed to be working. "You white men make me sick. You think you can rule the world," the short brown skinned army guard in an all-green Nigerian Army uniform looked at all the agents as he walked back and forth. "Why do you think you can come to my country and capture somebody and then take them back to your country to serve a jail sentence? My master has done nothing to deserve a long term jail sentence." He waited for a response but got none.

The last sentence by the stocky guard made all the agents wonder when they were going to get a chance to see the big boss, Gabriel Ogar. They also wondered what kind of note the security chief was going to send to the Embassy. They could now see the hatred in the eyes of the guards and this made them uncomfortable. This was beginning to look more like a hostage situation. Agent Johnson thought about asking the guard who seemed to be the second in charge what made the Nigerians think they can bring drugs to the United States and poison the people, but changed his mind when he saw how many automatic weapons were pointed at them by the other guards, including the officers that were supposed to be on the U.S. side.

"Was it your decision to travel here, sir," the guard asked, displaying anger and hatred in his voice as he now moved toward Johnson.

"No. It was the president's decision," Johnson answered calmly.

The look in the man's eyes told the agents that they may never see their families again. They hoped that help would arrive soon. They couldn't understand what the hold up was after almost three days in captivity. But, the more they thought about it, the more they realized how complicated it was to get inside the mansion without killing everyone on site. Also, negotiations could be done through the president but, then three agents were already dead. Knowing their president and his cabinet in Washington, this wasn't going to be left unpunished. This made the helpless federal agents more hopeless than they'd been in the past two and a half days.

After being released from the hospital for the minor injury he suffered, CIA agent, Joseph Albertson refused to go on medical leave. He wanted to get those who tried to take him away from his family, untimely. He sat at the conference table with his partners, Davidson and Spinard as the Ambassador and Nick Sandal read the content of the ransome note. The note arrived at exactly 9:06am by regular mail addressed to the Ambassador who immediately called Washington for advice. They were about to launch an attack with the Jet after getting the permission from the Nigerian government through diplomatic dialogue. But, Albertson, the designated Pilot, still had the anger in him and wanted to just launch a laser-guided bomb into the lavish estate of Gabriel Ogar.

"Good morning, gentlemen," Ambassador Paul Mason greeted with Nick Sandal, standing beside him.

The three remaining agents acknowledged by a head nod.

"The tactical team has been called off until the new agents arrive from Washington. We received a 'ransome note' today in the mail from the chief of security of Ogar's mansion, demanding one million dollars. That seems to be a good thing if he'll release the agents. Don't you think?" Mason stopped to get a feedback.

"What do you mean by that seems to be a good thing?" Davidson asked.

"Well, we figured if he can release them after the payment, then we can proceed to destroy the property and hopefully eliminate him and his organization."

"Do you really believe he's still in that residence? Even if he is still there, I doubt if anybody will be there after the payment of the ransome," Albertson said.

"You got a point but, that's not gonna stop us from making him pay one way or another. The destruction of that estate is the only recourse that would make some sense at this time," Sandal added.

"Something just doesn't seem to add up," Spinard commented, frowning his face and shaking his head.

"What do you mean, agent Spinard?" Mason asked.

"Well, the man has made millions dealing drugs and I just don't think he needs any money from us."

"In a way, you're right but you gotta look at it from the perspective of a desperate victim like us. We'll confirm the source before payment. Remember we have our ways and we're not as stupid as they may think we are."

"Mr. Albertson, it baffles me when I think about his security team ambushing our well-trained agents," Sandal intervened. He looked like a million bucks in the custom designed suit and shoes.

Albertson always wondered how Sandal lived above his means. He studied the director of operations closely before answering the question. "We were well outnumbered, sir, because of the unexpected betrayal by the local police that was supposed to be on our side. Plus agents Spinard and Davidson were on a surveillance detail at the time."

"I see." Sandal still had doubt, considering the sophisticated training provided by the federal government to its agents.

The Ambassador dismissed the agents as they waited for the arrival of the additional agents from Washington.

Alo had started buying gifts for Uma and the little boy to take to India with him when he thought about shaving his "head and growing a beard so that he can look different in the new Liberian passport he planned to get. He also thought about settling in India permanently. He wanted to cover all tracks so that he could get through any port of entry in the world without detection. On the other hand, Risky had decided to own up to his name as an African, He now believed he was actually David Okeke. The idea of building a house next to Alo's in the village was no longer under consideration by Risky, following the visit by the agents. This made him focus his mind on the nation's administrative capital of Abuja. Since the bulk of his money was still in the U.S., he had to come up with a plan to transfer most of it to Nigerian Banks.

The four fugitives sat in the big recreation area of the backyard, drinking and eating barbecued goat meat and oxtails.

"Anybody got any idea how I can get my money to Nigeria?" Risky asked, looking around, not worried about what Josephine thought.

As Risky waited for an answer from those who were present, Josephine walked over from the main building, looking seductive with a bottle of Hennessey in her hand. "Hello, baby. This is what I like," she said and sat on Risky's lap as others watched with interest.

"Oh, I see. Why don't you tell one of the maids to get us some glasses so that I can toast to our engagement," Risky said, shifting his eyes over to Mary and Nwoke.

Mary smiled with happiness as she now felt that she had hooked her cousin up with an eligible American bachelor.

Alo ignored the comment and studied the gold necklace he had bought Uma earlier. "Do you remember Cnote?"

"Yeah, the other yo from over East Bmore?" Risky answered.

"Good. That's who we're gonna have to call to get the message to your girl since Derrick changed his number. He would have to tell her in person and not on the phone."

The maid brought the tray of short and long glasses and set it on the table in front of Risky.

Josephine poured the drink in several glasses and handed one to Risky. "So, you didn't tell me about her. You still keep in touch?" she asked and fixed her eyes on Risky.

"My money is with her but you're gonna be my wife, baby." Risky kissed her on the lips and lifted the glass in a toast to all. He then sipped on the glass with a smile that didn't look too convincing to Josephine. "So, you think that's the safest way, yo?" he asked Alo.

Alo took his own glass of the cognac while Nwoke and Mary continued to devour the delicious goat meat and washing it down with Heineken. "I don't see why not. He's not under surveillance and the feds have no information on him as far as I know. Just tell'm to go to the beauty shop at Mondawmin mall and wait for her to show up, then relate the message as a customer. Simple as abc."

"Yo, I don't know how you do it but that shit sounds all that," Risky said and toasted the glass of Henney to Alo and, this time, tapped the glass.

After hearing the plan, Josephine decided to add her input.

"Don't forget you're in Liberia, so how are you gonna get a Bank account in Nigeria without being present?" she asked and sipped on the glass of Henney.

Mary decided to intervene. "That's okay, I think I can handle that. That's what I do."

Josephine smiled at her cousin. "How could I forget you were an expert on things like that, cousin?"

"When can you do this?" Risky asked.

"It all depends on how soon you need it," Mary responded and finished her bottle of Heineken.

"ASAP, if possible."

"Okay, since you wanna be smart. Give me your Nigerian passport," Mary demanded, standing up and extending her right hand as if Risky had the passport with him.

Risky smiled and finished his drink. "Okay, Mrs. James Bond, you sit back down, I'll get it.." Risky set down the glass of Henney and stood up, walked back to the main building and upstairs to his room. He returned in five minutes with the green passport in hand and handed it to Mary.

Mary, whom everybody thought was joking, let the crew and went to use the telephone in the reception area. She returned to the picnic area of the backyard in ten minutes and gave Risky back his passport. "It'll be done by tomorrow since the Bank is already closed for business today."

Risky was astounded at the ease of the illegal transaction.

"Yo, can I trust my money in this Bank?"

"Do you think I would mislead you?"

"Not that. You know how them peoples are with shit like that..... I just wondered." Risky stopped short.

"People got their money in those Banks, remember that. The people are good for some things, you know," Mary explained and sat down. "Besides, have you ever heard anybody losing their money in a Nigerian Bank?"

Risky thought for a minute. "Well, I wouldn't know, I ain't been reading the papers."

"You're in good hands, my man," Alo intervened.

"Thank you Alo. Now, David Okeke, tomorrow you'll get a Bank account number to transfer as much money as you want," Mary concluded and picked up another bottle of cold Heineken and opened it as she studied her cousin and her American fiancé.

Uzo and Cynthia were busy shopping and getting other things ready for the trip to Liberia and then back to London. They had spent the last few days at Uzo's father's home in Aba with Uzo's family. Cynthia now felt it was time they met her part of the family. They'd just got in from Ariara market when the phone rang and Uzo answered.

"Hello."

Nwoke was on the other end of the international line, wanting to know how long Uzo and family was going to be before joining them in Liberia.

"We're just about to leave for Port-Harcourt Airport," Uzo told him.

"Have you all heard what happened in Lagos a few days ago?" Nwoke asked on the other end of the line.

"Yes, I have. That man is really something else. Cynthia said she met him on the plane once. The news also said something about his partners fleeing from the U.S to Nigeria. Is that who you guys are involved with?"

Nwoke told him he couldn't discuss it on the phone and that he would see them when they got to Liberia. He ended the call, after saying goodbye.

Uzo and family finished packing and left for the airport. They arrived at the airport in Monrovia a few hours later. Mary and Nwoke picked them up in the Chevy Suburban, driven by one of Mary's drivers.

"Nigeria seems to be a little more advanced than your country, Mary," Uzo commented as he noticed the dust that covered the white SUV and the narrow road.

"So what. You don't like it?" Cynthia responded, not too happy about her husband's remarks of where she was born.

"I'm sorry. Now, how do you find it so far, buddy?" Uzo directed his question to his childhood friend, Nwoke.

"It's alright, even though I haven't really mixed with the people. I'm sure by now you know why," Nwoke responded, looking at Mary who was now holding little Patience with a passion.

"I'm gonna give you one, soon."

"Give me what?" Mary responded, looking at Nwoke.

"A baby."

"On the run?"

"Very funny. You can have a baby on the run, you know?"

Uzo intervened. "That reminds me. Tell me the entire story. You can trust me. Remember you couldn't tell me much on the phone," Uzo said, realizing his best friend was now a fugitive from the United States.

Nwoke enumerated the entire story, leaving out Cynthia as the unattentive driver drove the SUV back to Mary's house.

They arrived at Mary's house forty minutes later but, Cynthia suggested they leave the luggage in the vehicle so that the same driver could drive them to her house which wasn't that far from Mary's. They got out of the SUV and went straight to the family room where everybody was gathered to welcome them. They exchanged greetings and hugs.

"Those U.S. feds do not play when it comes to fighting crime, do they?" Uzo asked, looking to his right at Alo as he took a seat next to his best friend's uncle.

"No, they don't. I guess the news is all over the world by now," Alo responded, looking down on the ceramic floor.

Cynthia sat down next to her husband, carrying the little girl. "Yeah, Mr. Ogar is deadly but, then again, the U.S. sometimes go overboard. Who would've thought they would go that far just to catch a drug dealer? I can understand if he killed the president of the United States and then ran to another country," Cynthia added as she handed the little girl back to Mary.

"Remember, the BBC News said that one of his messengers who ingested one kilo of heroin died so they charged him with murder also," Uzo reminded his wife.

"But still, that was that person's choice to take the chance. It would be different if he forced the deadly drug down his throat."

Mary looked at her girlfriend, wondering why she was now speaking against drug smuggling when she was the real one. She thought about calling her outside to bring it to her attention but changed her mind after one looke at the happy baby in her hand.

"Well, it's almost dinner time and I think we should go to my place to see what my mom has prepared. She told me to invite all of you," Cynthia said and stood up, looking at her watch.

They all got up and left the family room. Mary called two of her drivers to take them to Cynthia's home which was only a few miles away.

"Yo, that's the man right there. I like his style, maybe those goddamn feds will learn something after this. That nigger jetted, right?" Risky asked Nwoke as they sat in the back of Mary's Toyota Landcruiser.

"He got us thinking he's in Morocco but, he might even be in Baltimore," Nwoke responded with a smile.

"You think he gonna kill the missing agents or what?" Risky asked.

"I don't know if he'll go that far. He ain't even doing the killings. The news said that it was his security people doing it."

"Who you think told them to, hah?"

Nwoke and Risky continued to go back and forth with the story for another fifteen minutes as Mary listened. Alo was in the Ford Expedition with Cynthia and Uzo. The driver made a right turn into a dirt-road that could only fit one SUV at a time. The two SUV's were the only vehicles heading one way on the deserted roadway that lead to Cynthia's house. They pulled up at Cynthia's upscale home five minutes later.

"Well, I'm encouraged by your progress, my dear wife," Uzo said as he stepped out of the SUV into the dry hot air. "How were your parents able to build this? I can understand Mary and her business but, baby, what's with you?"

"My father has a pretty good business, that's how. Now, can we meet my family?" Cynthia didn't want to discuss the forbidden subject any further. Things would have to remain the way it was, at least for the time being.

The crew entered Cynthia's home for the special dinner, prepared by Cynthia's mother.

CHAPTER NINETEEN

The three dead bodies of the U.S. Federal agents arrived at Washington National Airport on the 24th of January. They were transported to the Arlington Cemetery under heavy federal law enforcement motorcade, accompanied by the president and other dignitaries from his cabinet. Lasr respect was paid and the bodies were laid to rest.

In a live broadcast following the crowded funeral of the fallen heroes, the president of the United States vowed to bring Gabriel Ogar and his accomplices to justice. Thereafter, the selected ten CIA agents assigned to the mission, took off in the same specially-equipped Jet that flew the dead bodies back and headed for Nigeria.

The agents had an anticipatory clearance for the Nigerian Airspace from the president of Nigeria as the Jet landed thirteen hours later at the Murtala Muhammed International Airport in Lagos. President Osadebe, who deeply regretted the murders of the American agents, sent a special envoy to pick up the agents from the busy Airport. The special motorcade, headed by the Nigerian military, armed with submachine guns, went straight to the presidential palace under the watchful eyes of the CIA agents who were prepared for war. They were received by the vice president and his body-guards. The president and the vice president had flown in from Abuja to welcome the bereaved American federal agents.

"Welcome to Nigeria, gentlemen, greeted the tall and heavy-set vice president who wore a royal Dashiki with gold and diamonds that sparkled under the light. He shook the hands of the agents one by one as they took their seats in the presidential conference room. The brown-skinned vice president offered his condolences and apologized for the betrayal of the Nigerian police force He promised to deal with the officers severely upon capture. He then left the conference room to get the president.

The ten agents were joined by Ambassador Paul Mason and director of operations, Nick Sandal shortly after the Nigerian vice president left the room. They didn't trust the Nigerian politician.

Ten minutes later, the vice president re-entered the foreign government reception conference room, followed by the president of the country, Chief Osadebe.

"I thank you especially for landing during the day-time," the average-height, dark-complexioned president said and smiled at the agents. He didn't bother to shake their hands as he sat down in the royal chair at the head of the table. The physically-fit man apologized and offered his condolences to the agents and then appointed a special task-force to provide armoured security for the foreign agents. His speech lasted about ten minutes and he left the room.

The agents watched him leave in what looked like a custom-designed Italian suit, looking more westernized than the agents themselves. The agents were then escorted to the American Embassy for a briefing before they were taken to an undisclosed location,

The following morning, which was the 26th of January, the agents met at the conference room of the Embassy where they went into detail about the implications and alternatives surrounding the mission. To the U.S. government, one million dollars was not worth the lives of the six living federal agents. The head of the CIA, Joseph Albertson recommended they pay it and go from there. According to the ransome note, they were to contact a third party whose phone number was given and give him the cash and back off. The third party would notify an unnamed person of the receipt of the payment amount and then the six agents would be released to a location that was convenient to both sides.

The total -of thirteen U.S. federal agents, lead by Albertson, followed the directions and did as told. They did not want the special presidential task-force made up of Nigerian army personnel, involved so Albertson just told them to stand by.

Five of the newly arrived CIA agents, with their high-tech surveillance equipments, watched the little man who couldn't have been more than 5'4", pick up the bag of money and hop on a motorcycle that seemed pre-arranged. They took off with full speed, disappearing before the agents even realized what was happening. The agents were still able to tell the distance the pick-up men had gone and what direction by the GPS device. The agents just monitored the location of the individuals through the chip inside the bag of money until it became steady and, according to the GPS, they were only about one block from the mansion of Gabriel Ogar. The purpose of the monitoring was to keep track of the perpetrators until the six agents were released to safety. But, before the agents could make any moves or inform Albertson, the bag of money was moved to another location within the same vicinity but a different direction. The agents had a difficult time pinpointing the bag to a stable location for more than five minutes. In light of this, Albertson recommended they go to the location where the agents were supposed to be released. All thirteen agents positioned themselves in strategic spots around the Embassy, which was the designated location given by the kidnappers. Three of the CIA agents who were black, joined the visa-application line which stretched into the street, blending in with the local visa applicants. The other federal agents scattered around strategic points on the coast of the Atlantic ocean which was across from the Embassy building.

After about twenty minutes of waiting and watching, the signal from the GPS chip became steady for about eight minutes at an unexpected location about six hundred feet away on the water.

One of the agents with the sophisticated telescope, pointed it in the direction of the signal. "Hey what's that over there?" the agent asked his partner who was also looking in the same direction.

"It looks like a canoe with something on it. Let's find out," the agent responded and ran to Albertson, followed by the other two.

Albertson took one of the telescopes and looked in the direction of the canoe. "What? It's getting closer and now looks like six bags and I hope it's not what I think it is," he said, regretfully as all the other agents rushed to join him and see for themselves.

The agent with the GPS monitoring device told them that the bag that had the cash in it was also in the canoe.

"Can any of you swim that far?" Albertson asked, looking for a volunteer among the thirteen agents but got no response. "Okay then, agent Spinard go see if we got a plastic canoe in the building. I wanna find out what kind of games these goddam Africans are playing."

The special presidential task-force that was standing by, now joined the crowd in a spectator's capacity since nobody appeared to be in danger.

Spinard came back out ten minutes later with a plastic canoe, followed by Davidson with the inflator. They inflated a small canoe and carried it into the water. With each agent paddling on opposite sides, Agents Spinard and U.S. marshall Davidson, paddled their way to the floating canoe. They tied a rope on it and brought it ashore. Other agents carried the heavy canoe onto the main street that was now blocked off. They carried it to the back of the Embassy building for privacy and all the other federal agents gathered around the canoe. Albertson put some latex gloves on and reached inside between one of the bags and pulled out the empty bag that contained the one million dollar cash. He dropped it on the ground and then unzipped one of the brown bags to find the lifeless body of agent Billard. He stepped back as other agents stared in horror. Albertson knew that he did not have to open the remaining five bags to know what was inside.

After seeing Alo off to the airport, Nwoke, Mary, Risky and Josephine returned to the house. The crew decided to visit Cynthia. They rode in the Toyota Landcruiser, driven by one of Mary's drivers.

"Yo, I just can't believe how similar the two houses are. What, you two used the same builder or something?" Risky asked as they got out of the full-size SUV.

"Yup, we sure did. Cynthia and I are just like twins; we like the same things, can't you tell?" Mary responded and then pressed the doorbell.

"I see that alright. Hey, I'm starting to have second thoughts about transferring large amount of money to Nigeria, that's why I ain't done nothing yet," Risky said as the door opened and they walked into the reception room behind Uzo who opened the door.

"Look, it's up to you. I've already told you what I told and if you don't believe or trust me, then it's your call. Now, I'm finished on that topic," Mary sressed and took a seat next to her husband.

Cynthia joined them from upstairs and immediately took the remote control from the entertainment center and flipped the large screen television on to CNN International. "Hello, you chaps. Thanks for the visit and what can we get you all today?"

"You can start by bringing Patience in here so that I can hold her," Mary said.

"Will do and I'll just ask the maid to bring the usual refreshment," Cynthia responded and left the reception room.

Uzo grabbed the remote. "You all wanna stay in here or out back?" the response he got told him that everybody wanted to keep watching the satellite News station.

"I think we'll stay in here for now," Alo said, focused on the television.

Uzo was about to turn to BBC when the Anchor announced "BREAKING NEWS IN LAGOS NIGERIA TODAY, THE REMAINING SIX U.S. FEDERAL AGENTS WHO HAD BEEN HELD CAPTIVE BY GABRIEL OGAR, WERE FOUND IN BODY BAGS FLOATING ON THE COAST OF THE ATLANTIC

OCEAN, ACROSS FROM THE U.S. EMBASSY. ALL PREVIOUS EFFORTS TO SAVE THEM BY THE U.S. GOVERNMENT HAS NOW PROVED FUTILE. WHAT'S NEXT FROM THIS RUTHLESS DRUG DEALER." The Newscaster went on to elaborate on the details of the murders which brought the total of dead American federal agents to nine. There was no mention of the one million-dollar ransome and what was next for the American federal agents. The blonde female reporter quoted a statement from the U.S. president: "THOSE RESPONSIBLE WILL PAY."

The fugitives watched in shock as they all wondered what kind of problem Gabriel Ogar had created for the entire crew.

"Now, he's going a little too far. He didn't have to kill those agents," Nwoke commented, eyes glued to the set.

Josephine looked at Risky."Is that how you Americans kill, too?"

"Now, that question doesn't even make sense. The killer is that Nigerian drug dealer and not the American agents," Risky responded.

"I know but, I heard that's how you all kill over there, too."

"I ain't no American. I'm a Nigerian, okay. Remember, my new name is David Okeke. You dig?" Risky said and looked at Josephine who didn't know that her new boyfriend was a former drug dealer who could have done the same thing as Gabriel Ogar.

"Hey, you all, I see why he did that. If he had set them free, they would've done the same thing they'd planned to do for the previous three murders. I really think they might just blow up the mansion from the sky like they did in Libya and Iraq," Alo reasoned.

All eyes in the room turned to look at him, wondering if Alo could pull a trigger.

"You talk like you don't value life, uncle," Nwoke said.

"Stop it. Of course I value life but, I'm just speaking the facts. The Americans don't value life that's why they're gonna blow up the mansion and kill innocent people, too."

"Yo, I gotta go with my main man. Them white folks have been oppressing my peeps since slavery. You all should see what we go through over there. I'm kind of glad somebody stepped to the plate. That's right, so what's up?" Risky now had a serious look in his eyes.

Uzo and Cynthia had no comment. Uzo was getting a little scared as he wondered if he was in the company of some killers who did anything to make money.

The maid brought a tray of assorted drinks and goat pepper-soup in a big bowl so that everyone could scoop what they needed. They all chose their drinks of choice and helped themselves with the delicious soup.

After about thirty minutes, Risky asked Cynthia where the phone was. She showed him the phone on the porch and he picked it up and called Cnote. Risky told Cnote to give him an address for a message or get another phone and call him back on Cynthia's phone. He gave him the number and told him he would be there for a few more hours. Cnote gave him a P.O. Box address in West Baltimore and asked him if there was a need to call him back and Risky said yes.

One hour later, one of the caretakers came into the reception room and told Risky he had an international call. Risky went back on the porch and took the call. "Is this phone registered?" Risky asked Cnote.

"No, it's prepaid," Cnote responded on the other end of the international line..

"Good. I wasn't comfortable saying what I was calling on the old number that's why I asked you to get a prepaid phone." Risky then told him to go to Sherrie's shop at Mondawmin mall and let her no he's doing okay where he was and that he would send her a message through the P.O. Box address. "So, you alright, my nig?"

"I'm fine and after I heard about you all, I stopped and skipped town and just laid low, yo," Cnote said on the other end of the line. "Yo, that boss of their's is my Nigger. All the G's talking about him in the hood. Hey, he's the man!"

Risky noticed that the conversation was now heading elsewhere and decided to cut it off. "Yo, I don't mean to cut you off but, I may send this paper to the box and I want you to give it to her. Check the box in three days, you heard?"

"Yup. Say hello to Alo and the rest. Hit me on this number when you get a chance. I gotchu yo."

The conversation ended and Risky went back to the reception room and asked Cynthia where the closest DHL or FEDEX office was.

"Just write the message and I'll get one of the drivers to take it there, okay?" Cynthia suggested.

Risky got a piece of paper from the table and scribbled down something and then reached in his pocket and got the small address book he'd always carried. He flipped through several pages and stopped and wrote down the account number Mary had given him from the Nigerian bank. He asked for an envelope and Cynthia gave him one, he sealed it and gave it back to her. Cynthia then called one of the drivers and asked them to deliver it to DHL for speedy service.

Mary continued to play with Patience, wishing she had a baby just like Cynthia had. But when she realized the situation they were in, she knew the reality of the wish wasn't anywhere near.

In East Baltimore, Sherrie was getting ready for work when she heard the phone ring. "Hello."

"Hello, baby girl. You haven't met me but it's important I see you at your shop about some new hair products that just arrived," Cnote said on the other end of the line, trying to avoid being specific.

Sherrie wondered who the man was and how he got her number. "Who did you say you were again?" she asked, stopping what she was doing to pay a closer attention.

Cnote didn't want to give himself away so he decided to play it safe. "I'm a sales Rep. from New York and you sell most of our products in your shop. "You won't regret it. I'll see you when you get here." He hung up.

"Hey ma! I just got a call from a man who claims to have the latest beauty and hair products buy, I don't know how he got my phone number," Sherrie yelled to her mother from her room as she came downstairs to the family room.

Miss Washington, who was busy watching the stories on her favorite channel, didn't like being interrupted. "Oh, okay," she mumbled, not moving her face from the television.

Sherrie walked up to her and blocked her view. "Ma, did you hear what I just said?"

Miss Washington looked up to face her daughter. "What is it?"

Sherrie repeated what she said.

"Well, go see what he wants. Just don't meet him in a lonely place. Tell'm to come to your store. Now, can I finish watching my program?" Miss Washington advised and refocused on the television like she didn't think it was a matter of concern.

Sherrie moved out of her view and went back to her room to finish getting ready.

One hour later, Sherrie was looking for the closest parking space on the first-level of Mondawmin mall. She found one and parked the Range rover and got out, turning her swagger up a couple of notches. Cnote, who was sitting in his Cadillac Deville a few feet from where Sherrie had parked, noticed the classy and pretty Sherrie who fit the description he had from Risky and decided to follow her to see if she would open the shop that was closed.

"Excuse me, pretty ma," Cnote said as he got closer to Sherrie who was now about to open the door of the beauty salon.

Sherrie turned around, startled. "Yes?"

"I'm the man that called you on the phone." Cnote said and looked over his shoulder to make sure there was no one around in the empty mall. He then leaned over to her right ear with the envelope in hand. "I spoke to Risky a couple days ago and he sent this to my box." Risky handed her the envelope with the bank account number on it. "You wanna go get something to drink or eat?"

Sherrie studied the attractive Cnote and looked at the envelope, wondering if she should trust the stranger. She hesitated for about two minutes as they stood by the door of the shop and realized there was nothing to lose in hearing what Cnote had to say. "Okay, let's go to the second level."

They went to a food stand on the second level and sat down. They ordered two breakfast sandwiches and orange juice. Cnote told her what Risky told him and the reason why he hadn't called her and the more Sherrie listened, the more she trusted and liked Cnote.

"You made my day. I was so worried and didn't know what to think, especially when I heard about the murders on the News. He ain't tell you were he was?"

"Nah, but that envelope came from Liberia."

"Where in the world is that?"

"I think somewhere in Africa," Cnote answered and studied the pretty woman that seemed to be without a man as he took a bite out of the breakfast sandwich.

Sherrie then took the envelope out of her pocketbook and opened it. "I see. He seems to have plans. I wish him luck," she said, hoping it was a love letter or something telling her that he missed her.

"Everything okay?" Cnote asked as he noticed the depressed-look in Sherrie's eyes.

"Yup." Sherrie answered and started eating her sandwich so that she could get back to the store and let her employees in.

Agents Gomez and Burr, who had followed Sherrie from her house, sat at another food-stand across from Sherrie and Cnote and watched but couldn't make out what they were saying.

"I know he ain't no sales Rep," Burr said as he drank cup of coffee.

"What do you think they're up to?" Gomez responded.

"I don't know, I guess we just have to listen and watch just like we've been doing and, sooner or later, it's all gonna come to light." Burr took a sip of his coffee.

Ten minutes later, the two agents got up and followed Sherrie and Cnote back to the first level. They watched her from a distance as she opened the door to let her waiting Beauticians in. And then, they tailed Cnote to the parking lot and watched him drive away but couldn't leave their current assignment and follow him.

"You got that tag number?" Burr asked Gomez as they walked back to the van.

"Yup. I sure do," Gomez responded, sitting down in the driver seat of the well equipped surveillance van.

At his Rabat mansion in Morocco, Mr. Gabriel Ogar had been monitoring the news of the six American federal agents whose bodies were discovered floating on a canoe off the coast of the Atlantic ocean in Lagos, BBC and CNN made the coverage the most important news segment in the past few days. Ogar was pleased with the accomplishment of his security team, especially his chief of security, Santo. "They have learned their lesson and they'll never go to another man's country again and try to ruin his life for selling drugs," he said out loud to himself as he looked three inches taller due to the concrete patio he was standing on.

One of the armed guards he employed didn't speak english so he didn't have to worry about him hearing what he had just said while they stood only about ten feet apart. Ogar thought about the consequences of the action he had taken and realized it would be deadly and possibly swift from the American government. He picked up the satellite phone that was already on the patio and walked back inside and called Lagos to speak to Santo. "Hello, Oba," he said after Oba answered in one ring. "You must vacate the premises immediately, and tell everyone to do the same. I know most of the caretakers and drivers are gone. I will find you in due time. Make sure yo know where all the guards will be. I will talk to you another day and good luck. You have done a good job." He switched the satellite phone off and placed it back on its cradle. He figured the only way to get in contact with Oba would be through Cecelia, his wife. If there was any important message, Oba knew to let Cecelia know.

All the security personnel, including the extra five Nigerian police officers, who took part in the ambush and murders of the American federal agents, stopped whatever they were doing as the alarm sounded. Oba Santo called an emergency meeting and told all the employees to pack up and leave the premises. He told the security team to follow him as they escaped through the underground tunnel that connected the Bunker, not knowing where the danger was.

They got in two separate eight-passenger vans while the drivers were instructed to drive the regular employees to where they were going and hold on to the vehicles until further notice. They drove to a town called Surulere, which was similar to a ghetto in the U.S. Santo checked himself into the Kilo hotels and invited all the participating members of the security team and the five Nigerian police officers. The one million dollar ransome was shared, with the security chief getting the lion's share. Santo took two hundred thousand dollars and split the remaining $800,000.00 among the subordinate guards who were thirteen in number, including the five additional Nigerian police officers.

"I am entitled to more than this because I am the second in command," the lieutenant stated to Oba and looked for support from his subordinates but got none.

Oba looked at him and told him to be happy with what he got. This comment from Oba seemed to cause friction between the two men while others looked happy with what they got, which was a little over $72.000.00 each. They all then dispersed to various police stations throughout the country from which they were hired by Ogar. At least that's what Santo thought. The second in command, Mr. Uche was the last to leave the hotel room, without saying a single word.

The following morning, Uche saw the reward for fifty thousand that was being offered by the U.S. government for any information leading to the arrest and conviction of the ring leader, Gabriel Ogar. He was tempted to turn Santo in for the high reward to increase his share of the ransome payment since Santo pulled the trigger on the latest six dead agents. Uche wasn't too comfortable about going back to his base just yet so, he decided to check into a different hotel not far from Kilo, called Paragon hotel.

"Can I get a bottle of Star, please?" Uche ordered his favorite beer as he sat down on a high-stool at the hotel Bar.

"Yessir," the dark-skinned male Bartender responded, walking up to his second customer of the evening. He brought the lager beer a few seconds later. "Anything else, sir?"

Uche studied him for a minute and said no. He opened the beer with the can opener and poured himself a full glass and drank it, and then he poured another one and sat back. He started thinking about his next move. After thinking for about five minutes, he decided he wasn't going to let Santo get away with all that money if he could help it.

Meanwhile, the U.S. government, in cooperation with the Nigerian government, had launched an attack and a raid of the mansion of Gabriel Ogar, with the CIA agents leading the way. But, unfortunately no one came out of the big mansion after repeated tear-gas drops since they didn't want to destroy the mansion for obvious reasons that was going to materialize later.

"We're gonna have to go in. There may be something underground, like a Bunker," Albertson ordered as the men followed with their gas masks and submachine guns.

The agents busted several doors and finally found the entrance to the secret Bunker.

"Drop some more down there," Albertson,- wearing an AK-47 around his right shoulder, ordered as he moved and pointed the weapon directly into the Bunker, followed by others as the agents circled the entrance of the underground bomb shelter. They stepped down the steps one after another as each agent protected the other with his weapon.

After one our of searching through the entire mansion, agent Spinard became the first one to assume a defenseless posture, recognizing the empty estate in disgust as he stood outside in the middle of the backyard, absorbing a direct hit from the sunlight. "I can't believe we let'm all get away," he said to Davidson who now joined him in the yard.

"This is a disaster! I can't believe it. What now?" Davidson said and studied the waterfall pool a few feet from where they stood.

"I have plan. They're not gonna get away with this," Albertson promised as he and three other agents emerged from the 'Boys' quarters building on the other side of the backyard.

Uche turned on the small television set on the six O'clock News to find that the U.S. government had now doubled the amount of reward to one hundred thousand dollars. This made him change his mind immediately in his hotel room. He didn't think it was a good idea to show up at the hotel in person, so he had to find a way to get the information to the U.S. government without showing his face. After fifteen minutes of thinking, he concluded that his younger brother would be the perfect person to make the report to the U.S. Embassy or whoever was in charge. He picked up the phone and called his brother in a nearby town and invited him to Surulere. Ajengunle was also another ghetto-like town with terrible roads that caused heavy backed up traffic twenty four hours a day.

It took almost two hours for Ibe to get to the paragon hotel. "Yes, Uche and thank you for inviting me. What is the business you want to talk to me about?" the taller, skinny and darker Ibe said as he entered the hotel room. Uche showed him the flyer with the reward amount and explained the situation to him and how much he was going to get from it. "Can you now please rehearse what I've just explained?"

Uche recanted the entire plan twice and, satisfied with what he heard, Uche decided it was time to carry it out. Uche didn't let Ibe know about the ransome money just to be on the safe side in case his little brother decided to get greedy. He decided to place all the blame on Oba Santo, painting him as black as possible.

"The man seems very wicked," Ibe responded after listening to the entire lie.

"My brother, wicked is not the word. He's now on the run and I think he has gone back to Ikoyi Army barracks, but I'm not sure."

""Is that where they will find him?" Ibe asked, anxious to help catch the wicked man who took his brother's money.

"Yes."

"Why would he even go back there, knowing that's the first place the Americans will look?"

"We'll, right now, he's not wanted. The boss, Ogar is the one the Americans want because they think he was the one who killed those American agents. The U.S. don't even know who he is that's why we're going to tell them, get it?" Uche explained, smiling.

Ibe smiled back as he totally comprehended the object of the scheme.

"I'll get you a separate room till tomorrow and then after we go shopping, you will be on your own."

Ibe agreed, happily and stood up so that they could go down to the lobby and pay for another room, have dinner in the restaurant of the hotel and maybe get a couple of female company for the night. It was just like high school days to the two brothers who were only two years apart by birth. Uche was twenty-nine while Ibe was twenty seven. After high school, Uche decided to join the police while Ibe wanted to open up a clothing store after selling the land that his father gave him.

The following morning, Ibe and Uche went shopping for some new clothes and new looks to portray a professional image. When they came back, Uche paid for another day at the hotel and Ibe dressed up in a two-piece suit for the venture ahead. After one last rehearsal, Ibe got in a taxi and headed for the American Embassy in Victoria Island to file the report for information leading to the arrest and conviction of the perpetrators of the crime against the U.S. government, particularly, Gabriel

Ogar and his security chief. He arrived at the Embassy one hour later, paid the cab fare and stepped out of the taxi, looking like an attorney who was coming to apply for a multiple visa to travel to the United States. The white shirt and red tie gave him the image he needed to make himself believable. Ibe walked briskly past the line of visa applicants and asked the security guard to see the Ambassador. The big Nigerian security guard studied him and asked what it was in reference to and why he didn't join the line.

Ibe straightened his tie and looked the security guard in the eyes. "I have an important information he is waiting for," Ibe responded.

The security guard took Ibe's briefcase and put it through the metal-detector and when he didn't find anything suspicious he opened the gate and let Ibe in. The other security guard escorted him to the office of the Ambassador. Ibe took a seat in the front office where the secretary was.

"May I help you, sir'?" the pretty blonde American secretary asked.

'Yes, I am here to claim the reward for the information on the killers of the Americans," Ibe responded.

"Oh, okay. Hold on for just one moment, si," the secretary said and rushed into the Ambassador's office like she had an emergency.

One minute later, the Ambassador, Paul Mason, came out of the inner office, followed by the secretary. He walked straight to Ibe and studied him like an investigator who had a suspect in front of him. After about thirty seconds, Mason extended his right hand to Ibe for a welcome hand-shake. "I'm Ambassador Paul Mason and

I understand you came to see me with some important information?" Mason said as they shook hands.

"Yes, I did. It is about the killers of your agents," Ibe answered with a straight face.

Mr. Mason studied him for about twenty seconds and, when he realized it wasn't his expertise to psychoanalyze potential suspects, he decided to call in the professionals for assistance.

Ten minutes later, Albertson and Davidson came in, followed by Sandal minutes later. Ibe recanted what Uche told him in its exact rehearsed context as the American officials listened. Satisfied to some extent with the story, the four U.S. government officials decided to take Ibe to the conference room for a thorough cross-examination.

"Now, let me get this straight, Mr. what's your name again?" Albertson asked Ibe as they all sat down in the conference room.

"I'm Ibe, sir." Ibe maintained control.

"I mean, do you have a last name?" the trained CIA agent continued.

"Yes, it is Madu and please do not make it public," Ibe responded.

"Thank you, Mr. Madu; can I call you Mr. Madu while we're in here?"

"Yes. No problem as long as you don't let the public know."

"I promise I won't. You stated you heard this conversation in a crowded taxi-bus?"

"Yes, I did."

"And the suspect's name is Oba Santo?" Albertson continued as he looked deep into the eyes of the confidential informant who now wished to remain anonymous.

"Yes."

"And you know exactly where he can be found?" Albertson looked around the big conference table at his partners to see there reaction and then faced Ibe once again.

"Yes, they said he's at the Ikoyi branch of the army," Ibe answered, avoiding the agent's eyes as he looked straight at the wall in front of him.

Albertson looked at the agents again, thinking this sounded too good to be true as the other's, including Ambassador Mason, had a surprise-look in their eyes, too.

"Why do you think the man who said this on the bus, didn't come forward with this information, Mr. Madu?"

"I don't know. Maybe he is part of it or maybe he is... scared. I am sorry but I dont know." Nervousness was beginning to set in as body temperature brought sweat to the forehead of Mr. Ibe Madu.

Albertson noticed this and decided to meet with his partners. "Excuse us for a few minutes, Mr. Madu. Just stand out there in the hallway and don't go anywhere if you want this money," he said, knowing that the man couldn't go anywhere even if he tried.

Ibe left the room and the agents discussed their opinions in his absence. They decided to check out his story.

"If he's not one of the killers, he's very close to them," Albertson concluded.

The agents, unanimously had a problem believing that the real killers would discuss such sensitive subject on a public transportation.

Fifteen minutes later, Albertson invited Ibe back into the conference room. They called one of the security guards to keep an eye on Ibe while they check out his story at the Ikoyi branch of the Nigerian Army barracks.

"Guard, please escort Mr. Madu to the lunch room and see that he gets what he wants at the Embassy's expense. Thank you," Mr. Sandal ordered and went back to his office, along with the Ambassador to wait the outcome of the investigation.

Per order of the vice president of Nigeria, the thirteen U.S. federal agents and the special task-force appointed by the president of the country, left for the Ikoyi branch of the Nigerian Army in a seven vehicle motorcade, expecting the worse. They were hoping to find the chief of security of Ogar's mansion. Half way there, Albertson received a phone call on the car-phone of the U.S. government vehicle he was riding in. Nick Sandal called to tell him to send half of the agents back to the mansion for occupation until further notice. The assigned crew would keep a look-out for anyone trying to re-enter the premises. Agent Spinard was one of the those who went back to the mansion. Albertson and the other half of the crew would rejoin them to examine all documents ceased during the raid.

With the assistance of the Lagos state police commissioner and the Major of the Ikoyi branch of the Nigerian army, the selected agents were escorted into the barracks by Nigerian military men. To their surprise, there was, in fact, a Mr. Oba in a military uniform and he had no idea what the white men were doing in the facility.

"That is Mr. Oba, sir," the lead escorting Army captain said as he pointed to a man who was inspecting weapons, on "his post.

"Thank you," Albertson said and stepped forward to face the short military officer. "Mr. Oba?" He looked at the name tag which said Mr. Jonah Oba.

"Yes, may I help you?" the dark-skinned military man asked as he looked at the seven faces of civilian white men, lined up in the hallway. He wondered how the foreigner knew his name.

Albertson looked at his partners, including the escorting Captain and then looked at Mr. Oba again before he continued. "How long have you been active in this facility?"

"For about five years now. Why?" Oba responded and looked at the escorting captain for explanation.

The tall light-skinned captain intervened. "Please, Mr. Albertson, are you sure this is the man you want?"

"That's the name we have. Has he been here continuously for the past five years like he claims?"

"Yes, I am sure of that. He has not been on any outside assignment since he joined the force in 1993," the captain responded, studying the American agents and wondering if they were over-reacting because of the murders of their partners.

Albertson stood there for about four minutes, remembering the betrayal by the previous officers assigned to them and wondered if the entire Nigerian Army had been paid off by the rich Gabriel Ogar. "Captain, do you have an attendance record for your staff?"

"Yes, of course. Follow me so that we can verify what I just told you."

The captain lead the agents to his private office that was just around the corner from the weapons inspection unit. He pulled out the daily attendance sign in book that was almost as thick as an Encyclopedia and flipped to the desired page. The captain studied the page for about one minute. "Please come behind my desk, sir."

Albertson walked over to where the Captain was and looked at the page.

"Now, these are all the men assigned to this unit," he pointed with a pencil. "And, this is for this year." He stopped and looked at Albertson. "Do you follow me?"

"Yes."

The captain flipped backwards and showed Albertson year after year through 1994.

"Okay fine, let me see the past one month again, please."

The captain showed him where Jonah Oba had signed in daily for the previous thirty days.

After seeing this and convinced that the man was not who they were looking for, Albertson and the agents left the premises, disappointed. They would have to continue their interview with the suspicious Mr. Ibe Madu.

In Rabat, Morocco, the word of the U.S. occupation of his mansion reached Ogar and he was angry but happy that no lives of his employees were lost. He wondered what the purpose of the occupation was. How could the Nigerian government allow such invasion by a foreign government? He asked himself as he sat in his master-suite on the second floor of the mansion. He knew the U.S. was a super-power but he also thought of himself as a super-power after all the money he had invested in the Nigerian government over the years. His mind then wandered over to all the important documents he forgot to take with him, especially the deeds of all his homes around the world. Fear began to creep into the fearless mind of Gabriel Ogar for the first time since he left Nigeria. He had expected the U.S. to destroy the mansion with a laser- guided bomb like they did in Libya, years back. The sudden realization that the well-trained American agents might trace him to any of his houses in the world, made Ogar decide to relocate immediately. He picked up the land phone and called his lawyer in London, Mr. Clinton.

Mr. Clinton's secretary answered the phone in four rings since they were probably getting ready to leave for the day. Ogar checked the time and it said 6pm and there wasn't that much difference in time between the two countries.

"Can I speak to Mr. Clinton, please. This is Ogar," Ogar said on the international line, knowing that he paid a lot of money not to be placed on hold at anytime.

"This is Clinton, can I help you Mr. Ogar?" the voice of the British lawyer who specialized in international law said on the other end of the line.

"Can you please tell me what right the American government has to move into my house in Lagos?"

"With the permission of your government, yes they can, but only if there is treaty and in your case, yes. Now, did you kill all those American agents?"

Ogar wondered why his lawyer would ask him that question. "No, I haven't been to Nigeria for sometime now."

"Oh, I see but they presume you ordered the murders of those U.S. federal agents, so you better be hiding somewhere good. Where are you now?"

"In Nigeria. I have to go. Bye," Ogar lied and hung up." That's when he realized that his lawyer saw the story on BBc or CNN international. Then again, he thought about the possibility of his lawyer conspiring with the American government to catch him. He immediately started gathering a few things as the land phone he had just used may be traced to Morocco, knowing that America and Britain were brothers against the oppression of Africans.

In Monrovia, Liberia, the fugitives felt they were well protected since the masses didn't really pay too much attention to international news that didn't concern them and had limited access to satellite television. The ones that knew about the murders, never thought a Nigerian on the run would come to Liberia. But, despite all these advantages, the remaining fugitives did not want to take any chances as the news of the one hundred thousand American dollars was circulating around the world fast.

"I wanna have a baby, Nwoke," Mary said as she fed Patience.

Nwoke looked at his beautiful wife and smiled, cherishing the way she was feeding the little girl. "I'm ready whenever you are. All you have to do is stop taking the pills and ,, I'll take care of the rest," he responded, knowing full well that this was no time to be thinking about having a baby.

Mary gave Nwoke a seductive look with a smile. "Okay, young man."

Risky looked at Josephine and smiled. "You like babies?"

Josephine returned the smile. "Of course I do."

At that moment, the news of the U.S. government occupation of Ogar's mansion came on BBC and the crew got quiet to listen.

After about five minutes, the news went to another story and Cynthia stood up in the middle of the family room. "Now, don't you all think you're getting a little too comfortable, talking about having babies when that's going on. The American agents are nothing to play with! Look, they've moved into that man's house and probably will remain in it until further notice. Your pictures continue to flash and, remember, we have all kinds of greedy people out there in the world who will do anything for that kind of money." She stopped to look at her fugitive friends. "One hundred American dollars is a lot of money to most families around the world. You all need to figure something out and, Nwoke," she now faced Nwoke. "You need to put your brain to work!" Cynthia concluded and sat back down.

"Okay, you guys, we all gotta find a way to disguise ourselves and I'm gonna let each one of us come up with what they consider most appropriate for themselves. "I think I'll just grow a beard and shave my hair for a change." Nwoke said.

Everybody agreed with the idea and Risky and Mary said they would come up with something before the day was over.

"I may come up with something neat, yo. Just let me finish sipping on this Henney and my mind will work better cause that ain't shit and I don't need all day for it," Risky said and sipped on the glass of the cognac.

Josephine looked at her fiancé and wondered if she'd made the right decision to marry him.

The time was now 1:00pm and Risky, Nwoke, Mary and Josephine had spent the night at Cynthia's. Cynthia and Uzo had now been in Liberia for about six days and were making preparations to go back to London. Cynthia was happy she got out of the drug game just in time and wished Mary had done the same.

"Josephine, we might have to go back to the apartment 'cause I think better there," Risky suggested to Josephine, who was about to get some more drinks from the Bar.

"We just got here yesterday and I wanna spend some more time with my cousin before she leaves tomorrow. I promise it will be worth it to you, sweetie," Josephine said and continued to walk to the Bar, adding a. sexy switch to her steps, knowing that Risky was looking.

Risky changed his mind and continued to drink so that he could be very ready for the sexy Josephine who already knew what alcohol can do for them in bed. He had also just / received some Liberian weed from one of Cynthia's drivers and Josephine was yet to find out what the combination of Henney and weed can do for his Jimmy.

'The new apartment Risky and Josephine had moved into was closer to Cynthia's house than Mary's. Since becoming officially engaged, Josephine had stopped taking the herbal birth control medicine she was on. She had now fallen deeply in love with the rich American and didn't want to lose him so, she figured a baby was the best way to tie a man down and establish an everlasting bond.

On the other side of the room, Mary looked at Nwoke after hearing the exchange between Josephine and Risky. "What are you thinking about, Nwoke baby?" Mary asked, knowing that when her husband got quiet and started looking at the wall, he was upto something.

"Nothing. Excuse me a second, Uzo, can I use the phone to make an important international call? Nwoke asked as he thought about asking Alo for advice.

"Sure, go ahead," Cynthia intervened as she studied a piece of art she'd bought for one of their tight friends in London.

When Mary realized what Nwoke was about to do, she got up to stop him. "You had to call Alo, didn't you?" She confronted her younger husband. "When will you start making independent decisions for us?"

"Stop it, I've always made decisions for us and you know it," Nwoke said and brushed past her and walked to the wall where the cordless land phone was. He grabbed the phone and walked back to his seat and sat down while Mary was still standing, watching him. Nwoke reached in his shirt-pocket and took out a small phone and address book and flipped to the page where Uma's number was written and dialed. After listening to the international line ring for about fifteen seconds, Nwoke said: "hello."

Since it was a little past 1:00pm in Liberia that meant it was a little past 6:00pm in India. Uma answered the phone and then said hello and gave it Alo. "Hello nephew," Alo's voice said as Nwoke now switched the speaker on so that everybody could hear.

"'It's me, uncle, what's going on? I'm sure you've heard of what's become of Mr. Ogar, lately."

"Of course. Who hasn't? I've just been busy, trying to find out what's been going on with my wife, here in New Delhi She. might have cheated with one of her High school boyfriends who keeps calling for nothing," Alo explained.

Nwoke wasn't sure if he wanted everyone in the room to hear about her unfaithful sister-in-law but it was too late.

"Oh, sorry to hear about that. Uncle, what do suggest we do? We're no longer comfortable here. I shaved my hair and my beard is growing."

"I just got a face-lift myself. The Indian doctors are pretty good at cosmetic surgery and if you saw me now, you wouldn't even recognize me. The news of what Ogar did, made me and Uma so paranoid that I had to think of something. Who knows what's next."

A little static came over the international line and Nwoke paused a few seconds. "The surgery thing is a great idea. So, how's India, anyway?" Nwoke now sounded happier 'cause of the surgery which he wanted for him and Mary.

"It's okay. All black people look the same to them so, hiding amongst them is so much easier as long as you stay crime-free and out of the spot-light."

Nwoke looked around the big room at his co-conspirators, wishing they didn't have to live like they did. "I'm gonna discuss it with them and if they agree, we just might do like you."

"Good, let me speak to Risky if he's there." Nwoke gave the phone to Risky.

Risky and Alo spoke for a few more minutes on the international line and Risky told Alo that he would rather settle down in Nigeria, preferably, Abuja and get married to both Josephine and Ngozi since it had always been his dream to have two wives.

"I guess what goes around comes around, hah? I wonder if Sherrie is doing the same thing." Risky finally said and hung up the phone with a goodbye note.

"Okay, you guys, you heard the conversation. We're gonna have to make that move," Nwoke said after Risky got off the phone.

Uzo and Cynthia looked at him in total shock.

"What move are you talking about?" Mary asked, not sure it Nwoke meant running to India or just getting the plastic surgery.

"You heard me on the phone, right?"

"Listen; you are not going to have me looking like one of the Jacksons, okay?"

"Well, that's up to you but I'm headed that way. Risky, I guess you ain't going either."

"Nah. I may stay with Josephine and....." Risky didn't want to mention Ngozi's name in the presence of Josephine.

"Okay, Cynthia and Uzo, do you have a better idea since you look like you don't approve?" Nwoke waited for a few seconds for a response from Uzo and Cynthia but got nothing. "Indian visa is not a problem and that's it."

Uzo and Cynthia looked at each other and then looked at Mary, holding Patience who was now asleep. At that moment, the trouble-free couple decided they would have to make the trip back to London no later than the following day before things got out of hand.

In West Baltimore at Mondawmin mall, Sherrie had just finished having lunch with Cnote under the watchful eyes of DEA agents Burr and Gomez. Cnote left while Sherrie went back to her shop. After a few minutes, Sherrie came back out and walked briskly to the Bank which was on the same level as her shop. She went straight to the bank manager who had no customers waiting and requested to make a three hundred thousand dollar transfer to the National Bank of Nigeria in Abuja from her business account.

"Will that be all we can do for you today, Ms. Washington?" the beautiful brown-skinned female manager asked, recognizing Sherrie as a highly valued customer.

"Yes, that will be all for now. Thank you, Kathy and you have a nice day." Sherrie put the paper with the account number on it back in her Coach pocket-book and left the bank without wasting too much time, when she returned to her shop, she was surprised to see a white male and a hispanic-looking male, standing in front of one of her Beauticians, talking to her. The employee saw Sherrie walk into the shop and pointed at her to let the two men know that she was back. The men looked at Sherrie like they knew who she was and then proceeded toward her.

"Hello, maam," agent Burr said as they came face to face with Sherrie.

Gomez studied the young black woman who was also an entrepreneur and possible drug dealer.

"Hi, can I help you?" Sherrie asked, wondering what the men wanted since all her customers were black.

"We're looking for a woman that may have robbed a Beauty shop a few minutes ago and we thought maybe she came here to rob your store, too," Gomez lied as the two agents studied Sherrie's outfit, jewelry and shoes.

"Oh, well, I'm glad she didn't but if I see her, I'll let you know. Are you from the police or mall security?"

Gomez and Burr looked at each other. "Both," Burr answered.

The two agents left and went back to the surveillance van.

Sherrie called Cnote to let him know that it was done and avoided using her cell phone and disclosing what was done. She had taken a liking to the tall and handsome Cnote and wanted to see him again, not worried about what Risky thinks. "So, what time you wanna have dinner?"

"Whenever you want is cool with me," Cnote responded on the other end of the line.

"That's so gentlemanly of you. Are you a gentleman?"

"It all depends on what you call 'gentleman'. Are you a gentle lady?"

"Okay, stop it, boy. Question doesn't answer question. I'll just see you at six, bye." Sherrie hung up the business phone line of her shop.

Agents Gomez and Burr, who were now in a U-haul truck parked across from Sherrie's Range rover, "heard the conversation and looked at each other, smiling.

"You think the good girl has finally gone bad or going V. bad?" Gomez asked his partner as they sat in the front seat of the U-haul truck.

"I'd say, going bad."

The two DEA-agents smiled and then laughed out loud.

Ibe Madu was now being detained but not under arrest since his story did not seem to add up. He was now under tight security in the living quarters for the Embassy employees and fed after almost more than twenty-four hours of heavy scrutiny.

"Why would a fugitive go back to his employer or former employer since he knows that's the first place the law will look after "searching his home? That reminds me; now, we checked his listed address and they said they had never heard of the man, is that right, Davidson?" Albertson asked as he analyzed the situation with the agents outside Ibe's room.

"Yes sir. We figured he lived at the mansion just like the rest of the employees," Davidson responded.

The agents returned to the room where Ibe was being held to continue searching for the truth about the mystery man.

Albertson decided to repeat some questions to see if he would get a different answer. "Are you sure that's the name you heard, sir?"

"Yes," Ibe answered, now wearing a pair of jeans and t-shirt from the Embassy while they neatly hung his two-piece suit in the closet for him. Ibe was now scared to death and wished he'd never agreed to his brother's scheme.

Albertson scratched his head. "Hey, agent Spinard, call the captain at the barracks again and see if he found anything after we left."

"Yes sir," Spinard answered and left the room to make the phone call. He returned five minutes later and told Albertson that the Captain who escorted them at the barracks wanted to speak to him.

Albertson excused himself from the four agents and left the room. He walked out to the living room and picked up the phone and punched the blinking button. "Hello, Albertson here, and how can I help you?"

"Hello, Mr. Albertson. This is captain Olafemi and I have come across some good news," the army captain said on the other end of the line.

Albertson's face lit up. "Go ahead, sir."

"I was about to call the Embassy when your partner called me. After you left, I did my own investigation after somebody dropped us a note anonymously and disappeared. The note was a picture of the man you are looking for and his position with Gabriel Ogar's organization."

Albertson was elated. "Are you serious, Mr. Captain?" Albertson didn't try to pronounce the captain's name.

"Please, listen. I checked out the person and remembered him as Captain Oba Santo· who was assigned to an outside detail but did not come back to the army."

Albertson was dumbfounded for a few seconds and then thanked the captain and told him that somebody would be there to get the picture. He hung up the phone and returned to Ibe holding room to continue grilling him. "Mr. Madu, we think you know a lot more than you're telling us. Now, who dropped a note and a picture at the barracks?"

Ibe didn't know what to make of the question. Could it be his brother, Uche after not hearing from him? "I don't know, sir. I have been here for almost two days." Blood was now rushing to Ibe's head as confusion set in. "Who is in the picture, please?"

"We'll see in a couple of hours. Agent Spinard, why don't you and a couple of the agents take one of the members of the task force and got to the barracks and bring that note and picture back here."

The two men quickly left the room as Albertson resumed his questioning of Ibe in the presence of the remaining agents.

"Mr. Madu, do you have a brother?"

"Ibe hesitated, thinking maybe Uche got caught. "Yes."

"Is his name Oba Santo?"

"No," Ibe quickly responded, relieved the agent didn't say Uche Madu.

"Does the name sound familiar?"

"No."

"Very good. You're going to take us to him and if you don't you'll face the charges as a co-conspirator in the killings."

The threat from the blue-eyed white man sent a cold chill through the spine of Ibe Madu as he wasted no time in complying. He narrated the entire story of how his brother had persuaded him to seek the reward money.

Uche had just got in from the Ikoyi barracks of the army after dropping the anonymous note and picture of Santo. He was worried about something happening to his brother since he hadn't heard from him for almost two days. To him, the note would kill any suspicion the American agents may have had about Ibe, but unfortunately it didn't. As he sat in his hotel room watching the local news, a thought came to his mind as something told him to leave the hotel. He packed all his things and headed for a village different from his own after concluding that something must have gone wrong with the plan. He began to believe some the stories in some American movies about their agents and detectives might be true. Uche now believed that the well-trained American agents may have caught his brother in a lie. As he sat in the cheap motel located in Ikorodu village, Uche hoped that the taxi driver who took him to the barracks to drop of the note, would not be able to recognise or remember what he looked like, should the U.S. try to offer a reward like they always did.

After considering all options available to him, Uche Madu came to the conclusion that he was safe in the Lagos village.

Nathan Oba Santo was laying next to Gabriel Ogar's wife when the phone rang.

"Cecelia, answer the phone," Santo said.

But, Cecelia, who was exhausted from the hot sex they'd just had, didn't feel like talking. Santo had been in Abuja for two days now, since sharing the ransome money in Lagos. The phone stopped ringing and a few seconds later, started ringing again. Cecelia struggled to reach the phone but, Santo helped her by grabbing the phone from the End-table by the head-board of the king-size bed.

"Hello," Cecelia said in a tired voice, still laying down.

The forceful and commanding voice of her husband came over the international line. "What is the problem and why are you not answering the phone, my dear?"

Cecelia immediately sat up on the bed. Yes, honey and how are you doing? I am sorry but, I was sleeping," she said, still naked as her heart beat increased speed.

"Have you heard from Oba?"

The unfaithful wife didn't know whether to answer yes or no as she looked at Santo's naked body, laying there next to her. "No, am I supposed to hear from him?"

"I told him to make sure he called you after leaving the mansion in Lagos. I will try to locate him. Are you and the children doing okay?"

"We are fine. Where are you, dear?"

"I cannot tell you but, I may send for you and the children soon. Take care and goodbye." The international line died.

Cecelia hung the phone back on its cradle and got dressed. You must go back to the hotel you are staying. Gabriel is looking for you as we speak. I didn't know that you were supposed to call and update on the status of things," she said and walked to the bathroom.

The secret affair between Cecelia and Santo had been going on for about three years undetected. Ogar had enough mistresses to limit the attention he devoted to his wife. If he was interested in what his wife did, he would've caught her from the beginning. Understanding his boss and what he is capable of doing, Nathan Santo got dressed and quickly sneaked out of the Abuja home of Gabriel Ogar, who was now in London.

At the mansion of Gabriel Ogar, CIA agents pieced together evidence collected during the search. The

American federal agents had now occupied the luxurious dwelling, under heavy security provided by the Nigerian president and the United States government. The U.S. protected the Airspace over the mansion while keeping an eye on the Nigerian security force on the ground.via sophisticated satellite equipment.

"This is quite comfortable," Albertson said as he studied a deed to a Castle in France. "This guy must've been printing money."

Ibe had now been moved to the underground Bunker until he could find a way to get in touch with his brother, Uche, after two attempts at finding him at the Kilo hotel in Surulere had failed.

On the second floor living room of the mansion, the agents went through phone records they had obtained from the Nigerian Telecommunications Network (NTN).

Agent Spinard, who had the page of the special international line, saw something that caught his attention.

'Hey, look here. The last incoming call was from Rabat, Morocco. You think there's any chance that he might me there?" Spinard informed Albertson.

"Let me see that." Albertson walked over to where Spinard was and took the page from him and studied it. "Good observation agent Spinard. We're gonna have to check out where these calls came from." Albertson called one of the junior CIA agents had gave him the assignment of tracing the origin of the number. Albertson then walked to the middle of the floor and called for all the agents attention. "Okay, mow, we're gonna have to get the Artist to sketch a picture of Ibe's brother and then, with this picture of Mr. Santo, we can release their images to the press and offer a reward," He looked around the room to see where the CIA Master-sketcher was but, he wasn't sure which one of the recently arrived CIA agents was an artist, "if you're one of us, please come forward."

One of the black agents moved toward Albertson. I am the special artist, sir," the tall muscular brown skinned agent said as he stood in front of the slightly shorter Albertson.

"We're gonna go down to the Bunker and see what kind of description we can get from Ibe of his brother," Albertson said and lead the way to the underground Bunker.

Two hours later on the same day that the Master-sketcher drew the image of Uche Madu, Albertson wasted no time in submitting the picture of Santo and the sketched Image of Uche Madu, to the Nigerian press. As Cynthia and Uzo were preparing to leave for London, the pictures flashed on the 7:00pm News of the Liberian Television evening News. This was the only national News coverage in the former U.S. colony.

"Now, how in the world did they get that information?" Nwoke asked, startled at the picture of Nathan Oba Santo and the sketched image of his assistant. "The assistant's image looks just like the first pictures of Alo and I. I wonder if it's the same Artist that drew it."

Everyone in the living room, including Josephine, stopped whatever they were doing and paid attention.

"Now, we really gotta go. This is now an emergency," Mary said and walked over to the corner of the living room where Cynthia was standing and hugged her.

"I hope you'll be okay, sis," Cynthia said as she held her best friend.

"Okay, we have a flight to catch and we have to be at the airport at least one hour before boarding," Uzo intervened. "So, let's finish the topic on the way there, if you don't mind." Uzo left the living room for the Car-port where the drivers were waiting.

"Oh yeah, that's right. We're gonna take the eight-passenger Expedition so that we can all ride together," Cynthia suggested and lead the way out to the backyard.

Uzo told one of the drivers to stay while the one in the Suburban was now asked to drive the Expedition. After goodbyes and hugs from relatives and friends, including Cynthia's parents, the crew headed for the International Airport of Monrovia.

"I seriously think the plastic surgery idea is a good one, if not the best," Nwoke suggested as he got comfortable in the middle-row seating, behind Uzo and Cynthia. Risky and Josephine sat in the last row.

"I wish you all luck. I am home at last," Risky said and kissed Josephine, smiling.

"Thank you very much, dear Risky. One thing is that I don't know where we should get it done; here or wait till we get to India?" Mary asked, seeking opinion of everyone in the vehicle.

"Well, we have quite a few Indian doctors in London and they say the best surgeons are in their country. You are better off getting it done there if you can get there," Cynthia suggested.

"We'll just do what Alo did," Mary responded.

"But Alo's picture wasn't in the News," Cynthia countered.

Nwoke decided to intervene. "Here's what I think; we can always bribe our way out of this airport, and with my shaved head and beard on the new Liberian passport, no Indian Is gonna recognize me. Same goes for my wife, with her long fake hair and new name. Besides, uncle said that we all look alike to the Indians," he explained, convincingly.

"Sounds like a winner to me, doesn't it, baby?" Risky supported, looking at Josephine for approval.

"Yes, it does. "Josephine agreed with a smile.

The big SUV hit the main highway and accelerated to full speed as the crew continued to discuss the subject of evading international obstacles at Airports around the world. They also discussed exchanging visits between London and India, possibly New Delhi and the various loopholes available until the Expedition pulled alongside the British Airways terminal thirty five minutes later. The driver and the accompanying caretaker got out and brought out the luggage while Uzo and Cynthia held on to their Carry-ons.

"Well, I'm gonna miss you. I guess you can't risk coming to London after all we've discussed but, we're definitely going to come to wherever you guys settle at," Cynthia told Mary and Nwoke as they all stood beside the SUV.

"Well, according to Alo's lawyer, since they never arrested Mary and myself, we can actually go anywhere after seven years if they don't catch us," Nwoke informed Cynthia and Uzo.

"Word, yo?" Risky intervened, holding Josephine's hand as they stood by the vehicle while the driver and the caretaker unloaded the multiple luggage.

"Yup," Mary responded to Risky, studying her cousin who appeared to be very much in love with the American fugitive.

"That's great, man. Just stay out of trouble and I'll see ya in a few years," Uzo said as the driver and caretaker took the last piece of luggage out of the trunk of the

Expedition and placed it on the push-cart and wheeled it inside. Cynthia, holding the little girl and followed by Uzo, went into the terminal to take their position in line.

"I'm gonna have a baby just like you," Mary said to little Patience as they walked up to say their final goodbye to the departing family.

The fugitives waited until Uzo and Cynthia checked in forty-five minutes later before getting back in the SUV and heading back to Mary's house.

The CIA agents recognized a moment of silence for the last six fallen federal agents whose funerals were held in Washington on February 2nd, 1998. After watching the sad ceremony via satellite television in the first-floor living room of the occupied Gabriel Ogar's mansion in Lagos, all thirteen agents became even more motivated to find those responsible and punish them.

The team, lead by Joseph Albertson, continued to study all documents in their possession. The U.S. Embassy in Rabat had confirmed that the phone number was in fact, registered to the former owner of a mansion purchased by a Nigerian multimillionaire named Gabriel Ogar.

"I'm gonna take three of you guys with me to Morocco and the rest can stay here and monitor the result of the reward we offered," Albertson said to the team of agents in the living room of the mansion which had now been converted into a sub-division of the American Embassy.

In a London hotel, Gabriel Ogar was shocked to see the picture of his security chief on BBC. He had taken the precaution of checking into a hotel under a South African passport and name until he was able to find out what kind of information the U.S. feds had on him. Since he made it a habit not to take pictures, he knew it was impossible for the specially trained American agents to get a hold of his picture. He then wondered how they were able to sketch Santo's image. This thought made him uncomfortable when he realized that all his employees could give a description of him to a well-trained Artist. But, Ogar also knew that none of his associates nor employees would dare try such deadly act due to the consequences. The only thing that now worried him was Santo keeping in touch with his wife since he had become a wanted man, internationally. He decided it was best to end the communication between the two immediately as he picked up the hotel phone, but when he realized where he was, he replaced the phone on its receiver and retrieved his satellite phone and dialed the Abuja mansion.

Cecelia answered in two rings as she recognized the familiar untraceable line, "Hello, Gabriel. Where are you? You know its almost one O'clock in the morning," she asked in a sleepy voice.

"I told you not to worry about that, I am fine and it is also almost one O'clock here. Have you seen the news?" Ogar asked, sternly.

"You mean about Oba and his assistant, Uche?"

"Yes. You must stop communicating with him at once. The Americans may use him to get to us and that would mean you first. Do I make myself clear, Cecelia?"

"Yes dear. I will surely do so," Cecelia agreed on the other end of the satellite phone line.

"Goodnight. I will call you another day." Ogar hung up the phone and laid back down, trying to get some sleep in the comfortable king-size bed.

Assistant U.S. attorney, James Cohen arrived at the office early as he awaited the result of the mission to Rabat. The agents, lead by Albertson had now been in Morocco for twenty four hours. He sat in his office, gazing out of the window that overlooked the Baltimore convention center and the busy traffic on Pratt street. He was partly blaming himself for the loss of nine Ü.S. federal agents. What had he done so wrong in his decision to go after the drug dealers? Cohen tried to figure out a quick solution but, the ringing of the office phone interrupted his thoughts. "Hello," he answered as he pressed the speaker button.

"Yes, Mr. Cohen, this is Agent Albertson. Sorry to tell you that we have missed him again. We've swept through the entire home with the assistance of the Moroccan police and only his employees are here. The only one that spoke English, said that they don't know where he went or when he left. They thought he was still here," agent Albertson's voice paused on the speaker of the big office phone. "I think we may be dealing with more than what we had initially thought."

Cohen was highly disappointed at the news, and his anger showed in his voice. ""What do you mean? He's gotta be around there somewhere."

"I really think that the man has some kind of informant who alerts him to where we are and what moves we make. What I am saying is that, we may have underestimated the African and his partners."

Cohen wondered if Albertson was right. "Well, for now, just hang around and do some fishing. Do the same thing you did in Lagos to trace him there. He can't be that evasive." Cohen hung up the phone, confused. He contemplated what to do next as he stood up and walked to the window. He thought about the possibility of the rich drug dealer having an informant within the agents. This thought brought cold chill to his spine as he studied the cold weather which now seemed to grip him inside the heated office.

STAY TUNED!

ABOUT THE AUTHOR

The author was born in Nigeria and raised in the U.S. He earned a bachelor's degree in Criminal Justice and worked for the state of Maryland before falling on the wrong side of the law.

Printed in the United States
By Bookmasters